INTRIGUE

Seek thrills. Solve crimes. Justice served.

Protecting The Newborn
Delores Fossen

The Perfect Murder
K.D. Richards

MILLION

PROTECTING THE NEWBORN
© 2024 by Delores Fossen
Philippine Copyright 2024
Australian Copyright 2024
New Zealand Copyright 2024

First Published 2024
First Australian Paperback Edition 2024
ISBN 978 1 038 93548 9

THE PERFECT MURDER
© 2024 by Kia Dennis
Philippine Copyright 2024
Australian Copyright 2024
New Zealand Copyright 2024

First Published 2024
First Australian Paperback Edition 2024
ISBN 978 1 038 93548 9

Published by
Harlequin Mills & Boon
An imprint of Harlequin Enterprises (Australia) Pty Limited
(ABN 47 001 180 918), a subsidiary of HarperCollins
Publishers Australia Pty Limited
(ABN 36 009 913 517)
Level 19, 201 Elizabeth Street
SYDNEY NSW 2000 AUSTRALIA

Cover art used by arrangement with Harlequin Books S.A.. All rights reserved.

Printed and bound in Australia by McPherson's Printing Group

Protecting The Newborn

Delores Fossen

MILLS & BOON

Delores Fossen, a *USA TODAY* bestselling author, has written over a hundred and fifty novels, with millions of copies of her books in print worldwide. She's received a Booksellers' Best Award and an RT Reviewers' Choice Best Book Award. She was also a finalist for a prestigious RITA® Award. You can contact the author through her website at www.deloresfossen.com.

Books by Delores Fossen

Harlequin Intrigue

Saddle Ridge Justice

The Sheriff's Baby
Protecting the Newborn

Silver Creek Lawman: Second Generation

Targeted in Silver Creek
Maverick Detective Dad
Last Seen in Silver Creek
Marked for Revenge

The Law in Lubbock County

Sheriff in the Saddle
Maverick Justice
Lawman to the Core
Spurred to Justice

Visit the Author Profile page at millsandboon.com.au.

CAST OF CHARACTERS

Detective Ruston McCullough—While undercover, he's hired to kidnap his former partner and a newborn, but when the situation turns deadly, Ruston is forced to take them into hiding to protect them.

Gracelyn Wallace—A former cop whose last assignment may be responsible for the danger that's happening now. She has no choice but to trust Ruston so they can work together to save the baby Gracelyn loves.

Abigail Wallace—Gracelyn's infant niece, who was abandoned by her biological mom. Gracelyn and Ruston will do whatever it takes to keep her safe.

Allie Wallace—She gave birth to Abigail, but she's a danger to both herself and the baby.

Devin Blackburn—Allie's ex-boyfriend who not only has a police record but also criminal ties. He could be responsible for the attempts to kill Gracelyn and Ruston.

Charla Burke—An undercover detective who might be willing to do anything to cover up her past.

Tony Franklin—A high-ranking cop who could be dirty. Is he pulling the strings to try to have Ruston and Gracelyn killed?

Chapter One

Staying behind the cover of some sprawling oak trees, Detective Ruston McCullough pressed the night-vision binoculars to his eyes and got his first look of the place.

His target's house.

It was one story with a white stone exterior and was positioned dead smack in the middle of about three acres. Woods and old ranch trails formed a horseshoe around the house and the pasture.

Lots of places for someone to lie in wait.

Lots of places for a kidnapper or killer to hide.

Once, the house had belonged to a rancher and his wife, both now deceased, and their heirs rented out the place. The current renter, Lizzy Martin, had been living there for a little less than a month.

And she was Ruston's target.

Well, she would have been the target if he truly was a scumbag thug hired to kidnap the woman and her baby. He wasn't. He was an undercover San Antonio PD detective posing as a scumbag thug, but the slime who'd hired him didn't know that.

The slime, aka Marty Bennett, believed that Ruston was a dishonorably discharged army combat specialist with a rap sheet for assault who would do the job that Marty had hired him to do. That Ruston would kidnap the woman and baby and then bring them to Marty, so the baby could probably be sold on the black market and the woman could likely become a human-trafficking victim.

Ruston wouldn't be doing that.

No way.

Once he had the kid and woman secure and out of any harm's way, Ruston's fellow officers would move in to take Marty into custody at his San Antonio residence. Then Ruston would start creating another undercover persona while other detectives figured out for certain why Marty wanted this particular woman. Trafficking and the black market were always good guesses in situations like this.

But something about that theory didn't feel right.

If those were indeed Marty's motives, then Ruston wondered how the heck Marty had even seen her and the baby. This place in rural Texas wasn't on any beaten path, and judging from the gossip Ruston had picked up from his moles and snitches about this Lizzy Martin, no one had seen her in any of the nearby towns.

All three of those towns, including his own hometown of Saddle Ridge, were plenty small enough that folks would have recalled a stranger, especially one with a newborn baby. Added to that, he had siblings in law enforcement in Saddle Ridge, and neither of them had seen anyone resembling the description he had of Lizzy Martin.

Marty hadn't given Ruston a photo of the woman. Only her name, address and a few skimpy details. She was supposedly around five and a half feet tall, average build, brown hair and brown eyes. Considering that could apply to many women, Ruston had decided to run a background check on her —a skill set his undercover persona wouldn't have had, so Ruston had had to cover his tracks there in case Marty was monitoring him.

It had taken a while for Ruston to weed through all the possibilities with the name variations for Lizzy Martin, but he thought the one who had rented this place was a website designer who worked from home. Her driver's license photo showed a woman who was indeed as average as Marty's description of her. It seemed to Ruston that Lizzy was actually trying to fade into the background of that DMV photo. That was a lot to assume from a picture, but it had put him on further alert.

People who tried to hide usually had a reason for doing so.

That was why he'd come to the house earlier than planned. Ruston had told Marty that he would take the target at midnight, but he'd arrived four hours before that with the hopes that he'd catch a glimpse of her.

So far, he hadn't.

But someone was definitely inside the house, because he'd seen lights go on and off.

The breeze rustled through the trees around him, and he welcomed the somewhat cooler night air. It was late June, but in central Texas, it could still be scalding hot even at this time of night. Proof of that was the line of sweat already trickling down his back.

Ruston shifted the binoculars when he caught some movement in the front window. It was indeed a woman, and while he couldn't see her face, since she had her back to him, her height and hair color fit Marty's description. He watched as she picked up something.

A baby monitor.

She peered down at a little screen that he saw light up. The binoculars weren't clear enough for him to see the baby she was watching, but he could make out the outline of a crib on the screen.

Ruston continued to watch until she moved out of sight. A few seconds later, he saw the light go on in the front right window. Probably a bedroom or an office. Since he had verification she was indeed there, it was showtime.

Putting away his binoculars, Ruston eased out from the cover of the trees, and he crouched down to make his way closer to the house. He kept watch, looking and listening for anything or anybody, but the only sounds were an owl, some cicadas and the soft drumming of his own heartbeat in his ears.

He stayed low, not going toward that window with the light since he didn't want Lizzy to see him and then call the cops. Because there was a child on the premises, the locals would likely respond fast, and word of that could get back to Marty if he had his own moles and snitches in law enforcement. Ruston didn't want Marty to have a clue this was a sting operation until he had the woman and baby someplace safe.

Keeping up his slow and steady pace, Ruston went toward the back of the house, figuring he would first scope out all sides to see if there was an easy point of entry. He didn't like breaking in, but that was his best bet. Then he could sneak up on her, and before she could make that call to the locals, he could convince her that he was a cop and was there to help.

He stopped at the back corner of the house, peered around it. And because of the dim light coming from the porch, he saw the gun.

It was pointed right at his face.

He automatically drew his own gun. His body jolted, flooding with adrenaline, and he was ready to fight, to get that gun, but then he saw the face of the woman holding it. Not Lizzy and damn sure not the face of the woman in the driver's license. However, it was someone he instantly recognized.

"Gracelyn Wallace," he snapped.

His former partner at SAPD, and a woman he hadn't seen in nearly a year. Correction—a woman he'd been trying to find for ten and a half months. He sure as heck hadn't expected to find her here.

But she had obviously expected to see him.

There wasn't any surprise in her expression, just a steely anger. And some fear. Yeah, she couldn't mask that completely.

Her looks had changed plenty since he'd last laid eyes on her. No short, choppy blond hair but rather the shoulder-length brown that fit the description Marty had given him. Her face was thinner, as if she'd lost weight. And while she sort of resembled the photo on her driver's license, it was obvious that was a fake.

"What are you doing here?" Ruston demanded, though he was pretty sure that was a question she'd been about to ask him.

Her crystal green eyes narrowed even more. "I'm trying to stay alive," she snarled.

He hadn't been sure how she would answer, but Ruston hadn't expected that. "Alive?" he repeated. "Who's trying to kill you?"

Gracelyn huffed, lowered her gun. "Well, I guess it's not you." She tipped her head to the eaves of the house. "I didn't see anyone else with you. Are you alone?"

He glanced up at the eaves, and while it was too dark to spot a camera, one was obviously there. Hell. Whatever was going on, this was not the easy snatch and grab that Marty had said it would be.

"I'm alone," he assured her, "and you're in danger. But I'm guessing you already know that if you have cameras."

"I have cameras and perimeter security. You tripped one of the sensors, and my phone immediately gave me an alert." She made an uneasy glance around them. "Tell me why you're here and then leave. I don't have time for a long explanation."

Ruston mentally replayed each word. That was a lot of security for someone who was no longer a cop. It was more of a setup that a criminal would have. Or someone scared to the bone.

He was going with door number two on this.

And he thought he knew why.

Over ten months ago, Gracelyn and he had had the undercover mission from hell. Deep-cover infiltration of what was basically a baby farm. A place where pregnant women had been held and then their babies had been sold. Some of the women hadn't been there voluntarily either. Many were runaways who'd been scooped up by the SOBs who'd set up the operation. Others were illegal immigrants. Some were victims of human trafficking.

The operation hadn't been sloppy or easy to break into, but Gracelyn and he had managed it by being hired as security guards. They'd been in the facility for less than twenty-four hours and had managed to get absolutely nothing on the person or persons running the place when they realized their covers had been blown. That had become crystal clear when thugs had come into their quarters to murder them. They'd managed to escape, barely, but had then ended up in a seedy motel together, waiting for some fellow undercover cops to come and get them.

Ruston had a lot of nightmarish memories of that night.

And some memories that weren't of the nightmare variety.

Before that night, there had always been an attraction between Gracelyn and him. Always the heat.

Which they'd resisted because they were partners.

But they hadn't resisted enough after nearly being killed. They'd landed in bed, and a couple of hours later, when they'd been safely taken back to headquarters in San Antonio, Gracelyn had put in her resignation papers and had disappeared.

Ruston had not only looked for her, but he'd also continued to hunt for the person who'd run the baby farm. He'd ended up needing to hunt for the farm itself, too, since they'd moved locations. Of course they had. If the powers that be had figured out Gracelyn and he were cops, they would have known the place was no longer safe for their operation.

"I haven't been able to find the baby farm," he admitted. "You're worried about them coming after you?"

"And you're not?" she countered.

"I look over my shoulder a lot," he muttered, doing that now. He didn't like being out in the open like this. Even with all her security, that didn't mean someone couldn't gun them down.

"I have a new undercover identity," Ruston explained. "One that has no connections to the assignment we had together. But I've closely monitored the old identities we used, and there aren't any red flags." In other words, no one was searching for them under those names.

"Then why are you here?" Gracelyn's tone was nowhere close to being friendly.

Since Ruston didn't want to stand around outside any

longer, he just spilled it. "Someone hired me to kidnap you. You and the baby who's living here with you."

But then he paused. And did some thinking. Or rather some calculating.

"The baby who's living here with you," he repeated. "How old is he or she?" Because that was a detail that Marty hadn't given him. And it could be critical information, since Gracelyn and he had had sex ten and a half months ago.

Hell.

Was the child his?

"She's a newborn," Gracelyn muttered, her words rushing out as if to put a stop to the shock that must have been on his face. "She's only two weeks old."

Two weeks. So, the timing didn't fit. "She's your baby?" He had to ask because something else occurred to him.

That maybe Gracelyn had gotten the child from someone. Maybe from a baby farm or someone needing to put the baby in a safe place. That wouldn't explain why Marty had wanted the child kidnapped, though. But there were a lot of things that needed explaining right now.

"She's mine," Gracelyn finally said, but she didn't elaborate. However, she did take out something from the pocket of her jogging pants. The baby monitor he'd seen her looking at when she'd been by the window.

"Let's go inside and talk," he insisted. "Because something's wrong. I'm not sure what, but we need to figure out why someone hired me to kidnap you and the newborn."

She didn't jump at his request, but after another glance at the monitor, she motioned for him to follow her. Gracelyn still had her gun gripped in her hand, and even though it was no longer pointed at him, she didn't put it away.

Gracelyn led him into a small kitchen that at first glance seemed ordinary, with its outdated appliances and flowery wallpaper. Then he saw a tablet-sized device on the counter, and there were four images on the split screen that showed camera feed from all four sides of the house.

"Yeah," he remarked, "you would have seen me coming on that."

She made a sound of agreement and finally slipped her gun into what he realized was a slide holster in the back of her pants. She then triple locked the back door, took out her phone and showed him the same footage that was on the laptop.

"I get an alert if a camera or perimeter sensor is triggered," she explained.

"That's a lot of security," Ruston muttered, holstering his own gun. "Want to tell me why you need it?"

Gracelyn glanced away, murmuring something under her breath that Ruston didn't catch. "You might not have been tracked by anyone from our last mission, but I believe I have been. If not someone from the mission, then someone else."

Everything inside him went still. "What do you mean?"

She dragged in a long breath and kept her attention pinned to the baby monitor. "About a month after I resigned from SAPD, I was renting a place in Dallas, and I wasn't using my real name. It wasn't the same identity I'd used in the undercover op either, and I was being careful. *Very.* Anyway, I realized someone was following me. I set up cameras and got proof of it. I couldn't see his face, but he was definitely tracking me."

Ruston cursed. "Was it a tall, lanky guy about six feet, sandy-blond hair and chin scruff?" he asked.

That got her gaze shifting back to him. "No. Dark hair, about six foot three, muscular build. Why? Who's the guy you just described?"

"Marty Bennett, the lowlife who hired me to kidnap you and your baby." Now Ruston needed a long, deep breath. "I figured it was for trafficking or a black-market adoption. But maybe not," he added in a grumble.

Maybe Marty had a much bigger part in this.

One that had involved following Gracelyn long before he'd hired Ruston. But if Marty had known where she was all this time, why hadn't he taken her before now?

"Tell me about this Marty Bennett," Gracelyn insisted. "Is he connected in any way to the baby farm?"

Ruston shook his head. "Nothing in his background indicates that, and I dug hard and deep on him. Everything points to him being a somewhat successful money launderer and embezzler. He's got gambling debts, so I figured he somehow found out about you and the baby and thought he could earn some quick cash."

She didn't say anything, but he saw the muscles tighten in her face. Heard the shudder of breath she released. Gracelyn was worried and scared.

"Has anyone else followed you since you moved here?" he asked.

"Not that I know of, but I've moved twice since leaving that apartment in Dallas. I was within a week of leaving here because it doesn't feel safe to stay in one place for long."

Ruston wanted to curse again. And pull her into his arms. Not because of the heat, though that was still there. No, he wanted to try to ease some of that fear. But after what had happened between them, he seriously doubted a hug from him would give her much comfort.

"What about your sister, Allie?" he asked. "Does she know where you are?"

Allie was the only family Gracelyn had. Well, other than

the baby. And while Allie and Gracelyn hadn't been especially close, just the opposite actually, anyone wanting to get to Gracelyn could use Allie to do it. Allie had been pretty much a screwup most of her life, and Gracelyn had had to pull strings and call in favors several times to get her kid sister out of a jam.

"Allie doesn't know," Gracelyn answered, and then she swallowed hard. "And I don't know where she is either." She paused. "I'm not sure if she's safe or not."

Hell. Of course, she'd be worried about Allie. Worried about someone using her sister to get to her.

"You should have gotten in touch with me," he said. "You should have told me. I could have helped."

She laughed, but there was no humor in it. It was dry as West Texas dust. "Right. The man with one of the most dangerous jobs on the planet. The last person I wanted to contact was you."

Ruston's stomach twisted. But he couldn't deny what she'd just said. That last op they'd been on together, the one that had nearly gotten them killed, had obviously sent them in opposite directions. He'd kept up the deep-cover work, and she'd chosen to make her world as safe as possible. The pregnancy and the baby had no doubt factored into her lifestyle decisions.

And that brought him back to her newborn.

Two weeks old, which meant Gracelyn had hooked up with her baby's father six or seven weeks after she'd resigned from the force. Since they'd been partners, Ruston knew plenty about Gracelyn's personal life. And vice versa. She hadn't been involved with anyone when they'd had their one-off, and even though that night had been the culmination of the worst of circumstances, he'd thought it would be the beginning of a relationship since there'd always been an intense attraction between them.

Clearly, he'd been wrong about the relationship.

But not wrong about the attraction. It was still there, even now. Or maybe he was reading way too much into it. After all, Gracelyn had been with her baby's father roughly nine and a half months ago, which meant that was a month after Ruston and she had had that one night together.

"Is your baby's father in the picture?" he asked. Ruston watched her face to see if that was playing into this. Relationships went south all the time, and this man could be the threat to Gracelyn and her daughter.

It seemed to him that she tensed even more. Something he hadn't thought possible. After a long pause, Gracelyn opened her mouth but didn't get a chance to answer.

Because of the soft beeping sound.

Her gaze flew from his and went to the laptop monitor. "Someone or something just triggered the security alarm."

Chapter Two

Every nerve in Gracelyn's body was already on high alert, but that little beep of her security system gave her a fresh surge of adrenaline. She cursed herself for not having already moved. If she had, then the nightmare wouldn't have found her.

Maybe Ruston wouldn't have found her either.

She'd have to deal with him. But first, she had to handle this threat that could put the baby, Abigail, in danger.

While she hurried through a mental checklist of her security, Gracelyn went closer to the laptop monitor. She already knew all the windows and the doors were locked, and that every possible point of entry was equipped with sensors.

It hadn't been any of those that'd gone off, though.

That would have been a much louder beep. This softer sound had been because someone or something had moved past one of the sensors set up around the entire perimeter of the house.

She glanced through the various camera feeds and soon spotted the culprit, and she relaxed just a little. "A deer," she muttered. "There are dozens of them around, and they often set off the sensors."

Ruston moved closer to her, looking at the laptop screen as well. So close that she caught his scent. It stirred through her in a totally different way than the adrenaline and nerves.

A bad way.

Because it reminded her of the heat between them.

Reminded her of why they'd landed in bed. That couldn't happen again. Still, it was hard not to notice that face, that body that had drawn her to him in the first place. Ruston was very much the cowboy cop, though his dark brown hair was longer than most cops'. The length was no doubt to go along with his undercover persona. Ditto for the scruff that made him look like an Old West outlaw.

She kept her attention on the screen, looking for anyone or anything else that the deer's movements could have masked. When she'd set up the security, it had occurred to her that an intruder could sneak in behind a deer or some other animal, so she always looked for that. Always.

The seconds crawled by, turning into minutes, and she still didn't see any signs of an intruder. Gracelyn couldn't breathe easier, though. Not with Ruston standing next to her. She had to get rid of him fast so she could get out of there with the baby.

"I read about what happened to your father," she said to jump-start the conversation. Jump-start and then finish it as soon as she got any and all info from him.

He nodded, and she saw the pain flood his cool gray eyes. Pain because his father, Cliff, had been murdered seven months earlier. Gunned down by an unknown assailant. Since his dad had also been the sheriff of Saddle Ridge, Texas, the speculation around his murder centered on his investigations.

And his wife.

Sandra McCullough had left Saddle Ridge just hours before her husband's murder, and she hadn't returned. Of course, Ruston and his siblings, who were all lawmen, wanted to find her. To question her, too. But there was also the fear that she couldn't be found because she was dead. Or because she'd had some part in her husband's death and was now on the run.

"Among other things, your father was investigating the kidnapping of two pregnant women," Gracelyn continued. "According to what I've read, he thought that maybe the kidnappings were possibly connected to the baby farm where we were nearly killed." She stopped and waited for him to confirm or deny that.

Ruston was clearly still working through the horrible memories of losing his father and his missing mother, but he finally nodded. "He was investigating that. What no one has been able to do is link his murder to that case."

"Do you believe there's a link?" she came out and asked.

He didn't get a chance to answer though because his phone vibrated in his pocket. Ruston frowned when he looked at the caller. "It's Marty."

She didn't have to encourage Ruston to take the call. He wanted answers just as much as she did, and this Marty just might be able to give them some. It sickened her though to have to deal with the devil, but Gracelyn was willing to do whatever it took to keep the baby safe.

"Yeah," Ruston said when he answered, and he put the call on speaker. A sign that he had likely been up-front as to why he was here and had nothing to hide.

Unlike her.

Gracelyn wanted those answers. Desperately wanted them. But she also had to get Ruston out of there.

"Steve," the caller said, obviously calling Ruston by his cover name, "I need you to move things up. Get out to the woman's place right now and take her and the kid."

That tightened every muscle in her body. Judging from

the way Ruston pulled back his shoulders, he was having a similar reaction.

"Why?" Ruston asked. "What's wrong?"

"I just need her sooner than expected. I've had to work around some transportation issues."

Marty had said that so calmly, all business. There was no hint that he even thought of her and Abigail as anything more than objects.

"Transportation issues," Ruston repeated. "Am I still supposed to take her and the baby to the warehouse in San Antonio?"

"You are, but the people picking her up want her there earlier than planned. Make it happen," Marty insisted.

People. So, maybe Marty was just the middleman on this. Still, middlemen often knew who'd hired them.

"You didn't say, but why do you want this particular woman?" Ruston pressed.

"That's none of your business," Marty snapped, punctuating that with some profanity. "I didn't pay you to ask questions. If you can't take the woman and the kid, then I'll send someone else to do the job, and you'll pay me back every penny of the advance I gave you."

Gracelyn figured that wouldn't be all, that Marty would try to silence Ruston so he wouldn't blow the whistle on him.

"I said I'll get her and the baby and I will." Ruston's voice was a snap, too. "It just makes me uneasy when plans change. I don't want to grab them, show up at the warehouse and then have nobody there waiting to take them off my hands."

"Somebody will be waiting there for you," Marty growled. "Now, get them and finish this." With that barked order, Marty ended the call.

Ruston stared at the phone a few seconds and shook his

head. "I'd planned on dropping you and your baby at a safe house and then driving out to the warehouse with decoys."

Gracelyn had been so shocked at Ruston's arrival that she hadn't had a chance to ask him how he'd planned for all of this to play out. "Decoys?" she questioned.

He nodded. "Charla Burke," he said, referring to an SAPD detective they'd both worked with. "And a dummy baby. Obviously, Charla and I would both be armed, and we'd planned on arresting whoever was waiting in that warehouse. Other cops would be moving to take Marty at the same time." He paused a heartbeat. "I need to let Franklin know about this."

Lieutenant Tony Franklin, the senior officer in charge of undercover assignments in the SAPD Special Victims Unit. Gracelyn didn't have any reason to distrust Franklin or Charla, but she didn't care for them knowing her current location. Then again, Marty obviously knew, too, which meant heaven knew how many others did as well.

Yes, it was definitely well past time for her to leave.

"I have my own safe house already in place," Gracelyn said, and it got the reaction from Ruston that she expected.

His forehead bunched up, and he huffed. Obviously, he knew she could handle herself—most of the time, anyway— but he was probably still concerned. Heck, so was she.

"I don't want police protection," Gracelyn spelled out to him and left it at that.

No need for her to remind him that being a cop hadn't helped either of them on their last assignment. Yes, they'd both gotten out of there alive, barely, but that'd been more luck than training. At least two dozen bullets had been fired at them during their escape, and they'd received only minor injuries.

Well, minor *physical* injuries, anyway.

Gracelyn was still living with the nightmare of nearly being gunned down, and she figured it was the same for Ruston. Except Ruston had been able to go back to the job. She hadn't been.

A soft sound shot through the room. Not the security system this time, but a kitten-like cry that had come from the baby monitor. Gracelyn immediately looked and saw Abigail was squirming in her crib. That was her cue to get Ruston moving.

"You can leave now," she insisted, going to the bottom drawer beneath the stove and pulling out a go bag that had cash, fake IDs and a gun. She already had other supplies stashed in her SUV in the garage.

Ruston didn't budge. "I hate to see you on your own like this. I know you don't trust me, but I can help you."

She was ready to assure him that she didn't need his help, but the baby's fussing turned into a full cry. Gracelyn checked her watch, even though she knew it wasn't time for a bottle. She'd fed Abigail less than a half hour before Ruston had arrived.

"I'll be fine," Gracelyn said, and she hoped that was true.

She'd been so careful, and here at least four other people knew her current location. Ruston, Marty, Lieutenant Franklin and Charla. Soon, Gracelyn would want to dig into how Marty and his cohorts had found her. And why he wanted her and Abigail. For now, though, she had to move.

When the crying went up a significant notch, Gracelyn hooked the go bag over her shoulder and headed to the nursery. "I'll get Abigail and leave. Goodbye, Ruston."

"Abigail," he repeated. "You named her after your late mother."

She nodded. Then scowled when he followed her. "No need for you to lock up when you go," she insisted, stop-

ping outside the nursery door to stare at him. "I'll be out
of here within minutes."

Ruston stared back. And stared. Then he muttered some
profanity under his breath, reached around her and opened
the nursery door. He maneuvered around her before she
could stop him, and he made a beeline to the crib.

Gracelyn's heart went to her knees.

Somehow, she managed to get her legs working, and she
hurried to scoop up the baby. But not before Ruston got a
good look at her.

Ruston didn't say anything for several long moments,
and even though the only illumination in the room was from
a night-light, Gracelyn saw his jaw muscles turn to iron.

"Abigail isn't two weeks old," he said, his voice a low,
dangerous snarl.

"No. She's eight weeks old." And Gracelyn quickly tacked
on a huge detail that Ruston needed to hear. "She's not our
baby."

Ruston had already opened his mouth, no doubt to accuse her of not telling him that he'd gotten her pregnant,
but her comment stopped him. Temporarily, anyway. He
stared at her, and stared, clearly trying to figure out if she
was telling him the truth.

She was.

"Abigail's not my baby either," she added.

Again, Ruston had clearly been gearing up to accuse her
of all sorts of things that she wouldn't have done. Yes, she
was desperate. Still was. But if she'd had Ruston's baby, she
would have figured out a way to tell him about it.

"Then whose child is she?" he demanded. "Because she
looks like you." He stopped again. "Is she Allie's? Is she
your niece?"

Gracelyn nodded. Of course, that confirmation was

going to lead to a whole bunch of other questions. Questions that she couldn't answer. Still, she was going to have to give Ruston something or he'd never leave. Best to start at the beginning, which ironically had been at the end of her career as a cop.

"We didn't catch those people who were running the baby farm," she went on. "They were after us, and I couldn't dissolve into the background by taking on another undercover persona. Because I couldn't be a cop. So, I planned on...running. Hiding. Staying safe."

"You could have come to me," he insisted.

"No, I couldn't have." It was a truth that was going to cut him to the bone, but he had to hear it. "You still trusted the cops. I didn't. I knew you weren't dirty, but someone blew our cover at that baby farm, and that someone could have been another cop."

That was a reminder for her to get out of there with Abigail, since two cops she wasn't 100 percent certain she could trust—Charla and Lieutenant Franklin—knew her location. Well, they knew the location of Lizzy Martin, anyway. But it was possible that they knew it was an alias she'd been using.

"How'd you end up with Allie's baby?" Ruston asked.

Gracelyn gathered the long breath that she'd need. "Allie showed up shortly after I turned in my badge, just as I was about to go on the run. She was scared." And sporting a black eye and bruises on her arms. "She told me her boyfriend was abusive. And that she'd just taken a pregnancy test and was about two or three weeks pregnant. So, I took Allie with me."

She'd had no choice about that. Allie could be flighty and restless, but there was no way Gracelyn could have abandoned the child and her.

"Using an alias I'd set up for her, Allie gave birth to

Abigail eight weeks ago in Houston," Gracelyn went on. "Then, a week later, Allie disappeared. She left me a note, asking me to take care of Abigail, but that she wanted to try to make amends with Abigail's bio-dad, Devin Blackburn. He's bad news, Ruston."

She didn't get into the details of that, but Devin Blackburn had money and connections—and three restraining orders from previous relationships. He'd been arrested twice for assault and computer hacking, but the money and connections had kept him from doing any time in a cage.

However, there was one connection Ruston needed to know about. Except she could tell from his expression that he'd already figured it out.

"Devin Blackburn," he repeated. "He was one of the names that came up during the baby-farm investigation."

She nodded. There'd been dozens involved in that case, maybe hundreds, but Devin's name had popped up because he had known associations with a baby broker who'd worked for the farm. Since that particular broker had turned up dead, the cops hadn't been able to learn if Devin's association had led to anything criminal.

"I obviously couldn't risk Allie bringing Devin to the house in Houston, because I didn't know who else he'd let know I was there, so I brought Abigail here," Gracelyn added. "I keep a burner phone and a private Facebook account that Allie could have used to get in touch with me so I could let her know where I was." She paused. Had to. "But she hasn't contacted me, and I haven't been able to get in touch with her."

He shook his head. "If you'd come to me, I could have helped keep Allie, you and the baby safe," he insisted.

"You would have tried, but it would have meant giving up your badge," she insisted right back. "All four of us would have been in hiding until the people responsible for the danger are caught." She paused again, then drew in a long breath. "I think I'm close to finding those people."

That got his attention, and his glare morphed into a puzzled look. "Who? Is it Marty?"

She shook her head. "I don't have names. I have computer identities that I found on a website that's basically an auction site for babies. One of the identities is Green Eagle."

Gracelyn didn't have to explain why that was important. Ruston would recall it was what the person running the baby farm had called himself or herself.

"That can't be a coincidence," she added.

He made a sound that could have meant anything. Ruston certainly didn't jump to agree to that. "I looked for leaks in SAPD. For any signs that someone had ratted us out. I found nothing."

Gracelyn had known he would look, and if he had indeed found the culprit—if there was a dirty cop to find, that was—Ruston would have already told her.

"I did what I believed was necessary to keep Abigail safe," Gracelyn went on. "And if I had learned the identity of Green Eagle, I'd planned to contact you and give you the name so you could arrest him or her."

He went quiet again, but his gaze stayed intense. "We're going to talk more about Abigail and Allie," he said like a demand. "But for now, I want to know everything you have on Green Eagle and the baby auction."

She nodded. "Not here, though," she said and would have reminded him that it was too dangerous to stay here.

A sound stopped her.

It was that punch-to-the-gut beep from her security system, and even though it was possibly another deer, she whipped out her phone from her pocket and looked at the screen.

The slam of adrenaline knocked the breath out of her.

Because it wasn't a deer. In the milky haze of moon-light, Gracelyn saw the shadowy figure coming straight toward the house.

Chapter Three

Even though Gracelyn didn't say anything, Ruston instantly knew from the change in her body language that something was wrong.

She thrust out her phone screen so he could see what had put that alarm on her face. One look at the person in dark clothes, and Ruston was certain he was sporting plenty of alarm of his own.

He drew his gun and braced for an attack.

Ruston also took a harder look at the intruder to see if he recognized him, but he couldn't see the person's face because it was covered with a mask. He couldn't even be sure if it was a man or woman. He definitely couldn't rule out this being Marty. Or one of his hired guns.

But if Marty had come after him like this, then why not just take him when they'd had their initial meeting? They'd been alone for that with no obvious witnesses. Why wait until Ruston was here?

Unless both Gracelyn and he were targets.

Or maybe the target was the baby.

If so, that pointed right back to the baby farm and this mystery person, Green Eagle. And unfortunately, it could point right back to Ruston himself.

"I was careful," Ruston muttered to Gracelyn. "I didn't see anyone following me here."

That didn't mean, though, that someone hadn't managed to tail him. That caused him to mentally curse. Because, hell, everything about this could have been a setup.

"The windows aren't bulletproof," she whispered, grabbing a blanket from the chair next to the crib.

Gracelyn scooped up the baby, automatically trying to soothe her with gentle rocking motions and murmurs. A necessity, since any sound would alert an intruder to their specific location in the house.

"I have to get her to my SUV," Gracelyn added.

Gracelyn didn't invite Ruston to come along, but he did anyway. He had no intention of letting them out of his sight.

"Are the windows of your SUV bullet resistant?" he asked, following her out of the nursery.

"They are," Gracelyn answered, hurrying into the hall.

She had her hands full, literally, what with holding both the phone and Abigail. Plus, she had a backpack hooked over her shoulder, but she waved off Ruston when he tried to help her.

They'd barely made it another step, though, when they heard the sound. Definitely not something Ruston wanted to hear either.

A gunshot blasted through one the windows.

Ruston muttered some profanity and stepped in front of Gracelyn and the baby. They hunkered down seconds before the next shot. There was the sound of shattering glass falling on the floor, but Ruston didn't see any bullets coming through the wall near them.

"Give me your phone," he insisted. "I can see if he's alone and if he's using any kind of infrared." Infrared that would allow the person to track their every movement inside the house.

She passed her phone to him right as the third shot came,

and while Ruston listened for any sounds of the person trying to break in, he also studied the various frames from
the camera.

And he saw something he definitely didn't like.

"There are two of them," he relayed to her. "No infrared
device that I can see, but one is shooting at the windows in
your living room, and the other is on the front porch. How
hard will it be for him to get through the door?"

Gracelyn's groan was soft but heavy with fear. "Not hard
enough," she answered. "It's reinforced, but if he shoots
the locks…"

She didn't finish that. No need. It told Ruston everything
he needed to know. He debated making a stand since there
were only two of them, and if one of them came through
the door, Ruston would be able to take the guy out before
he managed to get inside. But it was a huge risk. If the intruder managed to get off even a single shot, it could hit
Gracelyn or the baby.

And that meant they had to move now.

Ruston took the bag from her shoulder and shifted it to
his so Gracelyn wouldn't have anything to slow her down.
He also pictured the location of the interior door that led to
the garage. It was just on the other side of the fridge. Not
ideal, since there was a window over the kitchen sink and
because the second attacker could be at the back door in a
matter of seconds.

Still, there weren't a lot of options here, and having the
baby in a bullet-resistant vehicle was better than staying
in the house that was currently under attack from two directions.

"Stay low and close to me," he instructed, though he
knew it wasn't necessary to tell her that.

Gracelyn had been a damn good cop, and she knew

how to stay alive. He hoped their combined skills would be enough to keep her infant niece safe.

They moved fast. Well, as fast as they could, considering they were crouching, and they'd just made it to the kitchen when the front doorknob rattled. Of course, it was locked. And as expected, the intruder was having none of that.

The next shot blasted into the lock.

And sent Abigail wailing.

The baby was clearly startled. And terrified. Ruston wanted to punch the intruder for doing that, for putting an innocent baby through this nightmarish ordeal.

Despite the baby's cries, Gracelyn and he kept moving. It seemed to take an eternity to go the twelve feet or so from the hall and into the kitchen, but they finally made it.

Only to hear another shot to the front lock.

And worse, someone jiggling the knob of the back door.

Clearly, these two thugs were going for a coordinated double attack. An attack where they no doubt would try to sandwich Gracelyn and him in, either to try to gun them down or force them to surrender.

Ruston felt a fresh surge of adrenaline. It was mixed with a fresh round of terror, but everything inside him managed to stay still. He relied on his training. On his instincts. And he shifted places with Gracelyn and the baby when they reached the garage door.

He hated sending her out to the garage ahead of him, but again, they didn't have a lot of options here. His shooting hand was free, and he needed to be able to return fire if those two thugs broke through the doors. Also, thankfully, there'd been no indications that someone had managed to sneak into the garage.

Gracelyn had to shift the crying baby in her arms, but the moment she opened the door, she moved into the garage. Ruston stayed put to give Gracelyn a chance to get the baby in the car seat. Once she'd finished that, he would hurry to the SUV as well.

There was a third shot to the front door, followed by what Ruston was certain was a kick and a swooshing sound. Then a single footstep. The intruder was inside.

Ruston glanced over his shoulder to see that Gracelyn was in the back seat of a black SUV and was struggling to get the baby into the infant seat. He couldn't wait any longer. He levered himself up from his crouch just enough to fire a shot in the direction of the front door. When he pulled the trigger, he heard exactly what he wanted.

Some cursing, and the sound of the guy staggering back.

Maybe he was hit, maybe he was merely scrambling to get out of the line of fire. Either way, this should give Gracelyn and him some extra seconds to escape.

Ruston aimed another shot in the direction of the back door, hoping it'd do the same to the intruder who was trying to get in there. But he didn't wait around to see or hear the results of his two shots. He bolted into the garage, hurrying to get behind the wheel.

"Stay in the back seat with the baby," Ruston told Gracelyn.

Since the keys were in the holder below the dash, Ruston was able to use the automatic starter to fire up the engine. In the same motion, he hit the remote on the visor to open the garage door.

"Stay down," he repeated to Gracelyn.

He caught only a glimpse of her face before she did just that. There was no argument in her expression, only the fear. Something he'd rarely seen in her when she'd been a cop. But this time the fear wasn't for herself or him but rather for the baby.

As soon as Ruston had enough clearance, he put the SUV into Reverse and gunned the engine. He truly hoped the thugs weren't parked nearby. Because if they had to run to their vehicles, that upped Ruston's chances of getting Gracelyn and the baby out of there.

Ruston made it out of the garage, but as he was shifting into Drive, a bullet slammed into the windshield of the SUV. It'd come from the gunman on the front porch, who was obviously very much alive. So was his partner, because Ruston caught a glimpse of the second one hurrying around the side of the house. Like his comrade, this one lifted his gun and took aim.

Two shots tore from their weapons.

Both hit the body of the SUV, causing Ruston's heart to drop. He prayed the bullets hadn't gotten through to Gracelyn and the baby. Still, he couldn't risk checking to see if they were all right. He just slammed his foot on the accelerator and got them the hell out of there.

The gunmen came after them.

Not in vehicles. Ruston didn't see any nearby. But the two men ran after the SUV with both guns blasting out nonstop shots. Most of the bullets slammed into the back window, and Ruston glanced to make sure the safety glass had held. Thankfully, it had.

He also managed to catch a glimpse of Gracelyn.

She'd gotten the crying baby in the infant seat and had positioned her body over the child. A human shield. Of course, that put Gracelyn at greater risk, but he couldn't fault her for it. If their positions had been reversed, he would have done the same.

Ruston sped to the end of the driveway, and with the tires squealing in protest, he turned right onto the narrow country road. Behind them, the shots finally stopped, but

Ruston figured that wasn't great news. It likely just meant the gunmen were running to their vehicle and would come in pursuit.

Even at the too-fast speed he was going, he was still ten minutes away from the nearest town, which happened to be Saddle Ridge. No way would backup reach them before that, even though Ruston would have loved to have a dozen police cruisers around right now. Not only would it prevent these gunmen from attacking them again, but backup would mean the thugs stood a chance of being apprehended.

And then Ruston could figure out who had hired them.

That was for later, though. For now, he focused on getting Gracelyn and the baby to safety. That started with contacting someone, and he was pleased to see that the SUV Bluetooth paired quickly with his cell so he could make a hands-free call.

He ruled out calling his sister Deputy Joelle McCullough, because she was seven months pregnant. Instead, Ruston called his brother, Slater, who was also a deputy in the Saddle Ridge Sheriff's Office. Ruston said a short prayer of relief when his brother answered on the first ring.

"Long story short," Ruston immediately said. "Get anyone you can out to the old Henderson Road. Have them head east. I want lights flashing and sirens blaring."

Slater had been a cop for a long time, and that was maybe why he didn't fire off any questions as to why Ruston would need such things. Within a couple of seconds, Ruston heard his brother make a call to Dispatch to request immediate backup and followed that by relaying the location that Ruston had given him.

"I'm on my way," Slater assured Ruston. "How far out are you from town?"

"Too far. Nine minutes." Which was an eternity. "Someone's trying to kill Gracelyn and me, and we have a baby with us."

No need for him to explain who Gracelyn was, because when Gracelyn had been his partner, he'd brought her to their family ranch several times.

"A baby," Slater muttered, and he added some ripe profanity to that. "Is anyone hurt? Do you need an ambulance?"

"No, not hurt." Ruston needed to keep it that way. "Two armed men attacked us at Gracelyn's place and will shortly be in pursuit of us again."

Ruston had barely gotten out the words when he glanced in the side mirror and saw the headlights of the vehicle barreling toward them.

"Correction," Ruston said. "The gunmen are in pursuit *now*."

That had Gracelyn shifting her position. She was still sheltering the baby, but she moved so she'd be able to use her gun.

"If they shoot out the safety glass, I'll return fire to try to get them to back off," she explained.

Ruston didn't like that plan at all, but if the bulletproof glass didn't hold, then the gunfire could get through to the baby. Having someone like Gracelyn—who was a darn good shot—returning fire could maybe get them to back off. And if she got lucky enough, she'd be able to take out the driver.

"You want to stay on the phone with me while I'm en route to you?" Slater asked him.

Ruston didn't want the distraction. He also didn't add for his brother to get there fast, because he knew Slater would. "No," he answered, and he ended the call so he could focus on the road.

Since Ruston didn't want to risk wrecking the car, he couldn't try to return fire as well, but he could do something to prevent these thugs from pulling up on the driver's side of the SUV and having an easier shot. He maneuvered into the center of the road. He should be able to see the headlights of any vehicle coming toward them and get out of the way in time.

He hoped.

Ruston kept up the pressure on the accelerator, but the gunmen must have had a more powerful engine in the big silver truck they were using, because they not only kept up, but they also gained ground. Their headlights were getting closer and closer. Worse, Ruston saw one of the thugs lean out from the passenger's window.

And take aim at the SUV.

"They're about to shoot at us," Ruston relayed to Gracelyn, hoping that would cause her to get back down.

His warning came a split second before the shot blasted into the rear window. The bulk of the glass continued to hold, but this bullet had created a fist-sized hole. It didn't seem nearly big enough for Gracelyn to get off a shot, but that didn't stop her.

She took aim. And fired. Not once. But four times.

The sound of each shot ripped through the SUV, causing the baby to wail again, but Ruston saw something positive. The truck swerved, the headlights slashing through the darkness. Gracelyn fired again. And again. Emptying the magazine.

She must have hit the driver, because the truck didn't just swerve this time. It practically flew off the road and crashed into a pasture fence.

Ruston felt some of the tightness ease up in his chest. Part of him wanted to go back and confront these SOBs, to make them pay for endangering Gracelyn and the baby. But he couldn't risk that. He just kept on driving and was about to use the hands-free system to call Slater to let him know what was going on. However, before he could do that, his phone rang.

"It's Charla," Ruston muttered when he saw the cop's name pop up on the dash screen.

"Don't tell her where we are," Gracelyn was quick to say.

She was still keeping watch out the hole in the back window but was also trying to soothe the baby. The soothing was working or else Abigail had just exhausted herself from crying, because her wails were now just a soft whimper.

"Don't tell Charla where we are," Gracelyn repeated, this time with even more emphasis.

Ruston wanted to bristle at the notion of not trusting a fellow cop. But Gracelyn was right. Someone had set him up, and only a handful of people could have managed that.

Charla was one of them.

Even though the woman had never given him a single reason not to trust her, Ruston was going to err on the side of caution here.

"What happened?" Charla demanded the moment Ruston answered the call.

Since that question could encompass a whole lot of things, Ruston took the safe route with this as well. "My cover was blown. Again. Any idea how that happened?"

There was silence for a long time, and then Charla cursed. "Blown? How? Are you hurt?"

Ruston didn't answer any of those questions but instead went with two of his own. "Why did you ask what'd happened? Why did you suspect something was wrong?"

That brought on more muttered profanity from Charla. "Because I've got a dead body on my hands. And judging from the crime scene, someone's trying to set you up for the murder."

Chapter Four

Gracelyn's heartbeat was still pounding in her ears, but she had no trouble hearing what Charla had just said.

Dead body.

Gracelyn had to choke back a sob because her mind instantly jumped to whose body that might be. Her sister's.

Sweet heaven, had Allie been murdered?

That was her first thought. Because if someone had come after Allie's baby and her, then they might have gone after Allie as well. Gracelyn needed to know the answer, but she wasn't sure she could handle it right now. Not coming on the heels of this attack that could have killed Ruston, Abigail and her.

"Who's dead?" Ruston asked.

Since Gracelyn didn't want Charla to know she was in the vehicle with Ruston, she stayed quiet. Waiting and praying.

"Marty Bennett," Charla provided. "He was found dead at his house in San Antonio. A single gunshot wound to the head."

Gracelyn felt the relief wash over her, but it didn't last. Yes, she was so thankful it hadn't been Allie, but Marty Bennett was the man who'd hired Ruston to kidnap Abigail and her.

Why was he dead?

Since he was a criminal, there could be plenty of reasons for his murder, but Gracelyn figured the man's death wasn't a coincidence. It had to be connected to this attack by those two thugs in the truck.

"Are you there, Ruston?" Charla asked.

"Yeah," he confirmed, and Gracelyn saw that, like her, he was still keeping watch around them while he drove. "I didn't kill him. Why do you think someone's trying to make it look as if I did?"

"Because whoever did kill him left your badge at the scene," Charla was quick to reply.

Ruston cursed under his breath. "My actual badge or a fake?"

"Looks like the real deal to me. Where did you last see it?"

He muttered yet more profanity. "In my apartment in San Antonio. Not the one I rent under my current cover, but my actual apartment under my real name. It's nowhere near the one I use for cover, and there are only a handful of people who know about it."

Gracelyn wondered if one of those people was Charla. Or any other cops. If not, it still meant the person behind this knew way too much about Ruston.

"I have a decent security system at the apartment," Ruston went on, "and I didn't get an alert that it'd been triggered."

"Do you have security cams?" Charla asked.

"No, but there are some on the street in front and back of the building."

"They'll be checked," Charla assured him. "I'll send someone over there now."

"No," Ruston said firmly. "Hold off on that. Uh, I'm not sure who to trust on this. With my cover blown, there could be some kind of leak."

Gracelyn hoped that his distrust extended to Charla. And maybe it did. Her distrust for Charla was certainly there. But it was possible Ruston was simply being cautious. There were plenty of reasons for that.

Maybe Ruston wanted to send up someone he'd be sure wouldn't plant anything or take something else. Then again, since the break-in had already happened, Gracelyn was betting any planting or taking had already happened.

"Where are you, Ruston?" Charla pressed a moment later.

"I'll get back to you on that," he said and ended the call.

Charla must not have cared for that abrupt dismissal, because she immediately tried to call him back, but Ruston declined it.

He looked in the rearview mirror to meet Gracelyn's gaze. "I don't know what's going on," Ruston said before he turned his attention back to their surroundings. "Do you?"

"No." And she wished her head would clear enough so she could think straight. Everything was still racing inside her, and it was hard to sort through the details when she wasn't even sure they were safe.

"Marty hired you to come after Abigail and me," Gracelyn spelled out, hoping that just going through the obvious would help them piece this together. "Then someone murdered him and tried to set you up. That someone killed Marty about the same time two gunmen were trying to kill us."

Saying it aloud worked. Something flashed in her mind. It must have come through in Ruston's, too, because he voiced what she was thinking.

"If the gunmen had killed me, then there's no way Marty's murder could have been pinned on me," he reasoned. "I spoke to Marty on the phone just minutes before the attack, which means it was probably minutes before he was murdered. I was at least fifty miles from Marty. So, the badge wasn't to set me up."

Gracelyn made a sound of agreement. "Maybe it was left to taunt you? To blow any future cover you might have?" If so, it would take Ruston off the market, so to speak. Since his face would be recognizable, he wouldn't be able to go back undercover.

Why would someone want that?

Again, Ruston supplied the answer. "This could have been done to discredit me with both the cops and the criminals." He stopped, shook his head. "And it just might work."

Yes, it possibly would, because even if Ruston had an alibi for Marty's murder, there'd still have to be an investigation. Gracelyn was betting that Ruston would be doing his own investigation, too. She certainly would be as well, since she didn't want another of these attacks.

"Either Charla or Tony could be dirty," she told him. "Of course, that's true about some other cops, but those two were in on every detail of our last assignment. And they were almost certainly in on every detail of your dealings with Marty. I've been digging into their backgrounds, and I believe there are some possible red flags for both Charla and Tony."

Thanks to the rearview mirror, she saw the concern flash in Ruston's eyes. Gracelyn didn't get to say any more, though, since there was the howl of sirens, and just ahead lights slashed across the dark road. Not solo ones either. There were at least three cruisers. In the same instant Gracelyn spotted them, Ruston's phone rang again, and this time it was Slater's name on the screen.

"Is that you coming my way in the black SUV?" Slater asked the moment Ruston answered.

"It is," Ruston verified. "We're not injured, but the SUV

is shot up courtesy of two gunmen in a silver truck. They went off the road about four miles back. It's possible one of them is injured, but they're dangerous, Slater. And they need to be caught so we can find out why they did this."

"Understood," Slater said. "Woodrow's right behind me, and the two of us will go after the gunmen. Carmen's in the third cruiser, and I'll alert her to turn around and shadow you."

Gracelyn didn't know who Woodrow and Carmen were, but she was guessing they were deputies. She was also guessing they'd come in separate cruisers to create that "lights flashing and sirens blaring" effect that Ruston had wanted. He'd gotten it, and it might be enough to put off any attackers who were nearby and ready to strike. Hopefully, though, those attackers didn't have a way to escape since they'd crashed their truck.

"Are you going to your place or the ranch?" Slater asked a second later.

"The ranch," Ruston verified, and he ended the call just as Slater and one of the other cruisers went past them.

Slater slowed just a little, probably so he could make brief eye contact with his brother and see for himself that Ruston wasn't hurt. Apparently satisfied with what he saw, Slater went off in pursuit of those gunmen with the second cruiser right behind him. The deputy in the third cruiser waited until Ruston had passed before she executed a U-turn so she could follow them.

"To the ranch?" Gracelyn questioned.

Ruston did another glance in the rearview, and he no doubt saw the concern on her face. And she didn't have to spell out why that concern was there. His father had been gunned down on the family ranch seven months ago, and

Gracelyn didn't want to jump out of the frying pan and into the fire.

"We've upgraded security since my father was killed," Ruston said.

Good, because she didn't want a killer to come waltzing in and try to finish what those two gunmen had started. Then again, she'd done plenty of security upgrades and look what'd happened. Still, there had to be a way to keep out a killer, and for Abigail's safety, she had to find it.

Had to.

Abigail wasn't her biological child, but Gracelyn couldn't have possibly loved her more. Of course, when and if Allie returned, her sister might take the baby. Or rather she would try, but Gracelyn couldn't let her do that unless she was certain the little girl was safe. At the moment, she wasn't.

Then again, maybe Allie wasn't either.

Gracelyn quickly had to shove that thought aside. No way could she let that fear take over her thoughts. She needed a clear head to keep watch. Because even though Ruston and she now had backup, they weren't out of the woods just yet.

"Red flags?" Ruston asked.

It took Gracelyn a moment to realize why he'd said that. Before Slater and the other deputies had arrived, she'd been telling him, or rather warning him, about her concerns about both Charla and Tony.

"Possible red flags," she emphasized. "It could be nothing, but I don't want to dismiss them and then have them turn out to be something." She paused a moment to gather her breath. "After our covers were blown, I did some research and found out that Charla's mother was a junkie and had a record for prostitution. When Charla was eight, her mother sold Charla's infant half brother to what was essentially a baby broker. Her mom did it again two years later with a baby girl but was caught and arrested. That's when Charla ended up in foster care."

She paused again to give Ruston a moment to digest that. It definitely fell into the "possible" red flag category, since it wasn't a strong connection to the baby farm that had come into existence some thirty years later.

"Is her mother still alive?" Ruston wanted to know.

"No. She died two years ago."

Which would have maybe been about the time of the start of the baby farm that Ruston and she had ended up investigating. Her mother's death could have been a trigger to start her on a very bad path.

Gracelyn went ahead and added the rest. "And, no, I don't have any proof that Charla stayed in touch with her mother and that the woman passed along her contacts for baby brokers to Charla. Even if she had, I know that doesn't mean Charla used those contacts to become the Green Eagle and start her own business."

Ruston muttered an agreement. What he didn't do was dismiss the possibility that it was exactly what'd happened. "And Tony? What do you have on him?"

"He was in serious debt. Not enough to draw the attention of Internal Affairs, but he'd gotten burned in a divorce settlement and was barely keeping his head above water. Until two and a half years ago, when his debts disappeared. The money appears to have come from an old army buddy of his who passed away, but I think the inheritance paperwork could be bogus."

Ruston met her gaze again. "You hacked into Tony's financials?"

Gracelyn knew she was about to admit to a crime. A crime that Ruston could use to have her arrested. But she wanted him to have the full picture here. And that picture was anything she'd learned about Tony's funds couldn't be used to launch an investigation.

"I didn't personally do the hacking," she admitted. "I don't have that particular skill set, but I hired someone to do it. An old friend of Allie's, Simon Milbrath, did it. I didn't use my real name when I contacted him. I set up an identity that I used just for my contact with him, and I never met with Simon in person."

Ruston muttered more profanity and took the turnoff to the main road. A road she knew would lead to his family's ranch.

"Simon Milbrath," he repeated as if committing that name to memory. "And Charla?" he pressed. "How did you find the info on her?"

"Not with any hacking," Gracelyn said right off the bat. "I dug through her background and found old newspaper articles about her mother's arrest. Then, using a cover that I was a reporter doing a story, I emailed the now-retired officer who arrested her mother. He was able to tell me that he had suspicions that Charla's mom had helped some of her junkie friends sell their babies through this broker. He also recalled Charla being furious when her mom was taken away."

"Did this retired cop have any computer expertise?" he asked after a short pause. "I'm just trying to get an idea of who could have found your location and then passed it along to Marty, who in turn gave it to me."

Gracelyn wanted to know the same thing, but she didn't have to consider his question for long. "I did a thorough check on the retired cop, Archie Ingram, before I ever contacted him. He's in his late seventies, and there's nothing in his background to indicate he's a computer whiz or that he was dirty. Just the opposite. He had a stellar record..."

Her words trailed off when the ranch came into view. She'd been here two other times when Ruston and she had still been partners, and it'd had a picture-postcard feel to it then, with its acres of pastures and the pretty pale yellow Victorian house. In the milky moonlight, it was still pretty, but she immediately spotted sensors on the fences, and the driveway along with the front and sides of the house had perimeter lighting. She was betting the back did, too.

"Who lives here now?" she asked. As he drove, even more lights flared on, obviously triggered by motion.

"My sister Joelle and her husband, Sheriff Duncan Holder."

She knew that Joelle was a deputy, so there'd be three cops. Maybe four if Carmen stayed. In some ways, even that didn't feel like enough protection. In other ways, it felt like too much, since Gracelyn figured she would be plenty uncomfortable around, well, anyone. That included Ruston's family.

"Do Joelle and the sheriff know we could be bringing danger right to their doorstep?" Gracelyn asked.

"They know. Slater would have told them."

She saw the tall man in the front window. Saw that he was armed, too. Duncan, no doubt, and Gracelyn recalled meeting him as well on one of her trips to Saddle Ridge. He'd been a deputy then and had obviously become the sheriff after Ruston's father had been murdered.

"A couple of months ago, there was trouble here," Ruston went on, stopping in front of the house. "Trouble at Duncan's and Joelle's houses, too. After it was over, they decided to move here and beef up security. Joelle's seven months pregnant, and they wanted to take precautions." He turned in the seat and looked at her. "They'll help us take precautions for Abigail, too."

She nodded and hoped any and all precautions would be enough. "Thank you. And thank you for helping Abigail and me to get away from those gunmen."

The corner of his mouth lifted just a little. "I suspect you could have gotten away from them yourself." The almost smile vanished. "Now, I need to figure out if I led those men to you or if they were already lying in wait to take both of us."

Yes, that was the million-dollar question, all right, but either way, the danger was still there. It could return. And despite what Ruston had just said, she wasn't so sure at all that she could have gotten away by herself.

The only reason she'd been able to return fire and cause the gunmen's truck to crash was because Ruston had been driving. If she'd been alone with Abigail and behind the wheel, it was entirely possible those thugs would have managed to overtake her and force her off the road.

When Ruston stepped out of the SUV, Duncan came out of the house, providing cover. Ruston moved fast, throwing open the back door so he could help her get Abigail unstrapped from the infant seat. The moment they'd done that, Ruston scooped up the baby. Gracelyn grabbed her go bag, and scrambling out right behind him, she hurriedly followed him into the house.

Once they were all inside, Duncan closed and locked the door. He used his phone to rearm the security system and then to make a quick call to Carmen to tell her to assist Slater. As much as Gracelyn wanted the extra backup here, it was best for Slater to have more help. That way, there was a better chance that the two gunmen would be caught.

Joelle was there in the foyer, and she was also armed.

Despite being mega-pregnant, Ruston's sister still looked more than capable of defending her family home.

"Gracelyn," Joelle said and didn't add the customary *it's good to see you*. Still, the woman didn't look upset or angry at the intrusion. Just the opposite. Joelle's face turned a little dreamy when her attention landed on the baby.

Dreamy and then suspicious. She aimed her suspicion at her brother.

"She's not our child," Ruston was quick to explain. "This is Abigail, and she's Gracelyn's niece."

Joelle seemed a little disappointed about that, and then her expression morphed again. She became all cop. "Slater said someone fired shots at you?"

Since the question seemed to be directed at Gracelyn, she nodded and hooked her go bag over her shoulder. "Two armed men. Slater and Woodrow and now Carmen are looking for them."

"I'll fill you in on the attack," Ruston added, aiming glances at both his sister and Duncan. "Any reports from Slater yet?"

Duncan shook his head. "But I've sent them out some more backup, and I've got a half dozen ranch hands patrolling the grounds."

Gracelyn was once again thankful for all these measures, but she wouldn't breathe easier until the two men were caught. Caught and questioned. Hopefully, they'd make some confessions, too.

"Any chance the baby's parents are responsible for the attack?" Duncan asked, aiming the question at Gracelyn.

She wanted to be able to say no, to deny that Allie could have had any part in this. But she couldn't. "I don't know where my sister is," Gracelyn admitted. "And Allie has a bad history with Abigail's father, Devin Blackburn."

Duncan jumped right on that. "Bad? How?"

"An arrest for assault and another for computer hacking. He also has several restraining orders from previous relationships. No jail time, though. When Allie disappeared a few weeks ago, she left me a note saying she was going back to Devin."

"Did she?" Duncan pressed.

"I'm not sure. I've been monitoring Devin's social media accounts, and there's no mention of Allie." That didn't mean, though, that Allie wasn't with him.

"Devin was also interviewed during the baby-farm investigation," Ruston supplied. "Interviewed after Gracelyn and I were attacked there," he clarified. "There was no evidence to charge him with anything."

"But you think he could be guilty," Duncan stated.

"I want to go back through the report of the interview, but Devin has the right skill set to have been involved. Computer hacker, money to set up an operation like that and a connection to a known baby broker."

Duncan nodded. "I'd like to read that report, too."

"I've gone through it many times," Gracelyn admitted. "Especially after my sister got involved with Devin."

"Was that involvement before or after the baby-farm investigation began?" Ruston asked.

"During," Gracelyn answered. "I pressed Allie about the timing, and she said she'd known Devin for years before they became lovers, and that their involvement had nothing to do with the farm. Or what happened to Ruston and me." She paused. "I don't know what's true and what's not."

But she needed to find that out fast.

Abigail whimpered, her arms flinging up in the air as if startled. Maybe from a nightmare. If so, Gracelyn hoped it was a nightmare the baby would soon forget. Still, she went to her and eased her out of Ruston's arms and into her own so she could try to soothe her.

"The nursery is already set up," Joelle explained, "so you can use that, or there's a playpen that I've already put in the guest room if you don't want to be away from her."

Gracelyn didn't even have to think about this. "The playpen." It was basically a portable enclosure that could also be used for sleeping. And it would keep Abigail with her.

Joelle nodded. "It's there and already set up. I can also have whatever you need delivered."

"Thank you, but I have some formula and diapers in my bag and there's more in the SUV." Well, unless that stash had been damaged in the gunfire. Even if it had, though, there was enough in the go bag to last for at least a couple of days.

Enough cash, too, along with a fake ID, a gun and a change of clothes for Gracelyn as well.

"Good," Joelle muttered. "But if you think of anything else, just let me know. Do you want to take her to the guest room now?"

Guest room. Not plural. And it made Gracelyn wonder if Ruston and she would be sharing it. Part of her hoped they would be. It wouldn't be especially comfortable to be in such close quarters with a man who'd once been her lover.

A onetime lover, anyway.

No, not very comfortable, but the discomfort would turn to something much worse—fear—if there wasn't enough protection for Abigail.

"I'll go ahead and take Gracelyn and the baby upstairs," Ruston offered. "Once they're settled, I'll help in any way I can with the investigation."

"I'll help, too," Gracelyn said. "I can get Abigail in the playpen and then make phone calls or anything else you need. I don't want her out of my sight, but I need to do something to help. And please don't say I should get some rest. That's not happening tonight, not after what we've been through."

No one disputed that. In fact, there were sounds of agreement all the way around, and one of those sounds was from Ruston as he led her up the stairs. The guest room was large and just off the right of the landing, and even though the playpen was indeed there, the lights were off. Gracelyn kept them that way. No reason to alert anyone outside that someone was in the room.

"I need to make a call," Ruston said, stepping to the side of the room while she put Abigail in the playpen. "I have to talk to a cop friend."

That gave her a shot of instant alarm, and it must have shown on her face.

"A cop I can trust," he added, already taking out his phone and pressing a contact number. "Noah Ryland."

She immediately relaxed. She'd worked with Detective Noah Ryland at SAPD and believed he was trustworthy. Since Noah was assigned to Homicide, Gracelyn figured that was why Ruston had chosen to call him.

"Noah," Ruston greeted once the detective answered. "I need two favors, and both are huge. I want you to secure any and all files from Marty Bennett's residence and office. He was murdered earlier tonight, and I don't want anything to go missing before it's had a chance to be examined."

She couldn't hear Noah's response to that, but after a few moments, Ruston added, "Yeah, Marty was connected to my current undercover." Another pause. "You heard right. Someone tried to kill me and also planted my badge at the scene of Marty's murder."

More silence, and since she couldn't even hear any immediate murmurings from the other end of the line, she figured Noah was sorting through that info.

"Good," Ruston said after Noah finally spoke. "The second favor involves Gracelyn Wallace…Yes, the former cop…No, she didn't have a part in Marty's murder either," Ruston explained when Noah must have asked about it. "She has a solid alibi. In fact, she was with me at the time of the murder."

He paused when Noah commented on that. "Yes, with me. And that leads me to my next favor. I want to try to stop anyone from going after her again, and I need answers. Gracelyn had contact with a computer hacker named Simon Milbrath and a retired cop, Archie Ingram. It's possible one of them leaked information to Marty or someone who ended up killing Marty. So, I'd like to know if there are any known connections between Marty and them. It's possible there'll be something at Marty's residence to verify those connections if they exist."

Again, she heard Noah murmur something that had Ruston's tight jaw relaxing a bit.

"I owe you," Ruston told the detective. He thanked him, ended the call and turned to her as he put his phone away. "Noah will secure Marty's things…if they haven't already been compromised, that is."

The odds were they probably had been, but maybe the killer had gotten sloppy. If the crime had been premeditated, though, she doubted it. Still, sometimes killers made mistakes.

"Along with looking for any connections between Marty and the hacker and retired cop, Noah's also going to get the surveillance from any security cameras outside my apartment," Ruston explained. "He won't have to do it under the table, so to speak, since he's gotten approval from his lieutenant for me to view the footage in case I see something on it that'll help with the investigation."

"Good." She was glad the lieutenant hadn't tried to stonewall this. Technically, Homicide could have kept this close to the vest, but that wouldn't have benefited anyone.

Ruston scrubbed his hand over his face. "Maybe the surveillance footage hasn't been tampered with."

Again, that was a strong possibility, but unlike removing documents from Marty's home, or planting incriminating ones, it'd be trickier to alter or erase footage from traffic and security cameras.

A cop could do it, of course.

"If I caused all of this to happen, I'm sorry," Ruston muttered.

Even though she had no idea who was responsible, Gracelyn didn't intend to let Ruston fall on his sword for this. "You asked Noah to look at Simon Milbrath and Archie Ingram, and that means you think the leak of my location could have come from one of them. And it could have," she emphasized.

He made a sound of agreement, but the guilt stayed in his eyes. Ruston didn't get a chance, though, to continue voicing that guilt, because his phone rang.

"Slater," he relayed to her and immediately answered it.

Again, he didn't put the call on speaker, maybe because he thought it would wake the baby. But after only a few seconds, Gracelyn knew that Ruston was hearing bad news from his brother.

That churned up the adrenaline again and caused the mother lode of flashbacks to come at her. Not just of this attack tonight but of the one from nearly a year ago. She had to fight hard to push all of that away just so she could try to steel herself up for whatever Ruston had just learned.

It took some effort, lots of it, but she'd just managed to re-gather her breath when Ruston hung up and looked at her.

"Slater found the truck. The license plates are bogus, and the gunmen weren't inside," he relayed. "They were nowhere in sight. Slater and the others will keep looking for them," Ruston added when she groaned. "A CSI team is heading out to examine the truck now and take a sample of the blood drops that Slater spotted. I guess I was right about one of them being injured."

Good, because the blood could lead to a DNA match. She hoped the injury was so serious that it meant this snake couldn't come after them again.

"Slater said it appears the gunmen ran from the truck on foot," Slater went on. "They left a lot of stuff behind."

There was something in the way he said the last part that put her back on full alert. She waited, fighting for her breath again, while Ruston spelled it out.

"Slater had a cursory look of the inside of the truck and found my wallet," Ruston added to his account. "He figures it was taken the same time my badge was. The gunmen's plan was probably to kill you and then set me up for your murder."

Gracelyn tried to mentally work her way through that. Yes, that could have indeed been the thugs' plan. They could have waited out of sight, out of range of her cameras, until Ruston had arrived and was inside. Then they could have broken in and tried to make it look as if some kind of gunfight had gone on between Ruston and her.

"But why would they want to set you up for my murder?" she asked.

Ruston shook his head. "I'm not sure," he said and then paused again. "But there was also an infant seat in the truck. And baby things."

Gracelyn felt everything inside her tighten into a knot.

"They were going to kidnap Abigail." Her voice broke. "She was the target."

Ruston came closer, met her gaze, and he took hold of her hand. Probably because spelling it out like that had shaken Gracelyn to the core, and he'd no doubt seen that. His gentle grip helped steady her. More than Gracelyn wanted.

And that was why she stepped back.

She couldn't do this, not with the nightmares pressing so close to her that she could feel them. Memories of coming so close to them being killed ten and a half months ago.

Ruston didn't move back toward her, but their gazes stayed locked. At least they did until his phone rang again. "It's Noah," he muttered when he glanced at the screen. This time, he turned down the volume and put the call on speaker.

"Is something wrong?" Ruston asked the moment he answered.

"Yeah," Noah confirmed. "Something's very wrong. On the drive to Marty's, I made a call to a computer tech I trust so I could get a background check on Archie Ingram and Simon Milbrath." He paused. "They're both dead, Ruston. Someone murdered them."

Chapter Five

Ruston sat in one of the chairs in the guest room and, well, multitasked. He was watching the sleeping baby while Gracelyn showered in the adjoining bath. But he was also working on a laptop while drinking coffee and hoping for a miracle.

One miracle was that the caffeine would perform some magic and make him feel as if he'd gotten a decent night's sleep and now had a clear head. He'd slept some in this very chair, but that nowhere near qualified as anything decent, and so far, his head was nowhere near being clear.

Judging from the glimpse of Gracelyn's bleary eyes as she'd headed for the shower, she was in the same boat. No surprise about that. Like him, not only had she been dealing with the aftermath of the attack on them but also the flood of information they'd gotten since arriving at the ranch.

Three murders.

And all of them people who'd had a connection to either Gracelyn or him. People who could have ultimately given them the identity of the person responsible for this nightmare.

Someone was clearly cleaning up after themselves. Tying up loose ends. And Ruston needed to find something, *anything*, that would give them a break so he could learn who wanted them dead.

Unfortunately, scouring the steady stream of reports coming in and going over Devin's old interview wasn't giving him anything he could use. He figured Duncan was no doubt going through those same reports in his home office, along with coordinating this end of the investigation. That included the CSI search of the gunmen's truck and the search of the grounds of the rental where Gracelyn had been staying.

Detective Noah Ryland was keeping both Duncan and him updated about the active cases there: the three murders and the break-in at Ruston's apartment. Noah had also managed not only to get himself assigned as one of the detectives on the murders, but also to secure Marty's laptop since there hadn't been any actual paperwork in the dead man's office. The laptop was now in the hands of the IT specialist that Noah trusted.

So far, the updates from Duncan, Slater and Noah had been disappointing. And outright frustrating. Someone, somewhere, had to know something that would help make sense of all this, but for now, there were still a whole lot of questions and very few answers.

He hoped some of those questions were about to be answered when his phone dinged with a text. But it wasn't from Duncan, Slater or Noah. It was from Charla.

Where are you? Charla texted. *Tony wants you at headquarters right away.*

Ruston frowned and then mentally cursed. Eventually, he was going to have to meet with Tony, but he didn't want that to happen until he learned who was trying to kill Gracelyn and him.

Tony wants Gracelyn in as well, Charla added a few seconds later. *You'll both need to give a statement about the attack last night.*

I emailed Tony a statement, Ruston quickly pointed out, knowing what he'd given wouldn't be nearly enough. It had been the bare-bones details.

You know how this works, Charla insisted. You need to be interviewed in person.

Ruston had a quick comeback for that, too. The attack wasn't in SAPD's jurisdiction. Technically, that would fall under the duties of the county sheriff, but Duncan had already spoken to him, and he'd relinquished authority to Duncan. Charla almost certainly knew that.

Again, he didn't respond, and a few moments crawled by before Charla attempted to call him. So that the sound wouldn't wake up the baby, he'd put his phone on vibrate, and it rattled in his hand. Shortly after the rattling had stopped, he got the ding for a voicemail and listened to it.

"Damn it, Ruston, talk to me. This is important." In the voicemail, Charla huffed. "We got an anonymous tip that Marty was Green Eagle. We could finally be close to solving the case about the baby farm, and I know you want to be in on that. Call me," she demanded.

"Anonymous tip," he muttered, and, yeah, there was plenty of sarcasm in his voice.

If such a tip had indeed been phoned in, it had likely come from Marty's killer. Or someone connected to the murder, anyway. Then again, if Charla was behind this, the tip could be a lie, a ruse to try to tie all of this up.

Ruston's attention zoomed to the makeshift crib when the baby whimpered. Gracelyn had fed her less than thirty minutes earlier, before she'd gone in to take her shower, and the baby had fallen asleep during the burping process. That was when Ruston had gone down to the kitchen to get himself and Gracelyn some coffee.

The burping and so-called uptime, which Gracelyn had

explained was to minimize baby reflux, had just been coming to an end by the time he'd returned, and Abigail hadn't stirred when Gracelyn had placed her in the crib. However, she continued to squirm now, prompting Ruston to get up and move closer.

The baby still had her eyes closed but was smiling.

That made Ruston smile, too, even though he'd read somewhere that babies this age didn't actually sport that particular expression. It certainly looked like the real deal to him.

The bathroom door opened, and before he could even glance in that direction, Gracelyn blurted out, "What's wrong?"

"She's fine," Ruston assured her.

Or rather that was what he tried to do. It was obvious the reassurance hadn't worked one bit. Gracelyn ran to the baby, practically pushing him aside.

"She was just moving around a little and smiling," he added to his explanation. In fact, that smile was still on her tiny mouth.

Gracelyn released an audible breath of relief, and he could see she had to work to rein in whatever emotion had sent her running to the baby. Fear, no doubt, mixed with a whole boatload of worry.

"Sorry," she muttered. "Nerves on edge."

"No apology needed." He attempted more reassurance by giving her what he hoped would be a soothing look. This time, he was the one who failed when he saw the blood on her forehead. "You're bleeding."

She immediately pressed her fingers to a spot just inside her hairline. A spot he hadn't noticed the night before since her hair hadn't been swept away from her face the way it was now.

"It's just a small cut that I must have gotten when the safety glass was shot out in the SUV. It's okay," she insisted, taking out a tissue from the pocket of her jeans and pressing it to the wound. "I must have aggravated it when I was trying to brush my hair."

"Do you have any other cuts?" He immediately wanted to know.

"I think there's one other," she said, turning and lifting her hair so he could see the already scabbed spot on the back of her neck.

He wanted to curse. Wanted to beat those gunmen to a pulp. Yes, an extreme reaction to seeing two small cuts, but they were reminders that they could have easily been gunshot wounds.

She turned back to face him and muttered, "Yes." Gracelyn knew exactly how close they had come to dying.

He was about to fill her in on the three texts and voicemail he'd gotten from Charla, but she continued before he could do that.

"If their plan was to kidnap Abigail," she said, "those men took a huge risk shooting into the SUV."

They had indeed, and thinking about that had been a big contributor to Ruston's lack of sleep. "Maybe they did that because they panicked?" He threw the idea out there. That was one of his theories, anyway. "Or maybe because their orders were to eliminate you and me at all costs?"

It sickened him to think that the "cost" could have been the precious baby.

"The men had the infant seat in their truck," he reminded her. "And if the plan wasn't to take Abigail, then they could have just blown up the house or set it on fire with us inside."

She made a sound of agreement. "How long had you known my address before you showed up?"

"About five hours." He'd already given this plenty of thought as well. "So, maybe those men learned when I did. Perhaps Marty told them, or they found out through a mole or some kind of listening device. Either way, they would have had those five hours to figure out how to come after you." He paused. "Did you do your own security or hire someone else to set it up?"

"I did it," she answered, "with items I bought with cash the day I decided to disappear nearly a year ago. In fact, I've lived mainly off cash since then. Both Allie and I got a share of our parents' life insurance money after they died in a car crash. Allie blew through hers, but I saved mine and have been living off it since my resignation." She shook her head. "Those thugs didn't locate me through the security system, and that takes us back to Marty or someone connected to him."

Gracelyn seemed to settle a little. Ironic, since they were talking about the attack. But they were doing more than that. They were looking at this like cops and not intended victims.

"Did you get any calls or new reports when I was in the shower?" she asked.

"A few," he verified, "and basically all said the same thing. Everything is still being processed and looked at. Including Simon's and Archie's murders. Times of death for those two are about an hour apart, so the same person could have killed them both and then gone after Marty." He stopped and went through the mental checklist. "I also got three texts and a call from Charla."

The worry returned to her eyes. "She's demanding you come in?"

He nodded. "And you."

"Me? How did she know about…?" Gracelyn stopped.

"Duncan would have had to do a report, and she could have accessed it. Of course, she wouldn't have needed to access it if she already knew I was an intended target."

"Bingo." It still didn't sit well with him to think of a fellow cop as being responsible for this, but there were bad apples in every career field, and she might be one of them. "Charla says they got an anonymous tip, claiming that Marty was Green Eagle."

Gracelyn's eyes narrowed. "That's convenient."

"Isn't it, though?" he quickly agreed. "It works both ways in the killer's favor. If Marty was indeed Green Eagle, then he can't spill about anyone else who was involved in the baby-farm operation. If Marty wasn't Green Eagle, then someone wanted to set him up, probably with the hopes that setting him up would end any further investigation."

"That's one neat little package," Gracelyn muttered. "Too neat for my liking."

Ruston couldn't agree fast enough. "Let's see how this neat little package plays out. Charla will likely say that because Marty was Green Eagle, he wanted the baby for his still-ongoing business."

Gracelyn picked up on that scenario. "And that Marty wanted to get back at us for infiltrating the baby farm and causing him to have to move locations. Probably costing him a lot of money because of that. So, Marty hired you, somehow already knowing who you were. You and I were supposed to die, with you being set up for my murder."

He nodded. "But it's equally possible that Marty didn't actually orchestrate the attack against us. He could have been merely a middleman who had no connection to the baby farm or to us before someone used or hired him to set up yours and Abigail's kidnappings. He might not have had a clue how someone else was intending for this to play out. In the meantime, the cops will focus on Marty, and the real killer could just fade into the background."

"Or come after us again," Gracelyn muttered, her voice barely louder than a whisper. He saw the punch of emotion hit her, but then she quickly shook it off. "And that brings us back to Charla and Tony. Maybe," she amended. "And maybe they're clean. If so, that leaves Allie and Abigail's bio-father, Devin Blackburn."

Yes, because those two were the only other known players in this potentially lethal puzzle. Ruston had to ask, though he knew it was going to give Gracelyn another of those emotional jabs. "Could Allie have been in on the attack? Does she have a motive?"

"Trust me, I've been giving this a lot of thought," she muttered.

Of course she had. Gracelyn was still a cop at the core, and motherhood was an obvious connection they couldn't overlook.

"There'd be no obvious reason for Allie to kidnap the baby and kill us," Gracelyn said. "Obvious," she repeated. "If she wanted Abigail back, Allie knows how to get in touch with me. She could have called or texted the burner phone in my go bag. I check it often, and there was no contact from her."

Ruston figured Gracelyn had already thought of one possibility, so he voiced it. "What if Allie believed that you wouldn't give Abigail back to her? What if she thought, or someone convinced her, that kidnapping the baby was the only way she'd get her child back?"

Gracelyn's groan was soft, but it seemed to rumble through her entire body. "I wouldn't have just handed Abigail over to Allie. Not until I was certain she wouldn't do anything else reckless. And not as long as she was involved with a man like Devin Blackburn. So, yes, Allie might have known that, and Devin might have convinced her to go along with the kidnapping."

"And our murders?" he asked.

She shook her head. "Allie wouldn't have agreed to that. And, no, I'm not saying that because I'm her sister. I'm saying it because Allie isn't violent. She's, uh, more of a doormat. A very pliable, easily swayed one who Devin could have used to help him set up the kidnapping. Allie would have known what kind of security I was using, and there's a slim chance she might have even had an idea of where I was."

Ruston jumped right on that. "How?"

"I had notes on my tablet," she admitted, her forehead bunching up. That in turn caused her to wince a little, and she dabbed at the cut again. "Notes about possible rentals that I could use to make quick moves. My tablet is password protected, but there's a chance that Allie could have seen me typing and then accessed the notes without me knowing."

"Why would she have done that?" he pressed.

"Not specifically to find the notes," Gracelyn assured him. "But maybe to try to contact Devin. Or to check his social media posts." She stopped and sighed in frustration. "One minute Allie would be cursing Devin for the way he treated her, and the next, she'd be going on about forgiving him. Right before she left, she had convinced herself that she was responsible for him hitting her."

That was classic battered woman syndrome, and apparently the urge to forgive him and reunite had won out. Or maybe it had.

"You're sure Allie voluntarily left to go to Devin?" he asked.

Gracelyn opened her mouth and then immediately closed

it, obviously rethinking what she'd been about to say. "You're thinking he somehow lured Allie away?" She paused, then groaned again. "It's possible. That could go back to Allie using my tablet to get in touch with him. If she did, though, she didn't leave a trace of that contact. No copies of emails in the Sent folder or trash."

"Allie could have deleted them. Or Devin could have instructed her to delete them. You said he had an arrest for computer hacking, so he'd certainly know how to do something that simple."

"Yes," she muttered, and a moment later she repeated it while she was obviously working through this theory.

Because he was watching her, he saw the exact second she followed the theory to one possible conclusion. A bad one.

She nodded, swallowed hard. "Devin has a violent temper, and he could have lured Allie to him in order to punish her for leaving him. He could have already killed her."

Yeah. That was a bad possible conclusion, all right. Abusers could escalate. Hits and slaps could turn into something deadly.

"Oh, mercy," Gracelyn whispered, and the emotion took over.

Ruston went to her, pulling her into his arms, and she didn't resist. Gracelyn just let him hold her. Let herself lean on him while she dealt with the sickening realization that her sister could be dead. Unfortunately, that might not be the end of this scenario.

He gave Gracelyn a minute. Then two. And he just kept holding her. Definitely not a chore. In fact, it felt good to have her close like this. It stirred memories, of course. Of the heat. Of the one time they'd been together when a hug of comfort had turned into a kiss.

And then so much more.

Obviously, Gracelyn hadn't been able to deal with that *more* since she'd left the following day. That was the reason Ruston couldn't do what his body was urging him to do and push this contact further. He darn sure couldn't kiss her. That would risk her going on the run again, and he didn't want to lose her.

"If Allie is dead, if Devin killed her, then he might want to get Abigail," Ruston said. He was whispering now, too, because even though Abigail was way too young to understand, he didn't want her to hear any of this. "He might not want any DNA evidence to link him to Allie, and the baby would do that."

He felt Gracelyn's muscles tighten. "I could link him," she muttered.

Ruston eased back enough to meet her gaze. "And that leaves me. Until you told me about Allie and Devin, I had no idea about that connection."

She made a sound of agreement. "It's possible Devin contacted Marty to arrange the kidnapping, and Marty hired you." She stopped. "So, if Marty was indeed Green Eagle and knew your real identity, he could have used this opportunity to get rid of both of us and get payment from Devin for the baby."

Ruston was about to continue that line of thought, but his phone vibrated again, and he saw Noah's name on the screen. He showed it to Gracelyn, and he answered the call.

"Noah," he said, "I have Gracelyn here with me, and I'm putting you on speaker." That would save Ruston from repeating any info Noah was about to give them. And hopefully, that info would be useful and not simply more bad news. They'd filled their bad-news quota for a while.

"Good," Noah replied, "because I had a question for

her. Do you recall when you contacted retired sergeant Archie Ingram?"

"About two weeks ago," she quickly provided. "If you need the exact date, I can get it."

"Probably not necessary," Noah assured her, "but you should know that thirteen days ago, Archie called SAPD headquarters and asked to speak to Lieutenant Tony Franklin. Tony wasn't available, so Archie left a message, saying it was important, that some reporter was asking about the baby-farm investigation."

Gracelyn and Ruston exchanged glances, and she was probably thinking what he was. That this could indeed be important. If Tony had gotten concerned about a reporter, then he could have attempted to nip it in the bud. But for that to fit meant that Archie, or Tony, had figured out that Gracelyn was the bogus reporter.

"Did Tony call him back?" Ruston wanted to know.

"I'm not sure, but it's something you might want to ask him. He's on his way to Saddle Ridge, Ruston. I suspect he'll find his way to wherever you're staying."

Ruston wasn't sure whose groan was louder, his or Gracelyn's, but he thought he was the winner. "Any idea when he'll be here?"

"My guess is soon. I saw him hurrying out of his office about twenty minutes ago. Emphasis on *hurrying.*"

That would have been about the time Ruston had ended his call with Charla, and he wondered if Charla had said something to Tony to make him rush out to Saddle Ridge. Probably.

Even if Tony didn't know where the family ranch was, he'd soon find out, and that could mean he'd be here in as soon as ten minutes. Too bad his other sister, Bree, wasn't home. Bree was a high-profile lawyer for the Texas Rangers and could create legal walls in a blink to stop Tony from getting near the ranch.

But Ruston immediately rethought that.

He didn't want to hide behind Bree and legal walls anyway. He'd talk to Tony, give whatever statement was necessary, all the while watching for any signs that the lieutenant could be a cold-blooded killer.

There was a knock at the door, and for a moment, Ruston thought that meeting with Tony would be even sooner than he'd thought. But it was Slater.

"It's me," Slater said, keeping his voice low, no doubt because of the baby.

"Thanks for the info," Ruston told Noah, and he ended the call before he opened the door.

His brother was indeed there and not alone. Joelle was with him, and she had a tray of breakfast items. Fruit bowls, pastries and some juice. "You're probably not hungry," she immediately said. "But I decided to bring it up anyway."

Ruston checked the time. Just past nine, so not late, but he realized he should have already gotten Gracelyn and himself something to eat since neither of them had had dinner the night before. And, yeah, they wouldn't be hungry, but they should still try to eat.

He thanked his sister, who had already set down the tray and was making her way to look at the baby. "How did she sleep?" Joelle asked.

"Pretty good," Gracelyn supplied. "She had a four-hour stretch before she woke up for a bottle. And now she's about an hour into a nap. She might nap for another three hours before I have to feed her again."

"Speaking of feeding," Slater said, handing Ruston a large canvas shopping bag. "Extra diapers and formula," he explained. "Joelle arranged to have it delivered."

"But I made a point of telling the store clerk I was having some serious nesting urges and that I wanted the items for the nursery," Joelle added. "That way, no one is blabbing about a baby being here at the ranch."

Gracelyn added her own thanks to Joelle. It was possible the ranch hands were aware that Abigail was here, but the fewer people who knew, the better.

They shifted their attention to Slater. Everything about Slater's expression conveyed that he didn't have good news.

"Did you find the gunmen?" Ruston came out and asked. He set the canvas bag in the chair where he'd slept.

"No, but we think we know who one of them is. The blood is at the lab, and that might take a while to process, but there was a single partial fingerprint on the passenger's-side door handle. The handle had been wiped down, but he must have missed this one. Probably because he was in a hurry to get out of there. Anyway, the CSIs ran the partial, and they got an immediate hit for a man named Terry Zimmer."

Ruston tested out the name by repeating it a couple of times, but it wasn't familiar. "Zimmer has a record? Is that why his prints were on file?"

Slater shook his head. "He was a cop in Austin and resigned after some complaints about excessive force. That was three years ago, and afterward he supposedly worked for a company that provides security for large parties, weddings and corporate events."

Ruston latched on to one word. *"Supposedly?"*

"He did work there, part-time," Slater confirmed, "but he quit a little over a year ago, and no one at the company has heard from or seen him since." He paused a moment. "The CSIs found something when they ran facial recognition on him."

Slater took out his phone, and Gracelyn and Ruston

stepped closer to look at the picture. It was a grainy shot but still clear enough for Ruston to realize what he was seeing. The sprawling Victorian house that had once been a small hotel. That'd been its purpose fifty years ago, anyway. But it had been converted into something else.

The baby farm.

This had been the place Gracelyn and he had infiltrated. The place where they'd nearly died.

Gracelyn had no trouble recognizing it either, it seemed, because Ruston heard her quick intake of breath. Despite the god-awful memories it held, though, she didn't back away. Neither did Ruston. That was because the house wasn't the only thing in the picture. There was a man dressed in dark camo, and he was armed. His stance suggested he was standing guard.

Slater zoomed in on the man's face. "This was a picture taken shortly before Gracelyn and you arrived there undercover. And that's Terry Zimmer."

Ruston's mind began to whirl with thoughts of what this might mean. One immediate question came to mind. Was this Green Eagle? Ruston's guess was no. The boss of an operation that made millions of dollars probably wouldn't have been doing guard duty.

"Why wasn't this match made after the attack?" Gracelyn wanted to know. "Why did it take so long to identify him in this picture?"

"Apparently, because there are hundreds of photos that were taken over a monthlong period when the San Antonio cops had the place under surveillance," Slater explained. "Or that's what the CSIs told me, anyway. Hundreds that are still in queues waiting to be processed. This picture was one of them, and it popped because it'd been scanned into the system, but that's about all that had been done with it."

Ruston knew it wasn't that unusual for evidence to take months to process. He only hoped that someone, like a dirty cop, hadn't purposely delayed the examination of this photo.

"Does Duncan know all of this?" Ruston asked.

Slater nodded. "I filled him in before I came up to tell you." He paused. "While I had the CSI on the phone, I asked for a quick background on Zimmer, and I got his employment history. As a rookie cop in Austin, he worked with your lieutenant."

"Tony knows him," Gracelyn muttered, sounding just as rocked by that tidbit as Ruston was.

Of course, just because Tony knew Zimmer, it didn't mean they'd stayed in contact with each other. Still, it was a connection that made Ruston very uneasy.

"Now that we have a name and a face," Slater went on, "we can put out an APB. The more lawmen looking for Zimmer, the sooner he'll be found." He locked gazes with Ruston. "Of course, the person who hired Zimmer could be sheltering him. Or trying to silence him."

Yeah, and either one of those wasn't good. Ruston didn't want Zimmer to disappear or die. He wanted answers, and after that, he wanted him in a cage for the rest of his miserable life.

"Text me a copy of that picture," Ruston said.

Slater did that before he continued. "The CSIs will continue to process the other prints they retrieved from the truck," Slater went on. But he stopped. All of them did. They froze.

Outside, Ruston heard something that tightened every muscle in his body.

A gunshot.

Chapter Six

The moment Gracelyn heard the sound, she hurried to the baby, scooped her up and scrambled away from the windows. Even though the drapes and blinds were closed, that wouldn't stop a bullet.

Part of her, the former-cop part, wanted to grab a gun and be ready to return fire, but the baby had to come first. She couldn't protect Abigail if she was doing what Slater and Ruston were doing. They had already drawn their weapons, and Ruston had hurried to one window while Slater had gone to the other. They both lifted a few slats of the blinds so they could look out.

Joelle pulled out a gun, too, from the back waist of her jeans, but instead of the window, she maneuvered herself in front of Gracelyn and the baby.

There was the popping sound of another gunshot. It didn't sound close, and neither bullet had slammed into the house. Maybe that meant the shots had come from a hunter or someone who was trying to scare off a wild animal. Gracelyn wanted to hang on to that hope, but after what'd happened the night before, this was most likely another attempt to come after all three of them.

It was an incredibly risky move.

The ranch had four cops and ranch hands, all armed.

Then again, these shots were likely coming from a sniper and it wasn't a close-range attack. It was possible the shooter thought he could pick off some of them before moving in to finish the job he'd started.

"Is everyone all right?" Duncan called out. Judging from the sound of his voice, he was downstairs.

"So far," Joelle answered. "Can you see the shooter?"

"No," Duncan replied quickly. "But it's not any of the hands." He paused a heartbeat. "Someone's coming."

Duncan added that last part just as there was a third round of gunfire. And just as Ruston muttered some profanity. "It's an SAPD cruiser," Ruston snarled. "Probably Tony."

Gracelyn shook her head. "He's not the one firing those shots."

"No," Ruston agreed. "It appears he's the one being shot at."

That definitely didn't tamp down any of Gracelyn's worries since the gunman could change targets at any second. But it did punch some holes in one of her theories that Tony might be behind the attacks.

She heard the sound of the vehicle then. The sharp squeal of brakes as it came to a stop.

"The cruiser isn't in front of the house," Ruston relayed, glancing back at her to make very brief eye contact. "He's stopped at the end of the driveway."

Gracelyn nearly asked if that was because the driver had been hit. The cruiser was bullet resistant, but that didn't mean shots couldn't get through. So, if this was indeed Tony, he could be hurt. Then again, it was also possible he hadn't wanted to come closer since the gunshots could endanger those inside.

The silence came, and it seemed to her that everyone was holding their breaths. Even Abigail wasn't making a sound.

Then Ruston's phone vibrated.

It barely made a sound, but it cut right through the silence. While he continued to volley glances out the window, he took out his phone. "Tony," he said, and he answered it on speaker. "Are you in the cruiser at the end of the driveway?" Ruston demanded.

"Yeah," Tony immediately verified. "Who's shooting at us?" There were hitches in his breath, and the question rushed out.

"I was about to ask you the same thing," Ruston countered. *"Us?"* he questioned. "Who's with you?"

"It's me," Charla said. So, their call was on speaker as well. "Are the shots maybe coming from one of the local lawmen or a ranch hand?"

"No." He huffed, and when he repeated it, there was plenty of frustration in his voice. "I think the shots came from the west. There are a lot of trees in that area, so check and see if you can spot a sniper."

Because Gracelyn was watching Ruston so closely, she saw when he shifted his attention in the direction of the road. "A Saddle Ridge cruiser is coming," Ruston relayed to everyone just as his phone dinged with a text. "Duncan says it's Luca. Deputy Luca Vanetti," he spelled out, no doubt to inform Charla and Tony. "And Duncan is Sheriff Holder. He's here inside the house."

"I don't see a sniper," Tony said. "In fact, the only people I see are the deputy in the cruiser and some cowboys with rifles back behind the house. You're sure they're not the ones who shot at us?"

"I'm sure," Ruston snapped, and this time there was

some anger in his voice. "I'm not a dirty cop, and I didn't set anyone up to be murdered."

Before Ruston could add anything to that, he got a text. "Duncan says one of the hands spotted someone in that area by the trees. It's probably the sniper, so the hands are going in pursuit."

That gave Gracelyn a jolt of both hope and fear. She wanted the ranch hands to catch the guy, but they weren't cops. And they weren't killers like the sniper almost certainly was. The ranch hands could be hurt. Or worse. Still, if they managed to capture him, then they might learn why these attacks were happening.

Or if this was actually an attack.

After everything that had happened, Gracelyn wasn't about to dole out any automatic trust to Charla and Tony simply because they'd been shot at. One of them could have arranged this, knowing their odds of being hurt while sitting in a cruiser were slim.

Slater got another text. "Luca will escort the two SAPD cops to the house. They'll stay downstairs," Slater added, glancing at Gracelyn, probably to try to reassure her that Charla and Tony wouldn't be a threat.

And they probably wouldn't be, in a house surrounded by lawmen. No, this wouldn't be an optimal time for them to try to tie up loose ends. If that was what one of them was actually trying to do, that was. But Gracelyn very much wanted to see their faces so she could maybe tell if they were trying to hide their guilt.

"We'll talk once Charla and you are inside," Ruston said to Tony, and he ended the call.

Gracelyn turned to Joelle. "Would you be able to stay up here with the baby?" she asked.

Joelle didn't jump to say yes. She looked at Ruston, and

he gave her a nod. Only then did Joelle ease Abigail into her arms.

"I'll stay up here with Joelle," Slater immediately volunteered, "but if things get dicey downstairs, let me know." He looked Ruston straight in the eyes. "Are those two cops killers?"

Ruston held his brother's gaze. "I don't know. They might both be clean, but I can't trust either of them until I know for certain they aren't behind this. Right now, I'm nowhere near certain."

Slater nodded. "Let me know if you need help," he repeated.

Ruston turned to Gracelyn, studying her, and she thought maybe he was looking for any sign that she, too, wanted to stay put. She didn't.

"I'm armed," she let him know. "And I want to hear what they have to say."

He didn't try to talk her out of it. Probably because he understood she needed to do this as much as he did. "We shouldn't accuse Charla or Tony of anything right now. Nothing to put them on the defensive. Agreed?"

Gracelyn huffed. She did agree, since the pair were more likely to talk if they thought they were all on the same side. "All right," she finally said. "I'll play nice if they do."

Ruston didn't challenge that either. "I'll text Duncan and let him know that, while both Charla and Tony are suspects, we don't have anything concrete on them. Not enough to treat them like criminals, anyway." He stopped. "I'll ask Duncan if he wants to go tough on them to try to get some answers. Duncan's instincts are good," he added. "If he senses trouble, he'll shut it down."

That was a lot of trust to put in Duncan's hands, but she reminded herself that if Ruston believed in the sheriff, then she should, too. Plus, there was that whole deal about this being a bad time for Charla or Tony to try to come after Ruston and her.

Ruston sent the text and then motioned for her to follow him. After she brushed a kiss on the baby's head, Gracelyn did just that.

Ruston didn't put away his gun as they started down the stairs, and Gracelyn kept her hand on her own weapon. There were some footsteps and movements in the foyer, and she heard Duncan.

Ruston and she followed the sound of his voice and those footsteps and found Duncan, their two visitors and a black-haired man she figured was Deputy Luca Vanetti. All four still had their weapons drawn, and it gave Gracelyn an immediate jolt. Her instincts were to take out her own gun, to be ready to defend herself, but she forced herself to stay calm.

Both Charla and Tony immediately turned to Ruston and her, and Gracelyn tried to interpret their expressions. They were both a little wild-eyed, perhaps cranked up on adrenaline from the attack. Of course, it could be a pretense, and Gracelyn wished she knew for sure.

Both Charla and Tony were what many people would call average and nondescript. Charla was five foot six with brown hair and brown eyes. Slim but not overly thin. Attractive but not beautiful. Tony was about five foot ten and had sandy-blond hair and a face that sported no scars and no unusual features.

Nothing about them stood out, which was an advantage in undercover work, something Charla still did. Tony, however, with his promotion to lieutenant, was a "suit" these days and didn't do fieldwork.

Gracelyn had always felt as if she, too, fit into that average and nondescript category. But not Ruston. No, he had one of those faces that people definitely noticed. Handsome. Hot. That should have been a disadvantage for him, but it hadn't been. He'd always managed to alter his looks just enough for undercover work, and sometimes, he'd even used those good looks to coax his way into places and situations.

"Gracelyn," Tony muttered as a greeting, and he shifted his attention to Ruston and said his name as well. "Are you two all right? Were there shots fired into the house?"

"The shots didn't come into the house," Ruston stated. "They all seemed to be aimed at your cruiser."

Ruston hadn't emphasized the word *seemed*, but Gracelyn thought it was a good addition to his explanation. Because if Charla or Tony had indeed orchestrated this, then maybe the shots hadn't even come near them.

"I heard you say the ranch hands spotted the sniper and were in pursuit," Charla piped in.

She, too, was still gulping in her breath and looking a little shell-shocked. But Gracelyn had had to do that a time or two herself when undercover and playing a role. Undercover cops had to be good actors, and that could be exactly what Tony or Charla were doing now.

It was Duncan who answered. "Yes, the hands are looking now," he confirmed, "but I have other deputies on the way. They'll set up roadblocks. We might get lucky if the shooter's still in the area."

Tony nodded, and he was visibly steadier when he looked at Ruston and her again. "We have a lot to talk about," he said, sounding very much like a boss now.

"If you're here to demand I come into headquarters—" Ruston started.

"I'm not," Tony interrupted. "Well, I was, but I'm sure as

hell not demanding it now. It's obviously not safe to try to get you into San Antonio. You either," he added to Gracelyn. "How's the baby? Is she safe?"

"She's with two cops," Gracelyn answered, rather than spell out that the baby was in the house. If Abigail was indeed the target, then there was no need to advertise her whereabouts. "Cops that I trust," she couldn't help but add.

Something flashed in Charla's eyes. Anger, maybe. And she looked ready to demand to know if that was some kind of dig. It was, of course. But Tony spoke before she could.

"I understand your distrust of the police after what happened on your last assignment," he said. His voice was oh so sympathetic. Perhaps too much so. "But we need to talk to you about the attack last night. Ruston emailed me a brief report, but we'll need your account, too."

Charla took up the explanation from there, turning toward Duncan. "We understand that this is your jurisdiction," she said to Duncan, "but we have three dead bodies, and that needs to be investigated."

Duncan glanced at Ruston, and Ruston nodded. That was apparently the only cue Duncan needed.

"We can do the interviews here," Duncan said, speaking boss-to-boss with Tony. He motioned for them to all take a seat. "And since the investigations overlap, it'd be a good time for you and your detective to answer some of my questions, too." That wasn't a suggestion. Duncan was in all-cop mode now.

Charla opened her mouth, and Gracelyn was betting she was about to protest, but she hushed when she met Tony's gaze. Apparently, Charla also responded to subtle cues.

"All right," she said, holstering her gun and reaching into her pocket.

That had Gracelyn reaching for her gun. And Charla noticed. Her eyes widened, then narrowed. "Really?" Charla snarled.

"Really," Gracelyn snarled right back. She didn't add more because she didn't want this to turn into a sniping contest. Not when she wanted those answers from Charla and Tony.

Charla made a show of taking her phone from her pocket and holding it up for Gracelyn to see. "I need to record this interview."

Duncan holstered his own gun, took out his phone and sat in one of the chairs. "And I'll record your responses." He clicked on the record function. "In fact, I'd like to start. Sheriff Duncan Holder conducting interview of... State your names for the record," he insisted.

Charla and Tony were clearly not pleased to be on the other end of what would likely turn out to be an interrogation, but they both gave their names and sat on the sofa across from Duncan.

Duncan stated the date and time and continued. "Someone blew Detective Ruston McCullough's cover while he was on assignment at a house in my jurisdiction, and it nearly got him and Gracelyn Wallace killed. Who did that? Who's responsible for not securing the location of an undercover officer?"

Gracelyn had to suppress a smile. She was so glad Duncan had taken over the bad-cop role, and he'd almost certainly done that on purpose so that Tony and Charla's venom would be aimed at him. Of course, some of that venom would no doubt still come at Ruston and her. And she welcomed it. Because angry people often let things slip.

"That's being investigated," Tony answered. Yes, there was ire, all right. "We're still in the preliminary stages of that, but it's my theory that no one in my department was responsible. I trust the cops who work for me."

"Including Ruston?" Duncan asked.

Tony blinked. "Of course."

"Then that means you don't believe he was responsible in any way for his cover being blown," Duncan quickly concluded.

Tony shook his head, maybe objecting to the *in any way* part, but Duncan didn't give him a chance to voice that.

"For the record, Lieutenant Franklin indicated nonverbally that he did not believe Detective Ruston McCullough compromised his undercover identity. Is that right?"

"That's right," Tony muttered.

"Good. So, if Ruston didn't tell anyone who and where he was," Duncan went on, "then who did? What's your theory?"

Charla huffed. "That the leak came from Marty Bennett, the man who hired Ruston's undercover persona."

"Marty, who's now dead," Duncan stated in a way that made it sound like "isn't that convenient" sarcasm. "And how would Marty have learned Ruston was a cop?"

"We don't know," Tony jumped in. He met Ruston's gaze. "Not yet. But we'll find out. That's why we're here. I need to know if there's any possibility that you gave Marty some information, no matter how small, that made him believe you were undercover and that this was a sting operation."

Now it was Ruston who huffed. "So, you do think I was responsible for the leak. Trust me, I wasn't. My life was on the line. Gracelyn's life and the baby's, too. No way would I have risked letting anyone know. Especially a lowlife like Marty."

Duncan sat back, and Gracelyn took that as another of

those subtle cues that he was relinquishing the interview to Ruston and her. Gracelyn went with it.

"I certainly didn't leak my location to anyone," Gracelyn stated, easing down onto the love seat that was positioned adjacent to the sofa and the chair where Duncan was seated. "And until Ruston showed up, I had no idea he was even coming. But those two gunmen who tried to kill us, they knew. They knew my exact location."

"Which they could have gotten from Marty," Charla interjected.

"And that leads us right back to the question of who told Marty," Ruston said, sitting next to Gracelyn. "It's not just Gracelyn's location either, but considering the break-in at my apartment, someone would have told either Marty or his killer about that, too. That's a lot of information for someone outside of SAPD to have."

"We're looking into that," Tony insisted, and he shifted his attention to Gracelyn. "Is it possible you alerted someone to Ruston's identity—"

"No," she interrupted, "because I didn't know his undercover identity."

"But you knew the location of his apartment," Charla quickly inferred. There was something in her tone that suggested Charla had guessed that Ruston and she had gone there because they'd been lovers.

"No," Gracelyn repeated. "I didn't."

Charla pulled back her shoulders, and it seemed as if she wanted to challenge that. "But you came here with him. Before last night, I mean. You visited Ruston here in Saddle Ridge."

Gracelyn let her smile come. "That wouldn't have been in any report, Charla. How would you know that?"

"I must have heard it somewhere," Charla muttered, but

her eyes were narrowed now. "What is this about?" she demanded. "You can't possibly think Tony and I had something to do with what happened?"

"Did you?" Ruston asked, and he used some of Tony's wording to phrase his next question. "Is there any possibility that you gave Marty information, no matter how small, that ended up blowing my cover?"

"Absolutely not," Tony insisted.

Ruston didn't miss a beat. He took out his phone, brought up the photo he'd gotten from Slater and held it out for Tony to see.

"This is one of the gunmen who tried to kill us," Ruston spelled out. "Recognize him?" His tone indicated he already knew the answer.

A muscle tightened in Tony's jaw. "Terry Zimmer. How the hell do you know he was involved?"

"Evidence gathered from the vehicle used in the attack," Duncan supplied. He checked the time. "It's been less than fifteen hours since that attack, and we—a small-town sheriff's office with limited resources—have identified a former cop who you personally not only know, but one who also tried to murder Ruston and Gracelyn. And he was connected to the baby farm. You know the one I'm talking about. Gracelyn and Ruston were nearly killed then, too."

"How do you know that?" Tony demanded, but then he waved off the question. "I haven't seen or spoken to Zimmer in over a decade."

"Good," Duncan said, and he breezed right on. "Because as we speak, I have the Texas Rangers doing a deep background check on Zimmer. Deep," he emphasized. "So, you want to rethink that answer?"

"No." Tony spoke through clenched teeth now. "And there was no reason to involve the Rangers."

"Beg to differ," Duncan argued. "I have a high-ranking cop in SAPD—that would be you—with connections to a man involved in both an illegal black-market baby operation and the two attempted murders of police officers. I don't want this swept under any rug. I want everything out in the open."

The anger came, flaring through Tony's eyes, and he whipped out his phone, his movement so fast that it had Luca, Duncan, Ruston and Gracelyn all drawing their weapons. That caused Tony to scowl.

"Since you've brought in the Rangers," Tony said, his tone icy now, "you'll want to let them know about Gracelyn's involvement in this. And, no, I don't mean the so-called attempts to kill her. I mean her involvement."

Gracelyn flashed him her own scowl, but the uneasiness fell on her like a dead weight. She didn't ask what Tony meant by that, but it was obvious he had something up his sleeve. Or rather on his phone, because he thrust it out for her to see.

She leaned in closer, looking at the image that was just as grainy as the one they had of Zimmer.

"This was taken from the security camera just up the street from Marty's house," Tony explained, keeping his steely stare on Gracelyn. "Notice the time stamp."

She did. It would have been around the time that Marty had been murdered. There was the vague image of someone dressed in dark clothes.

Tony enlarged the image and showed it to her. Gracelyn leaned in again. And saw the face. She managed to choke back a gasp. Barely. But inside, a firestorm of emotions came at her.

Because she was looking at her sister's face.

Chapter Seven

Ruston wanted to curse. Something that Gracelyn likely wanted to do as well, and like him, she was no doubt trying to absorb the shock of what they were seeing.

Allie.

Near a murder scene.

No way could Ruston convince anyone, including himself, that Allie had simply been in the wrong place at the wrong time. That would be way too much of a coincidence.

"That's your sister, right?" Tony asked.

Gracelyn nodded. "Yes, that's Allie."

Both Tony and Charla had smug looks on their faces. "And what was she doing there?" Charla demanded.

Gracelyn shook her head. "I don't know. I haven't heard from her in a while, so I didn't know where she was."

"Well, clearly she was at the house, or at least near the house, of a man who was murdered," Charla said. "So, it's highly likely that she's the one who compromised Ruston's identity."

"No," Ruston was quick to argue. "There's nothing highly likely about that scenario. I had absolutely no indication from Marty that Allie was involved with this."

Of course, Marty wouldn't have mentioned that if she had been, but the premise was still way off.

He hoped.

Because if Allie was truly involved, this was going to crush Gracelyn. However, it might not be that much of a shock once it all sank in, and Gracelyn would likely come to some conclusions.

There was one way this could have all fit.

One way to explain why Allie had been there.

Ruston, though, had no intentions of voicing it in front of Charla and Tony. Thankfully, he didn't have to, because Tony's phone rang, and he saw Captain Katelyn O'Malley's name on the screen. Tony's boss. That wiped any trace of a smirk off Tony's face, and he stood, stepping to the side and muttering something about having to take the call.

"Why was your sister there?" Charla demanded, obviously trying to continue this interview.

But Tony's call only lasted a couple of seconds, and when he turned back around, Ruston thought the lieutenant looked even more riled than when they'd been peppering him with questions.

"I have to go," Tony said, motioning for Charla to stand. He aimed those anger-filled eyes at Duncan and then Ruston. "Captain O'Malley got a call from the Texas Rangers, and they want to talk to me about my association with Zimmer. And it apparently can't wait."

Ruston could have managed his own smirk, but he didn't. He just considered this progress, because if there was something dirty going on with Tony's connection with Zimmer, maybe the Rangers could find it.

Charla clearly wasn't pleased with any of this, and she huffed. "The sniper could still be out there," she reminded Tony.

"Then we'll be careful." Tony looked at Ruston again.

"But it might not be necessary. The shots could have just been a way to try to ward us off."

Tony was obviously suggesting that Ruston and his family were behind the shooting. Of course, they weren't, but the gunfire could have indeed been a warning. The killer might want to discourage police interference if he wasn't linked to Tony or Charla.

And that brought him back to Allie.

Tony got Charla moving, and despite the intense exchange that had gone on during the interviews, Luca, Duncan and Ruston all provided cover as Tony and Charla hurried down the porch steps and to the waiting cruiser. Gracelyn drew her weapon as well, but thankfully stayed in the door.

Ruston held his breath when no shots came, and he rushed back in, mainly so he could get Gracelyn fully back inside. He expected her to still have that shell-shocked look on her face, but she had shaken that off.

"I need to try to call Allie," she insisted.

"You know how to get in touch with her?" Duncan asked, shutting the door and resetting the security system.

Gracelyn nodded, then lifted her shoulder as if not so certain of her response. "I gave her a burner before she left and told her if I needed to contact her, I'd call her with a burner I keep in my go bag. Or that I'd message her through a private Facebook page I'd set up. I'll try the phone first."

"I'll get your go bag," Duncan offered when she started for the stairs. "I want to check on Joelle anyway."

"And I need to text one of the ranch hands to see where they are in their search for the sniper," Luca explained, taking out his phone and moving away from them.

Ruston had no doubts that Duncan did want to check on Joelle and that Luca needed to make contact with the ranch hands, but he also figured this was about giving Gracelyn and him a moment alone. Gracelyn clearly needed it, because she went straight into his arms.

"Oh, God," she muttered. "I'm so sorry."

He'd expected this from her, but it still riled him. "You aren't going to take the blame for anything your sister might have done. If she did anything at all," he tacked on to that. "Someone could have lured her there to Marty's."

Gracelyn made a half-hearted sound of agreement. "But even if she had been lured, it means someone used her to get to you. To try to kill you."

"And you," he pointed out. As good as it felt to hold her, and it felt darn good, he pulled back just enough so he could look her straight in the eyes. "Play this through while thinking like a cop and not like the sister of a woman who's screwed up time and time again."

She stared at him, and he saw the shift. He saw Gracelyn tucking away some of the raw emotion that had to be eating away at her. "All right." She repeated that several times. "I don't recall Allie ever mentioning anyone named Marty, so she might not have even known him." She paused. "And she might not have been in that area because of him."

Bingo. "Where does Devin Blackburn live?" he asked.

"One of those upscale apartments on the River Walk in San Antonio. I've never been there, and he also owns a house in a gated community on the north side of the city. I've never been to it either," she was quick to add. "But after Allie told me some of the things he's done, I researched him."

"Are either of those two places anywhere near Marty's?" He pulled out his phone and showed her first the location of Marty's office and then the man's house, where he'd been murdered.

She looked at the addresses on the map, sighed and shook her head. "No."

"But maybe Allie is staying near there," he pointed out. "You don't know for certain she's with Devin."

That put some hope in her eyes. "True. Things might not have worked out between them." She paused, huffed. "Of course, that doesn't explain why Allie wouldn't have tried to come back to get Abigail."

No, it didn't. But there was something else that had to give Gracelyn hope. "Allie's alive, and she didn't appear to be hurt." He wanted to see the actual surveillance footage, though, so he could try to determine what direction she'd come from and if anyone had been with her.

Since Noah was one of the detectives investigating Marty's murder, Ruston sent him a text to request a copy of the security feed. Of course, Noah would almost certainly scour that feed for himself, looking for anything that would help him find Marty's killer.

"I swear, I won't fall apart," Gracelyn muttered.

Ruston looked down at her. They were still close. Very close with their bodies touching. "I never thought you would," he let her know.

She shook her head. "I fell apart nearly a year ago when we were almost killed."

"No." He pulled her back into his arms, creating even more contact, but hopefully giving Gracelyn something she needed right now. "You never fell apart. If you had, you wouldn't have been able to put together a plan to disappear the way you did."

Even though he could no longer see her face, Ruston suspected she was sporting a very skeptical expression. "I disappeared," she stated.

"Because you needed time to process what'd happened,"

he spelled out. "And while I would have preferred you process that with me around, I understand why you had to have
that time, that space."

She lifted her head and looked up at him as he looked
down at her. "Yes," she muttered. "You understand because
of your father."

Yeah, he did. And Ruston was well aware that his father's
life had ended just a few yards from where they were standing right now. Ruston had done his own version of disap-
pearing in the weeks following that. He'd thrown himself
into the investigation. He'd become obsessed with finding
his father's killer. That obsession was still there. Maybe it
always would be until his dad finally got the justice he deserved.

First, though, he had to unravel who was after Gracelyn and him. That was the only way to keep the baby and
her safe.

She groaned softly, causing Ruston to look at her again.
Not that his attention had strayed too far. And it didn't stray
now either. With their gazes locked, things passed between
them. The worry. The urgency to find their attacker.

The heat.

Yeah, it was there, all right, and it felt like a gut punch
of a different kind. It was also a complication. One that he
knew he shouldn't act on. But he did anyway.

Ruston dipped his head and kissed her.

Since he hadn't actually planned it, he wasn't sure if this
was for comfort or if the heat was calling the shots here.
When the taste of her jolted through him, he had his answer.

The heat was in charge.

That definitely wasn't a good sign, and he figured Gracelyn would realize that and push him away. She didn't. She
sank right into the kiss, pressing her mouth harder against

his. Deepening it, too, and skyrocketing the fire. Making every inch of him want every inch of her.

The sound of approaching footsteps had Gracelyn and him practically jumping away from each other. Not in time, though, for Duncan to miss what'd been going on. Duncan didn't question it, not verbally, but Ruston figured the look Duncan gave him was sort of a caution. *You're playing with fire.*

Ruston knew that was the truth. This heat between Gracelyn and him was strong and hot. It was also a distraction. One that could ultimately cause him to lose focus at a time when that could turn out to be a fatal mistake. Still, Ruston couldn't just flip a switch and put an end to the heat. He just needed to try to keep it in check until Gracelyn and the baby were no longer in danger.

Duncan handed Gracelyn the go bag. "Joelle says she'll stay with the baby as long as needed," he said while Gracelyn began to dig through the bag for the burner phone. "I'm hoping you'll let her do that."

Gracelyn looked up at him, and Duncan huffed. "I'm worried about her. She's a cop to the bone, but she's also pregnant. I'd rather her be with Abigail than facing down murder suspects."

Since Joelle was his sister, Ruston felt the same way. It was even more of a reason for them to find the killer and put a stop to the danger.

"With Allie on that surveillance footage, SAPD will bring her in for questioning," Ruston told Duncan. "If they can find her, that is."

"I'd like to question her, too," Duncan insisted. "And her boyfriend, Devin Blackburn."

That was exactly what Ruston had hoped he would say.

First, though, they had to locate Allie, and that started with the phone call.

"You'll probably want to record this in case Allie answers," Gracelyn said.

She waited until Ruston had hit the recording app on his phone before she used the burner to dial the only number in its contacts. Gracelyn then put it on speaker just as it rang.

And rang.

After what felt like an eternity, it went to voicemail, but there was no personal recorded greeting to invite the caller to leave a message. Just the beep.

"It's me," Gracelyn said. Ruston figured she purposely didn't leave her name in case someone other than Allie had access to the burner. "We need to talk. It's important."

She ended the call, slipped the burner into the pocket of her jeans and took out her other phone. "I'll leave a message on the private Facebook page, too," she added and did that as soon as she pulled up the app.

When Ruston heard the ringing, he at first thought it was Allie returning her sister's call, but it was his own phone.

"Noah," he relayed to Gracelyn and Duncan, and he took the call on speaker. Gracelyn stopped what she was doing and moved closer to listen.

"I just heard someone shot at Tony and Charla," Noah said right off the bat.

Ruston realized he should have added that to the text he'd sent to Noah earlier. "Yeah," he verified. "They're both okay. The sniper hasn't been found, but Tony and Charla are headed back to San Antonio."

"Glad to hear they weren't hurt. Does their departure have anything to do with the Texas Rangers being in Captain O'Malley's office?" Noah asked.

"It does." And this was yet something else he should have

told Noah about. "There was a fingerprint in our attackers' truck that belonged to former cop Terry Zimmer. He was also connected to the baby farm. And Tony. They were rookies together in Austin."

Noah said a few words of choice profanity. "Yeah, that would get him in the captain's office." He paused a second. "You really think Tony could be dirty?"

Ruston didn't want to think it, but there was no way he could deny the possibility. "Either that or someone came by a whole lot of information that shouldn't have been available to anyone but cops."

Noah made a sound of agreement. "Terry Zimmer," he repeated. "I'm plugging his name into a search engine I put together. It's sort of a cop's form of Google that taps into data pools of arrest histories, police reports and witness statements. I'll let that run while I tell you the main reason I'm calling." He paused. "There's a problem with Marty's computer files."

Now it was Ruston who cursed, and Gracelyn wasn't far behind him on that particular reaction. "What happened? Did they go missing?" Ruston asked.

"No, but they might as well have." There was plenty of frustration in Noah's voice. "The techs say it was some kind of complex computer virus that corrupted every file on the laptop. They'll see if they can get anything from the corrupted data, but it doesn't look promising."

Hell. Of course, Marty would put some kind of measure like this in place. Except Ruston rethought that. "Any chance the virus was added after the laptop was taken into custody?"

"I asked the techs about that, and they say the virus doesn't appear to have been uploaded remotely, that they think it was already on the computer."

So, the killer likely hadn't done that. If he'd gotten access to Marty's laptop, he could have just destroyed it. Unless... "Any chance those files were backed up on a storage cloud?"

"Yes," Noah verified, "and those copies were corrupted, too." He stopped, muttered something that Ruston didn't catch. "Hold on a second," Noah added. Then he cursed again. "You said Tony knows Zimmer, but you didn't mention that Charla does, too."

Ruston saw the surprise register on Gracelyn's face and figured it was on his as well. "Because I had no idea. And she didn't say a word about it."

"Well, she knows him, all right. According to a report Charla filed last year, Zimmer was her confidential informant."

Ruston went still. "Give me the details on that, please." He wanted one bit of info in particular. "Was it connected to the baby farm?"

"I'll read it thoroughly but just scanning through for now," Noah let him know. "But, no, it doesn't appear to have anything to do with the baby farm. This report was filed about a month after the attack on you and Gracelyn. Charla was undercover to investigate some illegal weapons being moved through and stored in a warehouse. The weapons were found, and Charla noted that Zimmer had provided her with info for which he was paid."

So, that might be why Zimmer had been actually named. The payment would have required an invoice.

"Anything in that report about Charla investigating Zimmer before she used his info?" Ruston asked. Because if Charla had run a deep background check, she might have found a photo of him at the baby farm.

"Nothing that I can see," Noah answered. "But like I said,

I'm skimming. I'll go through this line by line, and I'll keep running the search engines. If I find anything, I'll let you know. Oh, and you'll be getting a copy of the surveillance feed sometime today."

Ruston thanked him and ended the call just as another phone rang. The burner this time. Gracelyn yanked it from her pocket but didn't answer it on speaker until Ruston had the recording app going.

"I understand you want to talk to Allie," the man said.

"Who is this?" Gracelyn demanded.

"Devin Blackburn," he said without hesitation.

Ruston didn't like this one bit. Clearly, neither did Gracelyn. "Where's Allie? Why are you using her phone?"

Devin countered that with a question of his own. "Are you Gracelyn?"

Gracelyn hesitated but finally said, "Yes. Where's Allie?" she repeated.

Devin's sigh was loud and long. "That's what I was hoping you could tell me. I don't know where your sister is."

"But you have her phone," Gracelyn quickly pointed out.

"No, I have a phone that I found in her purse. It's not the one she usually uses. When I heard it ringing, I didn't get to it in time to answer it, but I listened to your voicemail. I figured from your tone that you're worried about her. Well, so am I. Do you have any idea where Allie is?"

The image of Allie on the security footage flashed into Ruston's head, and he was certain the same image was going through Gracelyn's.

"When is the last time you saw my sister?" Gracelyn pressed.

"Two days ago." Devin didn't hesitate, but then he sighed again. "I'm afraid Allie has gotten into serious trouble."

Some of the color drained from Gracelyn's face. "What do you mean?"

Devin wasn't so quick to answer this time. "We have to talk, and it should be in person. You can either come to me, or I can meet you somewhere."

Gracelyn paused, too. "Meet me at the Saddle Ridge Sheriff's Office."

Ruston expected Devin to balk about the location. He didn't. "Saddle Ridge Sheriff's Office," he confirmed. "I can be there in an hour. See you then."

"Wait," Gracelyn said before he could hang up. "What kind of trouble is Allie in?"

No sigh this time but rather a soft groan. "The kind that can get her killed. Let's see if we can prevent that from happening."

Chapter Eight

Gracelyn was fully aware this wasn't the safest thing to do. Meeting Devin meant leaving the ranch. Leaving Abigail. And Ruston and her going outside when there was a sniper still at large. But after talking it over with Ruston, they had decided it was a risk they had to take.

Because they needed to hear what Devin had to say.

And they didn't want to do the interview at the ranch. Better to have some distance between Abigail and him, even if that distance meant more of a risk to Ruston and her. A risk, though, that didn't compromise Abigail's safety.

That was why Ruston and she had arranged for plenty of protection, with Slater, Luca and Joelle all staying with the baby while the armed ranch hands patrolled the grounds. A sniper could still return to fire more shots, but any gunfire was more likely to be aimed at Ruston and her. That was why they were all keeping watch as Duncan drove them to the sheriff's office.

A drive that hopefully wouldn't turn out to be a huge mistake.

Gracelyn needed to know what was going on with Allie, and Devin might be able to give her answers. And if she was to believe what Devin had said, they were answers that might help save Allie's life. She wasn't close to her sister, wasn't even sure she could say she actually loved her, but Gracelyn certainly didn't want Allie hurt or dead.

What she wanted, though, was to talk to Allie. That was critical. And Gracelyn hadn't given up hope of that happening. It was the reason she'd brought the burner with her, and she'd also left a message for Allie on that private Facebook page. Since Allie didn't have the burner Gracelyn had given her—Devin did—maybe Allie would use her regular phone, see the Facebook message and get in touch with her.

Because Ruston and she were in the back seat of the cruiser, Gracelyn had turned to keep watch behind them. To make sure they weren't being followed. Ruston was watching the sides of the narrow road while Duncan focused on the driving and what was ahead. All of them were primed for an attack, and they stayed that way during the entire ten-minute drive, even though they didn't see another vehicle until they were in town.

Duncan parked, and they used the side door to enter the building to get to his office. Gracelyn had been here before, too, when Ruston's father was sheriff, and it appeared that Duncan had kept things exactly the same, down to the Texas landscape art on the walls.

His office front was all glass, so she had no trouble seeing into the large bullpen and reception area, where she immediately spotted two deputies. She was pretty sure they were Carmen Gonzales and Woodrow Leonard, and both were on the phone while Carmen was also using her computer. However, the moment she noticed Duncan, she ended the call and stood.

"Devin Blackburn's not here yet," she relayed to Duncan. "And we're still waiting on those two officers to come down and pick up the prisoner."

"What prisoner?" Ruston asked.

"A guy named Brent Litton," Duncan supplied. "Woodrow pulled him over for speeding, and when he ran the plates, it came up there was an outstanding warrant on him for a string of burglaries in Austin. Austin PD is supposed to come and get him sometime today." He looked at Gracelyn and must have seen the concern on her face. "This guy isn't the sniper. He's been behind bars since about ten last night."

Gracelyn wished he had been the sniper so they could have questioned him. Additionally, he would have no longer been a threat.

"I need you to sign some reports," Carmen continued, still speaking to Duncan.

The deputy picked up a folder and started toward him, but Duncan went to her in the bullpen. Again, Gracelyn thought he'd maybe done that to give Ruston and her a little privacy so she could settle her nerves. But there wasn't any time for that because Ruston's phone rang, and when he took it from his pocket, she saw Noah's name on the screen.

"Devin's not here yet," Ruston told Noah the moment he answered. Ruston had already filled Noah in on Devin's phone call, and Noah had to be just as anxious as they were to find out what the man had to say.

"I hope he hasn't had second thoughts," Noah muttered. "Up to now, he's been dodging my calls and requests to come in for an interview. And I don't have enough for a warrant. In fact, I don't have anything on him except his involvement with Allie."

Yes, and that was why they had to get more. Well, if there was more to get, that was. It was entirely possible that Devin had nothing to do with any of this.

"I'm about to email you the surveillance footage of Gracelyn's sister," Noah continued a moment later. "I wanted to take care of that because I think Tony's trying to have me taken off Marty's murder. He's pissed off, Ruston, and he knows we're friends."

"He also knows you're a good cop," Ruston snarled. "Is he purposely trying to compromise the investigation?"

"I hope not, but the possibility has occurred to me. I don't think he'll succeed in getting me removed," Noah added. "He's having to deal with both the Rangers and Internal Affairs. This is gossip, but word is there are some inconsistencies in his finances and that he'll be put on paid leave for a couple of days."

That definitely wouldn't make Tony happy, but Gracelyn was thankful this was being done. Because there were inconsistencies, and if they had anything to do with the murders and attacks, then that should come to light.

"What about Charla?" Gracelyn asked. "Is Internal Affairs looking at her, too?"

"Not that I know of, and she wasn't in the meeting with the captain and the Rangers." Noah paused. "Is Charla aware that the two of you know about her connection to Zimmer?"

"Not yet," Ruston answered. "I wanted to confront her with that myself to see her reaction, and then I'll pass the info along."

Normally, the passing along meant her boss would be the one who got that info, but since her boss was Tony, that would likely be elevated to the captain.

The front door opened, and a dark-haired man came in. Devin. She recognized him from his photos.

"Gotta go," Ruston told Noah. "Allie's boyfriend just showed up."

"Good. Let me know if he spills anything I can use," Noah added right before he ended the call.

Gracelyn's first impression of Devin was that he didn't look the sort to spill anything that wouldn't paint himself in a good light. But that left plenty of other areas where he might be helpful. First, though, she had to get past that initial feeling of disdain. This was a man who'd assaulted and stalked women. That made him slime in her book, but if she hadn't known his history, she might not have seen the sliminess.

He was dressed like a rock star in his designer jeans with rips in all the trendy places. He'd paired them with a black tee that she was betting he hadn't bought off the rack. Expensive boots and sunglasses completed the outfit.

Woodrow went to Devin, first checking his ID and then sending him through the metal detector. No alarms sounded, but then, Devin would have been a fool to come to a sheriff's office armed.

"Gracelyn?" Devin questioned once he'd cleared security. When she nodded, he thrust out his hand for her to shake. She did that while keeping her gaze pinned to him.

"We can use interview room one," Duncan said, and he introduced both himself and Ruston.

"We?" Devin challenged. "I thought it'd be just Gracelyn and me talking."

"Then you thought wrong," Duncan quickly replied.

Devin didn't scowl at that remark. In fact, the little twist of his mouth seemed to convey that he'd expected this to be an official interview with the cops.

"Detective Noah Ryland from SAPD has been trying to get in touch with you," Ruston said to Devin as they walked to the room.

"Really?" Devin said, and he checked his phone. "No messages from him. Oh," he added as if something had just occurred to him. "I have a new number. Guess he's probably been trying to reach me at the old one. Detective Ryland, you said?"

Ruston nodded. He, too, had a hard look in his eyes.

"All right, I'll call Ryland when I'm done here," Devin said once they were in the interview room. "I'm guessing he wants to talk to me about Allie," he added. "Has she done something else I don't know about?"

None of them answered, but Duncan launched right into reading Devin his rights. That finally erased some of Devin's cockiness.

"Am I under arrest?" Devin asked.

"No. Reading you your rights is for your protection, so that you know what's expected of you," Duncan explained. "And so you're aware you can have a lawyer. We can all wait here if you want to call one."

"That won't be necessary. I didn't do anything wrong," Devin insisted. "In fact, I'm trying to do what's right by coming here." He sat and looked at Gracelyn, who took the seat at the table across from him. Duncan sat next to her while Ruston opted to stand.

Gracelyn didn't waste any time getting the questions started. "On the phone, you said you were afraid my sister had gotten into serious trouble. Explain that."

Devin gathered his breath, and rearranged his expression by bunching up his forehead. "Allie's been using drugs again. Two days ago, I caught her trying to make a deal with one of her old dealers. She didn't even deny it. Didn't deny either that she'd taken money from my wallet to buy the drugs."

Gracelyn tried to ignore the initial emotional punch of that. It certainly wasn't the first time she'd heard someone say Allie was using. In fact, Allie had been arrested twice for drug possession when she'd been a juvenile. Her pattern was to stay clean for about a year, and then she'd have a relapse. Thankfully, she'd been in the clean stage when she was pregnant with Abigail.

"Allie and I had a big argument," Devin went on, "and I told her she had to leave. I've got a record." He added a dry laugh. "But I'm positive you already know that." He put his arms on the table and leaned in toward her. "I don't want to do anything that could land me in jail. Not only would that cause my folks to disown me, but it's not who I am now. New leaf and all that."

Gracelyn figured she failed at totally suppressing a scowl over the way he'd flippantly thrown in that last part. But she was betting he was indeed concerned about being disowned. From everything she'd read about his parents, they fit more of the mold of upstanding citizens.

"Where did Allie go after you argued?" Gracelyn asked.

"I have no idea." He paused, forehead bunching up again. "But she said if I didn't give her the money that she'd get it from you. She figured by now you were attached to the baby and that you'd be willing to pay for the privilege of keeping her."

Gracelyn felt sick to her stomach, and she wanted every word of that to be lies. But she couldn't be sure. When Allie was using, she would resort to anything to get her hands on drugs.

"So, you know about the baby," Ruston commented.

"Yeah, Allie told me about her." Devin stopped, and his eyes widened. "Wait. Is the kid okay? Is she safe?" The concern in his voice appeared to be genuine. *Appeared.*

"She's safe," Gracelyn settled on saying. "What did Allie tell you about the baby?"

"That I'm her father," Devin admitted without hesitation.

"Are you?" Gracelyn pressed, though she thought she

already knew the answer. It was the eyes. Abigail's eyes were a genetic copy of Devin's.

Devin shrugged. "It's a good possibility that I am. I mean, the timing fits. Allie and I had been together for a while before she left. Another argument," he tacked on to that.

"Yes, I remember seeing the bruises and her black eye," Gracelyn remarked. She sounded as if she had ice in her blood, but it was all fiery anger.

Devin held up his hands. "She didn't get those from me. Scout's honor." He made a crossing gesture over his heart. "She got those from her dealer."

"She wasn't using when I saw her with the bruises," Gracelyn argued, and this time the anger coated her words.

"No," Devin agreed, "but she'd agreed to sell some product for him and had reneged on the deal. He came after her, and that's why she ran. She didn't think I'd be able to protect her."

Duncan slid a notepad and pen at Devin. "Write down the name of this dealer."

She thought maybe Devin would refuse. He didn't. He scribbled down a name and passed it back to Duncan.

Gracelyn's stomach dropped.

Because he'd written *Terry Zimmer.*

"What?" Devin said, obviously noticing her surprise. "You know that guy?"

Now she was the one who hesitated. "How well do you know him?" Gracelyn countered.

"Not well at all, and I want to keep it that way." He leaned back in his chair. "But Zimmer came round a few times before Allie left that first time. I swear, at first I thought the guy was a cop."

"You didn't check out his background or anything?"

Ruston asked. "I mean, since you supposedly have better-than-average computer skills."

Devin's mouth tightened a little. Ruston had obviously managed to get under his skin. A small victory.

"Yeah, I did," Devin admitted. "Former cop turned drug dealer. Talk about a drastic turn in career paths. But other than meeting him a couple of times and checking him on the internet, I don't really know the guy."

"But you saw him with Allie two days ago," Gracelyn reminded him.

"I did, and that's why I wanted to talk to you. I'm worried she's with Zimmer, and if so, God knows what kind of trouble he can get her into."

Gracelyn was worried, too. Especially worried that the trouble involved murder.

"Did you ever hear Allie talk about a man named Marty Bennett?" Gracelyn asked.

"Marty," Devin repeated. "Sure. We both know Marty. Knew," he amended. "I heard he died."

"He was murdered," Ruston provided.

Devin shook his head in an "I'm not surprised" kind of way. "Marty had dealings with a lot of dangerous people."

"So, how did you know him?" Ruston added.

Devin didn't jump to answer this time. "I borrowed money from him twice." He glanced at Gracelyn's raised eyebrow. "I have a trust fund, but sometimes I run short. I paid Marty back every cent, and then some." He paused then. "You think Allie had some kind of run-in with Marty?"

"Did she?" Gracelyn pressed.

"I don't know. Maybe," Devin conceded. Then his eyes widened again. "You don't think she killed him, do you?"

That was the last thing Gracelyn wanted to think. But

she had to consider it. Especially if Allie was truly hooked up with Zimmer.

"Hell," Devin grumbled. "If Allie's gone that far off the rails, I wouldn't let her near the kid. Look, the kid may or may not be mine, but I don't want anything to happen to her, okay?"

"You're not interested in finding out if she actually is your child?" Duncan asked.

Devin shrugged. "If you want me to give you a sample of my DNA, you can check it. I personally don't need the results, but you might want them." He aimed that last part at Gracelyn. "I mean, just in case the kid asks about that sort of thing down the road."

"You don't want to know if she's your daughter?" Gracelyn managed to say, though her throat was very tight now.

"No," Devin insisted. "I'm not exactly the father type. And FYI, I told Allie that when she first suspected she might be pregnant. I told her if she had the kid, it was hers, not mine. I wanted no part of any of that."

Gracelyn hated the way he threw the word *kid* around. Then again, she hated Devin, so it stood to reason she despised anything that came out of his mouth.

"I'll get a DNA test kit," Duncan said, standing.

The surprise flashed through Devin's eyes, but he didn't go back on his offer to give them a sample. Good. This would expedite things. Since Devin had a record, they could go through the database and get his DNA, but this way, his sample could be sent directly to the lab. Then not only could they use the DNA for a paternity test, but they could see if it matched any of the evidence gathered from the multiple crime scenes. It was a long shot, but sometimes long shots paid off.

And that was why she went with another one while Duncan was getting the test.

"Last year your name came up in an investigation that dealt with a black-market baby operation," Gracelyn stated. "You were interviewed because—"

"Because I knew the wrong person," Devin interrupted. He huffed. "Freddy Dundee. I had no idea he was selling babies. And apparently he sold some kids to the so-called baby farm that the cops tried to bust." He stared at her. "You were a cop. Were you involved in the investigation?"

"No," she lied, and she watched his reaction to that. Another of the almost smiles. So, he knew she'd been involved, which meant he likely knew that Ruston had been as well.

"Probably for the best you weren't involved," Devin commented. "I mean, I heard it turned out bad for the cops."

"It turned out bad for the criminals, too," Ruston interjected. "The baby farm was shut down."

"Well, that's good," Devin muttered, and this time there was no reaction at all. Gracelyn wouldn't have wanted to play poker with this guy.

Gracelyn pushed some more. "I'm trying to work out a timeline for Allie and you. When did the two of you become involved?"

"Oh, I've known Allie for years. We met at a party... I'm not sure how long ago. But years, like I said."

"When did you start a romantic relationship with her?" Ruston asked.

Devin shrugged, glanced away. "I'm not sure," he repeated.

"Was it about a year ago?" Ruston pressed. "Longer, shorter?"

Now Devin's eyes hardened. No more poker face. "You're trying to pinpoint if I hooked up with her to get some insider info on the baby-farm investigation. I didn't. And it wasn't a romance. It was sex. Allie tried to make it out to be more than it was." He checked his watch. "Sorry, but I forgot I have another appointment back in San Antonio. Can we wrap this up?"

Gracelyn wanted to continue to push on the baby-farm connection, but Devin seemed right on the edge. She didn't want him walking out, especially before he'd done the DNA test.

"Have you ever had any dealings with Lieutenant Tony Franklin or Detective Charla Burke?" she asked. On the surface, it might seem as if she was changing the subject, but she was just shifting it a little.

Devin repeated the names as if trying to see if they sparked any recognition. He shook his head. "I don't think so, but again, you know I've been arrested." He stopped, smiled. "And I can't recall all the cops involved in every case."

She couldn't tell if he was lying, so she used her phone to pull up photos of both Charla and Tony. And she watched to see if there was any reaction.

Maybe.

There was just a slight tensing of his jaw before he shook his head again. "I don't know them. Why? Are they involved in this mess with Marty?"

Quite possibly. One of them, anyway. But it was equally possible that both Charla and Tony had had nothing to do with the attacks and murders. That could all be on the man sitting directly across from her.

Gracelyn wished there was something they could use to hold Devin while they continued to dig deeper into the investigation. There was his association with Marty. And Allie. But there wasn't any proof that Duncan or SAPD could use for an arrest.

Not yet, anyway.

Duncan came back into the interview room with the test kit, and he handed it to Devin, instructing him on how to use it. Again, Devin hesitated, but he went through with the cheek swab. He handed it back to Duncan and then checked his watch.

"I need to leave for that other appointment," Devin said, standing. "Do any of you have any more questions for me before I go?"

Ruston, Duncan and Gracelyn volleyed glances at each other. It was Duncan who answered. "If we think of anything else, we'll let you know. You'll need to check in with Detective Ryland," he reminded Devin. And he gave Devin the detective's contact information.

"Right. I'll do that." Devin started for the door but then stopped and tipped his head to the test kit Duncan was still holding. "Do me a favor and keep the results of that to yourself," he insisted. "I really don't want to know one way or another if the kid is mine."

He walked out, and for several moments Duncan, Ruston and she sat in silence. No doubt mentally going over everything Devin had just told them. That was what Gracelyn was doing, anyway.

Duncan went to the door and shut it. "You believe him?"

"No," Gracelyn was quick to say. "My gut says he's lying about something. I just don't know what," she admitted.

Duncan made a sound of agreement. "If any part of what he said was true, it doesn't look good for your sister."

"It doesn't," she admitted. "And that's not exactly a surprise. Allie has a history of drug use, and she can be very impulsive. I still don't believe she's a killer, though, and Devin didn't give us any concrete proof that she is."

Duncan tapped the notepad with Zimmer's name on it.

But then he shook his head. "That could be one of Devin's lies. There's no known evidence to indicate Zimmer is a dealer. No known evidence to indicate he's even connected to Allie. I've been digging through Zimmer's background, and nothing about Allie or drugs has come up."

That brought on another round of silence while they obviously thought that through. "So, why would Devin have lied about that?" Gracelyn muttered, and she already had her own theory forming in her head.

"Because Devin might have thought it would make us look at Zimmer and Allie and not him," Ruston threw out. "That way, we might not concentrate on Devin's admission that he knew not only Marty but Zimmer as well."

"And we might not concentrate on the fact that Devin is a known hacker," Duncan spelled out. "A hacker who could have maybe accessed any and all information that was used to murder three people and attack Ruston and you. Added to that, he was interviewed about the baby farm."

All of that was true, but it brought Gracelyn to one very important question. "Why would Devin have killed or hired someone to kill?"

Duncan shrugged. "That's what we need to find out. Maybe this is about money. He worked hard to make it seem as if he wasn't interested in Abigail, but she could be a money source for him. Kidnap her and sell her on the black market. That plan failed, so now he could be in the cover-up mode by implicating Allie." He paused. "But that doesn't explain the two murders of the hacker and retired cop."

Gracelyn could think of an explanation. A bad one. "Devin could be Green Eagle. That would make everything fit."

"Yes," Ruston muttered, and he took out his phone. "I'm calling Noah. I'm hoping he can get Devin in right away and grill him about Marty. And about any possible connection to the baby farm. Noah might be able to get something out of Devin that we missed."

Ruston called Noah, but the detective didn't answer. As Ruston was leaving a voicemail, his phone dinged with an incoming call.

"It's Slater," he relayed.

Every muscle in Gracelyn's body tightened, and she prayed nothing had gone wrong at the ranch.

Ruston quickly finished the voicemail and took the call from his brother on speaker. "Did something happen?" Ruston immediately asked.

"No, everything is secure here," Slater replied just as quickly. "I just got a call, though, from one of the hands. No sign of the sniper, but he found spent shell casings beneath one of those big oak trees near the road. I'll call the CSIs to come out and collect them."

Gracelyn forced herself to unclench some of the tightness in her chest. She knew the exact area of trees that Slater was talking about, and the location probably hadn't been a coincidence. The sniper had likely chosen it so he could make a quick getaway.

"I'll have the CSIs check the ranch trails nearby," Slater went on. "It's possible the gunman parked on one of those and left some tracks."

True, but a former cop like Zimmer would have known that. Then again, Zimmer had left his prints in the truck, so maybe he wasn't careful. There was a third possibility, though, that Zimmer had been set up.

Maybe by Devin.

That could have been why Devin had been so quick to volunteer Zimmer's name to them.

Gracelyn heard a soft sound come from the small bag

she'd brought to the station with her, and it took a couple of seconds for her mind to register what it was.

"It's the alert I set up for messages coming from the private Facebook page," she said, already hurrying to retrieve her phone.

And there it was.

What she'd been waiting for.

It's me, Allie. I don't have the phone you gave me. I must have left it somewhere. Give me your number so I can call you.

Since both Duncan and Ruston had moved closer, she showed them the message, and she fought the urge to fire off a quick response.

"It could be a hoax," she muttered. "Devin or someone else could have gotten access." Still, there was no way she could just ignore this. She typed in her number. And waited.

Gracelyn didn't have to wait long.

Within a couple of seconds, her phone rang, and she saw Unknown Caller on the screen. Holding her breath, she answered it.

"Gracelyn," the caller said, the single word rushing out with a long breath.

"It's Allie," Gracelyn whispered to Duncan and Ruston. The relief came, washing over her. Temporarily, anyway. And then came the worry.

"Allie, where are you?" Gracelyn asked. "Are you all right?"

"No. I'm not all right at all." A hoarse sob tore from her sister's throat. "I'm here in Saddle Ridge, and I have to see you right now."

Gracelyn had so many questions, but she started with an obvious one. "Why are you in Saddle Ridge?"

"I'll tell you when I see you." Allie sobbed again. "When can we meet? I can come to wherever you are."

Gracelyn debated how to respond, and she went with the truth. "I'm at the sheriff's office." She thought that might get Allie to hang up. Or change her mind about meeting with her.

It didn't.

"Okay," Allie finally said. Her voice broke on that single word. "I'll be there in about thirty minutes. I need help, Gracelyn. I need a deal with the cops. I need immunity."

Gracelyn opened her mouth to ask why Allie would need those things, but her sister had already ended the call.

Chapter Nine

Ruston watched Gracelyn pace across the interview room, and he could practically see the nerves coming off her. He was in the same boat, but he was trying to tamp down the worst of his worries.

That this was some kind of ruse for gunmen to try to murder Gracelyn.

Yes, they were in a police station with at least four cops in the building, but if Allie was desperate—and she was a killer—then she might have come here to try to go after her sister.

Ruston had no intention of letting that happen.

Duncan was on the same page with that, because right after Allie had ended her call, he'd gone to his office to let the other deputies know that Allie would be coming in. Or rather she had said she'd be coming in. If she did arrive, she'd be treated like a dangerous suspect and would be thoroughly searched before she got anywhere near Gracelyn.

"Immunity," Gracelyn muttered.

Yeah, Ruston hadn't missed that part. Immunity probably meant Allie had committed a crime and had useful information that she hoped to trade so the cops could catch a bigger fish. But if this was about murder, immunity probably wasn't going to be an option.

And that meant they might have to arrest Allie on the spot. That thought had no doubt already occurred to Gracelyn, and it had to be contributing to the nerves.

"Has Allie ever been to Saddle Ridge before today?" Ruston asked, hoping the conversation would help settle her before Allie showed up. That thirty-minute arrival was ticking down fast.

"Not that I know of," Gracelyn said, "but I'm sure she heard me mention you were from here."

Yeah, and that meant Allie had made the connection between Gracelyn and him when such a connection shouldn't have been obvious, since before yesterday, they hadn't seen each other in months. But it might have been obvious to Allie if she'd known they had been attacked and had had to flee with Abigail.

One way Allie could have known that was to be directly involved in the attack, but Ruston was hoping that hadn't happened. That instead she'd come by the information from someone else. Like Devin.

"Even though Devin claimed he doesn't know where Allie is," Ruston pointed out, "he could have been lying. He could have been with her when he arranged the meeting and told Allie he was coming here to see us."

Gracelyn nodded, and she seemed to latch on to that. But the hope didn't stay on her face long. Probably because she was well aware of her sister's checkered past. Also, there were those parts about needing immunity and cutting a deal.

There was a knock at the door, and Ruston steeled himself. But it wasn't Allie. It was Woodrow. "There's a cop here to see you. Detective Charla Burke."

Ruston groaned. They didn't need this now. "What does she want?"

"She wouldn't say. Only said it was important."

Ruston connected with Gracelyn's gaze, and even though she didn't look any happier about this intrusion than he was, she nodded. "Let's give her five minutes."

Ruston turned back to Woodrow. "Bring her back here."

That way, Charla wouldn't be in the front of the building when and if Allie came in. After seeing Allie on that surveillance footage, Charla would almost certainly recognize her, and he didn't want the cop trying to question, or intimidate, Gracelyn's sister.

"Duncan probably told you we're expecting another visitor," Ruston commented.

Woodrow nodded. "Allie Wallace. Duncan is keeping an eye out for her."

Good. That was just as they'd planned it since Duncan hadn't wanted Gracelyn in the front of the building either. The windows were bullet resistant, but if the sniper targeted her and used a powerful enough weapon, he might be able to get a shot through. The interview rooms were the only places in the sheriff's office without windows.

"If Allie comes in while Charla is still here, make sure the women's paths don't cross," Ruston spelled out.

"Will do," Woodrow assured him, and he walked away. It didn't take him long to return with Charla.

One look at her face, and Ruston knew she was riled to the bone.

"Make this quick," Ruston immediately told her.

"Quick," Charla snarled like profanity. "Because you're busy trying to ruin Tony's career."

"No." Ruston stretched that out a few syllables. "I'm trying to find out the truth as to why someone has been murdering people. And shooting at Gracelyn, me and you. I know you didn't forget about the sniper."

No way, but it was possible she knew the sniper wasn't an actual threat to her because he was working for her.

"What Internal Affairs is investigating has nothing to do with that," Charla snapped. "It's about some discrepancy in his finances."

"Which could in turn be linked to the attacks and murders," Gracelyn was quick to say. She huffed. "You're a cop, Charla. You know how this works. If there are funds that Tony can't account for, then that opens the door for an investigation into all aspects of his life. Internal Affairs might not find anything."

The anger, and worry, flashed across Charla's face again. "And if they do, it won't have anything to do with murders or attacks."

Yes, but the funds could still be illegal, and that in turn could indeed cost Tony his career.

"I think someone's setting him up," Charla muttered. She fired glances at both Gracelyn and him. "And it sure as hell better not be either of you."

"Or you," Ruston suggested.

Charla practically snapped to attention. "What does that mean?"

Since time was of the essence, Ruston went with a simple response. "Terry Zimmer."

For a couple of seconds, Charla just looked puzzled. Then she put on her cop's face. "What about him?"

"When we showed Tony and you Zimmer's picture, Tony owned up to knowing him," Ruston spelled out. "You didn't."

"Because I—" She stopped, groaned and pinched her eyes together for a second. "I didn't say anything because Zimmer was a confidential informant. And if I'd admitted that, you would have assumed the worst because of the photograph of Zimmer at the baby farm."

"I did assume the worst," Ruston confirmed. "I wouldn't have necessarily done that if you'd been up-front." That was possibly true. Either way, he would have kept Charla on the suspect lists, but she'd made herself look darn guilty by not owning up to knowing Zimmer.

"I swear, I didn't know Zimmer had any connection to the baby farm," Charla insisted.

"But he did," Ruston argued, "and he has a connection to you."

Charla huffed. "You can't possibly believe I was part of that. Why would I? I have no..." She stopped again. "Oh," she muttered. "This is because of my mother."

Bingo.

Charla laughed, but there was no humor in it. "I see. Because my mother sold babies, you believe I continued the family business. I didn't." She paused again. "The only thing I'm guilty of is not admitting I knew Zimmer."

Ruston decided to go out on a limb here. "And protecting Tony. How long have you known about those mystery funds in his accounts?"

Another bingo. Charla certainly didn't jump to deny it, and the look on her face confirmed she had indeed known. "Go ahead, report me to Internal Affairs. Better yet, I'll save you the trouble and do it myself."

Charla stormed out, and Ruston turned to Gracelyn. He didn't get a chance, though, to get her take on everything the woman had just said. That was because his phone dinged with a text.

"It's from Duncan," he said. "Allie just came in, and Duncan has her in his office."

Ruston didn't need to ask for her take on that. She was both relieved and anxious, and she immediately headed out of the interview room. He was right behind her.

When they made it to the front of the building, Charla was thankfully nowhere in sight, which meant she likely hadn't seen Allie. Then again, Ruston might not have seen her either if he hadn't been specifically looking for her. Gracelyn's sister was in the corner of Duncan's office, standing away from the large window, and she was wearing a purple hoodie that covered not only her head but a good portion of her face as well. Her shoulders were hunched, her gaze aimed at the floor.

Duncan was standing by his desk, and the moment Gracelyn and Ruston were inside the office, he shut the door.

"She's been frisked," Duncan told them. "No weapons. And I've already Mirandized her."

If Allie had objected to the frisking and Miranda warning, she didn't voice it. However, when she lifted her head and Ruston got a better look at her face, he could see the agitation in her bloodshot eyes. He searched her face, looking for any resemblance between Gracelyn and her. Or her and the baby. But it just wasn't there.

"Gracelyn," Allie muttered, and the tears came. Probably not her first of the day. "You have to help me."

Gracelyn didn't respond, didn't move. She just stood there for several moments and studied her sister. Then, on a sigh, she went to Allie and hugged her. It didn't last long. Allie ended it and stepped away from her.

"Go ahead," Allie said, defensiveness in her voice now. "Ask me if I've been using. That's what you always do."

"Have you been?" Gracelyn obliged.

"No," Allie snarled. "I'm clean." She paused and groaned. "I haven't used anything today," she amended.

That was possibly true. Possibly. And it drilled home for Ruston that Allie had to be beyond desperate to walk into a sheriff's office and admit that she'd recently used drugs. Something she could be arrested for if they found any illegals in her possession. Then again, she could be arrested for something a whole lot worse.

"You said you wanted immunity," Gracelyn reminded her. "Why? What did you do?"

Allie shook her head and folded her arms over her chest. "First, the immunity, and then I talk."

Gracelyn shook her head. "That's not the way immunity works. You tell us what you know, and then we talk about immunity or a deal."

Allie did more head shaking. "But how do I know you just won't arrest me?" She aimed the question at Duncan.

"You don't, but I could have arrested you the moment you stepped in here, and I didn't," Duncan spelled out. "That's because I want to hear what you have to say. Then I can decide how to help you."

Duncan had clearly sugarcoated that, but Ruston figured if Allie was a victim in all of this, if she had nothing to do with the murders, then Duncan would almost certainly follow through on that "help" if what Allie told them led them to the killer.

"I'll need to record what you say," Duncan added, holding up his phone. "That's for your protection," he said when Allie made a soft gasp. "The district attorney will need to hear your own words before she can work any kind of deal. I can't go to her and just give her a summary."

Not entirely true. Deals happened with summaries. But Duncan wanted anything Allie might say to be on the record. Of course, Allie could lie on the record as well.

"All right," Allie finally said, but she didn't launch into the reason she was here. She sat there until Gracelyn gave her a prompt.

"The San Antonio police have been looking for you," Gracelyn said. She had likely gone with that rather than a direct question to ease Allie into this.

Allie nodded. "I know." She stopped again, and this time she pressed her fingers to her mouth. Both parts of her were trembling, and she looked on the verge of having a full melt-down. "It's because of Marty, isn't it? Because he's dead, and they want to ask me if I killed him. I didn't. I swear, I didn't."

Duncan went to a small fridge behind his desk and brought out a bottle of water for Allie. He also motioned for her to sit in one of the chairs. She drank some water but remained standing.

"You were spotted on a security camera near Marty's around the same time he was killed," Ruston said, figuring it was something Allie might already know.

She did.

"Devin called and told me. He said that's why the cops wanted to talk to me."

Ruston and Gracelyn exchanged glances, and he saw the question in her eyes. Had SAPD released that info about Allie being on the security feed? He shook his head, though that was something that likely would have happened soon if the cops hadn't been able to locate Allie.

So, how had Devin known?

It was something Ruston would have Noah ask Devin if and when the man came back in to be interviewed.

"Why were you at Marty's?" Gracelyn asked her sister.

"Well, it wasn't to kill him," Allie was quick to say. "That'd be like killing the golden goose." She glanced away. "I was going to try to get a loan from Marty. I needed money so I could get back on my feet."

Interesting. "And you knew Marty loaned money be-cause he'd done that for Devin?" Ruston wanted to know.

"Devin," Allie spit out. She said the man's name like profanity. "Yeah, Devin owes Marty lots and lots of money. Some kind of investment deal gone wrong," she added in a mutter.

"Really?" Gracelyn asked. "I was under the impression that Devin had paid off his debts to Marty."

"As if," Allie snarled. "And if Devin told you that, he's lying. Then again, he lies about a lot of stuff." The tears came again, and she sank down into one of the chairs. "He told me he loved me, and then he kicked me out."

Gracelyn sat, too, probably so she'd be eye level with Allie. "Why did he do that?"

Allie stayed quiet for so long that Ruston thought she might just clam up, but she finally answered. "He claimed it was because I used just a little to help take the edge off my nerves. He called me names, said I'd never be anything but a screwup, and he kicked me out. That's why I went to Marty."

Ruston didn't like having to rely on hearsay to try to figure out the big picture here, but it was possible that things had played out that way. If Devin did still owe Marty a lot of money and was trying to resolve that in some way, then he might not have wanted a loose cannon like Allie around.

"Tell me what happened when you went to Marty's," Gracelyn pressed.

Allie drank more water and then took several long breaths. "I saw him twice. First, two days ago, and he was fine then." She had fixed her gaze on her thumbnail now and was scraping away some flakes of bright pink polish. "Then I went back last night to get the money, but Marty was dead when I got there." The water and breaths didn't help. Allie broke into a heavy sob. "He was dead, and there was so much blood. I'd never seen that much blood before."

Ruston got an instant flash of his father's murder. Of the blood. And he relived the shock of seeing that. The crushing pain in his chest that followed. But Ruston shoved that aside. Had to. He had to focus on what Allie was saying to finish creating that mental big picture.

"So, what did you do?" Gracelyn continued.

"I ran, of course," Allie was quick to say. "I got out of there as fast as I could because I thought the killer could still be there. He could have killed me if he thought I was a witness or something."

"He?" Gracelyn questioned. "You thought the killer was a man?"

Allie looked at her and then shook her head. "No. I mean, I didn't know. I just assumed it was a man who'd done something like that. I didn't want to hang around and end up like Marty."

"Or answer questions from the cops who responded to the scene," Duncan commented.

Allie's mouth went into a flat line, but at least she stopped crying. "Or that," she verified, her voice a snap now. "With my record, they would have thought I was responsible, and I'm not."

The cops would have indeed thought that, and Allie would have become their prime suspect with the means and opportunity to have done the kill. But Ruston wasn't sure of her motive.

"Where did you go when you ran from Marty's?" Gracelyn asked.

"To a hotel about six blocks away. I used cash so there wouldn't be a way to trace the room to me."

"Cash?" Gracelyn repeated. "You had cash for a hotel room, but you went to Marty for a loan?"

Allie huffed. "I needed more than what I had on me."

She quickly waved that away as if she didn't want to dwell on that particular subject. "With Marty out of the picture, I decided to try to convince Devin to give me some money. I still had a key to his place, and I slipped in. I wanted to make sure he was in a good mood before I asked him for a loan."

Or she'd slipped in to steal from Devin. But since he didn't want to disrupt the flow of her explanation, Ruston kept that to himself for the moment.

"I heard Devin talking on the phone," Allie went on. "And I heard him say he was coming to Saddle Ridge, and he said all that stuff about me being in trouble." The anger increased with each word. "I knew then he was coming to see you, to whine about me using a little."

"And you followed him?" Gracelyn pressed.

Allie nodded. "I took a taxi, and trust me, that ate up a lot of what little cash I have left, but I didn't want Devin to come here and tell you a bunch of lies about me."

"Why would he do that?" Ruston asked.

"Because he's a selfish SOB, that's why," she was quick to say. "He never once asked about our baby."

Ruston checked the time. Allie had been here for going on ten minutes, and this was the first time she'd brought up Abigail. Added to that, she hadn't mentioned her in the phone call she'd made to Gracelyn.

"So, did Devin tell you lies about me?" Allie asked.

Gracelyn shifted closer to her sister, a signal that she was going to deal with this answer. "He said you were using again and that he kicked you out. He thought you'd hooked up with your former drug dealer."

Allie huffed again. "There was no hooking up. I used, yes, but it was from a small stash I'd left at Devin's last year. I guess he didn't find it, because it was still there."

"Terry Zimmer," Gracelyn threw out there, and she no doubt wanted to groan because she couldn't have missed the flicker of surprise in her sister's eyes.

"I don't know who that is," Allie insisted. It was a lie and not a very good one at that.

"I believe you do," Gracelyn said, somehow managing to keep her voice level. "We've already told you that immunity can't even be considered until you tell us the truth about everything."

"I did tell the truth," Allie howled.

"No, you didn't," Gracelyn argued. "You know Zimmer, and you have to tell me if he's connected to the reason you need immunity."

"I don't know him," Allie practically shouted, springing to her feet. "I don't…" She stopped and locked gazes with Gracelyn, who wasn't pulling a visible punch. She was staring at her sister the way she would a murder suspect.

"The truth," Gracelyn repeated. "That's the only chance you have of me helping you. Lie again, and you'll be arrested."

Allie flung gazes at all three of them, and for a moment, she looked like a trapped animal ready to fight her way out of there. Then a sob tore from her throat, and she sank back into the chair.

"I didn't kill Marty. That's the truth," Allie stated. "And Zimmer isn't my dealer. In fact, I'd never met him until two days ago, when I went to see Marty." She lowered her head, shook it. "You're going to be so upset when you hear this. Really, really upset," she emphasized, "but I swear, at the time I thought it was the only option I had."

Hell. Ruston figured anything that came after this part of the explanation couldn't be good.

"What option?" Gracelyn insisted.

Allie sobbed again, and the tears returned, but thankfully that didn't silence her. "I thought Devin was going to take care of me, but when he didn't, I knew I was going to need some money. A lot of money so I could get away and have a fresh start. I'd heard Marty had connections, so two days ago I went to see him."

Gracelyn pulled in a sharp breath. "Why?" And there was a lot of emotion and strain in that one word.

Allie swallowed hard. "Because I had heard that he sometimes acted as a go-between for people looking to adopt. Good people," she tacked on to that. "I wouldn't want my baby going to just anyone."

Duncan and Ruston both cursed. Hell. She'd planned on selling Abigail.

Gracelyn stayed put in the chair, but her eyes had narrowed. "Say it," she demanded. Not yelling, but there was a dangerous edge to her voice.

"All right." Allie threw an indignant stare right back at her sister. "A couple wanted to adopt the baby, and they were willing to pay my expenses. You know, for carrying her for nine months."

"How much?" Gracelyn asked. That dangerous edge went up a notch.

"Ten thousand," Allie spit out as if she wasn't the least bit ashamed of it. "I knew you wouldn't just hand Abigail over, not without asking me a lot of questions, and I told Marty that. He said there was a way to get her. A fake kidnapping, but it wouldn't actually be a kidnapping because she's my daughter."

Ruston wasn't sure how Gracelyn managed to just sit there and not spew every word of profanity she knew. Maybe because this had shaken her to the core. Allie had been planning on selling that precious baby. And that was just the tip of the iceberg.

Gracelyn held up a hand, maybe to steady herself. Maybe to signal that she wanted to continue the questioning. "How did Marty know where the baby was?"

"I told him. Well, I guessed because I'd seen the file with places where you might be, and I'd taken a picture of it with my phone. You know, just in case I wasn't able to track you down."

So, that was how Marty had gotten the address. Ruston figured Gracelyn was mentally kicking herself for that. All those security precautions down the drain because of Allie.

"You said you saw Zimmer at Marty's," Gracelyn went on a moment later.

"Yes, but not last night, not when I found his body. Zimmer was there on my first visit. I got the impression he worked for Marty. Maybe like an assistant or something."

Ruston was going with the "or something" on this one, and it made him wonder if Zimmer had been around when he'd met with Marty. Maybe. Zimmer certainly hadn't been in the room with them, but it was possible Zimmer had seen him.

"So, how was the fake kidnapping supposed to work?" Duncan asked.

Allie lifted her shoulder. "I'm not sure. Marty said he'd take care of all of that. He just told me to come back when he had the baby and that he'd give me the money. But I didn't want to wait for him to call me. He'd said he'd have the baby last night, so I went to his place to wait."

"Did you know Marty intended for me to be kidnapped as well?" Gracelyn asked.

Allie dismissed that with an eye roll. "That was only so you wouldn't interfere with the men taking the baby. Marty would have let you go."

"Not a chance," Gracelyn muttered. She didn't mutter the rest, though. It came out loud and clear. "You set me up to either die or be sold. You set me up so that I had to fight to save Abigail, Ruston and myself. You did that." She jabbed her index finger at Allie.

Allie huffed once more and got to her feet again. "I did what I had to do to get my daughter. You can't just keep my baby. She's mine, not yours."

Gracelyn stood, too, and, oh, Ruston didn't like that her entire body seemed to make her sister pay. "Yes, biologically you're her mother, and you were planning on selling her. Hear this, Allie—I'll see you locked away for the rest of your miserable life before I let you anywhere near Abigail."

"You can't do that." Allie drew her hand back as if she might slap Gracelyn, but Duncan put a stop to that.

"Sit down and shut up," Duncan ordered Allie.

For a moment, Ruston thought Allie might launch herself at him, but she must have realized that assaulting a cop would only add to the mess she'd gotten herself into.

"I want that deal," Allie snarled. "I want immunity."

"Did you miss that 'shut up' part to my order?" Duncan growled. "Now, sit there and don't say another word until I'm ready for you to talk."

Duncan motioned for them to step out into the bullpen. "You're going to have to turn this over to SAPD, aren't you?" Gracelyn immediately asked him.

"Afraid so." Duncan didn't sound at all pleased about that either. "Every crime she committed, including the most serious ones, are in SAPD's jurisdiction."

Ruston knew that was true, and it was also true that Allie would need to go through this all again with the San Antonio cops. "I'll call Noah," he said. But before he could do that, Woodrow motioned to get his attention.

"You got a call on the station's landline," Woodrow said. "Actually, the caller wants to speak to both Gracelyn and you."

"Who is it?" Ruston asked.

"The guy says he's Terry Zimmer."

Hell. That caused the squad room to go quiet, and there was no need for Ruston to explain to Woodrow who the caller was. Or rather who he was claiming to be. Woodrow and Carmen both knew that was the name of their murder suspect.

"He used your rank, Ruston," Woodrow added. "He knows you're a cop. And he says there are some things you need to know."

Chapter Ten

Zimmer.

Of all the people who she thought might try to contact them, he wasn't one of them. Not unless he wanted to taunt them about the attack. But even if that was Zimmer's intentions, this was a call they had to take.

"Use the landline in the interview room," Duncan offered, glancing back at his office. "And I'll try to have the call traced."

Allie was still in the chair and had moved on to biting her nails instead of just scraping off polish. Just the sight of her made Gracelyn's stomach twist. She would never forgive Allie for trying to sell Abigail. But she'd have to deal with her sister later. For now, she wanted to hear what Zimmer had to say, so Ruston and she headed back to the interview room.

This particular landline had a recording function on it, and Ruston turned that on in the same moment that he answered the call on speaker.

"I'm listening," Ruston said in lieu of a greeting.

"How about Gracelyn?" the man fired back.

Gracelyn didn't think she'd ever heard that voice before. Not a Texas drawl but a quick clip pace that seemed to be void of any accent.

"Gracelyn will especially want to hear what I have to say," the caller insisted.

Ruston motioned for her to stay quiet. And she did. She couldn't think of a good reason to let a murder suspect know her location. It was possible, though, that Woodrow had already done that, but Gracelyn had no intention of confirming it.

"I'll pass along anything you tell me to Gracelyn," Ruston said. "Or you can just turn yourself in, and the three of us can have a face-to-face chat."

Zimmer didn't react to that. "I'm guessing she's there with you," he commented several moments later. "So, I'll just go ahead and direct this to her. And by the way, don't bother with the trace I'm sure you're doing. I'm using a burner."

Gracelyn figured that, but sometimes it was possible to trace the location of a burner. Of course, Zimmer would know that, so he could be either driving around or else planned on leaving the scene as soon as he was done with this call.

"I believe your sister was set up, Gracelyn," Zimmer went on to say. "And, yeah, I know what she tried to do. She wanted to sell her baby. But everything else is a setup."

That could be true. *Could be.* However, the attempt to sell her child and commissioning a double kidnapping wouldn't just end up a slap on the wrist. Allie would be going to jail.

"Did you set Allie up?" Ruston came out and asked.

"No." And there seemed to be genuine frustration in his voice. Zimmer didn't add anything to that, though.

"Then who did?" Ruston demanded.

"I'm not sure. That's the truth," he snapped when Ruston huffed. "At first, I thought it was Marty. I thought maybe he wanted a way out of paying Allie the ten grand he promised her. And maybe it was him and someone then pulled a double cross and put a bullet in his head."

Marty hadn't died from a gunshot to the head but rather to the chest. But Ruston didn't correct Zimmer. It was possible Zimmer already knew that and had doled out some false information so that Ruston and she wouldn't think he was guilty.

Gracelyn didn't buy it, not for a second, and judging from Ruston's expression, neither did he.

"Are you also going to tell me you didn't have any part in trying to kidnap Gracelyn and the baby?" Ruston asked.

Zimmer muttered something she didn't catch. "It's not what you think."

"Then tell me what the hell it was," Ruston snarled.

Gracelyn totally understood the surge of anger in Ruston's voice. The anger raced through her, too, at the thought of how close they had come to dying. And this scumbag was no doubt responsible.

"I've been investigating the baby farm," Zimmer said after a long pause. "Not officially, but I've still got enough cop in me that it doesn't sit well when someone buys and sells babies as if they were merchandise."

"You were working at the baby farm," Ruston pointed out.

"Yeah, so I could dig around and find out who was responsible. I wanted to bring him or her down. I wanted to put an end to it."

Ruston didn't appear ready to tamp down his anger or the sarcasm that went along with it. "You seem awfully dedicated to justice, considering you're a disgraced former cop. Or do you have an excuse for that, too? Maybe someone set you up?"

"No. I used excessive force, and I resigned." There was some anger in his tone now, too. "And I'm dedicated to justice in this particular matter because when I was a baby, I was sold to a couple in a private adoption. A couple who shouldn't have been given a pet rock, much less a kid."

Ruston used his cell to open the site where records of former police officers could be accessed. He used his password to access it and then handed Gracelyn his phone so she could check and see if there was anything in Zimmer's background to indicate there was a shred of truth in what he was saying.

"Because I wanted to find the person running the baby farm, I managed to get hired as a security guard," Zimmer went on. "Just like Gracelyn and you did."

Oh, that reminder didn't help ease any of Ruston's anger. Nor hers. "Were you the one who tried to kill Gracelyn and me that night, just like you did when you attempted to kidnap the baby and her?"

"No." Zimmer paused and repeated that through what sounded to be clenched teeth. "I don't know who shot at you at the baby farm. And I didn't shoot at you during the kidnapping attempt either. Yes, I fired shots, but I purposely aimed away from you. That was to convince the thug who was with me that he and I were on the same side. If he'd thought I had my own reasons for being there, he would have killed me."

Ruston paused a moment, probably to try to wrap his mind around all of that and figure out if it was true. While he did that, Gracelyn showed him what she'd accessed on Zimmer. There were no accounts of any childhood abuse. No reported accounts, anyway, but Zimmer was a former elementary school counselor, and when he'd been on the force, he'd routinely volunteered to work with troubled kids who'd ended up in juvie.

Another thing stood out, though.

The excessive-force charge had involved a couple who had gotten off child-abuse charges because of a botched investigation. Zimmer had been the investigator.

All of that presented a package of a man who seemed to want to help kids and get them away from scumbag parents. But that didn't mean Zimmer hadn't crossed some very big lines and turned criminal.

"Give me the name of the thug who was with you when you attacked Gracelyn and me," Ruston ordered.

"He used the name Buddy Bradley," Zimmer answered without hesitation. "Marty said Buddy had worked for him for years. I'm guessing the CSIs found his blood in the truck and sent it to the lab. If you don't have confirmation already, you'll soon get it and learn his real name was Robert Radley and that he had a record a mile long."

"Was? Had?" Ruston questioned as Gracelyn started looking for any info on him.

"He's dead. And, no, I didn't kill him," Zimmer insisted. "You did. Or maybe it was Gracelyn. Whoever fired that shot at him through the door. The bullet must have nicked an artery or something, because by the time I got him in the backup vehicle we'd left on one of those ranch trails, he'd bled out."

Gracelyn held up his phone so he could see the quick run she'd just done on Robert Radley. The man was forty-two and did indeed have a long criminal history that included B and E, assault and drug charges. He'd been in and out of jail since he was sixteen.

"I'd never met Buddy before Marty paired us up to do

the kidnapping," Zimmer went on. "But it took me about a half of a second to realize he was a dangerous hothead."

"And yet you went through with the job," Ruston reminded him.

Zimmer was quick to answer that, too. "If I hadn't, Marty would have just hired someone else. I figured if I was there, I could keep Buddy in check. Obviously, I failed at that."

"Yeah, you did," Ruston agreed. "Now, tell me why the hell Marty hired you and the hothead when he had already arranged for someone else to kidnap Gracelyn and the baby."

That was the big question, and Gracelyn automatically moved closer to the landline because she didn't want to miss a word of this.

"You," Zimmer said. "Marty hired you to do the kidnapping." He groaned. "I was at Marty's when he called you over. Marty asked that I stay out of sight in a little room he has off his office. He wanted me to listen to the conversation and make sure there were no red flags in anything you were saying. He wasn't sure he could trust you."

The muscles in Ruston's jaw turned to iron. "Did you recognize me?"

"I did," Zimmer admitted. "I'd gotten copies of the reports on the baby-farm attack, and I knew you were there. Gracelyn, too."

"Did your friend Charla get you those copies?" Ruston asked.

"No. I, uh, hired someone for that." Zimmer's voice lowered to a murmur. "A hacker. Simon Milbrath, and yeah, I know it looks bad that he was murdered, but I didn't kill him."

Gracelyn saw the mountain of skepticism in Ruston's expression. She was right there with him. So far, Zimmer had what was called the *categorical trinity*. Means, motive and opportunity. Zimmer could have killed both Marty and Simon to eliminate anyone who could have ratted him out. And since Zimmer had already admitted to hiring a hacker, that same hacker could have been keeping tabs on anything connected to the baby-farm investigation. The call Archie made to Tony might have fallen into that category.

"You told Marty I was a cop," Ruston said.

"I told him I thought you were an informant for the cops," Zimmer corrected as if that were a good thing. "And I did that, hoping that Marty would pull you off the assignment."

"Why? Because you knew I'd kill you for coming after Gracelyn and the baby?" Ruston's voice was pure ice now.

"No. I did it because I could tell Marty was suspicious of you. Why else have me listen in on the conversation? Marty didn't fully trust you, and I figured it was safer for you to be pulled off the job rather than risk Marty having you killed."

"That's generous of you," Ruston countered. "And why was Marty suspicious of me? Because of something you told him?"

"I think Allie must have said something about you, like maybe you could have helped Gracelyn go into hiding. If Allie had mentioned you, Marty would have looked you up. Hell, Marty had hackers on his payroll, and he could have discovered you were a cop and set you up to die. Marty didn't come out and say that to me, but Buddy was awfully fast on the trigger."

Ruston and she locked gazes, no doubt so he could see what her take was on this. Gracelyn had to shake her head. Like Allie, Zimmer wasn't innocent. He was a criminal, but maybe he hadn't gone to her place with the intention of killing anyone.

"Did Marty break into my apartment?" Ruston asked Zimmer.

"I'm not sure. When I showed up to do the job, Buddy had your wallet, and he said Marty had told him to leave it at Gracelyn's."

"And my badge?" Ruston added.

"I don't know about that," Zimmer answered. "If Marty or Buddy had it, they didn't share that info with me."

Again, Gracelyn had no idea if that was the truth. She was betting Ruston didn't either.

"Someone fired shots at an SAPD cruiser," Ruston said. "Was that you?"

Zimmer muttered some profanity. "It was," he verified and then paused. "After Marty was murdered, I got a call from a guy who said he was Marty's partner and that he had one last job for me. No, I don't have a name. He wouldn't say, but he told me he had photos and recordings of me with Marty from when I agreed to kidnap Gracelyn and the baby. He said he'd turn that over to the cops if I didn't do one last job."

"The job of trying to shoot the two police officers in that cruiser," Ruston snapped.

"No, the job of firing shots at the cruiser. The man told me to miss. I wouldn't have done it otherwise."

Ruston's gaze met hers. "Was Marty's partner your old friend Tony?" he asked Zimmer.

"No," the man repeated. "That wasn't him on the phone. I think I would have recognized his voice."

"Think?" Ruston challenged.

Zimmer stayed quiet for a while. "I don't believe it was him." Then he stopped and cursed. "Maybe it was. Anyway, I agreed to go through with it with one stipulation. That the so-called partner meet me in person afterward and hand over those photos and recordings. I had to figure the guy would keep copies and would continue trying to use them as leverage for future jobs, but I wanted that meeting to know who I was dealing with."

"And?" Ruston prompted when Zimmer fell silent.

"He didn't show for the meeting. And he hasn't contacted me since."

The partner could be Tony. Or Charla, for that matter, if she'd gotten a man to make that call for her. Devin could have done it as well.

"What is it you want me to do with what you've just told me?" Ruston continued a moment later.

"I want you to find out who killed Marty, Simon and the retired cop," Zimmer was quick to say. "And it wasn't Allie. Find out who it was, and I'll turn myself in. If I do that now, I'll end up dead. Find the killer," he insisted a split second before he ended the call.

Ruston ended the recording, and he immediately called Duncan. "Were you able to get a trace?" he asked.

"No," Gracelyn heard Duncan say.

And then she heard something else. Something that sent her stomach to her knees.

A woman screamed.

"Allie," Gracelyn said, her sister's name rushing out with her breath.

Ruston threw open the interview room door. In the same motion, he put away his phone and started running toward Duncan's office. Gracelyn was right behind him. They raced into the squad room.

And into chaos.

Allie was still in Duncan's office. Still screaming. Gracelyn soon saw why. There were two uniformed officers, and both had their weapons drawn. One of them, a beefy black-haired man, had Deputy Carmen Gonzales in a choke hold, and his Glock was pointed at her head. The other man, a lanky blond guy, was aiming at Allie.

He fired.

Just as Duncan tackled Allie and knocked her to the ground. The shot crashed through the office window, causing the glass to explode, but Gracelyn couldn't tell if the bullet had hit her sister. Or Duncan.

Ruston drew his gun. So did Gracelyn. Just as the lanky blond man turned his weapon toward them. Ruston dragged her to the floor as he fired.

There was the howl of some kind of alarm, loud and blaring, and Gracelyn saw Woodrow beneath his desk, where he'd taken cover. Either Duncan or he must have activated a security alert, and she hoped that brought officers responding to the scene. They might not get there in time.

Another shot came their way, blasting into the wall mere inches above their heads.

Mercy, what was happening? Gracelyn didn't have a full answer to that, but one thing was for certain. These weren't good cops. They might not even be cops at all, and they had probably used their uniforms and badges to gain access to the building.

And Allie, Ruston and she were their targets.

She cursed the call that'd just come from Zimmer. He'd phoned the landline, maybe to make sure they were there so he could send in these goons. If so, it'd been beyond gutsy to have hired guns come into a police station.

Gutsy and maybe extremely effective.

Ruston and she had a small amount of cover since there was a desk in front of them, but if the blond shooter came closer, he'd basically have them pinned down. That was probably why Ruston maneuvered himself in front of her. Shielding her. And in doing so, he was putting himself in the direct line of fire.

Gracelyn didn't want Ruston sacrificing himself for her, but this wasn't the time for her to question what he was doing. And what he was doing was getting himself into a better position to fire if he got a clean shot. At the moment, he didn't have one since both gunmen were using Carmen as their shield.

"Stop them," Allie yelled. "They're going to kill all of us."

Her sister might be right. If these fake cops had come here to eliminate Ruston, Allie and her, then they weren't likely to leave Duncan, Carmen or Woodrow alive either.

"They've locked the front door," Ruston whispered to her.

That didn't help her tamp down the wild surge of adrenaline. It meant no responders would be coming in that way. But there were other doors to the sheriff's office, and she doubted they'd managed to lock them all.

Around the squad room, phones began to ring, the sounds blending with the loud, pulsing alarm. Responders were probably trying to find out what was going on, but no one answered any of the phones. Well, maybe Duncan did. Gracelyn couldn't see Allie or him.

"If you want to save some lives, step out and let's finish this," the bulky gunman growled.

Gracelyn didn't have any doubts about what he meant. He wanted Ruston, Allie and her to sacrifice themselves. And she might have considered it. Might. But she went back to her original idea. These gunmen had no intentions of letting any of them live.

"Keep watch behind us," Ruston muttered.

That slammed her with more adrenaline, but she turned so she was essentially back-to-back with him. And got the mother lode of flashbacks. To survive the attack at the baby farm, they'd had to do this. They'd had to sit there with the threat of being gunned down and dying.

Gracelyn shook her head, forcing back those images. Forcing back the gut-wrenching emotions that went along with them. She couldn't let those flashbacks play into what was happening now. She just couldn't. Because it could get a whole lot of people killed.

"Five seconds," the gunman warned them. "That's how long you've got before we start shooting the hell out of this place. We won't kill Deputy Gonzales right off, but we'll make her wish she was dead."

Gracelyn couldn't see Carmen's face, but she knew the woman had to be terrified as the gunman started the countdown.

"Five…"

Ruston inched closer to the side of the desk. From Duncan's office, Allie quit screaming, making Gracelyn wonder if she had been hit after all. Or maybe Duncan had just figured out a way to silence her.

"Four…"

Gracelyn kept watch of the hall and the sides of the room, and from the corner of her eye, she saw Woodrow move as well. Like Ruston, he was adjusting his position, preparing for an attack.

"Three… Time's running out," the gunman added as a threat.

Woodrow looked in their direction, and even though Gracelyn couldn't see Ruston's face, he nodded. Woodrow and he had made some kind of silent pact. Maybe to leave cover and try to get that clean shot.

Gracelyn decided to help with that.

"Two," the gunman barked out.

She took off one of her shoes, holding it for a split second in Ruston's line of sight so he'd know what she was doing. Then she hurled it over the desk and in the direction of Carmen and the gunmen.

All hell broke loose.

There were scuffling sounds, and shots rang out. So many shots. With the alarms and the blasts, she couldn't tell what direction the gunfire was coming from, but it seemed to be coming from everywhere at once.

And maybe it was.

She caught a glimpse of Duncan crouched down in the doorway. Ruston and Woodrow had left cover and were both firing. Gracelyn continued to keep watch behind them, but she scrambled around to the side of the desk and saw Carmen on the floor. The deputy didn't appear to have been shot, but she was crawling toward Gracelyn.

The blond gunman pivoted to shoot Carmen, but he didn't get the chance. Gracelyn fired, but she was pretty sure that Woodrow and Ruston did as well. Maybe even Duncan. Multiple shots hit the gunman in the chest, and he dropped like a stone, his weapon clattering to the floor.

The beefy gunman dropped, too, but he wasn't shot. He was coming after Carmen, no doubt to get back his human shield.

He failed.

There was another round of gunfire. Gracelyn couldn't get in on this one because Carmen was in front of her, but her shot wasn't necessary. Bullets slammed into the gunman, and he used his last breath to snarl out some profanity. Gracelyn figured he was dead before he even hit the floor.

Gracelyn continued to hold her breath. Continued to

watch for another attacker. Someone, maybe Woodrow, shut off the alarm, but around the office, the phones continued to ring.

"Is anyone hurt?" Duncan called out.

"I'm okay," Carmen answered.

Gracelyn didn't answer. Couldn't. Because she couldn't unclamp her throat enough to speak. She just wanted to hear Ruston's voice. She needed to know he was okay.

"I'm fine." That came from Woodrow. "Are you hurt?"

"No," Duncan confirmed.

"I'm okay," Ruston finally said. "Gracelyn?"

"Okay," she finally managed. The relief came. Well, relief about Ruston and the others, anyway.

"Allie, were you hit?" Gracelyn called out.

Nothing.

No response.

Not for a couple of seconds, anyway, and then she heard Duncan curse. "Allie's not here."

Alarmed, Gracelyn stood, her gaze zooming to Duncan's office. Since the glass was now gone, she had no trouble seeing directly inside. And what she saw was the open side door that her sister had almost certainly used to escape.

Chapter Eleven

Ruston seriously doubted Gracelyn was actually sleeping, but since she wasn't saying anything, he stayed quiet as well.

And replayed every second of the nightmare that'd happened at the sheriff's office.

That'd been over twelve hours ago, and after the shots had ended, both Gracelyn and he had gotten caught up in the investigative whirlwind of trying to piece everything together. That had been both an exhausting and frustrating process that was merely on pause so everyone could get some rest.

In Gracelyn's and his case, they'd chosen for that "rest" to happen at the ranch so she could be with Abigail. Ruston had even managed to get Gracelyn to eat something before they'd gone to bed. Well, she had gone to bed, and he'd taken the chair again. She had offered to share the queen-size bed with him, and that'd been a damn tempting offer, but he didn't have a lot of willpower right now when it came to Gracelyn. What could start as a hug of comfort could turn into a whole lot more, and Gracelyn didn't need that right now.

Like him, she needed some rest so she could approach the investigation with a clear head.

Clearly, Duncan wasn't in the rest mode, because even though it was well past midnight, Ruston's phone lit up with a text from him. Ruston had put his cell on silent, even shutting off the vibration so that it wouldn't wake Gracelyn if she did indeed manage to fall asleep. But she must have seen the flash of light, because she sat up, her gaze racing across the room to him.

"Did they find Allie?" she whispered.

The only light was coming from the ajar bathroom door, but Ruston had no trouble seeing that she was not only wide-awake but that she was just as on edge as he was.

He shook his head. "Duncan got IDs on the two dead fake cops, though. And they were fake," he emphasized, trying to keep his voice as low as possible. Abigail was only an hour into what should be a three- or four-hour stretch of sleep for her, and he didn't want to disturb her.

Apparently, Gracelyn was concerned about disturbing Abigail, too, because she moved as if to get out of bed to come to him. Ruston fixed that by going to her. He sat on the edge of the bed so they could talk, but he hoped this would be a short conversation. He was still hanging on to the hope that Gracelyn might actually get some rest tonight.

She wasn't wearing the pajamas that Joelle had brought in for her but had opted for a loose pair of loaner jogging pants and a T-shirt. Her shoes were right next to the bed beside her freshly restocked go bag. All indications she was ready to get Abigail out of there if necessary.

Ruston was hoping like the devil it wouldn't be necessary.

"The dead men are Eddie Baker and Andre Culpepper," Ruston told her. "Both have criminal records. According to Carmen, when they showed up to escort a prisoner to Austin, she thought there was something suspicious about the paperwork they had. She was about to call Austin PD when one of them grabbed her."

That was a nutshell account of what'd happened. Of course, the emotional couldn't be put in a nutshell. There'd been an attack at the sheriff's office, and now two men were dead. No wonder Duncan was still at work.

"What about the prisoner they were supposed to transport?" Gracelyn asked. "Was he in on it?"

"Duncan doesn't think so. Austin PD was actually sending down two officers to collect him, but they weren't coming for another two hours."

She stayed quiet for several seconds. "So, these two fake cops would have had access to Austin PD info," she concluded.

"Looks that way," he agreed.

"Zimmer," she muttered. "He could have set all of this up."

She'd get no argument from him about that. In fact, it was possible Zimmer had orchestrated this and everything else that'd happened. The man had sounded somewhat sincere when he'd told them about his quest to catch those involved in the baby farm, but that could have been all smoke. A ruse to confirm Gracelyn and he were at the sheriff's office so he could send in the thugs to attack.

"We were the targets," she said. "Me, you and Allie. They came there to kill us." Her voice broke and she squeezed her eyes shut as if trying to hold back tears.

Cursing and breaking his promise to himself that he wouldn't try to soothe her, Ruston pulled her into his arms. A hug probably wasn't going to do much, but it was all he had. There was no good news to give her. Heck, he couldn't even dispute that part about them being targets. In fact, it all made sense if Zimmer was trying to tie up some loose ends.

"I'm not going to let Allie or Zimmer get to Abigail," she whispered, her words brushing against his neck.

Ruston rethought that notion about a hug not doing much good because Gracelyn sounded stronger than she had just seconds earlier. Of course, the baby could do that. Ruston would protect the little girl with his own life, and that included not letting Allie or Zimmer get anywhere near her.

"Allie doesn't even love her," Gracelyn went on. "She was going to sell her."

"I know," Ruston murmured. And he knew something else.

That Gracelyn did love the baby.

Heck, so did he. That added even more urgency to the need to keep Gracelyn and her safe.

"Has there been any sign of Allie?" she asked.

"No." And that had given him plenty to think about.

If Allie had told the truth about not having much money, she couldn't have gotten far. Not on her own, anyway. But it was possible Zimmer or another thug was waiting near the sheriff's office and scooped her up after she ran outside. If that hadn't happened, then whoever had hired those two fake cops would no doubt be looking for her.

If they found her, they'd kill her.

Ruston knew Gracelyn was well aware of that. Allie probably was, too, but so far, that hadn't caused Allie to seek out police protection, something she could get with one phone call to either Gracelyn, Duncan or him.

Gracelyn had left a message for Allie encouraging her to do just that. To accept that protection. But so far, there'd been no response from her sister.

She eased back from him, just far enough for her to make eye contact. "You moved in front of me," she said, and he must have looked confused, because she added, "During the shooting."

Oh, that. "Yeah," he admitted. "It has nothing to do with you being a woman. It was just instinct."

Since she wasn't exactly doling out any thanks, he geared up to add an apology to that. And let her know that his instincts would be the same if it happened again.

"You did that at the baby farm, too," she muttered.

Ruston couldn't recall that for certain. Those moments they'd been pinned down by gunfire were a blur. Then again, he'd worked hard to make sure they were. He didn't need images like that in his head.

She sighed. "What's going on here?" Gracelyn asked.

And he didn't think they were talking about gunfire any longer. Nope. There was just enough light for him to see the change in her eyes. Her breath hitched a little. He felt her muscles tense beneath his hands. A reminder that he was still holding her in his arms.

"I think what's going on is a complication," he admitted. "Something we'd like to postpone. But it doesn't seem to want to go away."

"No," she quietly agreed.

They sat there, face-to-face, body-to-body, and it seemed as if everything stopped. Only for a second or two. But in that brief span of time, Ruston managed to have an argument with himself as to why he should move away from her.

An argument he lost.

Gracelyn lost it, too, because she was the one who leaned in and pressed her mouth to his. And just that, just that brief touch of her lips, sent the heat soaring.

He tried to rein in that heat. That need. But it was a lost cause and not one he wanted to win. He wanted to kiss Gracelyn, so that was exactly what he did.

She moaned, the silky sound one of pleasure, and immediately notched up the intensity by deepening the kiss.

The taste of her hit him hard again, spearing right through him and instantly making him want more.

He took more.

Ruston tightened his grip on her and brought her closer to him. Until her breasts were against his chest. Until there was no space or distance between them. And even that didn't seem close enough.

Of course, his body was insisting on getting closer to her. His body was urging him on and on. And Gracelyn certainly wasn't putting on the brakes either. So, maybe she was using this to shut out the nightmarish thoughts if even for a minute. Maybe this was a kind of comfort after all.

That notion stayed with him until she skimmed her hand down his back and then snuggled even closer to him, adjusting her position until she was in his lap. The kiss didn't stop. It continued to rage on. So did the touching, and Ruston got in on that. He slid his fingers over her breasts. And enjoyed the hell out of that little hitch that came from her throat.

This was how things had started the night after the baby-farm attack. The hug that had led to a kiss. The kiss that had led to, well, a hot and heavy make-out session that had landed them in bed. Since they were already in bed, they wouldn't have far to go.

But was Gracelyn ready for this?

Physically, yeah, she was. He could feel the unspoken invitation she was offering him. However, going just the physical route here could cause her to have lots of regrets. That was what had happened last time, and it had sent her running. Ruston didn't want that again.

And that was why he pulled back from her.

Not easily. It took every bit of willpower he could muster, and even then, he wasn't sure it was a battle he was going to win with himself. If she'd kissed him again, that would snap the leash on the heat, and they would just have to deal with things like regret later.

But she didn't kiss him.

She didn't move off his lap either, and he was well aware that the center of her body was pressing against his erection.

Gracelyn stared at him. "I want you to know that after the shooting at the baby farm, I didn't leave because of you. I left because of me, because I couldn't stay and deal with what was going on in my head."

"I understand," he assured her. And he did. "There were times after my father was killed when I considered leaving for a while, too."

"But you stayed because of your siblings," she finished for him.

He nodded. Joelle and Bree had taken the murder so hard. Heck, they all had, but they had found strength with each other. Gracelyn hadn't had that with Allie.

"Once this is over and the killer is caught, we should go on a date," she said.

Ruston laughed and then immediately cut off the sound when Abigail squirmed a little. He waited until he was sure she was back asleep before he responded.

"I'd like to go on a date with you," he told her and brushed his mouth over hers again. Not a hungry kiss exactly, but then again, with Gracelyn, hunger was always right beneath the surface.

She snapped it straight to the surface when she leaned in and kissed him again. The real deal kiss.

Nothing held back.

And considering they were both already hot and primed, Ruston knew exactly where this was going.

GRACELYN FIGURED THIS was a huge mistake, but she simply didn't care. She wanted Ruston. Needed him. And she didn't have the willpower to fight off that need any longer. She just sank into the kiss and let Ruston and his incredible mouth perform some magic.

The magic happened, all right.

She felt the heat race through her, and Gracelyn just let it carry her away. It had been like this on that other night Ruston and she had been together. That one, too, had been fueled with spent adrenaline and need. So much need. And once again, Ruston managed to notch up the heat.

They were already face-to-face, body-to-body, center-to-center, and that made it easier for him to lower his mouth to her neck and light some fires there. He touched, too. Mercy, did he touch. There was an urgency, and a gentleness, in the way he slid his hand down her back.

Gracelyn nearly got lost in the fiery haze, nearly let Ruston carry her away. But she wanted to give as good as she was getting. She wanted to do her own tasting and touching, so she unhooked his shoulder holster, setting the weapon aside on the nightstand, and then rid him of his shirt.

And her version of touching and tasting began.

She lowered her head, kissed his chest, and she felt his muscles stir beneath her mouth. Gracelyn used her tongue. Heard the rumble of pleasure that came deep from within his throat. She kept kissing while she slid her hand to his stomach.

More muscles stirred. He made that sound again. And she just kept pushing, firing up the heat. Until Ruston could seemingly take no more. He pulled off her top and turned the tables on her by touching her breasts. It was an amazing sensation that became so much more when he rid her of her bra.

The urgency escalated. Of course it did. This level of heat couldn't last, and it demanded to be sated now. That was the word pounding through her head—*now*—when she reached for the zipper of his jeans. He stopped her, and Gracelyn muttered some profanity when he moved her off his lap and stood.

For a few horrible moments she thought he was stopping, but Ruston pulled off his boots before he fished through the pocket of his jeans and came out with his wallet. Then a condom.

Gracelyn wanted to curse some more because the heat and need had nearly made her forget the whole safe-sex thing. Thankfully, Ruston hadn't. Also, thankfully, he was prepared.

And naked.

That happened when he shucked off his jeans and boxers. A fully clothed Ruston could fire her up, but a naked one stole her breath. The man was drop-dead hot, and he was hers.

Well, hers for this moment, anyway.

And this moment was enough. Gracelyn wouldn't allow herself to think beyond it. She didn't want to deal with anything but this urgency that was building, building, building in every inch of her.

Ruston moved back toward the bed, anchoring his knee on the edge of the mattress while he leaned in and pulled off her sweatpants. And panties. He didn't lower on top of her, though. But he kissed her. A long, slow slide of his mouth that started at her neck and went lower. To her breasts.

Then lower. To her stomach.

Then lower still. And that was a kiss that had Gracelyn jolting. That had her nearly flying right over the edge of a climax. While she was certain that would be amazing, she didn't want to finish things like this.

She levered herself up, not easily, and took hold of Ruston to pull him down on top of her. She wanted his body on hers. And that was what she got. She wanted him to be as mindless and ready as she was, and she got that, too, when she wrapped her hand around his erection.

Judging from the profanity he grumbled, that was the best kind of torture for him, and it caused him to hurry to get the condom on.

They were face-to-face again when he pushed inside her. Face-to-face when the thrusts turned from gentle and testing to deep and demanding. Face-to-face when those thrusts made it impossible for her to hang on any longer.

Gracelyn let him finish her. She let Ruston take her to the only place she wanted to go.

With the climax rippling through her, they were face-to-face when she kissed him and took Ruston right along with her.

Chapter Twelve

Ruston lay next to Gracelyn while she slept. And she was indeed sleeping. He could tell from the now gentle, even rhythm of her breathing. Nothing like the urgent pace that'd happened when they were having sex. Then again, there were many things that took on that level of heat and need.

There weren't many things that could make him forget that a killer was after them. Temporarily forget, anyway. Now that the fire had been cooled for the moment, he remembered.

And he worried.

How the hell was he going to keep Abigail and Gracelyn safe?

For the moment they didn't have anyone trying to gun them down, but Ruston also knew they couldn't stay holed up like this. It was like being undercover. With a baby, no less. That had to stop.

But how?

He didn't even know who was trying to kill them, much less how to draw the person out in a way that didn't involve putting Gracelyn or Abigail in even more danger than they already were.

There was one bright thing in all of this. Gracelyn and he were fully on the same side now. They were together, and while he wasn't going to try to figure out what that meant for the future, Ruston knew they'd be working together to protect Abigail.

"I can practically hear you thinking," Gracelyn muttered.

Ruston silently cursed when he looked down and saw she was now wide-awake. He silently cursed again at the heat that instantly notched up inside him just by looking at her.

"I was hoping you'd get more than an hour's sleep," he said, and because he couldn't stop himself, he kissed her.

Gracelyn kissed him right back and made that amazing sound of pleasure that took the hunger up even more. And while his body was all for revving up, it wasn't a good idea.

"I don't have a second condom," he told her.

She winced a little, then smiled. A wistful kind of smile that had an edge to it. The kind of edgy vibe that lovers threw off when the heat was strong and wouldn't just go away.

Using a single finger, she slid a strand of hair off his forehead. That shouldn't have felt like foreplay. It did. Then again, at the moment her breathing felt like foreplay, too.

He kissed her, way too long, way too deep. Enough to fire them both up. He would have taken that heat to the center of her body for some very pleasurable kisses. But a flash of light stopped him.

It hadn't come from the window, so it wasn't headlights. It took him a second to realize it was the phone. It was on the floor mixed with their discarded clothes. And it grabbed his attention, all right. It grabbed Gracelyn's, too, because she tensed, clearly bracing for the worst.

He scrambled off the bed, located the phone and saw the name on the screen. "It's a text from Luca," he relayed to her.

Apparently, Luca wasn't getting any sleep tonight either.

Ruston read the message and quickly told her so she could release the breath she was holding.

"The search team found the dead man, Buddy, who Zimmer told us about," Ruston explained. "The body was just off one of the ranch trails. The medical examiner will get the body and give us a cause of death, but Luca says it appears the guy did bleed out. So, Zimmer hadn't lied about that."

But Ruston immediately rethought that.

"Zimmer could have been the one to kill him," Ruston amended. "I could have shot Buddy when he was at the front door of your house, but Zimmer could have finished him off. Zimmer might not have wanted to leave behind a loose end, especially one who's a hothead."

Obviously, that hadn't occurred to Gracelyn yet, but it would have soon enough. Zimmer could have told them only the details that would paint him in the best light possible. The bottom line, though, was Zimmer could be a cold-blooded killer.

"Duncan will look for any connection between Zimmer and the dead fake cops," Ruston assured her. Since it didn't feel right to be discussing this while he was naked, he began to dress. "But my guess is if there is one, it won't be obvious. Whoever set this up had to know it was risky."

She made a sound of agreement and must have felt the same way he did, because she got up and started dressing as well. "And yet he went through with the plan anyway." Gracelyn sighed. "That tells me the attacks aren't going to stop." She pulled on her top, and when she'd gotten her head through the neck opening, she looked him straight in the eyes. "You and I are the ultimate loose ends because the killer has to know we won't stop until he's caught."

Ruston couldn't argue with any of that, but he had a bad

feeling about where Gracelyn was going with this. Still, he sat there and heard her out.

"Before today, I thought Abigail was the target," she continued. She pulled on her panties and then the jogging pants. "But I think they wanted her only because they could sell her. They didn't come after her here at the ranch. Thank God," she added in a mutter. "They came after us instead. So, we're their priority."

Again, he couldn't argue. In fact, he could take this line of thought one step further. "You're thinking Abigail would be safer away from us."

She nodded, but he saw the dread that was causing. For all intents and purposes, Gracelyn had become Abigail's mother, and it would crush her to have to leave the baby. Still, it would crush her even more if Abigail was hurt because some thugs were coming after Ruston and her.

But there was even more to this.

More that had Ruston muttering some profanity.

"You're thinking of making ourselves bait," he spelled out. He cursed while he finished putting on his clothes and his shoulder holster.

"Bait with a plan," she said, and she continued talking despite his groan. "We could leave Abigail here with lots of protection. Lots," she emphasized. "I mean security that's so tight, there's no way anyone can get to her. Then you and I could draw out the killer. Because as you know, we'll never be safe until the killer is caught."

He did know that. But there was a part of this plan he didn't like, and that was a huge understatement.

"You could have that same airtight security," Ruston insisted. "You could be here with Abigail, and I could become the bait."

She stared at him and took hold of his shoulders. "They

want both of us, Ruston. If I'm here, they could come here. Or they just wait until something draws me out. I can't stay holed up in here forever, and they know that."

Ruston wanted to argue with her. Mercy, he did. Because he wanted to keep Gracelyn safe. He didn't want her anywhere near the line of fire again.

"We've done undercover together before," she added a moment later, "and this would be very similar."

"Yeah, and the last time we were undercover together, we nearly died," he reminded her.

"Because someone betrayed us or made us as cops. Maybe Zimmer. Maybe Charla or Tony. Heck, maybe it was Devin, since he seems to be connected to everything that's happening. But for this, we make the plan. This time, only people we trust will know what's going on."

That would be a given, but he still wasn't on board. "So, what? We set up somewhere and lure the killer to us? Because he won't be alone. And, heck, might not come at all. He could send more hired thugs like he did at the sheriff's office."

"He might be running out of hired thugs," she muttered. "But if he's not, then the plan should include capturing at least one of them and getting him to talk."

Ruston huffed because there were so many things that could go wrong with this plan, and Gracelyn no doubt saw the skepticism that was still all over his face.

"Let's map it out like an op," she went on. "Then we can identify any weak spots and fix them. Only then do we go in. Only then do we put this into motion."

"And what if the op is mapped out, and there are weak spots we can't eliminate?" he asked.

"Then we come up with another plan, one where we can make it as safe as possible."

Which wouldn't be very safe if they were literally putting themselves out there as bait. Unfortunately, he thought the bait would work. The killer seemed desperate to eliminate them. Still…

His phone lit up again, and this time, it was Slater's name on the screen. Yeah, no one other than Abigail was getting much sleep tonight. Slater hadn't sent a text but was calling instead.

Hell.

This couldn't be good, and he hoped the killer hadn't already launched an attack here at the ranch.

Since Ruston didn't want the sound of Slater's voice waking the baby, he didn't put the call on speaker. "Slater," he whispered. "What's wrong?"

"I just got a report that SAPD found another body," Slater said.

That caused everything inside him to clench. "Is it Allie?" he asked.

"No," Slater was quick to answer.

Even though he hadn't put the call on speaker, Gracelyn obviously heard that, and she made a sharp sound of relief.

"SAPD thinks this one is a suicide. Or at least it was set up to look that way, with a single gunshot wound to the head," Slater explained. "The dead guy is Zimmer."

Chapter Thirteen

Gracelyn sat in the family room at the McCullough ranch, holding Abigail and waiting while Duncan was talking on the phone to Noah about the latest updates in the investigation. She felt drained. Numb. But she knew those feelings would have been much worse had it been her sister's body that was found.

That was what she'd first thought when Slater had called hours earlier to tell them what had happened. Gracelyn had thought that Zimmer had gotten to Allie and had silenced her for good.

Instead, Zimmer was the one who was dead.

Gracelyn had read the preliminary report that Noah had done, and someone out walking their dog had spotted Zimmer slumped behind the wheel of his truck that was parked outside a long-stay motel. As Slater had said, he'd died from a gunshot wound to the head that appeared to be self-inflicted.

She wasn't buying that.

And apparently neither was Ruston, Joelle, Duncan, Slater or Noah. Like her, they were all convinced that Zimmer had been murdered. Probably by the same person who'd already murdered at least three other people and had hired those fake cops to come after Ruston and her.

"You should eat," Ruston said, tipping his head to the

breakfast sandwich that was on the end table to her right. It was one of many sandwiches that Luca had dropped off from the diner.

Ruston leaned in and smiled at Abigail. "Hey, sweet girl." He brushed a kiss on her cheek.

Abigail turned her head toward him, something she'd only recently started doing, and she studied Ruston for a couple of seconds before her tiny mouth bowed into a smile. The baby's attention then shifted to his badge that he had pinned to his shirt. It was shiny, since it was new and had been delivered earlier, courtesy of Captain O'Malley. Gracelyn was glad the captain had made that kind of effort, because it showed she still had plenty of faith in Ruston as a cop.

"Want me to hold Abigail while you eat?" Ruston asked.

Gracelyn wasn't sure her stomach was settled enough to handle any food, but it was obvious Ruston was concerned about her. Added to that, she really did need to try to eat something, since she couldn't even remember when her last meal had been. So, she handed him the baby and picked up the sandwich. Just as Duncan finished his latest phone call.

"Time of death for Zimmer was about ten last night. The medical examiner agrees that it's not suicide," Duncan said right off. "The angle of the shot is off. Good, but off."

"Close range or from a distance?" Joelle asked. She was in the chair next to Duncan and was eating a bagel that had been slathered with cream cheese.

"Close range but not point-blank," Duncan supplied. "Noah believes Zimmer's killer was waiting for him, and when Zimmer parked in front of his motel room, the killer shot him. Not through the glass. Zimmer had apparently lowered his windows."

"Because he knew his killer and was going to talk to him or her?" Ruston wanted to know.

"Maybe. Noah said the AC wasn't working in Zimmer's truck, so both the driver's and passenger's windows were down. He was shot through the passenger's window. The killer could have simply walked up to him, fired and then placed the gun in Zimmer's hand to try to make it look as if he'd pulled the trigger."

Gracelyn took a moment, fixing that scenario in her mind. "Is the gun registered to Zimmer?"

Duncan shook his head. "It was reported stolen about a year ago, so no way to trace it. Zimmer had a slide holster in the back of his jeans, but there was no gun inside it."

"Which meant the killer likely took it," Ruston said, shaking his head. "Was the motel parking lot well lit? And please tell me there are security cameras nearby."

Duncan's sigh said it all. "No cameras, bad lighting, and in a neighborhood where it's rare for someone to come forward and report what they saw."

The killer would have known all of that. Added to that, it'd been night, and the darkness would have given him an advantage.

Duncan washed down a bite of his breakfast burrito with some coffee and shifted his attention to Gracelyn. "There's been no sign of your sister. Why don't you go ahead and leave her another message on the private Facebook page? Tell her I want to talk to her about that deal she was looking to make."

"I will," Gracelyn said, taking out her phone to do that. "But I doubt she'll believe that."

"Probably not, but we need to find her. And, yeah, there's a slim-to-none chance of a deal, but if she cooperates, the DA might show some leniency."

Gracelyn didn't say aloud that Allie didn't deserve leniency. Not after what she'd tried to do to Abigail, but that wasn't for her to decide. Right now, Allie just needed to turn herself in or she would likely end up dead like Zimmer.

She left the message for Allie just as Duncan's phone rang. "It's Hank, one of the ranch hands," he relayed.

Gracelyn couldn't hear what the hand said, but whatever it was caused Duncan to get to his feet and make a beeline toward the front window. "We have a visitor," Duncan explained. "It's Tony. He said he's here to make a confession."

"A confession?" Ruston and she repeated in unison.

Mercy. Gracelyn hadn't seen this coming. Then again, maybe this was just another ruse to get close to Ruston and her so he could kill them.

Duncan must have had the same concerns, because he glanced back at Joelle. "Why don't Slater and you go ahead and take the baby upstairs?"

Joelle nodded, immediately got up and took Abigail from Ruston. Gracelyn figured Duncan was about to tell her to go with them, but he didn't.

"Tony's still at the end of the road, and the hands can and will block him from coming closer. It's up to you whether or not you want to see him," Duncan explained, looking at both Ruston and her. He listened to something else Hank said. "Tony's alone and volunteered to be disarmed before he comes in the house."

Before Duncan had added that last part, Gracelyn had figured they would be having this conversation with Tony on the porch and Ruston and she would be tucked back in the foyer.

"We'll talk to him," Gracelyn agreed after she got a nod from Ruston. "I want to hear what he has to say."

They had a lot of information about the murders and attacks. Info from plenty of sources that might or might not be reliable. Zimmer, Allie, Charla and Devin. If Tony was truly here to confess, then all of those pieces of info might actually fit. They might be able to make an arrest and put a stop to any other murders or attacks.

"Frisk him thoroughly," Duncan told the ranch hand on the phone. "Hold on to any weapons he has and then drive him to the house in your truck. If this is some kind of last-ditch effort, Tony's vehicle could be rigged with explosives."

Gracelyn hadn't even considered that, a reminder that she really needed to try to keep a clear head. If Tony was desperate enough to make a confession, then he might want to first do as much damage as possible.

Since Ruston and Duncan were already at the front windows and had their weapons drawn, Gracelyn moved to the side one and took out her gun as well. The ranch hands were keeping an eye on the yard to make sure no one tried to sneak into the house, but she needed to do something to make sure they weren't attacked.

It was a good five minutes before Gracelyn saw the truck coming up the road, and she lost sight of it when it turned down the driveway toward the house. Both Duncan and Ruston stayed in place until the driver turned off the engine, and then they went to the door.

"Hang back until we have Tony inside," Duncan told her. "I've got to turn off the security system for just a couple of seconds. Once Tony is inside, I'll turn it back on."

Gracelyn muttered an agreement and continued to keep watch out the side window, especially since there'd be that short pause for the security. It wasn't long before the footsteps on the porch had her turning in that direction. Tony stepped in, and while he frowned at Duncan and Ruston basically holding him at gunpoint, he didn't protest.

"I won't take much of your time," Tony insisted, spearing Ruston with his gaze before he did the same to her.

Duncan maneuvered Tony into the foyer so he could shut the door, and Gracelyn saw him rearm the security system. Only then did Gracelyn give Tony her full attention. He looked disheveled, with his clothes wrinkled and stubble that was well past the fashionable stage. Like the rest of them, Tony didn't appear to have gotten much sleep.

"I'm resigning from SAPD today," Tony stated. He'd somehow managed to keep the emotion out of his flat tone, but the emotion was there in his eyes. A mix of anger and frustration. And guilt.

"You said you were here to make a confession," Ruston pressed. No flat tone for him. There was a "get on with this" edge to his voice.

Tony nodded. "Internal Affairs is examining my financials, and it won't take them long to discover that I accepted money from Marty. Payment in exchange for redirecting investigations so they didn't lead to him."

Ruston uttered a single raw word of profanity. "You sold out Gracelyn and me at the baby farm?"

"No," Tony was quick to say. "Hell, no. Nothing like that." He groaned and shook his head. "I was broke and behind in my child support. My ex was going to report me, and I would have maybe ended up losing my job, so I borrowed money from Marty. I know it was stupid," he quickly added, "but I was desperate."

"Desperate enough to sell out your badge," Ruston snapped, taking the words right out of Gracelyn's mouth.

Tony sighed. "Yes, but I didn't see it as selling out. I thought, stupidly thought," he amended, "that I could get my ex off my

back and find another way to pay Marty what I owed him."
He paused. "But Marty didn't want payback in the form of
money. He wanted a cop in his pocket. He got one, but I never
compromised the safety of any officers. Like I said, I only re-
directed investigations away from Marty."

The anger and disgust rolled through her, and Gracelyn
had to tamp some of that down before she could speak. "Did
you tell Internal Affairs this?"

"No, but I will. I wanted to tell Ruston and you first, and
then I'll talk to Charla. Then I'll turn myself in."

"Charla doesn't know what you've done?" Gracelyn
asked.

"No, and she'll be crushed," Tony concluded.

Maybe. But if Charla was the killer, then she might be
pleased about this development, because in a way, it took
some of the focus off the person behind the attacks and
murders.

Tony pulled in a long breath. "I didn't directly do anything to put the two of you in danger, but by protecting
Marty, the danger happened anyway."

Yes, it had. And Internal Affairs would no doubt question him about that once he told them what he'd done.

If he told them, that was.

It occurred to her that Tony might be planning to go on
the run. But if so, why come here first? Was this actually
some kind of ploy to distract them? That thought flashed
in her head just as Duncan's phone rang.

"It's Hank," Duncan muttered, keeping his gaze on Tony
while he took the call. Gracelyn couldn't hear what the hand
said, but whatever it was prompted Duncan to mutter his
own word of profanity, and he shook his head. "No, search
them and bring them up. I'll call for every available deputy
to respond." And Duncan proceeded to contact Dispatch.

Gracelyn's stomach dropped. "Are we about to be at-tacked?" she asked Duncan the second he finished the call.

"I don't think so. Hank said that Devin just arrived," Duncan explained. "And he has Allie with him. Devin wants me to arrest her."

"Allie," Gracelyn murmured, and she looked at Ruston to get his take on this.

He was apparently on the same wavelength, because she could see the uneasiness in his eyes. Then again, that feel-ing had already been there for both of them with Tony's arrival. Now it was skyrocketing.

It could be a coincidence that two of their suspects, Tony and Devin, were there at the same time, but Gracelyn didn't like coincidences. Maybe Tony and Devin were working together. This could be the start of another attack.

Part of her was relieved her sister was alive. But there was no relief whatsoever in the fact that Devin was the one bringing her in. Well, supposedly he was, anyway. Gracelyn didn't trust Devin any more than she did Tony or her sister.

Or Charla.

Since Charla was the only one of their suspects who hadn't shown up, that made Gracelyn wonder where she was. Was she standing back, watching this all play out after she'd set it in motion?

Perhaps.

Or Devin could be the one playing games here. But if he was the one responsible for the murders and attacks, then why hadn't he just killed Allie? That didn't help settle Gracelyn's worries about Devin, since this could be a sort of reverse psychology. A way to try to make himself look innocent by keeping one loose end alive.

"I don't want Allie in the house," Ruston insisted. "She might try to go after Abigail."

Gracelyn was in complete agreement, and apparently so was Duncan since he didn't protest that. "Hank, let me speak to Devin," Duncan told the ranch hand. "I'm putting the call on speaker."

The downside to that was Tony was standing right there and would be able to hear everything, but that was better than the alternative of bringing Devin and Allie to the house. Or sending Tony on his way. If Tony had hooked up with Devin to do another attack, Gracelyn thought it would be best if they weren't together. Then again, it was possible Devin was counting on Tony to be his inside man in whatever might be about to happen. That was why Gracelyn kept her attention pinned to Tony.

"Don't," she warned Tony when he reached for something in his pocket.

Tony huffed, clearly annoyed at her warning. "I just want to call SAPD and get you some help out here."

"No calls," Duncan ordered, muting his phone so that Devin wouldn't be able to hear any of this. "Just stand there and don't say anything."

Tony's eyes narrowed, but he held up his hands as if in mock surrender. Oh, yes. Gracelyn was definitely going to watch him.

Duncan's phone began to ding with a series of texts, and Gracelyn caught glimpses of his screen. Carmen, Luca and Woodrow were on their way.

"Sheriff Holder," Devin said the moment he was on the phone. "I've got Allie with me."

"So I heard. How did you know I was here?" Duncan asked.

Devin seemed to hesitate as if he hadn't expected the question. "Allie told me about the shooting at the sheriff's office, and I figured the place was a giant crime scene right now."

It was, and since the CSIs were working the scene, the building was temporarily closed, and Duncan and the other deputies were working from home.

"I guessed you'd come back here with Gracelyn," Devin tacked on to his explanation.

"And you decided to bring Allie with you." The remark was heavy with skepticism.

"He brought me here against my will," Allie shouted. "He tied my hands and kidnapped me."

"I found her trying to sneak into my house," Devin countered. "I'd changed the locks, and she'd broken a window. When I confronted her, she tried to punch me. Then bite me. Then scratch me." He sounded riled about that. "I brought her here so you can arrest her."

"SAPD could have done that much faster," Duncan was quick to point out.

More silence from Devin. But not from Allie. She continued to curse and yell, and Gracelyn hoped she didn't break out of whatever restraints were on her.

"I thought you'd want to handle the arrest," Devin finally said. "SAPD might not turn her over to you to answer for what she did, and I know Gracelyn especially will want her sister punished."

"Abigail is mine." That came as another shout from Allie. "I can do with her what I want."

The words hit Gracelyn like a heavyweight's fists. Allie could be just ranting out of rage, but that sounded very much like the threat that it was. If Allie got her hands on Abigail, there was no telling what she'd do to the child.

Duncan sighed and scrubbed his hand over his face, and he checked the text messages that were lighting up his phone. "Stay put at the end of the road. Deputies Vanetti and Leonard will be there in just a few minutes. They can take custody of Allie and transport her to the county jail."

That brought out even louder shouts and cursing from Allie. "Gracelyn?" her sister called out. "I know you're there. Help me. Help your sister. Please," Allie begged. "Stop the deputies from taking me."

Gracelyn nearly spoke, not to give Allie any assurance she would stop the deputies, though. But to tell Allie that she would arrange for a lawyer to represent her.

"Gracelyn," Allie went on, and this time she spoke her name as if coated with venom. "So much for sisterly love, huh? You won't even help me. Well, to hell with you, Gracelyn. I wish the gunmen would have killed you. I wish you were dead." She was shrieking by the time she got out those last words.

Gracelyn wanted to be immune to them. But she wasn't. The words and her sister's hatred sliced her to the bone.

"Hell, Allie managed to get out of the car," Devin snarled.

Through the phone, Gracelyn heard Devin shouting her sister's name just as there was the squeal of brakes.

And the deadly-sounding thud that followed.

Chapter Fourteen

Ruston finished his latest phone call, this one an update from Slater. A call he purposely hadn't put on speaker since Gracelyn was talking with one of the ER nurses, Eileen Parsons, and he hadn't wanted Eileen to hear anything that might then end up as gossip. Added to that, if Slater had doled out some bad news, Ruston had wanted the chance to soften that news before passing it along to Gracelyn.

Gracelyn didn't look on the verge of falling apart, but he didn't want to add anything else to this already bad situation. Allie was now out of nearly seven hours of surgery, but she was critical. The surgeon had already told Gracelyn and him that Allie's chances of survival weren't good.

Ruston hadn't actually seen Allie since she'd bolted into the road and been hit by a rancher who just happened to be driving by at the time. But he'd heard the sound of the impact. He'd heard the urgency in Hank's voice, too, when he'd shouted for Devin to call an ambulance.

And Ruston had seen the blood on the road.

Gracelyn had seen it as well. No way to avoid it since Duncan, Ruston and she had left the ranch in a cruiser to come to the hospital, and they'd had to drive right past the spot where Allie had been hit.

Ruston had dreaded that drive for a lot of reasons, but

it hadn't been optional. Not after the hospital had called Gracelyn to ask her to come in and donate the rare AB negative blood that Allie and she shared. Gracelyn had done that, and now, ten hours later, they were waiting to see if it would save her sister's life.

Even though Allie's last words to Gracelyn had been to wish her dead, Gracelyn clearly didn't feel the same way about Allie. No way was she pleased with pretty much anything Allie had done, but Ruston understood her need to be here. Her need to do whatever she could to keep Allie alive.

Later, if Allie made it, she'd have to answer for the horrible crimes she'd committed. But *later* would have to wait.

Eileen looked over at him when Ruston put his phone away and made his way back toward Gracelyn and her. Not that he had gone far. For one thing, he wouldn't have let Gracelyn out of his sight, and for another, this particular waiting room was small, not much larger than a normal-sized kitchen.

Not many places to have a private conversation.

It was at the other end of the hospital from the much larger ER waiting room, which not only had way too many windows for Ruston's liking but also multiple points of entry. That was why Duncan and he had insisted on using this area, which had been set up for families to wait for surgical patients. No windows. Only one way in and out, and Duncan was guarding that.

Literally.

Duncan was pacing up and down the hall in front of the open archway entrance while he was on the phone, dealing with all the various moving parts of multiple investigations. That included making sure the hospital itself was secure.

Duncan had brought in reserve deputies for that as well, but there was always the concern that someone could slip in.

Or had already slipped in.

There had been well over a two-hour gap between the time that Gracelyn had gotten the call to ask if she'd donate blood and their arrival here at the hospital. There'd been no reserve deputies on the doors during that gap, so someone could have gotten in then.

"Any news about Allie?" Ruston asked Eileen.

The nurse had come in just as Ruston had gotten the call from Slater, so he hadn't heard anything of what she'd come to tell Gracelyn. But Ruston figured Eileen wasn't there to deliver the news that Allie was dead. That would almost certainly come from a doctor.

Eileen nodded. "They had to take her back into surgery to try to stop some internal bleeding. We're not sure how long the procedure will take." She sighed, checked her watch. "You guys have been here a long time, and I just wanted to check on the two of you and see if you needed anything."

Yeah, he needed a safe place for Gracelyn. Safer than here, anyway. But that wasn't something Eileen could fix.

Ruston looked at Gracelyn to see if she intended to take Eileen up on her offer, but she shook her head. "We're fine for now, but thanks," Ruston told the nurse, and he went to Gracelyn to pull her into his arms.

"What did Slater tell you?" she immediately asked. "Is Abigail all right?"

"She's fine. All the security measures are still in place."

All was a lot. Joelle, Slater and Luca were inside the locked-down ranch house with Abigail, and Slater had brought in his ranch hands to patrol the grounds with the other hands already keeping watch. A reserve deputy was at the end of the road to stop anyone from driving up to the house.

That included Tony or Devin. Ruston hadn't wanted them hanging around, so he'd sent them both on their way, though Devin would have to come in and give a statement about why he'd brought Allie to the ranch in the first place. But that would have to wait.

Part of Ruston had wanted to haul Devin in if only so he could keep him under a careful watch for a while, but the deputies and Duncan were already stretched thin. Added to that, the sheriff's office was still shut down, and with Duncan on guard duty, it would have meant bringing Devin to the hospital. Since that wouldn't have pleased anyone, Duncan had sent Devin home.

Hopefully that wouldn't turn out to be a fatal mistake.

"Slater said no one has gotten onto the ranch," Ruston emphasized before he told her the rest. "But one of the hands did see a vehicle driving slowly on the road that leads to the turnoff to the ranch. He didn't recognize the car, so he got the license plate and phoned Slater. When Slater ran it, he learned the vehicle belongs to Charla."

Gracelyn huffed. "What was she doing there?"

"I'm not sure. And it might not have been her behind the wheel. The hand thought the driver was a man."

"A hired gun?" But she immediately dismissed that with a head shake. "No, Charla wouldn't have let a hired gun use her car."

"Probably not," he agreed. "If she's not behind the attacks, someone could have stolen her car to make it look as if she was in the area."

He thought of another possibility, though. That Charla had hoped this mystery driver would be mistaken for her and therefore give her some kind of alibi.

"Slater did try to call her," Ruston added, "but it went straight to voicemail, so he left a message for Charla to contact either him or me."

Whether or not Charla would call back was anyone's guess. Ditto for her revealing what she was actually doing there. She could have been setting up another attack. Or she could have simply been looking for Tony. Ruston had no idea where he was. Then again, he could say that about all of their suspects except for Allie.

"You're thinking how vulnerable we are here at the hospital," Gracelyn muttered, and when he pulled himself out of his own thoughts, he realized she was staring up at him.

Ruston nodded. "Vulnerable here and anywhere else we happen to go," he admitted.

Gracelyn matched his nod. "Once Allie's out of surgery and we're back at the ranch, we should talk about that plan for us as bait. And, no, I don't like it any more than you do," she was quick to add. "But the truth is, we're no closer to catching this killer than we were two days ago. You and I are what he or she wants. We're what could cause the killer to slip up and get caught."

Every word of that was true, but it didn't minimize the risks they'd be taking. That was why he tried again to offer her a plan B. "I can be the bait, and you can be part of the security setup. You can be the one to help pen in the killer."

Ruston could tell from the look in her eyes that she was going to argue with that. She didn't want to be tucked away somewhere while he was basically dealing with a serial killer. But she didn't get a chance to voice that because of the sound of footsteps.

Both Gracelyn and he put their hands over their guns, proof of just how on edge they were, but it was Duncan who stepped into the doorway.

"Anything on Allie?" he immediately asked.

"She's back in surgery," Gracelyn answered. "Internal bleeding. It doesn't sound good."

Duncan muttered an "I'm sorry" and then paused. "The medical examiner found something on Zimmer's body."

That got their attention, and they pinned their gazes on Duncan.

"Zimmer had homemade tats between his toes," Duncan explained. "Recent ones. It appears to be a username and password. For what, we don't know, but I just got off the phone with the tech guys who are going to try to find out what they could mean."

Ruston thought back through all the things Zimmer had told Gracelyn and him in that phone conversation. "If Zimmer wasn't lying about investigating the baby farm, this could be his notes or something. Heck, it could give us the name of the killer."

"Yeah," Duncan muttered, not sounding overly hopeful, yet there was some hope there. Maybe because they didn't have any other leads.

"Did Slater tell you about Charla's vehicle being spotted near the ranch?" Ruston asked him.

"He did," Duncan verified. "Any chance your pal Noah Ryland can locate her and ask her about that?"

"I'll check," Ruston said, taking out his phone. "While I'm at it, I'll see if he can get any feed from security cameras near Devin's. It'd be interesting to see if his story about Allie trying to break in meshes with what shows up on the cameras."

Ruston started the text but then glanced up when the lights flickered. He frowned because there wasn't a storm to cause any interference. Frowned, too, because any and everything that wasn't normal was suspicious.

His suspicions skyrocketed.

The lights went out, and the room was plunged into total darkness.

GRACELYN HEARD HERSELF GASP, and she thought maybe her heart had skipped a beat or two. She immediately fumbled for her phone, but before she could take it out, a light came on. Not the overhead ones. This was a much dimmer one that was fixed on the wall.

"The generator kicked in," she heard Ruston say.

Obviously, he didn't think the loss of power was a fluke, because he'd stepped into the doorway next to Duncan and had already drawn his gun. Duncan and she did the same.

And they waited.

Her heartbeat started to race and thud as she thought of all the things that could go wrong. The killer could be coming after them. Right now. He could be using the dim lights as a way to get closer. But Ruston, Duncan and she were ready for that.

She hoped.

Gracelyn prayed the killer hadn't come up with a way to get to them that they couldn't stop. Or a way to crush her without even being near her.

"Abigail," she muttered, and the fear came, soaring.

Because if the killer had arranged for this, there could be an attack at the ranch. Her hands were far from being steady when she took out her phone and made a call to Joelle.

More waiting. Each fraction of a second seemed to take an eternity, but Joelle finally answered.

"Is everything okay?" Joelle and Gracelyn blurted out at the same time.

Apparently, Joelle was just as much on edge as she was. "The power went out at the hospital," Gracelyn explained. "We're okay, though," she quickly added when Duncan shot her a pleading glance. He obviously didn't want his pregnant wife to worry about him. "I just wanted to make sure everything was all right there."

"We're okay here, too," Joelle assured her. "No power outages. No signs of anyone trying to get near the house. Abigail just had a bottle and is asleep." She paused a moment. "Is Allie out of surgery?"

"Not yet."

"Okay, keep me posted," Joelle said, and she paused again. "You think the killer messed with the power, don't you?"

Gracelyn considered lying, but Joelle was a cop and would likely see right through that. "It's something we're considering. But the three of us are together, and we'll stay that way to give each other plenty of backup."

"All right." Joelle's voice was more than a little shaky now. "Just be careful, and tell Duncan I love him. Wait, don't do that," she quickly amended. "Because that sounds like a goodbye. Tell him to come home when he can."

"I will," Gracelyn assured her. She ended the call and relayed the message. "Joelle says to come home when you can."

Duncan made a sound of agreement, but heaven knew when that would be. For the moment, though, they weren't going anywhere. If the killer was indeed in the building, then it was best to stay put and have him or her come to them. Three against one. Well, three against an army, if the killer had backup.

But Gracelyn had to pray that wouldn't happen.

Duncan was looking to the left of the hall while Ruston was keeping an eye on the right. Gracelyn was between them and volleyed glances in both directions and at a stained glass window high on the wall across from them. She seriously doubted it would open, but it was possible someone could shoot their way through it. If that happened, she'd have a fairly good shot to stop anyone coming in that way.

A phone rang, the sound slicing through the silence, and Gracelyn saw the screen of Duncan's cell light up. "It's Anita Denny," he said, referring to one of the reserve deputies he'd posted around the hospital.

Duncan answered it, sandwiching the phone between his ear and shoulder while he continued to keep watch in the hall. He hadn't put the call on speaker, probably because he didn't want the sound of the deputy's voice to interfere with the sound of any approaching footsteps. That, and he likely didn't want Anita to give away anything that might help a killer pinpoint their location.

"Are you okay?" Duncan asked, and there was plenty of alarm in his voice.

Oh, mercy. Something had happened.

"Describe him," Duncan insisted a moment later, and then he paused, no doubt to listen to what Anita was telling him. "And you're sure it was a man?" Another pause, followed by some muttered profanity. "All right. Stay put, and I'll get someone to you," he said, ending the call.

"Who do you need me to call or text?" Ruston immediately wanted to know.

"Text Woodrow," Duncan was quick to say. "He's with the medical examiner and can be here in about fifteen minutes. I want him to go to the east side of the hospital to check on Anita. She says she's okay, but I'm not convinced."

"What happened to her?" Ruston asked Duncan while he sent the message to Woodrow.

"Someone tossed some rocks from the roof of the hospital. A few of them hit her, and when Anita looked up, she saw a man looming over the side. Just the top of his head, though, not his actual face. Anita called out to him, but he disappeared from sight."

So, it could be either Devin or Tony. Or someone that Charla had hired.

Or none of the above.

Gracelyn wanted to believe this was some kind of prank. But it didn't feel like one at all.

"Who can I call to get someone onto the roof?" Gracelyn wanted to know.

"Anita's already done it," Duncan explained. "Two hospital security guards are headed up there now. I'm contacting Dispatch to see who they can get up there to help them."

Gracelyn had no idea if the guards could handle something like confronting a killer, but she suspected the confrontation wouldn't happen. The killer wanted Ruston and her, not the guards. So, maybe this was some kind of distraction? Certainly, the killer wasn't hoping to lure them up to the roof, too?

But maybe that would work.

Partially, anyway.

If the killer managed to hold the security guards hostage, Duncan might go up there. Might. And that would leave Ruston and her alone. But even then, they certainly weren't defenseless.

Duncan had just made his call to the dispatcher when Gracelyn heard something that had them all stopping cold.

A gasp.

It had come from the direction of the nurses' station just up the hall, and they all turned in that direction, each of them bringing up their guns. The light was dim in that area, too, but not so dim that Gracelyn didn't see the nurse lying face down on the floor. For a horrifying moment, Gracelyn thought she was dead, but the woman lifted her head and then tried to scramble away from something.

Or rather someone.

There, in the shadows, Gracelyn saw a figure wearing all black who was crouched down behind the nurse. Gracelyn couldn't see his face. Heck, couldn't even tell if it was a man.

Like Ruston and Duncan, Gracelyn took aim at him, but none of them had a clean shot because the person grabbed the nurse, hooked an arm around her neck and used her as a shield. That was when Gracelyn realized why she couldn't see the person's face.

Because there was a gas mask covering it.

A split second later, there was the thudding sound of something hitting the floor. A small canister, and white smoke immediately spewed from it. One whiff, though, and Gracelyn knew it wasn't smoke.

It was tear gas.

Her eyes started to burn like fire, and she began to cough. She tried to bat the gas away from her face but couldn't. It was everywhere, engulfing them in the thick cloud, and it was having the same effect on Ruston and Duncan, too, because they were coughing as well.

Not the killer, though.

That thought was loud and clear in her head. The killer had on that mask, which meant he could walk right through the gas and get to them.

Gracelyn tried to run. Tried to get to some fresh air so she'd have enough breath to fight back. To protect anyone who was now in this killer's path. But the coughing overtook everything, and she couldn't see. She had no choice but to drop to her knees.

Gracelyn felt someone take hold of her arm. Not a gentle grip. A hard, wrenching one that dragged her to her feet and ripped the gun from her hand.

"Move," the voice snarled.

The person's crushing grip made sure she did that. Moving her away from the waiting room. And toward the exit. That was when Gracelyn realized what was happening.

She was being kidnapped.

Chapter Fifteen

With his pulse racing and adrenaline firing on all cylinders, Ruston could hear the sounds around him. Footsteps, coughing, gasps for breath. He was doing plenty of coughing and gasping of his own, and he was on his knees. He couldn't see anything but the ghost-white tear gas.

He couldn't see the person who'd set off the canister.

Ruston figured the guy was there, though, and had done this so he could kill Gracelyn and him. The tear gas would make that easier for him to do that since he was wearing a mask, but first he'd have to get to them, and Ruston needed to do something to prevent that from happening.

Hard to do anything when his throat and lungs were on fire, and the coughing was making it impossible to do much of anything. He tried to call out to Gracelyn, to tell her to stay right next to him. However, he failed. Everything inside him was yelling for him to get away, to breathe in some fresh air. But he also needed to protect Gracelyn, and at the moment, he clearly couldn't do that.

Ruston wasn't even sure where she was.

He tried to move. Tried to listen. And he could hear more of the shuffling of footsteps mixed in with the other sounds. What he couldn't hear was Gracelyn or Duncan.

Along with essentially blinding him and sending him

into a coughing fit, Ruston was disoriented and couldn't tell exactly where he was. He kept his gun gripped in his right hand and reached out with his left. He felt what he thought was the hall wall and not the archway opening of the waiting room. If so, that meant Gracelyn was probably behind him.

He staggered in what he hoped was the right direction to find her, and he'd made it a few steps when he heard a door open. That was followed by a rush of light and the fresh air that his lungs were screaming for. It cleared out some of the gas mist, but his vision was still plenty blurry.

But not his mind.

The thoughts were racing through him. One bad thought in particular. If someone had opened a door to the outside, then it could mean the tear-gas thug was escaping. Not alone, though. He could have Gracelyn with him.

"Gracelyn?" he tried to call out and managed it despite the coughing.

No answer.

He wanted to believe that was because her throat didn't allow her to respond, but his gut told him it was something much worse.

Ruston gathered up every bit of his strength and got to his feet so he could get to that open door. He made it there one staggering step at a time, and he hoped Duncan was doing the same. Someone was moving in his direction, anyway. If it was the killer, then he'd no doubt have a clean shot.

But no gunshots came.

"Where's Gracelyn?" he heard Duncan ask through the strangling coughs.

That gave Ruston another jolt of adrenaline that fueled him to move even faster to the door. He stepped out, the fresh night air engulfing him, and he nearly tripped over something. No, not something.

Someone.

For a horrifying moment, he thought the person on the ground was Gracelyn, but it wasn't. It was Nelda Martin, one of the deputies guarding the doors. She was in a crumpled heap, and there was blood on her head.

Cursing, Ruston stooped down to check for a pulse while he frantically scanned the parking lot that was just on the other side of a grassy area. There were some vehicles, including a Saddle Ridge cruiser that Nelda had likely used to come to the hospital, but there was no sign of Gracelyn.

"Hell," Duncan snarled when he stepped outside. "Is Nelda alive?"

Ruston nodded. "She's got a pulse." He kept looking. Kept listening. And he finally heard something. The sound of an engine being revved. A few seconds later, he saw the black SUV speeding out of the parking lot. He caught a glimpse of the driver.

Someone in a gas mask.

And he saw Gracelyn. Just for a second.

His heart dropped.

Because, like Nelda, she was unconscious and there was blood on her head.

"Gracelyn!" he called out, running into the parking lot.

"She's in that SUV?" Duncan asked.

"Yeah," Ruston managed, and he tried to tamp down the panic that was crawling through him.

"Use the cruiser," Duncan insisted. He rummaged through Nelda's pocket, came up with the keys and tossed them to Ruston. "Go. I'll be right behind you as soon as I get her some help. I can use one of the other cruisers to track you."

Ruston caught the keys and didn't waste a second. He

ran straight to the cruiser, jumped in and started driving.
Fast. As if Gracelyn's life depended on it.

Which it did.

He practically flew out of the parking lot, and some of the
tightness in his chest eased up just a little when he spotted
the SUV. Again, it was just a glimpse before it disappeared
around a curve. But at least Ruston knew what direction it
was going.

Out of town.

Well, maybe. A sickening thought occurred to him, that
maybe there was more than one SUV, that the one he saw
was meant to lead him in the wrong direction. That was
possible, but since he didn't have a lot of options, he went
after it. He had to get to Gracelyn and stop her from being
killed.

The image of the blood on her head flashed in his mind,
but he had to shove that aside. That would only tear apart
his focus, and right now, he needed all the focus he could
get. He had to catch up with that SUV.

The plates on the SUV were almost certainly bogus,
so Ruston knew he wouldn't be able to rely on that even if
he got the license numbers. He had to keep the vehicle in
sight and follow it to wherever they were taking Gracelyn.

And that gave him another flood of thoughts.

Gracelyn must have been alive if the driver had taken
her. If he'd already killed her, he would have just left her
in the hospital. So, this was a kidnapping.

Why?

Again, that brought some bad thoughts. Maybe to use
Gracelyn to lure him out? But why not just take him along
with her?

Ruston thought back to what had gone on in the hall
of the hospital. He'd only seen one person, so it was pos-

sible the kidnapper couldn't get both of them out. Even if he'd managed to hold both Gracelyn and him at gunpoint, it would have been difficult to get them out of the hospital and into the SUV. Gracelyn and he would have fought back.

The image of the blood flashed again.

She likely had fought back. And the thug who had her had hurt her. Had probably knocked her unconscious. Or drugged her. Either way, when she came to, she'd try to escape. The kidnapper wouldn't just let that happen, which meant Gracelyn could end up being killed in the fight. That was why Ruston had to keep the SUV in sight. It was the only way he had now of getting to Gracelyn.

The SUV sped out of town, and the driver must have had the accelerator floored, because Ruston wasn't gaining on him. Thankfully, he wasn't losing either. The SUV stayed ahead, tearing across the rural road, and so far there were no other vehicles around. But the road wasn't straight either. There were plenty of curves just ahead. Since the driver might not be familiar with that, Ruston hoped he didn't lose control and crash.

Ruston had to hit his brakes when he got to the first of that series of curves, but once he was through it, he immediately sped up again. Keeping the SUV in sight.

He cursed when his phone rang because it took some effort to get it out of his pocket while keeping the cruiser from going off the road. Duncan's name was on the screen.

"I'm in a cruiser and am tracking your location," Duncan said the moment Ruston answered it on speaker. "You're heading toward the interstate."

"Yeah," Ruston verified. And that wasn't good. It'd be much harder to follow the SUV once it was in traffic.

Ruston didn't add more to that because he had to fight to keep control through another of those curves. Then he cursed when he was through it and saw the SUV. Not on the road but rather turning off onto what appeared to be a ranch trail. That could mean Gracelyn had regained consciousness and was now fighting her captor. Or this could have been the plan all along, for the captor to meet up with someone else.

Ruston followed.

"Keep tracking me," Ruston told Duncan, and he ended the call so he could focus on his driving.

The cruiser bounced over the uneven rock-and-dirt surface. Ahead of him, the SUV did, too. Then it stopped, and Ruston saw the driver bolt from the SUV and break into a run through the woods.

Ruston braked, bolted from the cruiser and began to run, too. Not toward the driver but to check on Gracelyn. Once he was sure she was all right, then he could go in pursuit.

He hurried to the passenger's-side door.

And his heart went straight to the ground.

Because she wasn't there. No one was. The SUV was empty.

He didn't see any blood, and he certainly hadn't seen her with the escaping driver, but he fired glances all around in case the thug had tossed her out of the vehicle.

Still, nothing.

Ruston tried to tamp down his fear and kept searching. His heartbeat was drumming in his ears now. He was breathing way too fast. But he still heard a ringing sound. Not his phone. He followed the sound to the driver's seat of the SUV, where a cheap-looking cell was ringing. A burner, no doubt.

He didn't have any evidence gloves on him, and it was a risk to touch the phone and contaminate any possible evidence. Still, he knew this call had to do with Gracelyn, so he went ahead and answered it.

"You can save her," the mechanical voice immediately said. "No other cops. Just you, Ruston. If you want to save her, you'll come alone."

He had to get his throat unclamped before he could speak. "Where? Where are you taking her?"

"To the baby farm. Get there fast," the voice warned him before the call ended.

GRACELYN FOUGHT HER way out of the dream. A nightmare. With images of blood and the sound of gunfire. The crushing sensation in her chest of not being able to breathe.

She forced her eyes open, slowly. She had no choice about that. Her head was throbbing, the pain pulsing through her, and she didn't want to make any sudden moves. So, she just sat there, glanced around and listened.

She was in a vehicle, belted into the front seat, and her hands were cuffed together at the wrists. That sent a jolt of panic through her, but she tried not to cry out. She didn't want to make a sound until she had figured out where she was and who had taken her.

The images and memories were all tangled up in her head. Everything swirling. And the pain. Mercy, the pain was still there, too. So, that was why it took long moments for her to latch on to anything. Then it all came together.

And she suddenly remembered what had happened.

The tear gas at the hospital. Being dragged out by a man wearing a mask. Once they were outside, she'd seen the injured deputy on the ground, and she'd managed to break away from her attacker. She ran. For only a second or two, though, before he'd grabbed her by the hair and then slammed her onto the ground.

She'd felt the sharp stab of pain in nearly every part of her body. Then she had fallen and hit her head. After that, everything went dark. Until now. Until she'd woken up in this vehicle. But where was she?

That question quickly faded when another, more important one flashed in her mind.

Where was Ruston?

Was he hurt? Or worse? And what about Duncan? Gracelyn was almost certain they'd still been in the hospital when she had been taken.

She moved her wrists a little, testing out the restraints. Flex-cuffs. It was what cops used to restrain perps. But it was also what Devin had used on Allie.

Allie.

Her thoughts went there for a moment. She wasn't sure how much time had passed since she'd been dragged away from the hospital, but Allie had still been in surgery then. Had been critical. Would the killer send someone after her, too?

Maybe.

But Gracelyn had to hope that the medical staff and the deputies would be able to stop that. Even if they couldn't, she couldn't help Allie herself. Not from here. She'd have to escape to do that.

"You awake?" the driver said.

It was a man. She didn't know who he was, but she thought it was the same person who'd barked out that order for her to move at the hospital.

"Who are you?" she asked, and she tried to make that sound like a demand. It didn't.

Her throat was still burning from the effects of the tear gas, and her vision wasn't 100 percent either. Everything was swimming in and out of focus, but she could see that the man was still wearing a gas mask that concealed all of his face. That blurred vision wasn't helping any with her figuring out where they were either. A country road... somewhere.

"My name's not important," he said, his voice a low, rasping growl. "Just consider me a lackey. A well-paid one," he added with a chuckle. The laughter turned her stomach.

"A lackey," she repeated. So, not the killer. Well, maybe not. She didn't think it was either Devin or Tony, anyway, but the killer could turn out to be someone who wasn't even on their radar. "Where are you taking me? And where's Ruston?"

"Ruston's on a wild-goose chase." He chuckled again.

Oh, that didn't help the panic building inside her. If he was telling the truth, Ruston wasn't coming for her. That could be good, she supposed, since she was probably going to become bait. That was the only reason she could think of as to why she was still alive.

"Why didn't you just take Ruston when you took me?" she asked.

"Too risky to have you both together. My orders were to get you, and once I drop you off, then I can wait around for your boyfriend to show up."

Her bait theory was right. She didn't ask why the lackey was so certain Ruston would come for her. No need. Because Ruston *would* come, and she knew there was nothing she could do or say to stop him. That meant she had to try to end this before Ruston walked into a trap.

But what exactly was this?

Gracelyn sat up in the seat and stared out the windshield at the scenery. Oh, God. She knew where he was taking her. Back to a nightmare.

Back to the baby farm.

"Now, don't go hyperventilating on me," the man said as if it was part of his continuing joke. "Before I drop you off, I'm to give you a message. My boss knows the medical examiner found the username and password for an online storage site that Zimmer set up. If you give it to him, he won't gun down Ruston."

So, that was what the killer wanted. Zimmer had hidden away something that could ID the killer.

"I don't know that information," she said.

"Then you'll get it." He pressed the phone function on his dash screen, and she saw Ruston's name and number pop up. "Tell Ruston what you need and ask him to bring it to you."

He didn't give her a chance to respond or even gather her breath. He just pressed the number, and Ruston immediately answered.

"Who is this?" he demanded. "Do you have Gracelyn?"

"I do indeed have your little darlin'," the man verified, "and this is how you'll get her back. Tell him, Gracelyn. Spell it out for him."

"Ruston," she managed to say. She wished she sounded stronger. Because she was. Despite the nightmare bubbling up inside her, she was a heck of a lot stronger than she sounded.

Think, she told herself. Ruston would be just as frantic as she was, so she had to be smart about what she said.

"I'm okay," she told Ruston and hoped he believed that. If he thought she'd been injured, that might cloud his judgment. He might be willing to do anything to get to her.

"Where are you?" he asked, and yes, there was a sharp intensity in his voice.

"Apparently, on the way to the baby farm."

Ruston cursed, and she heard the sound of a vehicle engine. He was coming for her.

"The lackey who took me didn't tell me the name of his boss, but the killer wants the username and password of Zimmer's accounts," she explained. "The ones he tatted on the inside of his wrist."

Gracelyn had purposely added that last bit of wrong information to confirm to Ruston something he no doubt already knew. That if he showed up at the baby farm, it'd be a trap to kill them both. Once the killer had the username and code, then he'd have no use for Ruston and her.

"Now, here's the deal, Ruston," the lackey said. "You gotta come alone and you gotta bring that username and password. Understand?"

"Yeah," Ruston said, his voice flat and cold. "If you hurt Gracelyn, I'll kill you. Understand?"

The lackey chuckled. "We'll see about that when you get here. Hurry, and if you're not alone, then Gracelyn dies on the spot."

With that, he ended the call and turned onto a familiar road. She had memorized this road and the surrounding area before Ruston and she had gone in undercover. It hadn't changed in a year. The trees that lined the narrow road seemed just as menacing. So did the building that sat just ahead. Not an actual house, but a compound that had once been owned by militia members. It was a mishmash of structures that had been cobbled together. Some parts freight containers, other parts prefab houses, all joined together by what she knew were mazelike halls.

There were no lights on that she could see. No obvious security either. The place looked deserted.

But she was betting it wasn't.

No. There was likely at least one person inside, waiting for her. Waiting for Ruston, too. And she wondered if it was Devin, Charla or Tony.

This would be a way to tie up many loose ends if the killer managed to get access to Zimmer's files and eliminate Ruston and her. But why was the killer so sure that Ruston and she had anything that would incriminate him?

One answer came to mind.

Because the killer knew they wouldn't stop until they got to the truth. They would hunt until they had eliminated the threat to Abigail. Any one of their suspects would know that, too.

The gravel crunched between the tires of the SUV as the driver pulled to a stop. "Man, oh, man, this mask is hot. Sweatin' up a storm underneath."

"You can take it off," she challenged.

He laughed again, that low chuckle that made her want to punch him. This wasn't a joke. This was her life. Hers and Ruston's, and this snake was playing a huge part in putting them in danger.

"Now, now," he scolded. "You don't want to see my face because then I would have to kill you. If you're gonna die, it won't be by my hands."

"No, you'll just turn me over to a killer and pretend the only thing you did wrong was take money to bring me here." This time, she was pleased with her tone. Anger. So much anger. She was channeling every bit of what was churning inside her. "Is that what you plan on telling yourself to help you sleep at night?"

"I sleep just fine," he snarled. He got out and began walking to the passenger's-side door to open it.

Gracelyn got ready. Well, as ready as she could, considering her hands were cuffed. No way to get out of that, and even though she fumbled with the seat belt, she couldn't unlatch it. So, she turned her body and tried to get into a position to do some damage.

The man opened the door, and he leaned in to unbuckle her seat belt. She smelled the sweat on him and could see that the moisture had built up behind the eye coverings of the gas mask. She hoped that meant he also had limited vision.

And that he wouldn't see the attack coming.

The moment he stepped back to pull her out of the SUV, she swung her legs around and kicked him. She aimed for his throat. Missed. But managed to land a kicking blow into his chest.

Cursing, he staggered back, but before he could get out of the way, she kicked him again. This time in the stomach. The air wheezed out of him, and he dropped.

Gracelyn bolted out of the SUV, and she started running as if her life depended on it.

Because it did.

Chapter Sixteen

Everything inside Ruston was a tight tangle of nerves and adrenaline. He'd been in high-stakes situations before, one of those with Gracelyn, but that had been different. She'd been armed then, and they'd been together. Now she was alone, hurt and with a thug who'd kill her in a blink.

And he'd taken her to the baby farm.

Ruston didn't want to think about what kind of mental torture that was for her. He didn't want to think about what her captor might be doing to her either. That would only shatter what little focus he had, and right now, that focus was what he needed to get to her in time.

He used the hands-free system while he sped down the road, and he called Duncan. "Where are you?" Duncan immediately asked.

"I got a call from the man who's got Gracelyn. He's taking her to the baby farm."

Ruston heard Duncan slam on his brakes. He was obviously changing directions as well, and since he didn't ask for the address, it meant he already knew the location. Then again, just about everyone in local law enforcement did.

"Did you recognize the guy's voice?" Duncan asked.

"No, because he was using a voice distorter," Ruston was quick to say. "He wants the username and password that Zimmer had tatted on him. He says I'm to come alone or Gracelyn will die."

Of course, Ruston knew the plan would be to kill both Gracelyn and him once he had what he wanted. Ruston had to figure out a way, fast, to make sure that didn't happen.

"How the hell did that...?" Duncan started, but he stopped and cursed. "Zimmer might have told someone about the tats, someone who then passed along that info to the killer. Or else the ME's office has a leak," he concluded.

Either was possible, but Zimmer didn't seem as if he trusted anyone enough to share that kind of info. But Ruston immediately rethought that. He could have trusted Tony or Charla. Especially Charla since he'd been her confidential informant.

"I'm guessing the ME filed a report," Ruston said, "and it was either hacked or accessed."

The hacking would point to Devin. The accessing to either Charla or Tony. Which meant they still couldn't use this to confirm the identity of the killer. But Zimmer had likely known that, or had had such strong suspicions, anyway, that he'd then put in that file.

"I can text you the username and password," Duncan said, the hesitation coating his voice. "But we don't know what's in that file yet. Heck, we don't even know where the file's been stored. The techs say it's like looking for a tiny needle in a massive cyber haystack."

"I'm guessing the killer knows that," Ruston concluded. "So, he could have knowledge of where the file is. Maybe he got that from something he found when he killed Zimmer."

Maybe, though, the killer would have to do the same search of that cyber haystack as the tech guys. If so, it'd be a race to see who got there first. If the killer did, then he'd certainly erase everything. But all of that would take time.

Time that Gracelyn didn't have.

"I'm about three miles out from the baby farm," Ruston explained. "Once I'm closer, I'll turn off my headlights. They'll know I'm coming and will be looking for me, but I'm hoping to get close, park and then go on foot."

Duncan cursed again. "I'm at least five miles out. I would ask you to wait for me, but I know you won't. I wouldn't if it were Joelle being held."

"I can't wait," Ruston confirmed. "But when you get here, do a silent approach. I don't want to give the killer any excuse to pull the trigger."

"Will do," Duncan confirmed. "I'll text you the username and password after I hang up. Be careful, Ruston."

"I will." And he would. But that might not be nearly enough. "You, too."

Ruston ended the call and had to slow down to take the final turn toward the baby farm. He drove way too fast on the poor excuse for a road, and as he'd told Duncan, he turned off his headlights when he was about a half mile out. That certainly didn't make driving any easier, but at least there was a moon tonight, and the meager light might stop him from running off the road.

Might.

He rethought that when he hit a deep pothole, and he had to grapple with the steering wheel to stay out of the deep ditches that were on both sides of him.

And that was when he saw it.

The movement from the corner of his eye. Someone running, not on the road but through the grassy area adjacent to it.

His heart crashed against his ribs when he realized it was Gracelyn. Her hands were cuffed in front of her, and she was firing glances behind her. Someone was chasing her.

Since there was no way he could drive to her, Ruston

stopped and got out. He couldn't call out to her because he didn't want to alert the killer to their positions. Instead, Ruston jumped over the ditch and started toward her.

He knew the exact moment when she spotted him. Her head whipped up, and she changed directions. She ran to him.

She didn't get far before a shot rang out.

Ruston felt the slam of fear. The fresh adrenaline. The need to get to Gracelyn now, now, now. If the bullet had hit her, she hadn't gone down. She was still running, and he quickly ate up the distance between them. Ruston immediately took hold of her and dragged her to the ground.

Just as another shot slammed into the dirt a few feet from them.

Ruston followed the direction of the shot and saw the gunman. He had his gas mask shoved up on his head, giving Ruston a look at his face. He didn't recognize him, which meant this was a hired gun.

The thug was trying to take aim while he was running. That was probably why he'd missed with the other two shots. That wouldn't last, though. He'd soon stop, and then Gracelyn and he would be way too easy targets.

"Stay down and let's move," Ruston instructed. He wanted to pull her into his arms, wanted to tell her…so many things. But that was going to have to wait. Maybe he'd get the chance to say those things when this was over.

A third shot came. And a fourth. All too close but still thankfully not hitting the intended mark.

The moment Ruston reached the ditch, he dropped down into it with Gracelyn. It was about three feet deep, so they crouched down, but Ruston knew they couldn't stay this way. The gunman would almost certainly be coming for them, and if he managed to approach at the right angle,

Gracelyn and he wouldn't be able to see the guy until it was too late.

Ruston quickly took out his small pocketknife so he could cut the cuffs from Gracelyn's wrists. It twisted away at him to see that blood on her forehead, but she didn't seem to be in pain. Like him, she was firing glances at the rim of the ditch, watching for the gunman.

The second he'd removed the cuffs, he took out his backup weapon and handed it to her. Then he peered over the top of the ditch. He braced for a shot to be fired at him. But it didn't come.

And the gunman was nowhere in sight.

Hell.

Where had he gone? There were some wild shrubs, and he could have ducked behind one of those. It was too much to hope that he'd just run off.

He saw some movement from a high patch of grass that was about five yards away, and Ruston turned in that direction so he could take aim. And he waited. Watched. Listened. Knowing that Gracelyn was doing the same thing.

There was a soft clicking sound, and he was pretty sure it came from the same grassy area. Moments later, a cloud of white smoke spewed out into the air.

More tear gas.

It wouldn't have the same potent effect as it had inside the hospital, but it could be just as dangerous, considering it was coming right at Gracelyn and him. Once the gas got to their eyes and throats, they wouldn't be able to defend themselves.

"Stay low and move down the ditch," Ruston whispered.

There was a huge disadvantage to that since the thug would be behind him. He'd no doubt be wearing a mask and could use the cloud of gas to conceal himself until he was right on them.

They moved, not as fast as he wanted, but Gracelyn and he scrambled away from the gas. But even over their movements, he heard another of those clicks. Heard the canister drop into the ditch.

And more tear gas came their way.

The moment the gas hit him, Ruston was right back where he'd been at the hospital. Coughing. Eyes burning. No way to fight back. Gracelyn was ahead of him, and she thankfully kept moving. Ruston tried to do that, too, but he heard another sound. Not the click of a canister being triggered.

The thud of someone dropping down into the ditch behind him.

Before Ruston could even turn, there was more movement. And he felt the barrel of a gun press against the back of his head.

"Cooperate," the man snarled, "or I shoot your woman in the back."

GRACELYN KEPT MOVING. Her eyes were stinging, but she thought she was staying just ahead of the worst of the gas. It wasn't a thick cloud but more of a mist. Added to that, the night breeze was dispersing what there was of it. If Ruston and she could just make it a few more feet, they wouldn't get the worst of it and would be able to defend themselves.

She glanced behind her.

And her heart stopped. It certainly felt like it, anyway.

She saw Ruston, not crouching. He was standing now, and not by choice either. There was a man wearing a gas mask behind him, and he was holding Ruston at gunpoint.

"You both throw down your guns," the guy in the gas mask ordered.

Ruston was coughing, but it wasn't nearly as bad as it had been during the other attack. Gracelyn just wished she could better see Ruston's eyes so she could tell if he'd been hurt. But her own eyes were still stinging, and the moonlight was creating plenty of shadows on his face.

"Guns down now," the thug insisted. "I've got a clear shot of your woman," he added to Ruston.

And he did. All the gunman had to do was aim in her direction and fire. There was nothing she could dart behind for cover, and if she tried to scramble out of the ditch, he'd likely just shoot her.

But why hadn't he just done that already?

And why hadn't he finished off Ruston instead of putting a gun to his head?

Because with both Ruston and her alive, they could be used against each other. Leverage. This snake and his boss had to know that she would cooperate to keep Ruston from being killed and vice versa.

"Last chance," the guy warned them. "Guns down now."

Ruston's Glock slid from his hand and dropped on the ground at his feet. Gracelyn knew what that had cost him, to lose the primary way to defend them. But he'd had no choice.

Neither did she.

Gracelyn dropped her gun as well, but she didn't toss it. She wanted it as close to her as possible. That way, if she got the chance to use it, she wouldn't have to reach that far.

"What now?" Ruston demanded.

"We walk and get the hell away from this gas," he answered right away. "Go to the baby farm. You got somebody there who's anxious to see you."

Gracelyn felt the fresh jolt of adrenaline, and she forced herself not to think of the other attack. Those images weren't going to help her think more clearly, and right now, she had to think. She had to figure a way out of this.

"Out of the ditch," the man ordered. "And remember that part about me shooting one of you? I will, you know. In fact, I'll get paid a bonus, so don't test my patience."

A bonus. She hadn't needed more proof that this was a hired thug, but there it was. Someone—maybe Charla, Tony or Devin—had paid this guy to do the dirty work. That could include murder. In fact, that was no doubt the killer's plan after Ruston spilled the username and password.

The thug shoved Ruston out of the ditch first, following quickly behind him and putting the gun back to Ruston's head. A silent warning for Gracelyn not to try anything. Not yet. But leaving the ditch meant leaving their guns behind, and Ruston wouldn't have a backup weapon on him since he'd given it to her.

But there would be backup.

No way would Duncan let Ruston come here alone. The sheriff was no doubt on his way, but he couldn't just come in with sirens blaring. He'd have to do a silent approach, but hopefully that meant he was making his way to them now.

"You stay ahead of us," the thug told Gracelyn. "And go ahead and put your hands on your head so I can see them."

She did as he said, and they started walking. The air cleared even more as they moved away from the ditch and back on the road. Her eyes were still stinging a little, but she could clearly see the building ahead.

And the shadowy figure that stepped out from it.

Gracelyn couldn't tell who it was, and the person stayed back enough so that she couldn't get a good look at him or her.

"Good," the thug muttered. "The boss is coming out to meet us. Might get home in time to watch the game."

It sickened her that he was being so flippant about this. Then again, she figured the other hired guns had been pretty much the same. Well, maybe not Zimmer. But the one who'd attacked with Zimmer had fired shots at the SUV with Abigail inside, and the two goons in the sheriff's office hadn't seemed to care how many people they killed to get to their targets.

"So, it's just you and the boss," she remarked.

He chuckled. "Honey, I'm the only one the boss needs to finish this."

She thought he was telling the truth. Hoped he was, anyway. She didn't want an army of hired thugs waiting for them.

Gracelyn purposely slowed her steps just a little, not because she wanted to delay facing down the killer. No. She was to the point that she wanted to know the person responsible. But she slowed down so that she could try to get closer to Ruston. If the thug was right, this was a two-on-two situation, and while Ruston and she weren't armed, that didn't mean they were defenseless. If they couldn't stall the killer until backup arrived, then they might have to fight their way out of here.

Again.

"And before either of you think about running again," the gunman went on, "my orders are, I lose you two, then I'm to go after the kid."

Oh, the anger came. Boiling hot. A full rage that Gracelyn had to fight to tamp down before she turned and clawed out this snake's eyes. How dare he threaten that little baby. And he was going to pay for that threat. She wasn't sure how, but he would pay.

So would the piece of slime that was waiting for them.

"Glad you could come," the killer said.

And he stepped out so Gracelyn could finally see his face.

DEVIN WAS SMILING when he walked toward them.

Smiling and gloating.

Ruston intended to make sure Devin didn't have those reactions for long. The goon's threats to Gracelyn and Abigail had been more than enough to fuel Ruston's anger, and it had seethed and soared with each step toward this miserable person in this miserable place.

Devin was armed, of course. He had a SIG Sauer in both hands, which he probably thought made him look like a cool bad guy.

"The Green Eagle," Ruston said like a mock greeting.

Devin shrugged. "I'm not going to come out and admit that," he said. "I mean, since I'd be incriminating myself. Oops." He laughed. "I guess I just did. There goes some of my bargaining power." Using the guns, he put those last two words in air quotes.

"Your plan was to tell me that you'd let Gracelyn live if I gave you what you wanted," Ruston spelled out for him.

"Why, yes." There it was again, that smugness that only fueled Ruston's anger. "But you would have never fallen for that anyway. Gracelyn wouldn't have either. You both know how this has to end."

"Yeah, you eliminate everyone who can put you in a cage," Gracelyn muttered.

"True. And so far, so good," he bragged.

Ruston wished he could have disputed that, but with the exception of this lone gunman, the others were dead. Marty, Simon, Archie and three hired guns. There were likely others who had been silenced in the aftermath of the baby farm.

"So far, so good," Devin repeated. "And that's why I need the info that Zimmer left behind."

"How did you know about it?" Ruston asked, shifting his weight so he'd be able to either drop down or lunge at Devin. Ahead of him, Ruston could see Gracelyn doing the same thing.

"Computer leaks," Devin admitted. "The ME isn't very careful about what he puts in his reports. He mentioned the tats, but he didn't give specifics." He paused. "I want specifics. Oh, wait. You need a reason to give it to me. How about a quick, easy death for Gracelyn? As opposed to me making it very, very painful."

"Your hired gun said you would go after Abigail," Gracelyn said, and Ruston heard the razor edge in her voice.

Again, Devin shrugged. "Only as a last resort."

Ruston saw the lie on Devin's face. Devin wouldn't come out now and say that he had planned on taking the baby all along because he probably hadn't wanted to give Gracelyn and Ruston a reason to stay alive.

A reason to fight.

But Gracelyn and he already had that reason. They both loved Abigail, and if they literally rolled over and died, it would leave the baby at the mercy of this monster. That wasn't going to happen.

"You were going to kidnap and sell your own daughter," Gracelyn spit out. "Or maybe she isn't yours."

"She is," Devin verified. "Allie brought me a sample of her DNA because she wanted to prove that I was the father. I'm not sure why she thought it was so important to prove, because I didn't give a rat. Still don't."

Ruston was glad Gracelyn was keeping Devin talking. Anything to distract him. Anything to buy them some time. And right now, he needed a weapon.

"You didn't kill Allie, though," Gracelyn pointed out. "Is she still a loose end?"

He laughed. "Your sister knows nothing, but I figured I could use her in a roundabout way to get the baby. I mean, if Allie ends up in jail, then I get custody. After I prove paternity, that is, and I can prove it. So can you now that the good sheriff took my DNA. He probably did that, hoping to find something to incriminate me, but the only thing that DNA will prove is that I have a legal right to my biological child."

A child he'd end up selling first chance he got.

And that wasn't all the dirty dealings this SOB had done.

"You're the one who blew our covers," Ruston snapped. "How did you even know we were cops?"

Devin shrugged as if that were nothing. No big deal that Gracelyn and he had nearly died. "I make a habit of using a hacker to check out anyone and everyone I do business with. A hacker who breaks many rules to tap into things like police databases and such." He narrowed his eyes at them. "If you two had died then and there, I wouldn't have to be going through this mess right now."

Ruston was already fuming, but that only added to the flames. He glanced around for something, anything, he could use to fight back. There wasn't anything, which meant he was going to have to do this with his bare hands. He was gearing up to ram his elbow into the thug's gut when there was a flash of headlights. They cut through the darkness at the end of the road and then disappeared.

Both Devin and the thug glanced in that direction.

And Ruston made his move.

With the thug's slight shift of his body, Ruston went for a more direct attack. He turned and slammed his fist into the guy's face. He heard the satisfying sound of cartilage breaking. Blood spewed, and the man howled.

From the corner of his eye, Ruston saw Gracelyn dive toward Devin's legs, tackling him and knocking him back against the building. Ruston cursed, though, when he saw that Devin had managed to hang on to both his guns, but the disadvantage of that was it didn't free up his hands to fight back. Then again, he wouldn't need to actually fight if he could get off a shot.

He did.

The blast tore through the air, the sound tearing through Ruston, and he was terrified that Gracelyn had just been shot. He latched on to the still-howling, still-bleeding thug and dragged him in front of him.

Just in time.

Because there was another shot, and Devin had aimed this one at Ruston. But the bullet meant for him slammed into the thug's chest. He dropped like a stone, giving Devin a clear path to shoot Ruston.

But Gracelyn stopped that from happening.

She kicked the gun from Devin's right hand and sent it flying. Devin pulled the trigger of the second gun, but it was a wild shot that didn't come anywhere near Ruston or her. Thank God. However, Devin immediately tried to shift the weapon to his right hand.

And worse.

During the shift, he bashed Gracelyn on the head, knocking her away from him.

Everything seemed to shift to slow motion. Even the sound of Gracelyn's voice yelling to him, "Get down."

Ruston did get down. He dived to the ground, scooping up

the thug's gun, and the second he had hold of it, he took aim. Even though she was clearly dazed from the blow, Gracelyn scurried away from Devin, giving Ruston a clear shot.

Which he took.

It seemed as if Devin and he pulled the triggers in that same heartbeat of time. Devin missed.

Ruston didn't.

He double tapped the trigger and sent two shots directly into Devin's chest. Devin froze, the shock registering on his face as his gun slid from his hand. Then he flashed that cocky smile one last time before he took in his dying breath.

Gracelyn's gaze connected with Ruston's. For just a second. And they moved. She toward the thug and Ruston toward Devin. Both of them checked to make sure killer and henchman were truly finished.

"He's dead," Ruston verified after touching his fingers to Devin's neck.

"He is, too," Gracelyn confirmed. She stared down at the goon, and her face tightened. She cursed the dead monster.

"Are you all right?" someone called out.

Ruston automatically took aim a split second before he realized it was Duncan. He was on foot, and he was running up the road toward them.

"We're alive," Ruston settled for saying. "But Devin and his hired gun aren't."

Ruston considered calling that in, but it appeared Duncan was already doing that. Instead, Ruston focused on Gracelyn. In addition to the blood on the side of her head, she had a nasty bruise on her face from where Devin had hit her.

Seeing that made him want to go after Devin all over again, but he pulled her into his arms. And held her.

"They were going after Abigail," she muttered. "They were going to kill us and go after her."

"Yeah," he managed to say through the vised muscles in his throat.

Gracelyn's head whipped up, and she looked him straight in the eyes. "We need to check on her. We need to make sure Abigail is okay."

Ruston didn't argue. They started running toward Duncan and the cruiser.

Chapter Seventeen

Gracelyn felt both exhausted and pumped up as if every nerve in her body was on high alert. And on the verge of crashing. Her mind was a tangle of thoughts and fears as Ruston sped toward his family's ranch.

It'd been nearly a half hour since the shoot-out with Devin. Time when they'd had to wait for backup to arrive so that Duncan wouldn't be left at the crime scene alone. During those thirty minutes, Gracelyn had spoken with Joelle not once but twice, and Joelle had assured her that all was well, that no one had come for Abigail. Gracelyn believed her, but she wouldn't breathe easier until she saw the baby for herself.

The moment Woodrow and Luca had arrived, Ruston and she had left, and she'd gotten one last glance of the baby farm in the rearview mirror. Despite nearly being killed there tonight, it no longer held that bogeyman fear for her. It was just a place that bad people had used to do bad things.

And now the leader of those bad people was dead.

Gracelyn didn't feel a drop of grief about that. Just the opposite. A monster was dead, and his death made the world a safer place. Devin wouldn't be around to hire any more henchmen. Wouldn't be around to try to kidnap and sell babies.

"I would suggest you go to the hospital for those injuries," Ruston said, "but I'm guessing you'd rather have an EMT come out to the ranch and examine you."

"The EMT," she immediately agreed. "And you should be checked out, too. We both got some heavy hits of tear gas tonight."

Ruston made a sound of agreement and glanced at her. "How are you, really?"

She did a quick assessment. Her head was hurting, but it wasn't a throbbing pain. "I'm okay enough. How about you?"

"Okay enough," he repeated, and he reached over, took her hand and gave it a gentle squeeze. "I thought I was going to lose you."

There was plenty of emotion in his voice, and she thought they were on the same emotional wavelength here. Well, maybe they were. She had been terrified when she'd thought she would lose Ruston. But there had been an extra layer to that terror.

That she might lose him before she even got the chance to tell him how she felt about him.

She was in love with him.

Gracelyn nearly blurted that out now, but Ruston's phone rang, and she saw Slater's name pop up on the dash screen. All her fears about Abigail came rushing back. It must have been the same for Ruston, because he answered it right away on speaker.

"Nothing's wrong here," Slater said right off the bat. "Abigail is fine."

Gracelyn's breath of relief came out like a loud moan. Ruston did his own version of a breath of relief by muttering something she didn't catch.

"How far out are you?" Slater asked.

"About fifteen minutes," Ruston answered. "Thirteen," he amended when he sped up. Good. The sooner they got there, the better.

Slater made a sound to indicate he was pleased about the shorter arrival time as well. "I thought Gracelyn would want to know that Allie came out of surgery, and she's critical but stable."

Gracelyn had to fight through the fatigue to try to process that. Unlike Devin, she didn't wish her sister dead. Yes, Allie had done some horrible things, but she didn't deserve to die.

"When Allie came out of the anesthesia," Slater went on, "she asked the doctor to give Gracelyn a message."

Everything inside Gracelyn went still. And she waited for Slater to finish. Her sister had done so many reckless, dangerous things that Gracelyn wasn't sure what kind of message she'd want to have passed on to her.

"Allie said that Abigail is yours, Gracelyn, that she'll sign over custody to you," Slater spelled out. "She also won't fight going to prison either."

It took a moment for that to sink in. A long moment where her stomach unclenched. Where so many of her nerves settled.

Abigail was hers.

"Why the change of heart for Allie?" Ruston asked.

"I think nearly dying must have given her some clarity," Slater suggested.

Yes, Gracelyn knew all about that. Being near death did have a way of pinpointing everything. Of making you see what was important.

She certainly had.

And Abigail and Ruston were at the very top of her list of important things.

"I alerted SAPD about Allie coming out of surgery," Slater went on a moment later. "Duncan agreed that they'll be the ones charging her. Conspiracy to kidnapping, human trafficking, obstruction of justice, child endangerment and accessory to attempted murder, including the attempted murder of a police officer. The last two are because she was involved in hiring Zimmer and Robert Radley, who attacked you at Gracelyn's place."

Gracelyn mentally repeated all those charges. With Devin dead, Allie wouldn't have any bargaining power for a deal, which meant she would likely spend the rest of her life in prison.

"See you in a few minutes," Slater said, ending the call.

Ruston gave her hand another gentle squeeze and then brought it to his mouth and brushed a kiss on her fingers. "Are you okay?"

She sighed. "Part of me aches for my sister, but this means Allie won't be able to endanger Abigail again."

Ruston nodded, kissed her hand again. She wished the kiss had been on her mouth. While he'd been holding her. She needed that right now.

She needed him.

Soon, she wanted to tell him that, but for now, she sat in silence, mourning the loss of a sister. Yes, Allie had done some unforgivable things, but she'd also given her the greatest gift. Abigail.

Ruston took the final turn to the ranch, and Gracelyn pushed aside her thoughts to prepare herself for what felt like a homecoming.

She was pleased when she spotted the still-armed ranch hands at the end of the road. Standing guard. Keeping Abigail safe. Gracelyn would owe them all a deep gratitude that she'd never be able to repay. The same was true for Duncan, his deputies, Ruston and his family.

Ruston pulled to a stop in front of the house, and Gracelyn hurried out of the cruiser. Slater was already opening the door before she reached it.

"Uh, are you sure you're okay?" Slater asked when he saw her face.

She nodded, though Gracelyn figured she looked pretty bad for him to have that reaction. However, that was yet something else she'd put on the back burner. For now, she raced up the stairs and straight to the guest room. Carmen and Joelle were both there.

And so was Abigail.

She was sleeping, but Gracelyn picked her up anyway and held her close. The tears came. The tears she'd fought so hard to hold back. But there was no holding back now. Abigail was safe. She was also a little riled at being awakened, and she let out a protesting wail that made Gracelyn smile. She hadn't given birth to Abigail, but this child was hers in every sense of the word.

Gracelyn kissed her cheek and looked back at Ruston when he stepped into the room. He went to them, sliding his arm around Gracelyn's waist and delivering his own kiss to the baby's cheek. Abigail immediately stopped her fussing and smiled at him.

"You've already charmed her," Gracelyn muttered.

"One down, one to go," he muttered back.

Their gazes met for a moment, and Gracelyn saw the love. Well, maybe that was what it was. Love for Abigail, anyway, but what had he meant?

His phone rang, and she saw Duncan's name on the screen. Since Gracelyn wanted to hear what he had to say, she eased the baby back in the crib, thanked both Joelle and Carmen and then stepped out into the hall with Ruston.

"You two back at the ranch yet?" Duncan immediately asked.

"We are," Ruston answered. "Just a couple of minutes ago. Slater filled us in on Allie."

Duncan sighed. "Yeah," he muttered like an apology that Gracelyn knew was meant for her. "I have some good news," he added. "The techs located Zimmer's online file."

Gracelyn saw the surprise flash through Ruston's eyes. "How? They said it'd be a needle in a haystack."

"It would have been, but Zimmer had a clue to the storage site in the password, so the techs were able to narrow it down. They not only found the file, but they were also able to access it."

Something Devin would have certainly been able to do had he gotten the username and password.

"The file is huge and filled with photos and details that would have apparently gotten Devin the death penalty," Duncan explained. "Zimmer confirms that Devin was Green Eagle. And there are other names of people involved in the baby farm, people who probably thought they'd escaped justice."

"Are Tony or Charla on the list?" Gracelyn asked.

"No," Duncan was quick to say.

Gracelyn felt nothing but relief about that. Yes, she would apologize to Charla and Tony for believing they were guilty, and she was glad they hadn't been dirty cops.

"Archie, Marty and Simon were on the list," Duncan went on, "and that explains why Devin had them murdered. Devin was basically eliminating anyone who could link him to the baby farm."

Yes, that made sense. It was the reason Devin wanted to

eliminate Ruston and her, too. And Allie. But maybe he'd let her live, with the hopes that she would end up taking the blame for not only the attacks and murders but also for the baby farm itself. Gracelyn could see Devin trying to use Allie as the ultimate scapegoat.

"I'll be tied up here a while longer, but I'm hoping to be home in about two hours," Duncan added. "Is everything and everyone okay there?"

"Yes," Ruston and Gracelyn muttered in unison, and for the first time in nearly a year, Gracelyn could say that was the truth.

She was okay.

The past would always be with her, but it wasn't the past she was looking at now. She was looking at a future.

Gracelyn was looking at Ruston.

And he was looking at her.

He ended the call, slipped his phone into his pocket and immediately pulled her into his arms. He took her mouth in a deep kiss that notched up her "okay" to something much, much more.

But how much more?

What she said in the next few minutes could change everything, but Ruston might not be ready to hear it. Still, she needed to tell him what she'd been holding inside. And she would. As soon as he finished melting her with this kiss.

When he'd left her breathless and on cloud nine, he eased back from her and flashed that incredible smile again.

"I'm in love with you," she said. Gracelyn braced herself for the shock. Maybe for him to back away and tell her that he needed more time.

That didn't happen.

Ruston kissed her again, and this one was so hot that

Gracelyn wasn't sure how she managed to stay on her feet. The man had a way of firing up every inch of her.

"Good." He muttered that single word while his mouth was still against hers.

But he added more words to it.

"Because you and I are of a like mind here," he went on. "Because I'm in love with you, too."

Now she didn't stay on her feet. Or at least she wouldn't have if Ruston hadn't caught her. Her heart filled with so much emotion. Not the bad ones this time either. All the very best ones. Happiness. Need. And love. So much love.

But Ruston added to that, too.

"I say, since we both love Abigail, that we raise her together," he threw out there. "What do you think about that?"

"I think it's perfect," she managed to say.

And it was just that. Perfect. Still, Ruston managed to add to that, too. Because he pulled her back to him for a long, slow kiss.

* * * * *

Don't miss the stories in this mini series!

SADDLE RIDGE JUSTICE

Protecting The Newborn
DELORES FOSSEN
November 2024

Tracking Down The Lawman's Son
DELORES FOSSEN
December 2024

Child In Jeopardy
DELORES FOSSEN
January 2025

MILLS & BOON

The Perfect Murder

K.D. Richards

MILLS & BOON

Books by K.D. Richards

Harlequin Intrigue

West Investigations

Pursuit of the Truth
Missing at Christmas
Christmas Data Breach
Shielding Her Son
Dark Water Disappearance
Catching the Carling Lake Killer
Under the Cover of Darkness
A Stalker's Prey
Silenced Witness
Lakeside Secrets
The Perfect Murder

Visit the Author Profile page at millsandboon.com.au.

K.D. Richards is a native of the Washington, DC, area, who now lives outside Toronto with her husband and two sons. You can find her at kdrichardsbooks.com.

CAST OF CHARACTERS

Chelsea Harper—A teacher investigating the wrongful conviction of her father.

Travis Collins—West Investigations private detective and former police officer.

Franklin Brooks—Chelsea's father, convicted of a crime he didn't commit.

Gabe Owens—Travis's friend and a police detective.

Victor Thompson—Chelsea's cousin and best friend.

Brenda Thompson—Chelsea's aunt.

Bill Rowland—Franklin Brooks's best friend.

Chapter One

He'd worried for years waiting for Franklin Brooks to exhaust all of his appeals. And now the last appeal was over, and he should be able to relax, confident that another man would be paying for the crime he'd committed. But he couldn't relax. Because Chelsea just wouldn't let it go.

He couldn't believe Chelsea Harper, a third-grade teacher, had the skills to hack into the LAPD's computer system, but whoever she'd gotten to do it had been good. If he hadn't had the foresight to flag Lily Wong's case file, he would have never known it had been accessed and downloaded remotely. The hacker hadn't left a trail, either. Thank goodness he'd been notified the moment the file was accessed. Knowing about the hack while it was happening was the only reason he'd been able to follow it back to its source. After that it had been easy to search through the hacker's computer and find out who'd hired him to steal Lily's file.

He hadn't meant to kill her. His precious Lily. He'd tried to make her understand they were meant to be together. She wouldn't listen.

Killing her had been an accident. His rage had exploded, and before he realized it, she was dead.

Franklin getting blamed for it had been a fluke. A convenient fluke.

He hadn't had to run. He hadn't had to leave his life.

But if Chelsea Harper succeeded in her quest to clear her father's name, he might have to now.

No. No, he wouldn't let her destroy his life.

He finished his breakfast, loading his dishes into the dishwasher and straightening the kitchen before he prepared to leave for work. Years of monotonous, solitary drudgery among boxes and in dark rooms had given him a superpower. Invisibility. It would come in handy. He'd need to keep an eye on Chelsea. And, if he had to, deal with her the same way he'd dealt with Lily.

Chapter Two

Chelsea Harper paused for a moment just inside the West Security and Investigations West Coast offices. The private investigations firm was located in a single-story brick building in West Hollywood. She passed through double glass doors into a small lobby where an attractive twenty-something Latina woman typed on a computer behind the reception desk. The decor was sleek and masculine with dark leather sofas and an uninspired snapshot of the iconic Hollywood sign on the white wall.

"Hello," she said, giving the receptionist, whose name plate read Bailey Lee, a smile. "I'd like to speak with Travis Collins, please."

Bailey returned her smile with one that looked genuine. She tapped a few keys, her smile slightly dimming when her gaze returned to Chelsea's face. "Is Mr. Collins expecting you?"

"No." Chelsea bit her bottom lip. She had considered calling to make an appointment, but she'd been afraid that Travis Collins would refuse to see her, so she'd opted for an ambush instead. "But I'm hoping he can make time for me."

"And your name is?" Bailey asked, reaching for the phone receiver.

"Chelsea Harper."

Bailey spoke quietly into the receiver for a moment. "Mr. Collins will be right out. You can have a seat while you wait if you'd like." She motioned to the leather sofas with one hand and reset the phone receiver with the other.

Chelsea was too nervous to sit. She backed away from the receptionist's desk but stayed standing. She examined the photos on the wall, not really seeing them. For maybe the hundredth time, she wondered if she was doing the right thing bringing on an investigator. Especially this particular investigator. For a second, she considered turning around and leaving, but Travis Collins rounded the corner before she could make a break for it.

She'd seen him on the news and had read several online articles that mentioned him while she was investigating PIs, so she knew he was thirty-five years old and an attractive man. Real-life Travis Collins was not just attractive, he was impressively masculine. He was tall and lean and wearing a suit that fit him like he had been born in it. His short, cropped hair was shot through with the beginning of gray. He moved toward her with a stride that was both confident and noble. His dark brown eyes fell on her face, and she watched as he quickly sized her up from head to toe.

His gaze met hers as he approached, and she saw the moment he recognized her. It had been a long time since anyone recognized her like that, but she wasn't surprised that he had. Her face had been in the papers almost as much as her father's during his trial, reporters hounding her to no end. And Travis was a detective and a private investigator, trained to remember details.

"Chelsea Brooks?" His expression was a cross between surprise and shock.

"It's Chelsea Harper now."

"You got married?"

She shook her head. "I took my aunt and uncle's last name after..." The press and social media had made it impossible to keep her father's name even during the years she'd lived in San Francisco immediately after college.

He nodded. "I understand."

She doubted that he did but kept that thought to herself.

"What can I do for you?"

"I'd like to hire you."

One of his eyebrows cocked upward. "Hire me?"

"Yes. I understand you have left the LAPD and are a private investigator now." She waved a hand vaguely to encompass the lobby. "I want to hire you to help me prove my father's innocence."

His brow came down now as his eyes narrowed suspiciously. "Let's go into a conference room. We can talk more freely there."

He led her down a hallway to a small glass-walled conference room. She took a seat at the large round table, and he offered her coffee and water, which she declined. She was too anxious to drink.

Travis sat across from her at the table. He looked like he wasn't sure how to start the conversation. Finally, he said, "Why don't you tell me exactly what you're hoping West Investigations can do for you?"

She cocked her head to the side. "As you know, my father was convicted of the murder of Lily Wong, his former girlfriend."

Of course he knew. He had not been involved in her father's case, but he had been on the force, and Lily's murder was big news for more than a year. Chelsea knew it might seem odd for her to seek his help in proving her father's innocence. She'd spent countless hours debating whether he was the right man for the job. But West Security and Investigations was one of the best PI firms on either coast, and in the years since her father had been convicted, Travis had proved he was willing to go up against the system in general and the LAPD in particular to do the right thing. She was going to need that kind of courage and conviction if she had any hope of winning her father's freedom.

"He's exhausted all his appeals. The only way to get him out of jail now is to prove he was wrongly convicted."

Travis's expression remained sympathetic. "These past seven years must have been hard for you," he started.

"You have no idea, Mr. Collins."

"Call me Travis, please."

"Travis. And you can call me Chelsea. Travis, my father is innocent. He did not kill Lily Wong."

She watched him stiffen in his chair. "Ms. Harper—"

She held up a hand, stopping him. "I'm sure you heard that a lot as a police detective, but you're not a cop now, so I hope you'll hear me out."

He hesitated before nodding that she should continue.

"My father has always maintained his innocence. In the years since his trial, I've gathered as much information as I could, news articles, police reports, whatever I could get my hands on, and I've pored over them." She wasn't sure how he would react to the conclusions she'd drawn from her review of the police investigation, but if there was any chance of them working together, it was best to get everything out in the open now. "Frankly, the police investigation was lacking. They homed in on my dad and never looked at anyone else."

The look he gave her was one of disbelief. "It may seem that way to you, but a jury convicted your father."

"Based on the limited evidence collected by the cops and presented by the prosecutor," she responded fiercely.

"Ms. Harper, I know we are talking about your father. I'm sure you love him, but I don't have time—"

"I'm not here to waste your time, Mr. Collins," she interjected sharply. "I'm here to hire you. I want to clear my father's name and get him out of prison. But more than that, I want Lily's real murderer to pay. Whoever killed her has gotten away with the crime for all these years. My dad wants to rectify that." She paused for a moment before adding quietly. "And my dad wasn't the only one who cared about Lily."

"Chelsea, it has been seven years. I wouldn't even know where to begin."

He may have thought that statement would deter her, but it showed he was thinking about where to begin. A good sign in her book. "There are discrepancies in the witness statements." She reached into her handbag and pulled out a crinkled letter-size envelope. "My aunt received this note last week. I think the witness who placed my dad at Lily's house, Peter Schmeichel—"

Travis gave her a look that drew a smile from her along with a shrug.

"Hey, I didn't name him. Take it up with his parents. As I was saying, I think the witness who placed my dad at Lily's house perjured himself on the witness stand."

She handed him the letter and envelope and watched as he read it once, then once more. She knew the words by heart.

Peter Schmeichel lied. He didn't see your brother at the dead girl's house that night.

Travis shook his head. She was losing him. "This isn't evidence." He turned the envelope over, looking, she was sure, for a return address or some indication where it might have come from. There was nothing but a postage stamp indicating it had been mailed from California. No help.

"I know." She nearly growled the words. "The police detective I took it to all but laughed at me and the prosecutor wouldn't even meet with me. But if it's true—"

He cut her off. "If, and that's a very big if. We don't even know who sent this." He held up the note.

She didn't need to hear the suspicion in his voice to know what he was getting at. "You think my father, or I, sent the note. To what end? If I could get anyone to believe me, they'd just go find Peter, and he'd stick to his story. What would sending the note to myself get me or my dad in the end?"

Suspicion still clouded his face, but he said, "I'm willing to concede that it makes no sense for you or your dad to send the note, but that doesn't make the note true."

"But it's worth looking into. It might be my father's only chance." She hated the pleading tone of her voice, but if pleading was what it took to get him to help her, she'd do it. She reached out and took his hand in both of hers. His brown skin was smooth, and she couldn't help noticing how perfectly her hand fit with his. "Please. Please. Just come with me to visit my father tomorrow at the prison. Listen to his story. If you still don't believe him, I'll never bother you again."

The expression on his face was inscrutable.

She took her hand back. "At the very least you'll get paid for a day's work."

"One day. That's all I can promise you."

"And you listen with an open mind," she countered.

"And I'll listen with an open mind," he agreed.

The tension she had been carrying inside of her eased. Over the first hurdle and only hundreds more to go.

"If you give me your contact information, I will have the paperwork emailed to you. You can read it and sign it tonight and give it to me tomorrow. What time are we expected at Chino?" he asked, referencing the California Institution for Men by its common nickname.

Chelsea nodded. "Yes. Visiting hours start at eleven."

"I'll pick you up at your place at ten then. Let me walk you out."

He walked her to the entrance and shook her hand before she pushed out into the Los Angeles heat. She could feel his eyes still on her as she stepped off the curb. She was in the middle of the street when the roar of an engine came from her right. She froze as a black sedan careened toward her. Seconds passed as she processed the moment. Then her brain finally sent the message to her feet to move.

She leaped for the opposite curb. A sharp pain whipped through her hip right before she hit the pavement and rolled between two parked cars.

It felt as if the pain was coming from everywhere. She struggled to take in a breath.

Then Travis Collins's face appeared, hovering over hers. "Chelsea? Are you okay?" His voice sounded as if it was coming from a distance even though he was centimeters away.

She wasn't sure how to answer that. She struggled to push herself up into a sitting position, but gentle hands held her down.

"Don't move. An ambulance is on its way." He lifted her head gently and rested it on his knees.

"I don't need an ambulance."

"You were clipped by a car. You definitely need to be checked out at the hospital."

Sirens wailed in the distance. A man in a suit jogged to Travis's side. "I tried to catch him, but he got away."

"Did you get a look at the license plate?" Travis asked the man.

The man was hunched over, hands on his knees, trying to catch his breath, but he shook his head. "Sorry, dude. The guy must have been drunk or something."

"That was no drunk driver," Travis said, looking down at Chelsea, his gaze serious. "I think someone just tried to kill you."

Chapter Three

Travis rode with Chelsea in the ambulance to the hospital and didn't leave her side while the doctor checked her over. She was lucky. She had a few bruises and a deep gash on her arm that needed a handful of stitches, but she had no broken bones or permanent damage. She sat on a gurney in the curtained area of the emergency room, clutching Travis's hand in a death grip while the doctor stitched her arm.

The day had taken a very unexpected turn. He had planned to wrap up his current case, a fraud investigation for an insurance client who suspected a business owner of faking a series of thefts from his store. Travis had caught the owner on camera taking stock that had supposedly been stolen from the store from a self-storage locker and selling it out of his home. He'd already forwarded the photos to his client, but he needed to put the finishing touches on his report. That had been the plan for the day before Chelsea Harper walked into the West offices.

Chelsea squeezed his hand, and he glanced down at her face. He could tell she was trying to hide it, but she was in pain. That thought sent a bubble of anger rising in his chest.

Over her shoulders, he saw the automatic doors to the

emergency room open. Kevin Lombard, his boss and West Security and Investigations' operations manager, strode in with Tess Stenning, head of the West Coast office.

He gave Chelsea's hand a squeeze and rose. "I'll be right back."

Chelsea clutched his hand. "Don't leave me?"

"Of course not. I'm just going to talk to my boss. Right over there." He jerked his head to where Tess and Kevin waited for him.

He could feel Chelsea's eyes following him as he crossed the emergency room.

"How is she?" Kevin asked. Like Travis, Kevin was a former cop who had signed on with West Security and Investigations when the firm opened up its West Coast office.

"Okay. She had a gash on her arm that required stitches, but otherwise she was unharmed."

"That's a relief," Tess said. "I don't know how I would have explained to Ryan and Sean if a client got seriously injured right outside our offices." Although Tess was the head of West Security and Investigations West Coast division, she reported to Sean and Ryan West, the co-owners who remained in the firm's New York headquarters.

"Were you able to get any info from witnesses about the car or driver?" Travis asked. He'd given Tess a quick description of the hit and run before leaving for the hospital with Chelsea.

Tess shook her head. "Nothing. But we're working on getting security footage from the surrounding businesses. Unfortunately, the angle wasn't good enough to get a clear shot from our own cameras."

"Someone knew Chelsea was coming to see me. This wasn't an accident."

Tess nodded. "That or they were following her, but either way I agree this doesn't look like an accident."

"Do you think it was a warning or..." Kevin let the rest of the sentence hang.

Travis shook his head, his rage barely contained. "I don't know, but you better believe I intend to find out." His jaw clenched, and a hot rage bubbled in his gut. "Let me know when you get that security footage from the nearby businesses."

There was no reason for him to feel so protective of Chelsea—he barely knew her—but he did.

"Already on it," Kevin responded.

Tess gave Travis a searching look. "Bailey said Ms. Harper came in without an appointment and asked for you specifically. Do you two know each other?"

"Yes and no. She's Franklin Brooks's daughter. I wasn't involved in the case, but he was convicted seven years ago for killing his former girlfriend."

"And why did Ms. Harper want to speak with you?" Tess pressed.

"She wants to hire West Investigations to prove her father's innocence."

"Wait." Kevin held up a hand. "You said her father has already been convicted."

Travis sighed. "He was, but he never stopped professing his innocence. He's exhausted his appeals, but Chelsea says she's found evidence that a key witness may have lied at his trial."

Both frowns deepened.

"Okay," Kevin said. "That's all fine and good, but her father has been convicted and his appeal denied. I don't see how we can help."

Travis held his hands up, hoping to ward off his bosses'

arguments. "Hey, I know what it sounds like. So does Chelsea. She's asked me to meet with her father tomorrow, and I've agreed." He held a hand up higher stopping the oncoming protest. "I've made it clear to her that's all I'm agreeing to. One meeting. I'll hear Franklin Brooks out, but I've promised nothing."

Tess and Kevin groaned.

"I know. I felt the same way. Until the hit-and-run," Travis responded pointedly.

"The two things may not be related," Tess countered.

Travis shot her a look.

She shrugged. "I said they may not be related."

"Unlikely." Travis ran a hand over his head. "Chelsea comes to me about proving her father's innocence, and she's not ten steps from the office when someone tries to run her down? Something is going on here whether Franklin Brooks is innocent or guilty."

"And she's willing to pay our fee for this investigation?" Tess, ever the businesswoman, asked. "It may be a lot of expense for nothing."

"I'm not going to lead her on. One day. Limited expense, then I'll let her down as gently as possible." He thought about Chelsea having to take her uncle's name just to get away from the press, and anger bubbled. Whatever her father had done, she didn't deserve to be punished for it.

"You know digging into this could put you at odds with your friends at the LAPD, right?" Tess stated the obvious.

Travis frowned. "I doubt very much anyone at the LAPD considers themselves my friend. At least not anymore. And if, and I know it's a very big if, Chelsea is right, I want to make it right."

"I don't know how much of her father's story is true, but

the lady has definitely acquired an enemy," Kevin said, shooting a glance at the bed where Chelsea was still getting stitched up. "There is one thing we should consider." Kevin hesitated before continuing, "Chelsea could have set this up herself. Hired someone to drive that car at her."

The look on Tess's face said she'd thought of this as well.

Chelsea's fear-filled brown eyes popped into Travis's head, and he instinctively rejected the idea. "You didn't see her face when she was lying there in the street. She was stunned and terrified. She didn't do that to herself." He glanced over his shoulder to where Chelsea lay on the rolling bed alone now, the doctor having finished her stitches. He turned back to his colleagues in time to catch them sharing a look. "What?"

"Do you think you might be too close to this to be objective?" Tess asked.

"No," he answered quickly. Maybe too quickly. "Look, do I feel sorry for her? Yes. She was twenty-two years old when her father was convicted. The local media around this was not kind to her. She had to take her aunt and uncle's last name to get away from it. But every convict professes their innocence. Franklin Brooks is guilty."

"But…" Kevin cocked an eyebrow.

"But something is going on here, and my gut tells me Chelsea might have put herself in real danger."

Tess shook her head. "Not another one. I'm surrounded by knights in shining armor."

He was no knight. But he was convinced something dangerous was going on, and he was going to find out what it was.

TRAVIS DROVE CHELSEA home after taking her to have the prescription the doctor had given her filled. He had suggested she call someone to come stay with her. She'd told him she would consider it, but she really just wanted to be alone. Still, she did leave a message for her cousin Victor, telling him she'd had a minor run-in with a car but that she was okay and resting at home. She was sure she'd have to answer for that less-than-descriptive message but hoped it would wait until tomorrow.

She swallowed two of the pills the doctor had prescribed and made a large bowl of popcorn for dinner. She usually loved to cook, but she didn't have the energy tonight, nor a taste for takeout.

When the popcorn was ready, she carried it and a large glass of water (since alcohol and painkillers didn't mix) to the sofa and flipped through the movie channels. *Batman*, the one with Michael Keaton, was on, and she'd just settled in to watch when the sound of the front door clicking open drew her attention.

Only Victor and her aunt Brenda had keys to her house, so she wasn't surprised when her cousin appeared in the doorway between the kitchen and family room a moment later.

"Chelsea Antoinette Harper, are you okay?"

"I'm fine, Victor. I told you that in my message," she said, moving the blanket covering her legs to the side and starting to rise.

"Do not get up." Victor marched across the room and sat next to her on the sofa. Gently, he pulled her into his arms and gave her a sideways hug. "I can't believe you didn't call me."

"I knew you were at work."

Victor was a teacher just like her, but he had elected to teach summer school. Chelsea usually did, too, but she'd planned to devote this summer to doing everything she could to finally free her father.

"I would have dropped everything if I'd known you needed me. You know that."

"I do. But like I said, I'm fine, and I wasn't alone."

Victor's eyebrows went up.

"The private investigator I hired was with me."

"Private investigator?"

"Yes. I hired him to help me with my father's case. I've done a lot by myself, but I think I could use some professional help."

"Chelsea—"

"I know you think I should just get on with my life, but—"

"It's not that I don't believe in Uncle Franklin's innocence," Victor started. He had taken a more measured approach to her father's predicament than his mother, who wanted nothing to do with her older brother, but Chelsea knew Victor had his doubts. He'd never laid them all out for her, preferring to remain Switzerland between Chelsea and Brenda.

"I get it, Victor, I do."

"I'm just worried about you. You said you were at the hospital with your private investigator. Was he with you when you got hit?"

"I was leaving his office. He was inside, but he saw it."

"Does he think the hit-and-run is connected to your investigation?"

"I'm sure it isn't," she lied.

"Uh-huh."

"Are you going to do something pedestrian, like order me to stop investigating?"

"You know me well enough to know I would never do anything pedestrian. I am worried about you, though."

"Don't be."

"Oh, don't be. Well, poof, I'm no longer worried. You know it doesn't work that way. You're family."

"So is my dad."

"I'm not saying he's not…"

"I know, and I know you don't mean anything by it, but I can't drop this."

"Do you really think you can turn up something the police didn't? Even after seven years?"

"I don't know," she said, exasperated. "Maybe not. But I have to try everything I possibly can to get my father his life back."

Victor bumped her shoulder with his. "You're amazing, you know that?"

"Well…" Chelsea flipped her hair over one shoulder and vamped.

"And so humble, too." Victor tossed a piece of popcorn at her. "By the way, this—" he circled the popcorn bowl with his index finger "—does not qualify as dinner. I'm going to call Novita's. Do you want me to order something for you?"

Chelsea sighed inside. It looked like she wasn't going to get her quiet, restful night at home, after all.

Chapter Four

Travis suggested rescheduling their appointment to meet with Franklin Brooks, but Chelsea insisted they keep it. If they missed their prearranged visitation time, it would be at least another week, probably considerably longer, before Chelsea could get set up another time to visit her father.

Travis had taken her home after her discharge from the hospital and promised to return the next morning at ten to take her to the prison. When she opened her front door to him that morning, she only looked slightly more rested than when he dropped her off the day before. But she grabbed her purse and locked the front door to the house, ignoring his renewed suggestion of putting off the visit.

It was a forty-minute drive to Chino. They passed the time with pleasantries. Chelsea told him all about her plans for her third-grade class in the fall. It was clear she was a passionate and engaged teacher, dedicated to doing her best for each of the kids who passed through her class-room doors. He wasn't surprised, given how zealously she was championing her father's cause.

The prison was a blocky, red-brick, one-story struc-ture. A high fence topped with razor wire wound around the perimeter. Travis drove through the main gate and to the visitors' parking lot. He parked the car, then led Chelsea into the prison.

Prisons always felt like…well, prisons. The air was thick with the smell of disinfectant and despair. It hit him the moment he walked in. He and Chelsea got in line behind another family queued up to sign in and go through the series of indignities required in order to see their incarcerated family member or friend. The guards at the desk were efficient, checking names on driver's licenses against the names on the list of visitors allowed inside, then waving each person on to the lockers.

Travis and Chelsea showed their identification and stored their personal items—his wallet and her purse—in a locker before going through a set of metal detectors. After lining up again, they were led along with the other visitors to a large cream-colored room.

Fluorescent lights flickered overhead, and a half-dozen cafeteria tables lined the walls on either side of the room. The visitors trampled down the middle aisle, claiming seats at various tables. A mechanical buzzing echoed through the room after they were all seated.

Prisoners clad in drab gray jumpsuits, with Department of Corrections and their prisoner numbers penned on the left side of their chests, shuffled into the room.

Franklin Brooks was one of the last men to enter. He had aged quite a bit in the seven years since Travis had last seen him. His dark brown dreads had gone mostly gray. He'd lost weight but gained muscle. His skin was sallow, and his eyes were hooded, undoubtedly from the horrors he'd seen behind bars. But his smile when his gaze landed on Chelsea was pure and filled with love.

"Hi, Daddy." Chelsea stepped into her father's arms.

Brooks's arms tightened around his daughter, and his

eyes closed. The hug went on long enough to draw a cough and a frown from a nearby prison guard.

The prison had strict rules about touching. Brief touches such as hugs and handshakes were allowed at the beginning and end of visitation hour.

Brooks pulled away, his gaze moving to Travis. His smile fell into something more akin to a grimace. "Mr. Collins, thanks for coming."

Travis took Brooks's outstretched hand and shook it briefly. Travis sat next to Chelsea on one side of the table, and Brooks sat across from them on the other side.

"I wasn't sure Chelsea would be able to convince you to come see me, but I should have never doubted my girl." He smiled across the table at Chelsea.

Chelsea reached for her father's hand, giving it a quick squeeze before pulling back. "Travis has agreed to hear you out before he decides whether to help me investigate."

Travis frowned. He still had no intention of taking on investigating Franklin Brooks's case. As far as he was concerned, the justice system had spoken. He was more inclined toward investigating who had attempted to hit Chelsea.

"It would be best if you went over the details of your case. Starting at the beginning."

"The beginning," Brooks said acidly. "I'm not sure where that is, but I'll try." He took a deep breath and let it out slowly. "I wasn't a good father."

"Daddy—" Chelsea reached across the table for her father's hands.

"No, sweetheart. I wasn't." Brooks gave her hands a quick squeeze before pulling back. "If it wasn't for your aunt Brenda and uncle Darren taking us in and doing the lion's share of rearing you, I don't know where we would have been." His gaze went back to Travis's face. "Brenda is my sister. She and her husband took care of Chelsea like she was their own. Making sure she did her homework. Had clean clothes. Stayed away from the wrong crowds when she was a teen. She acted as Chelsea's parent after her mother died and while I drank too much, too often. Catted around with women when I should have been home, raising my daughter. I'm ashamed to say I never really grew up. At least not until I got here." He motioned to the prison walls. "And didn't have a choice."

Travis hadn't traveled all the way to Chino to hold a therapy session with Brooks. If the man was feeling remorse over how he'd lived his life, he was sorry, but he wasn't a therapist. "I understand," he said, nodding for Brooks to go on.

Brooks smiled knowingly. "Yes, of course. I don't want you to think I'm wasting your time, Mr. Collins. I just want you to understand what our life was like back when—"

Travis tapped into his store of patience. "When Lily Wong was killed."

Brooks glanced at Chelsea who nodded her encouragement. "Yes. Like I said, I dated a lot of women back then, but Lily was different. I loved her."

"How did you meet Lily?"

Brooks smiled, his eyes going glassy as if he was remembering. "At the park. She'd gone to a yoga class, and when she got back to her car, it wouldn't start. She called the garage where I worked, and I was sent out with the tow truck to see if I could get her car started. I couldn't. I had to tow it in, and by the time we got back to the shop, I had a date for the weekend."

"So, you two hit it off right away?" Travis asked.

"Right away. She was just so beautiful and so fun. And

funny, a real quick wit. Everybody loved being around her. You remember, don't you, Chels?"

"I do." Chelsea grinned. "She always made me laugh."

Brooks laughed then, too. "Always."

"When did the relationship start to sour?" That was one thing Travis remembered clearly from the trial. As good as things may have been between Franklin and Lily at the beginning of their relationship, it definitely hadn't been good around the time of Lily's murder.

Brooks's face fell. "When my drinking picked up. I'll be the first to admit it got out of hand. I've been in AA since I got to this lovely establishment. But it took me a long time to admit I had a problem."

"What happened the day Lily was killed?" Travis asked, getting to the reason he was there. It hadn't been his case and he only remembered bits and pieces of the news reports that had come out about Lily's murder and Franklin's conviction. And it was always best to hear a story directly from the source.

Brooks let out a sigh. "I've gone over it hundreds, thousands of times in my head. I convinced Lily to meet me at Billiards, a bar we like to go to. She had broken things off with me about a month earlier, sick of my drinking. And yes, my cheating on her. I had been trying to get her back. Cleaning up my act and proving to her that I could be the man she deserved." Brooks paused, looking down at the table.

Chelsea shifted in her seat. It couldn't have been easy for her to hear her father talk about his faults, but her expression remained nonjudgmental.

"Lily and I had a couple drinks. We talked, but she wasn't buying that I had changed. She said she was through. She deserved better, and she'd moved on." Brooks's gaze rose. "She said she'd met someone new. I got angry. I yelled at her. Said horrible things. Things I didn't mean. She left the bar, and I followed her to her house."

"And then what happened?" Travis pressed. Visitation was only for an hour, and they were already nearing half an hour in. He wanted to make sure he got as much detail from Brooks as possible before he left.

"Lily wouldn't let me in her house. I can't say I blame her. I was angry. We argued some more on her front porch, and then I left. That's the last time I saw her. I swear. I went to another bar, I could never remember the name of it, just some dive, and drank myself stupid. I'm not sure when I left or how I got to the park where Lily and I met, but I know I woke up there in the parking lot the next morning with one helluva hangover. I went home, and I was sleeping it off when the cops showed up and took me in."

It was a story full of holes, which was probably why the lead detective had homed in on him in the first place. "And you have never been able to recall any specifics about what you did or where you went after leaving the bar? Not in the last seven years?" It didn't seem likely.

Brooks shook his head. "It's like the hours after I left Lily are just gone."

Travis's disbelief must have shown on his face.

Brooks's expression hardened. "Mr. Collins, I know you don't believe me."

"Your story is hard to believe."

Chelsea turned an angry gaze on Travis. "You said you would listen with an open mind."

"And I have. I just don't believe the story I'm hearing. Open mind or no."

Chelsea's cheeks mottled in anger. "What about the hit-

and-run? How do you explain that, or do you think it's just a coincidence that the very day I seek your help proving my father's innocence someone tries to run me down?"

"What?" Brooks's roar had most of the heads in the room turning in their direction.

Two of the guards headed toward them. "Keep it down, Brooks, or I will cut this party short," a beefy guard with a shaved head said in a gruff smoker's voice.

Brooks never took his gaze from his daughter. "What is this business about a hit-and-run?"

Chelsea's expression slipped from one of anger to one of chagrin. She clearly hadn't intended to tell her father about the hit-and-run, but the cat was out of the bag now. "I wasn't going to say anything. I didn't want to worry you." Her gaze slid from her father's face to the guards, who were still standing close by, and back to him nervously.

"Chelsea Antoinette Brooks. What is going on?"

Travis sat silently, watching the family drama play out.

"It's nothing to worry about. I was crossing the street yesterday when a car almost hit me. You know Los Angeles traffic. It was probably just some jerk racing off to an appointment."

Brooks held Chelsea's gaze for several long beats before turning to Travis. "You were there, yes?"

"It happened outside my agency's offices. I was inside the building, but I saw the whole thing from the window."

Brooks's eyes probed Travis's face. "Do you think it was just a drunk driving too fast and not paying attention?"

Travis could almost feel Chelsea willing him to say yes. But this was a father concerned about his daughter. If the roles were reversed, he would want the truth. So, he gave it to Brooks. "No, I don't. It looked like the driver was aiming for Chelsea."

Chelsea growled angrily next to him.

"I don't want you to investigate," Brooks said determinedly.

"Daddy—"

"Mr. Collins," Brooks said, looking Travis in the eye. "Thank you for coming out here today, but your services are no longer needed."

"It's not your decision to make," Chelsea ground out.

"It's my case and my life. That makes it my decision," Brooks shot back.

"It's my money," Chelsea countered.

The guards were looking their way again, and Travis didn't like the expressions on their faces. "Okay, let's just take a minute, and both of you cool down," he said. "I may not believe you, Brooks, but I don't not believe you, either. I don't know. The prosecutor's evidence against you was strong. But your sister recently received a note saying that Peter Schmeichel lied about seeing you at Lily's house around the time of her murder."

"Of course he lied. I may not be able to tell you exactly what I did after I left the bar that night, but I know—" Brooks pressed a fist over his heart "—in here that I didn't kill Lily."

"That's not going to be enough to get you out of jail," Travis responded.

"That's why I need your help," Chelsea countered.

"No," Brooks hissed. "I will not put you in danger."

Chelsea opened her mouth, but Travis spoke first. "It may be too late to avoid that."

"Then I want to hire you to protect Chelsea," Brooks said. "I don't know how much you charge, but I'll get it."

"Daddy, I don't need protection."

"Mr. Brooks, I'm not a bodyguard."

"You're a former cop. You served and protected for a living."

Chelsea slapped her hand on the table. "Is anyone listening to me? I don't need a bodyguard."

They had pushed the guards to their limit. The bald one came up behind Brooks. "All right, Brooks. That's enough. Time to go back to your cell."

Brooks didn't move.

Travis knew the situation could very easily and very quickly escalate. "I'll keep an eye on Chelsea," he said.

Beside him, another growl rumbled in Chelsea's throat.

Brooks's shoulders relaxed a fraction of an inch. "Thank you," he said, rising.

The guard put a hand on his shoulder and started turning him away, but Brooks resisted, looking at Chelsea. "Baby girl, be careful. You mean more to me than anything. Including my own life. I love you."

Brooks turned with the guard and let them lead him away then.

Chelsea fumed silently beside Travis while they collected their things and exited the prison. She didn't speak until they got to his car.

Travis opened the driver's-side door, but Chelsea glared at him over the car's hood. "What the hell was that?" she asked.

Travis sighed. He'd been asking himself the same question for the last several minutes, but he knew the answer. "That was me taking your case."

Chapter Five

Travis stood on Chelsea's welcome mat waiting for her to answer the door and wondering if he had made the right choice, agreeing to help her. Kevin hadn't been thrilled when Travis told him they were officially on the case. But something about Franklin Brooks's desperation to protect his daughter had gotten to Travis. That and the nagging suspicion that despite the evidence against her father, Chelsea might be onto something. When he'd dropped her off after leaving the prison, they'd agreed to meet up at her place later that evening to go over the files she'd collected.

Now the door opened, and Chelsea stood in front of him clad in yoga pants and a long-sleeve T-shirt, her feet bare. She'd put her hair atop her head in a messy bun from which curly tendrils fell to frame her heart-shaped face. The overall effect was sexy as hell.

"Hi," she said.

"Hey," he replied. "Can I come in?"

"Sorry. Yes, of course." She stepped back to allow him inside.

He followed her down a short hall, trying not to stare at her figure as he did, but it was hard not to. He'd always been attracted to curvy women, and Chelsea definitely had curves in all the right places. There was a grace to her that only came from being completely comfortable in her own skin. Her dark brown skin looked as if it had never seen a blemish, but it was her eyes that really pulled him in; violet-colored orbs that made him think of seduction.

He pulled his attention away from her and noticed that they had reached a living room, which opened up to the left, and a dining room was to the right. The dining room table was covered with boxes, and two big blue binders were stacked on top of one of them.

Chelsea paused in the entrance to the dining room. "This is my war room so to speak. Everything I have been able to find on my dad's case is in here."

"It seems like you've been able to get a lot."

"In some respects, yes. In others, not nearly enough." She began walking again, leading him to the kitchen at the back of the house. There was a second hall off the kitchen, and he could see three doors that opened onto it. Two bedrooms and a bathroom, he presumed. The house was small but cozy.

He sat on one of the two stools at the island counter. "What is all this?" He eyed the pots on the stove across from where he sat.

"I'm fixing us dinner. Beef shank ragù. I hope you like beef."

The smell had his stomach growling. He hadn't eaten since breakfast, and he suddenly realized he was ravenous. "I definitely do. But that sounds fancy."

Chelsea lifted the top of one of the pots and peeked inside. Obviously satisfied with what she saw, she placed the top back on. "Just a few more minutes. And it's really not that fancy. The pressure cooker does most of the work. I'm just cooking the pasta now. I figured we could eat and then get started going through the files."

"That works for me."

She smiled. "Great. Can I offer you something to drink? Water. Soda pop. Wine. I've also got beer."

"Beer for me, please."

"Is Corona okay?"

"Fine."

Chelsea pulled two bottles of Corona from the fridge and opened them both before sliding one his way.

He was glad she seemed to have gotten over her anger at him from that morning. It would definitely be easier to work together. He took a sip before speaking again. "So, I take it you like to cook?"

"Yeah." She took a pull from her bottle. "I find it relaxing. My aunt is an amazing cook, and I learned a lot from her. When I moved out on my own after college, I didn't want to get into the habit of eating out all the time. Not that I could afford to. How about you?"

"Do you mean do I cook? No. Not really." There were a handful of things he could make, but nothing like what she was talking about. "I'm pretty good at breakfast foods. Pancakes. Waffles. Even French toast, but nothing approaching beef shank ragù. I'm not even sure what a ragù is. Assuming we aren't talking about Chef Boyardee."

She laughed, and he felt warmth spread through his chest and limbs. "No. Definitely not. A ragù is basically just a meat-based sauce. The meat is braised and cooked in the sauce slowly over several hours. It's common for it to be served over pasta."

"So fancy spaghetti and meat sauce."

"Fancy spaghetti—" She fisted her hands on her hips, but her eyes sparkled, so he knew he hadn't actually offended her. "Go sit at the table." She pointed to the round table in the kitchen. "I'll show you fancy spaghetti." She laughed again, a slow sexy turnup of her mouth that sent a jolt through him. This felt a lot like flirting, something he did not do with clients.

Not that he didn't date. He did, usually quite regularly, although he'd been in a slump for the last several months. What he didn't do was relationships. Too messy, too likely that someone would get attached.

He never wanted to feel the pain of losing someone he loved again. The car accident that had taken the lives of his parents and his older brother, and had nearly taken his own when he was only ten, had left a wound that he wasn't sure would ever heal. He didn't think he could live through losing the woman he loved, and he was going to do everything he could not to ever put himself in that situation.

Maybe it was time to call one of his friends with benefits who understood that he was not looking for anything more than a pleasant weekend between two consenting adults. He'd been working a lot lately, so maybe after he put this case to bed, he'd take some time off. Maybe take a trip to Las Vegas or even splurge and fly to Hawaii. He lived frugally, so he could afford it.

He glanced at Chelsea, wondering if she'd ever been to Hawaii. He was positive she looked fabulous in a bikini. His groin tightened, and he shook the mental image from his head. She was a client, he reminded himself.

"Do you mind if I wash up before we eat?" he said, feeling the need to put a bit of distance between himself and Chelsea.

"Oh, sure. The bathroom is just down the hall." She pointed to the hall off the kitchen, confirming his earlier guess. "Second door to the left."

The bathroom was on the dated side but clean. He washed his hands, taking more time than usual to give

his body a chance to settle down. On the way back to the
kitchen, he passed the open door to what looked to be
Chelsea's bedroom. He surveyed the room from the hall.
A queen-size bed was on the far wall, with a night table
and lamps on either side of the bed. On the other side of
the room was a dresser with a bunch of bottles—perfume,
hair products and who knew what else—on top. There
were also framed photos. Several of her, Franklin and a
woman who had to be Chelsea's mother based on the resemblance. One of her father, Chelsea and a woman Travis
figured must be Chelsea's aunt. The second photo was of
a younger man he didn't recognize. Maybe a boyfriend?

A knot of jealousy formed in his stomach.

"Everything okay in there?" Chelsea called out.

"On my way," he called back, leaving the doorway and
striding back into the kitchen. "I'm ready to try this ragù."

Chelsea had set the table while he'd washed his hands.
She plated the food and brought it to the table.

He took a bite, the flavors bursting in his mouth.
"Wow," he said. "This is amazing."

Chelsea's eyes sparkled. "See, I told you. Better than
spaghetti and meatballs, right?"

He agreed, and they ate in silence for a few moments,
enjoying the meal. A part of him felt as if he should make
conversation, but then he remembered this wasn't a date.
And the silence wasn't bad. It was actually quite comfortable.

After a while, Chelsea cleared her throat. "Can I ask
you a question?"

"Sure," he said hesitantly.

"Going to the state's attorney about the corruption in
your department. That had to be hard."

That was an understatement. Two years after Brooks's

conviction, the FBI indicted several LAPD officers and detectives for bribery, money laundering and other crimes related to accepting money, gifts and other favors from local gang members to look the other way regarding their criminal activities. Not long after the initial news reports came out, Travis's name was leaked to the media as the source of the investigation that ultimately led to the charges. And then the organized campaign to ruin him kicked off. It had worked. Most of his colleagues wouldn't talk to him, refused to be partnered with him and certainly couldn't be trusted to have his back. He'd had no choice but to leave the force.

His stomach twisted. "That's not a question," he responded.

"I know. The question is why did you do it? I mean, you had to know you would be vilified even if the corrupt officers were arrested and charged."

He looked into her eyes. "I did it because it was the right thing to do."

She held his gaze for a long moment. She looked as if she was on the verge of a response, a response that he was surprisingly eager to hear, but the doorbell rang before she spoke.

"Excuse me," she said, getting up from the table and going to the door.

He waited until she disappeared from the kitchen to follow her. He heard the front door open, and then Chelsea spoke.

"Simon, what are you doing here?" she asked, irritation lacing her tone.

"One of my colleagues told me you were in the hospital last night. Why didn't you call me?"

Travis peeked around the corner, careful to stay out of

sight. Chelsea's back was to him, and the man—Simon, Chelsea had called him—hadn't noticed him. He took in the man's wavy black hair, blue eyes and beige-colored skin that shone in a way that could only be achieved with regular facials. He wore pressed chinos with a crease down the front and a starched white button-down. All he needed was a sweater thrown over his shoulders and the preppy look would be complete.

"Why would I call you?" Chelsea said.

The man sighed as if the answer was obvious, but Chelsea was just too dim-witted to see it. "Just because we aren't married anymore doesn't mean we can't care about each other, does it?"

"I haven't seen or heard from you in months, Simon. And when we were married, you cared so much about me that you cheated on me. Repeatedly."

Simon sighed again. "Chelsea, I want us to get past the past. We should look toward the future."

"We don't have a future."

"Can I please just come in? I don't want to have a conversation with you on the front porch for the whole neighborhood to hear."

Travis stepped around the wall separating the foyer from the rest of the house. "Chelsea, is everything okay here?"

Simon leaned around Chelsea. His eyes narrowed, and he made a show of sizing Travis up. "Who is this?"

"None of your business," Chelsea answered.

"This is my house," Simon shot back.

"Was your house. You seem to have forgotten I got the house in the divorce. You said it was a dump and you wanted to move to a condo on the beach."

Simon's expression turned contrite. "I said some things during our rough patch that I didn't mean. That's one of the things I wanted to talk to you about."

"I don't care what you want to talk about, Simon. I want you to leave." Chelsea started to close the door.

Simon's hand shot out, preventing it from closing. "Chelsea—" He stepped forward as if he was prepared to force his way into the house.

Travis crossed the few remaining steps separating him from Chelsea. He filled the space Simon would have used to slide past her into the house. "The lady asked you to leave," he said.

Simon was an inch or two shorter than Travis, but he looked up at him now with a glower. "I think you should leave. This conversation is between me and my wife."

"Ex-wife," Chelsea corrected. "Ex being the most important part, and if you don't leave now, I will call the cops."

"If you don't leave now, you will need an ambulance, not the police," Travis amended in a voice so cold it served as a warning.

Simon must have heard it. Anger still blazed in his gaze, but his hand dropped to his side, and he took several steps away from the door. His gaze swung to Chelsea, his expression turning pleading. "We need to talk, Chels. It's important. I'll call you to find a better time," he said.

"You do that." Chelsea closed the door. She turned to face Travis. "Sorry about that. I don't know what possessed him to show up here out of the blue. He's never done that before."

Travis held up his hands. "You don't owe me an explanation." And she didn't. Her ex-husband was clearly an ass, but he had reminded Travis why he didn't do relationships. "I think we should take a look at those files now," he said, turning his back on Chelsea, but not before he saw something resembling hurt flash across her face.

Chapter Six

Chelsea cleared the kitchen table of their dinner plates and got a pot of coffee started while Travis moved into the dining room. The evening had taken on a decidedly chillier tone after Simon's unwelcome visit. She couldn't help but be annoyed at Travis's change in attitude after Simon left. She hadn't invited Simon over. But her ex-husband did have a way of rubbing people wrong. Unfortunately, she hadn't noticed that character flaw until after they'd said *I do*.

"Would you like some coffee?" Chelsea asked, heading for the kitchen ten steps away. Nothing in her small house was more than ten steps from anything else. Small was all she could afford, but she made the space feel like home.

"Yes. Black please," Travis answered.

She finished loading the dishes in the dishwasher and poured two cups of coffee. She brought the mugs to the table, setting his next to him, then carrying hers to sit across from him.

"You have done a lot of work in a short time." He flipped through the binder that held a timeline of Lily's last days.

"I've tried to reconstruct as much of the timeline as I could. It's been years, though, and there are still missing pieces." Chelsea reached across the cluttered table and pulled the second binder in front of her. She'd constructed biographies for each of the witnesses who testified in her father's case, including Lily's friends and family and the cops who had testified. She also had copies of relevant reports, news articles, internet posts and anything else that she could find relating to the case, but she could save those for later.

Her father had already told Travis about the last time he'd seen Lily. Now, she walked Travis through her father's trial and appeals, pulling documents from binders and boxes to support her statements as she went along. The recitation took hours, and by the time she was finished, she had covered the dining room table with papers.

She took a sip of the now-cold coffee, exhausted but also energized. She could see doubt about the case against her father in Travis's eyes. He'd taken copious notes and had asked a lot of questions, good questions, some of which she hadn't thought of.

He flipped through the binder to Lily's biography. "You've tried to contact Lily's friends and family?"

She nodded. "I was hoping someone might listen and at least concede that the police work wasn't as thorough as it could have been. Maybe support my dad's appeals, but none of Lily's family or friends would speak to me when I approached them about my father's possible innocence."

That wasn't completely true. A few of Lily's friends had plenty to say about what a monster her father was and how much they hoped he rotted in jail, but they wouldn't talk to her about anything that could help her prove his innocence. Even when she'd pointed out that if she was right and that her father was innocent, Lily's killer was still out there. She understood why Lily's friends and relatives didn't want to talk to the daughter of her accused murderer. She didn't blame them, but it made her investigation harder, and she couldn't help feeling some resentment toward them for it.

Travis flipped to the autopsy report. The description of Lily's wounds and the photos were gruesome. The brutal nature of the attack was one of the reasons the cops had been convinced the killer had to be someone who knew Lily and whose anger was personal.

"How did you get this?" Travis asked.

"If I told you, I'd have to kill you," she joked flatly.

The autopsy hadn't been easy to get. It had been part of the trial but wasn't included with the transcripts that were available to the public. She'd had to resort to searching the dark web for hackers and praying that she wasn't walking into a scam or a police sting. It had not been cheap, but it had worked. The hacker had gotten her the autopsy report and the police report in the case. She paid and hadn't asked any questions.

Travis's eyebrows rose.

"It's better you don't know. Let's just say with enough money, anything is attainable."

He seemed to let it go. For now. "How long have you been trying to free your father?" Travis asked.

She met his gaze straight on. "Since the day he was arrested."

Travis's brow rose. "You believe that much in his innocence?"

"Yes," she said, steel in her voice. "He is innocent." She'd never believed in anything more than that her father, for all his faults, would never kill anyone. "My father loved Lily. And she loved him. I think that's why she met him that night at the bar. She may not have wanted to be with him, but she still cared about him. He didn't do this." It didn't escape her notice that her statement echoed Simon's comments from earlier. "And I won't stop until I prove he's innocent."

"Okay," Travis said with a nod.

Her shoulders relaxed when she saw that even if Travis didn't quite believe in her father's innocence yet, he at least believed that she believed it. That was a start. At least she wasn't completely alone in this anymore. Her father now had one person on his side with the knowledge, expertise and resources that could lead to his freedom.

Travis flipped several pages in the binder. "We need to speak with Peter Schmeichel and Gina McGrath. If Peter admits that he lied and Gina confirms it, that could go a long way to getting a judge's attention."

"Gina used to live next door to Lily. She worked as a nurse. I went to the house after I got the note about Peter's confession, but Gina doesn't live there anymore. The current occupant has been living there for years and had never heard of Gina." Chelsea grabbed the photos she'd taken of Lily's old house. She'd taken them more than a decade after the murder, but the home hadn't changed much in those years. "In the statement Gina gave the police on the night of Lily's murder, she says she was taking the trash out and saw my dad and Lily arguing on the porch. That was hours before the medical examiner says Lily was killed. My dad admits to the argument, but he swears he left and Lily was alive."

"Gina didn't see him leave?" Travis's eyes darted over the testimony.

"No. She went back into her house before my dad left."

Travis gave the note accusing Peter of lying a quick

once-over, then flipped through the file until he got to the section on Peter. "And what can you tell me about Peter?"

"He was Gina's boyfriend back then," Chelsea admitted. "According to Peter's testimony, he left Gina's place the night of the murder around 1:00 a.m. He says he saw my dad leaving Lily's house at the same time. That my dad was disheveled and in a rush. His statement is what put my father at Lily's house around the time the medical examiner says she was killed." She flipped to a different page in the binder. "Mr. Schmeichel has a criminal record for dealing drugs, assault and burglary. Amazingly, he's managed not to do all that much time in prison even though he's a career criminal. He was arrested a week after Lily's death and that's when he told the cops about seeing my dad at Lily's house."

"And you find that suspicious," Travis stated the obvious.

"Of course I do. Why wouldn't he have approached the cops earlier if he'd really seen my dad that night?" She turned to yet another page in her binder. "And Gina's statement says Peter was at her house all night. No mention of him leaving at 1:00 a.m."

Travis frowned. "Could be an oversight. Witness statements often don't match exactly."

"The cops didn't interview Peter right after the murder. At least, there's not a statement from him that I could find."

"We need to talk to him," Travis conceded.

"His last known address is in the binder, but he's not exactly what I'd call stable. I can't say for sure that he still lives there."

"We'll find him wherever he is," Travis said with confidence. He looked up from the notebook, the gaze he pinned on her intense. "You've done a good job with this so far. Better than some professional private investigators I've had the misfortune to run into."

She nodded her thanks for the compliment and lowered her gaze to the papers on the table. Her cheeks were on fire, and her heart was thundering. "You guys should consider hiring more teachers. There's no one more resourceful on the planet."

Travis grinned and her stomach did a flip-flop. "I'll keep that in mind," he said.

CHELSEA WAS DAMN IMPRESSIVE. When Travis thought about what life must have been like for her since her father went to prison, he felt for her. "Tell me about Lily," he said.

Chelsea moved to open the binder to Lily's page.

Travis put his hand over hers, stopping her from flipping the pages. "You knew her. Tell me about her in your own words."

He could see genuine grief on her face when she thought about Lily. "What do you want to know?"

"Tell me how she and your father met. What was their relationship like? What did you think about her?"

"I was nineteen when they met. Between work and school, I was busy and not around very much, but she was nice. I was glad my dad had someone who seemed to care about him. He and my mother had married young, and then they had me. My mother passed away when I was ten, and my father dated a lot while I was growing up, but Lily was his first serious girlfriend after my mom passed. She did my hair for me for free, and we both loved action movies, so we'd always catch opening weekend of the new ones together. She was just great. She treated me more like a little sister than her boyfriend's daughter."

It was clear Lily's father hadn't been the only one who'd loved Lily. "How did you feel about her breaking up with your dad?"

Chelsea's gaze slid away from his. "I didn't really have an opinion."

Travis waited a beat, but Chelsea didn't add any more. "If this is going to work, you have to be honest with me. About everything."

"I'm not lying." But Chelsea still wasn't meeting his gaze.

"Maybe not, but you're holding back."

Chelsea sighed. "You already know my dad was a heavy drinker back then. He was never violent, but he could be really mean when he had too many. I suspect Lily got tired of it."

She flipped to the page with Lily's biography. Hers was one of the only profiles that had a photo with it. Lily had been quite beautiful with a slim, heart-shaped face and straight dark hair. Her dark brown eyes were ringed with gold on the outer edges, and laugh lines creased the edges of her mouth.

Chelsea rubbed her thumb over the photograph as if she could touch Lily's cheek. Her gaze shifted out the window. It was clear that she'd been transported back into her memories. Travis wanted to reach across the table and comfort her. He suspected that she needed it. With her aunt not believing in her father's innocence and her father in prison, she was isolated. Alone.

And he needed to remember that. She was vulnerable, and she'd come to him for help.

"I skimmed Lily's half sister's testimony at the trial," Travis said. "She said Lily was finished with your father. That it was over, and she made that clear to him.

Lily was dating someone else. But she didn't say who that person was."

"We never found out who the other man was. If there was another man. If Lily was seeing someone new, why did she meet my dad at the bar that night? And it seems odd that Lily told no one about him."

"Your dad also said Lily told him she was seeing someone new."

Chelsea shrugged. "Maybe that was her way of letting him down easy. I don't know. But I know that Lily's family, the cops, the prosecutors, everyone decided my father had committed the murder just hours after Lily's body was found. They never looked at anyone else seriously."

They were going to have to find a way to get Lily's friends and family to talk to them if they wanted to find out if her mystery man existed. He didn't anticipate that it was going to be easy.

Chelsea looked deflated, and he didn't like it. He preferred the aggressive, take-charge, uber-organized woman on a mission to save her father. He wasn't sure he believed her father was innocent, but he admired her determination. And he wanted to give her closure. One way or the other. He had a feeling that it had been some time since she had genuinely smiled. For one fleeting moment, the urge to be the man who put that smile on her face consumed him.

"Do you know the name of the salon where Lily worked?" he asked instead.

"The salon she worked at closed a few years ago. But I know Lily's best friend and former coworker, Rachel Lamier, opened her own salon, Snips, in Venice. She wouldn't talk to me when I called her, though."

"We have to start somewhere. Maybe I'll have better

luck. If you're up for it, we can pay a visit to Rachel to-morrow morning."

"I'm up for it, definitely."

"Great." Travis looked at his watch. "It's getting late so I think I should go." He rose.

She stood and walked him to the door.

"Make sure you lock this behind me." He tapped the lock.

"Don't worry about me."

But he was worried about her. He'd made a promise to her father to watch out for her, and he intended to keep that promise. "Good night, Chelsea. Sleep tight."

Chapter Seven

Chelsea spent a restless night flitting in and out of sleep.
A part of her was excited. She felt like there was finally
some movement behind her investigation. Another part
of her was nervous. This was her father's last chance. If
she didn't find some evidence to convince the authorities
that they'd convicted the wrong man for Lily's murder,
her father would spend the rest of his life in jail.

At 7:00 a.m., she gave up trying to sleep and went to
the basement where she kept her treadmill. A forty-five-
minute workout burned off some of her nervousness, but
her injured hip throbbed afterward. She took a long hot
shower to soothe the pain and, when she got out, found a
text message from Travis telling her he was on his way
over. She dressed quickly in a yellow floral dress and
braided her long light brown hair into a goddess braid
encircling her head. She was still debating which pair of
sandals went best with the outfit when the doorbell rang.

Travis stood on her doorstep, two steaming to-go cups
in hand. Despite the already warm late June morning, he
wore blue jeans. He'd paired them with a white short-
sleeved collared shirt that brought out the flecks of gray
in his brown eyes. Not for the first time, she noted how
devastatingly handsome the man was.

Travis's brow quirked up. "Can I come in?"

Chelsea's body flooded with embarrassment at how long she'd been standing in the doorway thinking about him. "Yes. Of course. Sorry."

She stepped back to allow him to pass by her into the house. He headed straight for the dining room, where she had cleared a small square of space on the table for her laptop. She'd spent some time after he left the night before scouring social media for more of Lily's prior co-workers with no luck.

"How was your night?" she asked, accepting the cup of coffee Travis handed her. "Thank you." She popped the lid off her coffee and took a sip. She was pleasantly surprised to find it was exactly how she liked it, with milk and more sugar than she probably should have had. She was touched that he had paid attention to the several cups of coffee she'd plowed through while they'd worked the day before. She closed her eyes and wrapped her hands around the warm cup, taking another sip. It was good. Almost as good as the expensive stuff she bought from the specialty coffee shop not far from her house, her one splurge.

She opened her eyes and found Travis watching her, his gaze intense. Sexual awareness flooded through her. "What?"

"Nothing." He shifted his gaze away, focusing on setting up his tablet next to her laptop. "How are you feeling? Any pain?"

Part of her wanted to push to know exactly what he was thinking when he was looking at her, but she let it go. "A little. Nothing a couple of ibuprofen can't fix. Did you have any luck finding our eyewitness Peter Schmeichel?"

"I think I have a line on him."

"Really?" She felt herself perking up at the news. "That's great."

"Don't get too excited. I don't have anything concrete like a location yet, but I'm working on it."

"Still, great." She took another sip of her coffee. "Hopefully, Rachel will give us some useful information as well. Snips opens at nine."

Travis looked at his wristwatch. "It's still early. The shop won't be open yet."

Chelsea put her coffee down and eyed her phone. "Are you sure it wouldn't be better for me to call and make an appointment when they open? Rachel might be more receptive to answering our questions if we don't ambush her."

Travis shook his hand. "I come from the school of thought where it's better to ask forgiveness than permission."

"Alrighty then. An ambush it is," Chelsea teased. "I'm just going to go finish getting dressed."

In the bathroom, she popped open the bottle of ibuprofen and took two pills, then brushed her teeth and reapplied her lip gloss before rejoining Travis.

"What are you doing now?" She looked over his shoulder at the screen of his tablet.

"Just pulling on some of the threads, one of which I hope will lead to Peter Schmeichel. He's done a good job of staying under the radar. He hasn't filed taxes in years or applied for disability or unemployment. I can't find any relatives or even an address for him."

Chelsea frowned. "I thought you said you had a line on him."

"I have other oars in the water, don't worry," he responded confidently. "I'll find him. It's just unusual for someone to disappear so completely."

"Do you think there's something to it? Like maybe he's disappeared to avoid someone or something. Like the law?"

Travis shrugged. "Maybe. I'll keep digging."

Since they had an hour to kill before they needed to leave for Snips, Travis continued his search for Peter while she tried to locate as many of Lily's former coworkers as she could. It was slow going; most salons didn't list their stylists by name, so she had to cobble together information from old websites and social media. Travis didn't seem to be having much better luck based on his grunts and sighs.

At ten minutes to 9:00 a.m., Travis closed the cover of his tablet. "Are you ready to head out to see Rachel?"

Chelsea closed her laptop. "As ready as I'll ever be."

They climbed into Travis's car, and he headed for Venice. Rachel had opened her shop, Snips, six years earlier. Based on its fashionable location, it seemed like she was doing very well as a business owner. Rachel had been interviewed by the police during their investigation, but she hadn't testified at Chelsea's father's trial. Chelsea didn't know what or if Rachel could tell them anything that might be helpful in proving her father's innocence, but she hoped the woman would be less hostile toward now that more time had passed. She was still hopeful Rachel might be able to tell them something about Lily's life around the time of her murder that they didn't already know. Maybe point them in the direction of this mysterious boyfriend, assuming he existed at all.

They parked in a garage and walked the two blocks to the salon. Chelsea noticed several women turn and shoot very feminine gazes and smiles at Travis as they made the trek to the salon. A pang of jealousy stirred inside her, but Travis didn't seem to notice the women's stares. Or maybe he was just used to them. He was a very attractive man, there was no doubt about that. Maybe if they'd met under different circumstances… But they hadn't. And she needed to focus all her attention on her father's case.

One of the women passing by them tripped on some uneven pavement she hadn't noticed because she'd been staring at Travis.

He reached out a hand, steadying her. "Are you okay?"

"Yeah…yes. Thank you." The woman's words came out breathily.

Chelsea rolled her eyes and shot a death glare at the woman. The woman's cheeks pinked, and she hurried on.

Travis turned to her, his eyes sparkling with mischief. "That wasn't very nice."

"She's a grown woman falling all over herself because you have a nice—"

He looked like he was trying not to laugh. "A nice what?"

"I'm sure you know you're a very attractive man."

"Am I now?" Travis said in a teasing tone.

"Can we just get to the salon, please?" Chelsea picked up her pace.

Now Travis did let loose with a hearty laugh. "Slow down. I want to hear more about how attractive you find me."

"I did not say I found you attractive," she shot back, heat flooding into her cheeks. "I said you know you are an attractive man."

"A very attractive man, you said."

"Is this really the time for this conversation?" she asked, nearly sweating with embarrassment.

Travis caught her arm as they arrived in front of Snips. "I think it's a great time for this conversation."

A gust of wind blew a napkin down the street, but it did nothing to cool the heat burning through her.

Travis stared at her with an odd look she couldn't place on his face. "I think you're very attractive, too."

Chelsea's heart thumped in her chest, her pulse picking up even more steam when Travis took a step closer to her. She could see that his brown eyes were rimmed in gold. She saw heat in them.

Travis reached out a hand, running two fingers down her cheek, sending her into a full-body blush. He leaned in closer, and she closed her eyes.

Someone bumped into her shoulder. Chelsea glanced at the woman and recognized her as Rachel from her social media accounts.

Rachel Lamier had shiny, bouncy, shoulder-length red hair that only a professional could have achieved. It framed her square-shaped face and deep-set blue eyes. Rachel appeared to be about the same age as Lily would have been. Chelsea couldn't help but feel a twinge of sadness at the thought that Lily hadn't had the opportunity to live the years that Rachel had.

Rachel tore her gaze from Travis, who was seemingly the cause of their minor collision, and turned to Chelsea. "Oh, sorry. I wasn't looking where I was going."

Chelsea chuckled knowingly. "That's okay. I understand. You are Rachel, aren't you?"

The slightly amused expression on Rachel's face changed to suspicion. "Yes. Do I know you?"

"I'm Chelsea Harper. I'm actually here to speak with you."

Rachel's shoulders relaxed. "Oh, well, I have a client scheduled in a few minutes but if you can come back this afternoon, I'm free after 1:00 p.m." Rachel shot another glance at Travis, no doubt wondering about his presence.

"I'm not here to have my hair done. I was hoping to speak to you about Lily Wong."

Rachel started. "Lily? Why?"

It was Chelsea's turn to shoot a glance at Travis. He picked up on her train of thought right away. "Ms. Harper is Franklin Brooks's daughter." Travis handed Rachel a business card. "She has hired me to look into her father's case."

"I don't have anything to say to you," Rachel spat.

"My father is innocent," Chelsea replied firmly.

"We'll only take a moment of your time," Travis interjected. "Please."

The seconds stretched until Chelsea was sure Rachel was going to say no and walk away. But Rachel surprised her. "Ten minutes. Then I have to prepare for my client. What do you want to know about Lily?"

RACHEL LED CHELSEA and Travis to her office at the back of the salon and closed the door. The office was no bigger than a closet and so cluttered as to be claustrophobic. Rachel cleared off the sole chair in front of her desk, and Travis gestured for Chelsea to take it. She did, and he stood next to her facing Rachel who took a seat behind the desk.

"I don't know how I can help you," Rachel said. "It's been a long time, and the cops caught Lily's murderer as far as I'm concerned." She shot a venomous look in Chelsea's direction.

Even though he understood where Rachel was coming from, Travis felt a surge of protectiveness. Chelsea didn't deserve anger from Lily's friends and family. Even if her father was a murderer, she'd done nothing wrong. And if she was right, and Franklin was innocent, she was one of the bravest women he knew.

Chelsea didn't seem to be letting Rachel get to her, though. Her expression remained polite, almost as if she hadn't seen the nasty look Rachel shot at her, although Travis knew that she had.

"We understand why you feel that way," Travis said soothingly. "You want someone to pay for what was done to your friend."

"I do, yes."

"But what if the wrong person is in jail? What if Lily's killer is still out there? Walking free? You wouldn't want an innocent man to pay for a crime he didn't commit."

Rachel bit her bottom lip. "Of course I wouldn't want that."

"Me, either. That's why I agreed to take this case. If Lily's killer is still out there, we need to find him and have him brought to justice. Anything you can tell us, no matter how insignificant you might think it is, could help."

From the look on her face, his words had gotten through to Rachel. "I'll tell you what I can, but I warn you it probably won't be much."

"Thank you." Travis smiled, melting more of Rachel's iciness. "Can you tell me what Lily was like?"

Rachel smiled. "She was the most caring person you'd ever meet. Everyone from her coworkers to her clients loved her." It was similar to the way Franklin and Chelsea had described Lily. Of course, people tended to speak well of the dead even when they hadn't been very nice people in life, but he had a feeling that Lily had genuinely been a good person who was liked by many.

"Did you and Lily hang out a lot outside of work?" he asked.

"I wouldn't say a lot, but we did hang out a few times."

It looked like Chelsea had wisely decided to let him take the lead on questioning Rachel, so he forged on. "Did Lily ever mention a new boyfriend?"

Rachel's face scrounged as if she was thinking back. "No, not that I remember. She broke up with Frank a few weeks before she was killed." She shot another look Chelsea's way, but this one was far less venomous. "I don't remember her talking about dating anyone new."

"Did she ever talk about Frank with you? Do you know why they broke up?"

Rachel nodded. "Yes, she talked about him all the time. She really loved him, but I got the feeling that she was fed up with his drinking near the end. I don't think she wanted to end it, but she didn't know what else to do. Or how to help him. She stopped hanging out with me as much after work once they broke up. I don't know much about the relationship after that."

Travis poked and prodded along that line of questioning for a bit more, but Rachel didn't have more to offer about Lily and Frank's relationship.

"Is there anything else you can remember about that time?"

"Well, there was one thing. Lily had been having some trouble at her house."

Chelsea sat up straighter in the chair next to him. "What kind of trouble?"

"She complained a couple of times about some strange stuff that was happening. Her car had been vandalized with someone throwing eggs on her hood. And she thought someone had been in her house, but nothing was missing. I told her it was probably just teenagers goofing, you know. It didn't seem serious."

"Did she call the police?"

"I don't think so. Like I said, we both thought it was probably just some of the rowdy teens who lived in her neighborhood. And it wasn't like there was anything missing or permanently damaged." Rachel shrugged. "What were the police going to do?"

Probably nothing, but he made a mental note to check if Lily had filed a police report anyway. "Did you tell the police about the vandalism when they interviewed you?"

"Oh." Rachel seemed surprised by the question. "I'm not sure. Probably not. They seemed so sure that Frank had done it when they talked to me. Most of their questions were about him, and his and Lily's relationship."

Travis shot a look at Chelsea. She was pressing her lips together as if she was trying not to let certain words spill out of her mouth.

Rachel pressed a hand over her mouth. "You don't think the stuff with her house had anything to do with her murder, do you? I mean…" She cut a look at Chelsea. "If Frank is innocent, and I didn't say anything…"

"Right now, we are collecting information. We don't know what is relevant and what isn't, but you've been very helpful." Travis rose as did Chelsea next to him. "If you think of anything else, give me a call."

He opened the door, but Rachel spoke again before he and Chelsea stepped out of the office. "I met Frank a couple of times. When a cop said he killed Lily, I couldn't see it. I know people have dark sides, but he just didn't seem like the type. He loved her. You could see that whenever they were together. Even when they were fighting and arguing."

Chelsea gave a small smile. "Thank you for saying that."

Rachel tapped the side of Travis's business card against the palm of her hand. "Would you let me know what happens? If it wasn't Frank who killed Lily, I'd like to know. I want to see the person who hurt my friend in jail."

"I will." Chelsea nodded. "And like Travis said, if you can think of anything else, please let him know."

They headed out of the salon. Travis glanced at Chelsea as they walked to the car in silence, but she looked lost in her thoughts. He'd give anything to know what she was thinking, but her face gave away nothing. They were back in the car before she spoke again.

"Well, what do you think?" she asked, fastening her seat belt.

"The vandalism and possible break-in are something to explore. I take it you didn't know about that." Travis started the car and pulled out of the parking lot.

"I didn't. And if my dad did, he never said anything to me. And it didn't come up during his trial either," Chelsea added bitterly.

He could understand why she might be bitter. It certainly would have helped her father if the jury had heard that Lily had been the victim of vandalism and possible break-ins just weeks before she was murdered. Of course, it might have also hurt him if the prosecution had been able to imply that Franklin was behind the vandalism and break-in. You never knew with a jury.

"Rachel wasn't sure if Lily called the police, but I'm going to check into whether she made a police report about the events at her house," he said, laying out his next steps.

"Okay, and what should I do?"

"Did Lily have any social media presence?"

Chelsea nodded. "Yes, she had a couple social media pages. Why?"

"Take another look at them. We need to figure out if this boyfriend really existed. If he did, it's likely he's in those feeds somewhere. Don't just look for the obvious, though. Look for anything out of the ordinary for Lily. A new restaurant. Changes to her normal routine. Anything that might have changed between the time she and your father broke up until her death."

Chelsea frowned. "Rachel didn't seem to think Lily had a new man in her life."

"That's what she said, but I noticed some hesitation. Like maybe there was something she didn't want to say. Often people don't want to say anything that might make their friends look bad, especially when those friends can no longer defend themselves."

Chelsea shrugged. "Okay, I'll see what I can find."

"In the meantime, are you up for a little field trip?"

"A field trip? Where?"

"I want to get a look at Lily's old house. Get a feel for the place and the neighborhood and how someone might have gotten in and out without being seen."

The air in the car stilled. Lily's old house...which also happened to be the scene of her murder.

"I understand if you don't want to go with me. I can drop you off at your place if you want."

"No," Chelsea said quickly. "No, I'll go with you."

"Chelsea, you really don't have to—"

"It's okay. It's been a long time, and I want to be involved in every part of the investigation."

"Okay. Let's go back to the beginning." Travis said, turning the car in the direction of Lily's old San Fernando Valley neighborhood.

Chapter Eight

Chelsea gave Travis an address that she knew by heart, and he plugged it into the GPS and drove. He stopped the car across the street from Lily's old house. It looked bigger, cheerier the last time she'd seen it. Lily had been proud of her little home, keeping the square patch of front lawn neat and trimmed and the window boxes full of flowers and herbs. Now it looked as if the current owners hadn't put any effort into its upkeep.

Travis turned to her. "You can stay in the car. I just want to take a quick look around."

Her gaze didn't leave the forlorn little house, but she answered him. "No, I want to go with you."

They climbed out of the car together. Chelsea stopped at the top of the cracked walkway and looked at the house. The house itself hadn't changed, but it had lost its sheen. Gone were the colorful flowers in the flower beds. The lawn was overgrown. The windows were filthy with grime and dirt.

Chelsea pointed to the house to the right of Lily's old place. "That's where Gina McGrath lived."

The neighboring house looked only slightly better kept than Lily's. Chelsea knew from her investigation that Gina no longer lived there.

She and Travis made their way up the cracked walkway to the front door. Travis knocked on the door, then peered through the front window. "I don't think anyone is living here at the moment."

Somehow that made her even sadder. Lily was gone, and her house was empty.

"I'm going to head around back," Travis said. "See if I can find an open door and take a look around."

Chelsea nodded. "Let's go."

Travis hesitated for a moment, searching her face. Whatever he found there clearly didn't please him, but it must have been enough to let him know she wasn't going to fall apart on him.

They walked through the tall grass around to the back of the house. Although the back door was locked, it was flimsy enough that Travis needed only to give it a good shove to get it to pop open.

"Travis," Chelsea hissed. "That's illegal."

"I'm just going to take a look. Get a feel for the crime scene. You can stay here if you want."

They both knew she wasn't going to do that despite her protests.

She hadn't been in Lily's house since before the murder and then only a handful of times. There was a generously spacious living room/kitchen/dining room setup followed by a short hall. Travis was right. There was clearly no one currently living in the house. There was no food in the fridge, and the water and electricity had been shut off. The sun was still high in the sky, but with no lights to turn on inside the house, shadows crisscrossed the space.

Travis aimed the flashlight on his phone toward the hall. Chelsea followed him past a bathroom and a small bedroom. Lily's bedroom was at the end of the hall. A king-size bed still rested against one wall, its headboard leaning precariously forward.

Chelsea's mind flashed back to the crime-scene pictures from the file her hacker had gotten for her. Lily lying on the bed. Cuts on her face, neck and hands. Her sheets were covered with blood. The report indicated she had fought. Her nails had been broken off in several places. And she had been stabbed six times. *Overkill*, Chelsea remembered reading in the detective's notes. It was one of the reasons the police believed Lily had more than likely known her attacker.

Chelsea was suddenly overwhelmed by a wave of emotion. The room was too small, and everything in it was too close to her. She'd looked at the crime-scene photos dozens of times, but somehow, she'd been able to detach in a way she couldn't while standing in Lily's old room. In the space where she'd been killed.

Almost as if he could feel her inner turmoil, Travis reached out and pulled her into his arms.

"Breathe. Just breathe slowly."

"All the violence, the anger. He stabbed her six times. Why?" Tears slid from her eyes.

Travis laid his cheek on her head, pulling her in closer. "I don't know, honey. I do know whoever did this is a coward. And we are going to figure it out."

She leaned into his warmth, letting the spicy scent of his cologne wrap around her. Despite the circumstances, in that moment, she felt safe. Protected. She stepped out of his arms, wiping the tears from her cheeks. "Can we get out of here?"

They retraced their steps through the house to the back door. They rounded the house just as a man got out of a red Mazda in the driveway next door.

He looked at them, surprise on his face. "Hello? Can I help you?" A curly mop of brunette curls bounced on the man's head as he pulled himself the rest of the way out of his car and slammed the driver's-side door.

Travis made his way forward, his business card extended toward the man. "I'm Travis Collins, a private investigator. This is Chelsea Harper, my associate. We're looking into the death of the woman who used to live here."

"Lily," the man said.

Chelsea shared a quick look with Travis.

"Yes," Travis confirmed. "Did you know her?"

"A little," the man answered. He looked to be a few years younger than her father, mid- to late-forties.

"Would you mind if I asked your name?"

"I'm Jace Orson."

"And how long have you lived here, Mr. Orson?"

Jace darted a glance at his house as if he was thinking about making a run for it. "About eight years. A little closer to nine."

"So, you lived here when Lily lived next door," Chelsea said.

"Yes. It was so sad when she was... Well, you obviously know if you're investigating. I thought they caught the guy who did it. A boyfriend or something."

"There have been some new developments," Travis said quickly.

Jace's face registered surprise.

Chelsea frowned. She had a feeling he'd spoken up so quickly to cut off her chance to argue that the man in jail for Lily's death had been wrongly convicted.

"Do you remember seeing anything unusual around the time that Lily was killed?" Travis asked. "Maybe a stranger hanging around? Or a vehicle that seemed out of place?"

"No." Jace shook his head. "But it's been a long time. I would have told the police if I had."

"Do you remember seeing or hearing Lily argue with anyone? Ever see her upset with anyone?"

"Well, sometimes she and the boyfriend of hers got into it." He rolled his eyes. "Loudly. I don't know what she saw in him. I could tell he was a loser. I wish she had listened to me."

Chelsea stopped angry words from springing forward and instead asked, "Listened to you?"

"Yeah, I may have mentioned that she could do better than the bum she was seeing. For a while there, I actually thought she had taken my advice."

"Why?" Travis asked.

"Because a new guy started coming around for a while, but he wasn't around for long before the loser boyfriend was back."

Chelsea's heart pounded. "The new guy, do you remember his name?"

"No, sorry. I don't think I ever knew it. Like I said, I didn't know Lily that well."

Well enough to call her boyfriend a loser, Chelsea thought, still fuming.

"Can you describe the man you saw?" Travis pressed.

"Oh, man. No, I don't think so. I'm only even thinking about this stuff because you guys asked. I try not to remember what happened right next door to me."

"I understand," Travis said in a conciliatory tone. "Do you happen to remember where you were when Lily was killed?"

Jace frowned. "I don't think I like what you are suggesting."

"Trust me I'm not suggesting anything," Travis said with a smile. "I'm just trying to draw as complete a picture as possible of the last moments of Lily's life."

Jace hesitated for a moment before answering. "Well, I do remember where I was as it happens. I was out with friends that night."

"One more question for you. Do you know where the neighbor on the other side of Lily's house moved to?"

Jace looked over Chelsea's shoulder at the house that used to be Gina's. "Sorry. She hung around for a little while after Lily died, but a lot of people got freaked out by a murder happening on their street. And, well, a lot has changed over the years."

"Thanks anyway for your help," Travis said, grabbing Chelsea's hand and backing away. "If you think of anything else, could you please give me a call at the number on the card? Anything you remember could be helpful."

"He's not going to call," Chelsea said as they got back into the car. She watched Jace watch them for a moment before he went into his house and shut the door.

"That's okay. He confirmed that another man had been visiting Lily around the time of her death. We need to find that man."

Chapter Nine

"Where to next?" Chelsea asked when they were back in the car.

"I'm headed back to my office to see if I can track down Peter and Gina. I'm taking you home so you can get some rest."

"I don't need to rest." But something about saying the word set off a yawn.

"You do need to rest. You could have been killed, and I noticed that hitch in your step back at Lily's house. Your hip is hurting you."

"I'll be fine."

"Rest. Investigations take time. A lot of the work is waiting for something to break."

Frustration swelled in her chest. "My father has been in jail for seven years now. I don't want to waste any more time."

Travis glanced across the car at her. "I get it, I do. I'll call you if I get any news. Until then, there's nothing for you to do."

She didn't like it, but she wasn't willing to argue with him about it. Not when she had an idea about who might be able to help them. But she knew Travis would want to go with her, and in this case, she was sure she needed to make this visit alone.

He turned into her driveway moments later. Travis walked her to her door and waited on the porch until he heard the lock click into place. She watched as he backed out of her driveway and waited five minutes before she grabbed her purse and keys and headed back out.

She'd made the short drive from her place to her father's best friend's house hundreds of times over the years. Bill Rowland, or Uncle Bill as she'd called him since she was a little girl, was a second father to her...

She turned the radio to her favorite nineties pop station and willed the tension in her shoulders to let up.

A short time later, she pulled to a stop at the curb in front of a suburban brick ranch in Winnetka. The flower beds lining the front of the house were filled with neatly trimmed flowers and hedges, and the grass was freshly cut. A tall maple tree stood stoically in the yard, his green leaves waving in the slight breeze cooling the day. Uncle Bill had taken up gardening in his semiretirement with the same passion he'd had for his auto mechanic business.

She walked to the front door and rang the bell. Seconds later, the door swung open, and Uncle Bill stood before her.

Uncle Bill smiled, happy to see her as always. The joy on his face sent a pang of guilt through her for not visiting more often. Uncle Bill had never married or had children. He had a brother in Arizona, but for the most part he'd always been on his own. Chelsea and her father were his family. He had been there for her as much as Aunt Brenda had, even though the two hadn't always seen eye to eye. Brenda Harper was conservative, quiet, a rule follower at heart. And Uncle Bill...was not. Gregarious, outgoing, always up for a laugh, that was Uncle Bill. He'd kept the same boisterous personality into his retirement years.

"How's life treating you, kid?" he asked, grabbing her into a bear hug. He held her there for a moment before pulling back and searching her face. "Everything good?"

Uncle Bill was one of the most empathetic people she knew. Which was why he'd always known when she was feeling down or nervous or needed someone to talk to.

Chelsea nodded and forced a smile. "Yes, everything is fine."

"Are you teaching this summer?" he asked as he led her into the small living room where a glass of lemonade and a small plate of cookies rested on the coffee table in front of his lounger.

"Not this summer. I decided to take some time off."

"Good for you. Oh, let me get you a glass of lemonade. I got chocolate chip cookies from this new bakery near the grocery store. They aren't too bad," he said, turning for the kitchen.

"No, Uncle Bill, I'm not thirsty or hungry. I just need to talk to you."

He turned back to her. "Are you sure?"

She assured him that she didn't want any refreshments, and he reclaimed his glass of already poured lemonade before settling into his battered brown easy chair.

Despite an active lifestyle, he'd begun to develop a little pouch in his tummy. At fifty-four years old, Uncle Bill was fortunate to have worked hard, built a sound business and saved enough that he only went into work a couple of days a week now. The rest of the workweek he left to his shop manager and employees, most of whom had worked for him for years, to handle. Her father had been one of those employees before he was arrested and convicted of Lily's murder. Uncle Bill had never believed his best friend was a murderer and had even offered to pay to hire a better lawyer for her father. But Franklin's pride hadn't allowed him to accept what he considered charity. Not even from his best friend.

"So, what brings you to an old man's door today?"

"You are not an old man, and I'm sorry I don't visit more often."

Uncle Bill waved her comment away. "Ah, don't worry about it. You're young. You have a life to live. I get it. So, what brings you by today?" he repeated.

Chelsea sat on the edge of her uncle's brown leather sofa, considering how to ease into the conversation she needed to have. Deciding that there was no easy way to ask, she just plunged in. "I need to ask you something, and it might be a little upsetting."

Uncle Bill frowned. He placed his lemonade on the coffee table. "You're scaring me. Are you sick?"

"No, no, it's nothing like that."

"Is it your aunt?" Aunt Brenda and Uncle Bill didn't get along, but Chelsea knew he would do anything for her aunt because of her.

"No, she's fine, too. We're both fine." Chelsea took a deep breath. "I've hired a private investigator to help me prove Dad didn't kill Lily."

Uncle Bill looked at her, his face twisted with surprise. It took him a moment to speak. "What? Why?"

"Why? Because he's innocent. And I need your help proving it."

"Chelsea—"

"Could you just answer some of my questions, please?" she interjected before he could argue with her.

Uncle Bill sighed. "Sure, you know I'll tell you whatever you want to know."

"Well, during my investigation, I found out a couple

of things that I didn't know about Dad and Lily's relationship."

"Things like what?"

"Did Dad ever tell you that Lily was seeing someone else?"

Uncle Bill looked uncomfortable. "I don't know if I should be talking to you about your father and Lily's relationship."

"Uncle Bill, I'm not a child. This could be important."

"At the end there, when your dad and Lily were finally calling it quits, he might've suspected she was seeing someone else. But I don't think he had any real proof."

"I spoke to Dad. He said Lily told him she was seeing someone else."

Uncle Bill's eyes went wide, and he pushed himself up straighter in his chair. "Yes...yes, but your father said she wouldn't tell him who the other man was."

"That's right. She didn't tell anyone his name, and the prosecution wasn't able to figure out who he was."

Her uncle slumped back down in his chair. "Honey, you know how emotional breakups can be."

That she did. Her recent confrontation with Simon flashed through her head before she shook it away. This wasn't about her and Simon. It was about her father and Lily.

The police never even considered this new guy, but if Lily had been seeing him, the man could know something about her murder. Or be her murderer. "I know you were only friends with Lily through Dad, but did you suspect she was seeing someone? Do you have any idea who this person might be?"

Uncle Bill's gaze slid away from hers. "I don't know, honey. It was all a very long time ago."

It felt as if he was holding something back, but she didn't know how to get him to tell her what it was. Just like her father, Uncle Bill's first concern was always protecting her even when she didn't need protecting.

"Why are you digging into this now?" he asked. "I thought your father's conviction had been upheld on appeal?"

"It was. The only chance he has now is to prove his innocence. And that's what I'm going to do."

Uncle Bill sighed. "I'm sure your father wouldn't want you to spend your time like this."

"Like what?" She threw her hands up in frustration. "Getting an innocent man out of jail? I can't think of a better way to spend my time."

Uncle Bill scooted to the end of his chair and reached out to take her hands. "I'm just worried that this obsession isn't healthy for you."

"Uncle Bill, an injustice has been done." She knew she sounded like a zealot. Maybe she was, but was zealotry in the interest of justice so wrong?

Uncle Bill dropped her hands and looked away.

"What is it?" she asked.

He held his gaze on the picture window for a long moment before turning back to her. "Chelsea, your father has exhausted his appeals. Every court that has looked at his case has determined he is guilty."

"What are you saying?"

His sigh this time was heavier and laced with something she couldn't quite name. Regret, maybe. "Maybe we have to face a hard truth."

"A hard truth? You mean that my father killed Lily? It sounds like you have already faced this truth."

"I've offered to hire better attorneys for your father, several times. He's always refused."

"He's proud."

"Or he feels guilty. Maybe he feels like he deserves the punishment he's getting."

"He has always professed his innocence. And he has appealed his conviction."

Uncle Bill shook his head. "He pursued that appeal for you. Because you wanted him to."

A heavy silence fell over the room while Chelsea struggled against fury and a sense of betrayal. Uncle Bill was supposed to be her father's best friend. He stood by her father even when Aunt Brenda, his own sister, didn't believe in him. He'd known her father for longer than she'd been alive. If he didn't believe in her father's innocence, what chance did she have convincing anyone else? She couldn't remember ever feeling so alone.

"I need to go," she said, surging to her feet.

"Oh, Chelsea. Don't leave like this. I just don't want to see you get hurt."

"I've already been hurt. I have spent the last seven years without my dad. I've had to change my name in order to get the press to stop hounding me. My own aunt believes her brother is a murderer. Everyone has turned against Dad, but I won't. I know he loved Lily. He didn't kill her. And I'm going to prove it. To you. To everyone."

Chapter Ten

After dropping Chelsea at her house, Travis fought the Los Angeles traffic to the West Security and Investigations offices. He strode through the glass entrance and nearly ran into his boss.

"Just the man I was looking for," Kevin said with a smile.

"Really? You must have ESP."

"Well, I looked for you in your cubicle a moment ago. You weren't there, so I was headed out to grab a decent cup of coffee, but seeing as you're here now, it will just have to wait."

"You got something?" Travis asked, following Kevin across the polished tile floor to his office.

Kevin gave them a brief nod and kept walking. "How is Chelsea recovering from the hit-and-run?"

"Better than I'd be. She's still got some pain," Travis said, recalling the ibuprofen she'd swallowed with her coffee that morning, "but she's going to be fine. She's tough."

Kevin slid a sidelong glance at Travis, appraising him. "I have to agree. That was quite a tuck-and-roll she did to get out of the way of that car's path."

They stepped into Kevin's corner office. Light streamed in from the bay of windows. The office was decorated in a minimalist fashion that was simultaneously masculine with lots of dark wood and leather. Kevin's office was one of the largest on the floor, second only to Tess's. Dual sleek silver monitors sat on a desk. Kevin tapped on the keyboard, and the large flat screen mounted to the opposite wall glowed to life. A black-and-white image of the street a few yards from their office building appeared.

"We were able to get security footage from several of our neighbors," Kevin said. "You can take a look at all the tapes, seven in total that caught glimpses of the car that hit Chelsea. I've spliced them together to approximate the route the car took." He tapped the keyboard again, and the tape began. "There's the car. A late model sedan. It sits across the street there idling while Chelsea is inside our offices. It appears this guy followed her to her meeting with you."

The black Oldsmobile sat about twenty feet from the front of the West Investigations building. Waiting.

Travis hoped to see the outline of the driver, but he or she had the sunshade pulled down, covering the top of their face. The recording was too grainy and from too far of a distance to make out any distinguishing features on the driver.

He and Kevin watched as Chelsea walked out of the front of the building and started to cross the street. His body tensed, anticipating what was about to happen. The Oldsmobile pulled away from the curb as Chelsea stepped into the street and accelerated toward her. Travis's heart thundered, watching Chelsea turn toward the danger and freeze for a moment. Then she was in motion, running for the opposite sidewalk. The car swerved into her path. She leaped for the sidewalk as the right front side of the car clipped her hip. That leap had probably kept her from suffering far greater injuries. It may have even saved her life. Chelsea hit the pavement just short of the curb and rolled between two parked cars. The sedan sped off.

"Can you rewind the tape and slow it down? Focusing on the sedan's driver."

"I've pulled some still photos, but there hasn't been a good enough shot to get an identification," Kevin said while he rewound the video. He handed Travis the photos, but he was right. They were worthless.

They watched the video again at a slower pace, but the driver wore a baseball cap pulled low over his brow and sunglasses in addition to having used the sun visor to conceal his identity.

"Did any of the cameras get a shot of the license plates?"

Kevin shook his head. "There were none."

Travis's stomach sank. The lack of license plates along with the driver's efforts to shield his identity confirmed what he already suspected. The hit-and-run hadn't been an accident. Someone had specifically targeted Chelsea. The still unanswered question was, had the driver meant to kill her or was this just a warning to back off investigating her father's case?

Either way, it meant Chelsea was in danger. It was impossible to believe that the hit-and-run wasn't connected to Chelsea's efforts to prove her father's innocence. Had Lily's killer somehow found out about Chelsea's investigation into the murder and decided to put a stop to it? If so, how had the killer learned about the investigation? There were dozens of names in Chelsea's binder, and Chelsea had said she'd reached out to several of Lily's friends and family before coming to him for help. Any one of them might want her to drop her investigation, either because they believed Franklin Brooks was in jail where he belonged or because they wanted to protect themselves or someone else. But right now, the hit-and-run driver appeared to be a dead end.

"Have we had any luck tracking down Peter Schmeichel?"

Kevin shook his head. "Peter doesn't appear to have a fixed address. I pulled his criminal record. It's as long as my arm, mostly drug offenses. A couple of assaults and batteries." He handed Travis a sheaf of papers. He hadn't been kidding about Peter's criminal history. The guy was a career criminal.

"Humph." Travis wasn't buying it. "What about locating Gina?"

"I've had better luck with that." Kevin tapped his keyboard, and Travis's phone chimed with the incoming text. "That's her current work and home address. She moved to San Bernardino about a year after Lily's death."

"This is great, thanks." Travis noted the address was about an hour away from Los Angeles. He could have just called Gina, but interviews were always more fruitful face-to-face. Plus, he wasn't convinced Gina had told the police everything she knew about Lily's murder. But she would tell him.

"Can you also check if Lily ever filed a police report for vandalism or a burglary at her place?" He explained what Rachel had told him and Chelsea, as well as the information that Jace, the neighbor, had given them about a possible new boyfriend.

"I'll see what I can do, but it might take a bit of time

to search police reports from seven-plus years ago that may or may not exist."

Travis's phone rang. He looked at the screen and saw the call was from Chelsea.

"Hello?"

"Did you call my aunt?" Chelsea asked without preamble.

"What? No, why?"

"I went to my uncle Bill's house—he's my dad's best friend—to ask him what he remembers about Lily and my dad's relationship, and my aunt called me as I was leaving. Someone called her asking a bunch of questions about me."

"You were supposed to be home resting," he said, tamping down his anger that she'd gone out alone.

"You said I should rest. I never agreed to it. Anyway, my aunt is more important."

"What kind of questions did the caller ask?" Travis said.

"I don't know," she answered, her voice rising. "Aunt Brenda said a man called saying he was a friend, and he asked questions about me and Dad. Then he said that it could be dangerous for me to continue on my quest to get Dad out of prison."

"The caller threatened you?" Travis growled.

"Not in so many words. I'm headed to my aunt's house now to check in on her."

"Send me her address," he said, already moving toward Kevin's office door.

"If you need any backup, give me a shout," Kevin said as he left.

Travis nodded to let Kevin know he heard him and

kept moving. His phone dinged in his ear. He pulled it
away long enough to see that Chelsea had sent him her
aunt's address.

"I'm on my way. I'll meet you there in twenty minutes,"
he said, racing from the office.

Chapter Eleven

He ate his lunch. A turkey sandwich on wheat, light mustard, heavy on the mayonnaise with a diet Coke. He ate alone as usual. His coworkers barely acknowledged him. He bet if asked most wouldn't even know his name. Some might not even recognize him if pressed. He knew how to blend in. How to go unnoticed. How to be unseen even when people were looking directly at him. That gave him space. To remember. To think. To plan.

She hadn't backed off after the hit-and-run. Chelsea Harper was tough, a fighter. Part of him admired her for it. But the other part, the bigger part, hated it. Hated her for making him feel this way. For turning him into a ball of nerves. For making him sneak around, hiding in the shadows, jumping at every shape and sound.

This would not do.

She was going to cause trouble, he knew it. But he couldn't just get rid of her.

She was going to keep asking questions. Ask even more questions, better questions, now that she'd hired a private detective. Dammit to hell and back.

Why wouldn't she just give up investigating Lily's case? Everyone else had. The whole world was convinced that Franklin Brooks killed Lily Wong. They'd convicted him and thrown away the key. No one cared anymore. No one except Franklin Brooks's daughter.

She was bringing it all back to the forefront of everyone's mind. What if someone remembered seeing him? What if that drugged-out fool grew a conscience? Admitted he'd lied? What if Chelsea and her private investigator succeeded in getting the police and prosecutor to reopen Franklin's case?

He couldn't let that happen. Too bad just killing her wasn't an option. But that would surely attract more attention than he wanted. Franklin Brooks's daughter getting killed when she was pressing for his case to be reopened. Shouting from the rafters to anyone who would listen that her father was innocent. The cops wouldn't be able to just write it off as coincidence.

He wasn't sure what it would take to get her to back off, but he had to figure it out.

He had to stop her.

He'd made it this long without anyone suspecting him. He didn't intend to go to jail.

Chapter Twelve

Chelsea pulled into her aunt's driveway just as Travis pulled to a stop in front of the house. She didn't slow down to let him catch up with her as she headed to the front door. The door opened as she lifted her hand to knock.

"Aunt Brenda, are you okay?" Chelsea let her gaze roam over her aunt from head to toe.

Aunt Brenda was a willowy woman with dark brown hair that had gone mostly gray and keen hazel eyes. She'd had surgery on her knees two years earlier that had left her with a slight limp, but she kept in shape by swimming regularly at the local recreation center.

"Of course I'm okay. You don't think a little old phone call is going to do me in, do you?"

"Well, no," Chelsea said, "but you seemed upset."

"I was upset for you, not me." Aunt Brenda leaned to her right, looking around Chelsea. "Who's he?"

Chelsea glanced over her shoulder at Travis, who was standing several feet behind her. His eyes swept over the street before coming back to land on her and her aunt. "This is Travis Collins, the private investigator I hired to help me get Dad out of jail."

Her aunt's face twisted into a scowl. "Waste of time and money if you ask me."

She hadn't asked, and it was her money, Chelsea thought, but she bit back that retort.

"Ladies, might I suggest we take this discussion inside?" Travis nodded toward the interior of the house.

Her aunt's scowl deepened, but she stood aside and let Chelsea and Travis in. The door snapped closed behind them, and Aunt Brenda turned, crossing her arms over her chest. "Is he the friend who called me?"

"No," Chelsea said through gritted teeth. "We don't know who called you. That's what we are hoping to find out."

"Chelsea, you know I try to put your father and all that nastiness that came with his trial behind me. I don't want to dredge all that up. I would think that you'd feel the same way. Picking at this scab could ruin your life."

Chelsea took a deep breath. Her aunt looked so much like her father, especially when she was mad, it was hard to look at her and not see him. In some ways, it was comforting, like still having a piece of her father with her. In others, it made her yearn for all that she had lost. "Seeking the truth is not going to ruin my life."

Aunt Brenda threw her hands up in the air and stomped past Chelsea and Travis into the kitchen. "Well, I want no part of it. Tell your friend never to call me again."

"Aunt Brenda, you aren't listening. I didn't tell anyone to call you."

"I don't understand you." Aunt Brenda looked around the kitchen as if understanding might be hiding on top of a cabinet or behind the toaster. "Why can't you just go on with your life? Forget about your father. Find a nice guy to settle down with and have a family of your own."

"I have a family. You, Victor, Uncle Bill and Dad." Chelsea emphasized her last word.

Her aunt let out a sigh of frustration, but her eyes were tinged with fear. "If you dredge this up again, people may realize who you are. Who your father is. What will they think of you?"

"I don't care what people think about me."

"That's obvious," her aunt shot back.

This was an argument they'd had dozens of times before, and neither was going to give in to the other. It wasn't why Chelsea had come to her aunt's house, either, so it was best to move on.

"On the phone, you said that the person who called was a man. Did he give you a name?" Chelsea asked.

Aunt Brenda shook her head, her expression contemplative. "I don't think so. He just said he was a friend of yours."

"Did the call come in on your home phone or your cell phone?" Travis asked.

Aunt Brenda nodded to the black handset and cradle on the kitchen counter. "Home. I hardly bother with that cell. Only a few people even have the number."

"Do you mind if I take a look at the incoming call log?" Travis asked.

"Knock yourself out."

"How long ago did you get the call?" Travis reached for the handset and pressed a button.

"Maybe an hour ago." Aunt Brenda glanced at the clock on the microwave. "I called Chelsea right after."

"Can you remember anything else about the call?" Chelsea asked, pulling her attention back to her. "Background noises? Did the man have an accent? Anything you remember could help us identify him."

"I don't know, Chels. It was a regular call." Her aunt

grabbed a dishrag from the sink and wiped haphazardly at the counter.

Chelsea knew her aunt cleaned when she was worried. She felt a moment's guilt for being the cause of that worry, but not enough to stop investigating.

"He said he was a friend of yours and that he knew we were investigating your father's case," Aunt Brenda continued. "He was concerned that you were in over your head. Those were his exact words, in over your head and that you could get hurt." Aunt Brenda scrubbed at a mark that had been on the counter for as long as Chelsea could remember.

She reached out and covered her aunt's hand with her own, stilling it.

Aunt Brenda's gaze met hers. "I asked what he meant by saying you could get hurt, but he just hung up."

Chelsea pulled her aunt into a hug. "I'm not going to get hurt."

"The number the call came in from was blocked," Travis said, replacing the phone on its cradle.

Chelsea pulled back from the embrace with her aunt but kept one arm around the older woman. "Now what?"

"Now you stop this madness." Her aunt shrugged out from under Chelsea's arm. "I've already lost a brother and a husband. I won't lose you, too."

"You won't lose me," Chelsea said.

"No?" her aunt spat angrily. "You think I don't know what's going on here? That call was a warning. A threat."

Another stab of guilt cut through Chelsea. She hadn't told her aunt about the hit-and-run earlier because she didn't want to worry her. But now didn't seem like a good time to tell her, either.

"I'm sorry, Aunt Brenda, but I have to do this. I'll be

careful, and I have Travis to help me. He's a former cop and a private investigator. We've already turned up some good leads that the police didn't follow up on seven years ago. I'll be careful, I promise."

Her aunt shook her head, a single tear falling over the crest of her cheek. "I can't talk you out of this, but I won't be a part of it." She turned and rushed from the room. A moment later the sound of a bedroom door slamming carried into the kitchen.

Chelsea let out a heavy sigh.

"She loves you," Travis said, coming to stand next to Chelsea.

"I know."

His voice lowered. "She's not wrong about the potential danger."

Chelsea studied him. "Did you learn something at West's offices this afternoon?"

"We probably shouldn't talk about it here." Travis had a look down the hallway where her aunt had disappeared.

"Come on. I haven't eaten since breakfast, and I'm starved," Chelsea said. "You can tell me the bad news over food."

"Do you have any particular place in mind?"

Chelsea flashed a weary smile. "My favorite place isn't too far. Follow me."

Chapter Thirteen

"Eight fish tacos coming up." The teen behind the food truck window shot a toothy grin at Chelsea as she passed him the cash for the food. He made change and handed it back to her.

"This is your favorite place to eat?" Travis asked when they stepped back to wait for their food.

"One of them, yes." She held up a finger. "It's afford-able. The tacos are the best on the West Coast." She held up a second finger. "And the views can't be beat." She spread out a hand to encompass the waves lapping against the sands of El Segundo Beach. Tucked under her other arm was the blanket she kept in the trunk of her car.

The views were spectacular, which was why this was one of her favorite places on earth, even with the crush of people mobbing the shoreline along the water.

"Eight fish tacos," the teen called out.

Chelsea grinned up at Travis. "And the service is quick," she added, walking back to the food truck to grab their order. She handed the bag of food and two canned iced teas to Travis.

At the edge of the beach, they shucked their shoes, and Chelsea carried them and the blanket down the beach until they found a spot that was not as crowded. She spread the blanket out over the flat sand, and they sat down.

"Do you do this often?" Travis asked. "Dine on the beach?"

Chelsea handed him two tacos. "I spent a lot of time here with my dad when I was growing up. It's not too far from Aunt Brenda's place, and it's cheap, so it fit right into our budget."

Travis unwrapped one of the tacos and ate half of it in one bite. "It must have been nice to have a beach so close to home."

"It was great. I take it you didn't grow up in Los Angeles."

Travis shook his head. "I grew up in the Midwest." He didn't give her any more information, instead stuffing the remaining portion of the taco in his mouth.

"I like to come here and think. After my dad was arrested, it was one of the only places I could go for a while where people didn't recognize me. I could blend into the crowd of beachgoers."

"It must have been hard for you after your father was arrested."

"It's like everyone—not just the cops, but my friends, my aunt—everyone believed that my dad did it. And because I didn't, I became one of the bad guys, too."

"I'm sorry."

Chelsea took a bite of taco, chewed and swallowed. "Victor was really the only person to stand by me. I mean, I know he thinks my dad is where he belongs, but he doesn't treat me any differently than he did before." She brought the iced tea to her lips.

"Victor?"

"My cousin. More like my brother. He's my aunt Brenda and uncle Darren's only child. We grew up together."

"Is he in one of the photos on your dresser?"

Chelsea made a face. "My dresser?"

"I noticed the photos that you have on top when I went to the bathroom at your place yesterday. I didn't go into your room," he added quickly. "I promise."

"Oh, yeah, that's Victor."

"Your cousin." Something passed over Travis's face.

"Yes. My cousin. Why?"

"Nothing. I just thought he might be a boyfriend."

She laughed. "You met Simon, so you know my track record with men isn't good. I haven't even had a date in, I don't remember how long."

He wiped his hands on a napkin, but not before Chelsea saw a satisfied smile on his face. Wait… He'd thought Victor was her boyfriend, and now that he knew he wasn't, was he happy she was single? Maybe he'd even been a little jealous. The idea of it made her insides do a happy dance before she reminded herself they could only have a business relationship.

Travis cleared his throat. "Listen, I wanted to tell you what the team at West has been able to turn up." Whatever he might have been thinking or feeling, it was gone, replaced by his usual professionalism.

She sighed internally, wiped her own hands on a napkin and set her iced tea to the side. "Great. Shoot."

"We got video of the hit-and-run from the businesses surrounding the office. This was no accident, Chelsea. The driver followed you to the office and waited for you to come out. He never swerved. In fact, he aimed for you."

Travis's words stole her breath. She'd suspected the hit-and-run wasn't an accident, but to have it confirmed was to face the fact that someone out there wanted to hurt her. Badly.

Travis put a hand on her arm. "Are you okay?"

Chelsea nodded slowly. "Yeah, just processing."

"We weren't able to get a good look at the driver's face or the tags on the car, but we know to watch out for a black sedan now."

"Okay," Chelsea said on a long breath.

"And this might be a good time to mention how bad an idea it was to sneak off to speak with your uncle earlier—"

Chelsea scowled. "I didn't sneak anywhere. I'm a grown woman. I can go where I please."

He held up his hands. "*Sneak* was the wrong word. But that hit-and-run was intentional. You need to be careful. At least let me know your plans so I can have your back even if I disagree with them."

She felt her ire dissipate. "Okay. I'll keep you in the loop from now on."

"Great. Now, can I ask what you and your uncle discussed?"

She filled him in on the conversation with her uncle. "Unfortunately, he didn't remember anything that could help us."

"Well, I do have some good news. We got an address for Gina. She's living in San Bernardino now."

"That's great. Are you going to give her a call or—"

"I was thinking we could take a trip up there and talk to her in person."

"Even better. Let's go," Chelsea said, starting to push to her feet.

Travis laid a hand on her arm again, keeping her on the blanket. "Slow down. I have to get some things in order first. Gina is working as a nurse at a local hospital. I don't want to have to ambush her at her job, so I need to try to get her schedule to see if we can catch her at home."

Frustration bubbled in Chelsea's chest, but she'd hired Travis for his help so she needed to take it. "Whatever you think is the best plan, I'm on board. When do you want to go?"

"I'm thinking about tomorrow afternoon."

Chelsea collected their trash and stuffed it into the taco bag. This time when she stood, Travis stood with her. Her feet sank into the sand and combined with her excitement and haste, she lost her footing.

Travis grabbed her, his hands winding around her waist, steadying her against his hard body. She angled her head to look up at him and saw desire in his eyes. The same desire that she felt.

Travis sucked in a breath that made her knees go weak again. He bought his mouth down, nearly touching hers. They stood there a moment, hovering at the edge of an invisible line.

A shriek ripped through the air a moment before a young girl came tearing down the sand.

Travis's arms dropped from her waist, and he took three large steps back. "I should get you home." He turned away, bending down to collect the blanket and their shoes.

Chelsea let out the breath she'd been holding. The young girl's parents ambled by, their arms loaded down with stuff, completely oblivious to the moment they'd interrupted.

But it was good that they'd been interrupted. She and Travis were obviously attracted to each other, but crossing the line could have repercussions neither of them needed at the moment. But now she just had to figure out a way to forget how she felt in his arms.

THAT WAS A near miss, Travis thought as he followed Chelsea to make sure she got home without incident. He'd almost kissed her. The way she'd melted against him had almost made him forget that she was a client. And that he didn't do relationships. He also knew Chelsea wasn't the kind of woman who did casual relationships. Luckily, that screaming kid had come along and brought him back to his senses. As soon as he was sure Chelsea was safe and sound inside her house, he'd head home and take a long cold shower and pretend nothing had happened.

He pulled into Chelsea's driveway behind her car and got out.

"I'm fine, Travis. You don't have to see me to my door."

He stopped next to her. "I do, actually. I promised your dad I'd watch out for you, and I mean to keep that promise."

"Fine," she huffed, turning and marching to her porch. She opened her front door and froze.

Travis immediately grabbed her and moved her behind him so he was between her and the interior of the house. It looked like a cyclone had blown through her living room. Bloodred paint splattered the soft gray walls and just about everything else in the living room. A single word—*Stop*—had been written across one wall, red paint dripping down from each letter like a horror movie.

"Stay here," he ordered before entering the house. He swept through the living room, dining room and kitchen as well as the bedrooms. They'd all been trashed, but only the living room had been splattered with paint.

He returned to the doorway to find that Chelsea had ignored his admonishment to stay outside. She reached for the wall.

"Don't touch anything," he began, but her fingertips were already covered in paint.

"He did this. The man who called my aunt and tried to run me over," she said, sounding as if she was in a daze. He recognized that she was in shock. "The man who killed Lily."

Travis strode over to her, tilting her chin until she was looking at him, really looking at him. "We're going to get this guy. I promise you." He took her into his arms, not caring if it was professional or not. Her home had been invaded and violated, and she needed comfort. Hell, he could use a little comfort himself. When he first stepped up to the door and saw all that red, he'd thought...

Of course, that was what this psycho wanted. To scare Chelsea. Scare her enough that she'd back off. Her home looked like the site of a grisly murder.

"Let's go outside, and I'll call the police." He led her back to his car and got her safely inside before bypassing 911 and punching a familiar number into his cell. Less than ten minutes later, a gold sedan screeched to a stop behind his car.

Travis stretched out his hand toward the man who approached. Detective Gabe Owens was the only person from his police days that he kept in touch with, and only sparingly. Owens had joined the LAPD a couple of years after Travis and had still been in uniform when Travis left the force. That was probably the only reason Owens hadn't shunned him like the rest of his former colleagues. He'd still been idealistic enough to believe that Travis had done the right thing.

But it had been over a year since he and Owens had last grabbed a drink together. Gabe had aged, as they all had. The flaming red hair Travis remembered was more orange now, at least the part that hadn't completely turned gray. But more than anything it was Owens's eyes that had changed. He had the eyes now of a man who had seen too much.

"Hey, thanks for getting here so quickly," Travis said.

"No problem. I wasn't far. So, you said someone vandalized your friend's home."

"My client," he responded automatically, then remembering their near kiss, he added, "and friend kind of."

Owens shot him a knowing look. "Okay, tell me about this client/friend kind of."

Travis shoved off the embarrassing description of Chelsea and gave Owens a quick rundown of the investigation, the recent threats against her life and now her coming home to a paint-splattered mess.

"You always did like the complicated ones," Owens said.

Travis wasn't sure whether Owens was referring to cases or women. He wasn't sure he wanted to know.

Owens insisted on clearing the house himself. Travis and Chelsea waited on the front step until he returned.

"It doesn't look like anything was stolen, but would you come inside and have a look?" Owens asked Chelsea.

Travis and Chelsea followed Owens back into the house. The way the place had been trashed, but it didn't seem like the perp had been looking for anything in particular. He'd just been bent on destruction. The televisions in the living room and Chelsea's bedroom had been smashed as had most of her china and several lamps. Her clothes were thrown around her bedroom, some clearly destroyed, and nearly every cabinet and drawer had been pulled out and their contents dumped. The papers Chelsea had collected in her investigation had been torn to shreds and littered the dining room floor.

"Where's your binder, Chelsea?" Travis asked.

"My binder—" Chelsea looked at him for a moment, confused, until understanding took over. "Oh, thankfully I had one in my car with me, but I think I left the second one on the dining room table."

Travis followed her around the house, an arm that he hoped was comforting around her shoulders. Finally, they returned to where Owens stood, making notes for the incident report, in the living room.

"It's hard to tell for sure," Chelsea said, "but I don't think anything is missing, just destroyed." She pointed to the dining room where the files she'd compiled on her father's case had been ripped and torn to shreds.

"Do you have any idea who could have done this? An ex-boyfriend?" Owens glanced at Travis. "A current boyfriend?"

Travis caught the look Chelsea shot at him before she answered, "Not exactly."

Owens's bushy brows rose. "What does that mean, exactly?"

"My ex-husband paid me an unexpected visit the other day, but I don't think he would do something like this."

Travis had taken an instant dislike to the man, but he had to agree with Chelsea. Whoever had done this had exhibited a lot of uncontrolled rage. Simon seemed like the type of guy who wouldn't have wanted to muss his hair. But looks could be deceiving, so he was glad Owens insisted on taking Simon's information down. Travis would also be checking into Simon more closely, something he should have thought of earlier.

"Can you think of anyone else who may be angry with you?" Owens asked Chelsea.

Chelsea shot Travis a look that seemed to say *where do I start?*

Travis stepped in, adding more detail to the brief explanation he'd given Owens outside. He explained Chelsea's theory that her father was innocent of the murder he was in jail for and that they were revisiting the case.

"And you think whoever did those things did this?" Owens summarized.

"Who else?" Chelsea responded sharply.

"I'm just trying to understand, Ms. Harper."

"I think it's the obvious answer, Owens," Travis seconded.

"And you think that person also really killed Lily Wong?" Owens asked.

"Yes," Chelsea answered definitively.

At the same time Travis said, "We don't know."

Chelsea shot him a look that would have turned him to dust if it could have.

Travis knew she thought her father's innocence was an absolute certainty, but he still had questions. Someone clearly wanted her to stop investigating, but that didn't mean that person was Lily Wong's true killer. It was just as possible that someone didn't appreciate Chelsea making waves.

Owens gave them both a long look. "Well, we don't usually dust for prints when nothing has been taken, but as a courtesy to you, Trav, I can have the boys come out. It may take them several hours to get here, though."

"Thanks," Travis responded. "I appreciate it."

"I'll write up the incident report. You need it to file a claim with your insurance company for the damages and replace your things."

"Thanks," Chelsea responded.

"Do you have a place to stay until the lock gets fixed?" Owens asked.

"She will be fine," Travis interjected before Chelsea spoke. "I'll take care of it."

Chelsea shot him a second disgruntled look.

"Here's my card." Owens handed a card to Chelsea. "I'll have the report ready for you in a couple days. You can call me directly if you have any more trouble."

"Thank you," Chelsea repeated, this time in a voice so small it tore through Travis. She didn't deserve this. To have her home violated in this way.

Owens started for the door, and Travis followed him outside. "Owens, look, I know I'm not a favorite citizen of the LAPD—"

Owens held up a meaty hand. "Look, man, you did what you felt was right. I respect that."

Travis was surprised. It had been some time since he'd spoken to a former colleague. At best he'd been treated like a pariah after he turned several of his colleagues into internal affairs for evidence tampering. At worst, he'd fielded threats that had him sleeping with his gun by his side. No one had ever indicated they believed he'd done the right thing by turning his colleagues in. "Thanks."

He said goodbye and went back inside the house.

"You can't stay here tonight," he said as Chelsea picked up the shattered remnants of a photograph of her and her aunt.

"Where else am I going to go?"

"You can get a hotel room."

She let out a strangled laugh. "You're kidding. I live on a teacher's salary. I can barely afford my mortgage and I've had to cut back in order to pay West's fee, and I can't leave with the lock smashed in like that."

"I can fix the lock, temporarily at least. But it's too dangerous for you to be here. Whoever is doing this is currently escalating. You shouldn't go anywhere alone until we find this guy and put him behind bars." He hesitated for a moment, considering the idea he'd been tossing around in his head. "You could stay with me. I have a spare room."

Chelsea studied him. "What did you mean when you said you didn't know if the person who did this is the person who killed Lily? You can't possibly believe all this—" she spread her arms out encompassing the destruction in the house "—isn't related to her death."

"It's definitely related, but we have no proof that the person who is doing this is Lily's killer."

"You still think my dad did it, don't you?"

"I haven't made any conclusions yet."

Chelsea stared at him for another long moment before turning and starting down the hall toward her bedroom.

"Chelsea, you might be angry with me now, but your safety—"

"I'm not stupid or foolhardy, Travis. I'll take you up on your offer of your spare bedroom."

He breathed out a sigh of relief.

"I'm going to see if I have enough undamaged clothes to pack a bag," she said, still not looking at him. "You should be able to find something to keep the door closed until I can get a locksmith here."

He watched her disappear into her bedroom, all the while something tugged at his insides. He was losing the battle to ignore his growing feelings for Chelsea. And even scarier, he was realizing that he wasn't sure it was a battle he really wanted to fight.

Chapter Fourteen

The next morning, Chelsea blinked her eyes open, her heart racing as she took in the unfamiliar room, then settled when she remembered where she was. In Travis's guestroom. In Travis's apartment. Because her home was not safe. Although the temperature in the room was a tad on the warm side, a chill went through her.

Travis had shored up her front door enough that it would hold for a night as long as the vandal didn't return to inflict more damage. She glanced at the clock on the nightstand—8:00 a.m. She'd slept later than usual.

She supposed she shouldn't be surprised. The day before had been long and trying, and she'd spent an hour after Travis got her settled in the guest room searching Lily's dormant social media pages for any hint of her mystery boyfriend, to no avail. It was enough to make her contemplate pulling the covers up over her head and hiding. One day in bed, a very comfortable one at that, was that too much to ask? But she had too much to do to hide out, no matter how much she wanted to or how enticing the mattress was.

She took a quick shower, then gathered her hair into a bun. Efficiency was going to have to trump fashion until she was back in her own place with all of her own things.

She slipped on a pair of black slacks, a burgundy knit top and black ankle boots. As she stepped out of the guest room, she smelled coffee and sautéed onions.

She found Travis in front of the stove making omelets. His back was to her. He wore a pair of gray sweatpants that clung to well-shaped buttocks. A black T-shirt stretched over the muscles of his arms and back. She allowed herself a moment to take him in completely before reminding herself that romance wasn't in the cards for them, no matter how delectable the man whose house she was now sharing. She gave herself a shake and entered the kitchen.

"Good morning," she said as she walked over to the coffee pot.

"Good morning," Travis responded without turning. "The omelets are almost done."

Chelsea poured herself a cup, adding cream and sugar, which Travis had already placed next to the carafe. She turned to find him staring at her. "Is everything okay?"

Travis blinked and turned back to the omelets. "Yeah, these are done. Have a seat."

Chelsea sat at the kitchen table, contemplating the look she'd seen on Travis's face. It was almost as if the sight of her had stunned him speechless. But that couldn't be, could it? He had been the one to pull away from her the day before at the beach. She was sure he'd been about to kiss her, and she would have let him. Heck, she wanted him to kiss her. As much as she'd tried to keep things professional between them, there was undeniably an attraction there.

Travis slid an omelet onto the plate in front of her.

"This looks great," she said as he slid a second omelet onto the plate across from hers.

He put the pan back on the stove and took his seat. "Thanks," he said. "I'm not much for cooking, but as I said, I can handle breakfast and a few simple meals."

She took a bite. "This *is* great. You can be in charge of breakfast every morning as far as I'm concerned." Heat rose in her cheeks as she realized what she'd implied. That they would be having breakfast together every morning. Hopefully, she'd be able to get a locksmith to her house today, and this would be the only time they had breakfast together. The thought made her sad.

They ate in silence for a few minutes. Finally, Travis spoke up. "I got Gina's schedule at the hospital. She works the 9:00 p.m. to 9:00 a.m. shift. I thought we could drive out to speak with her after we get your door fixed."

"That's great, but I haven't even contacted a locksmith yet."

"I hope you don't mind," he said. "I contacted the locksmith that West Investigations keeps on retainer. He'll meet us at your place whenever you're ready."

"That's great. Thank you. Could you arrange for him to come by this morning? Detective Owens left me a voicemail while I was in the shower to say he'd finished dusting my house for fingerprints, so I can get out of your hair today."

"You're welcome. And you're not in my hair. Actually, I wanted to talk to you about staying here for a few more days."

"Staying here?"

"We could stay at your place, but I do think you'd be safer here. For one thing, I have a security system, and you don't."

"Wait. Slow down. Why would I need to stay here or you stay with me if I change the locks?"

"Even with your locks changed, you'll still be in danger. I don't think it's safe for you to be at your place. Or alone generally."

"I can't hide."

"I know. And I'm not asking you to. Staying with me or me staying with you at your place would be a deterrent to whoever has been targeting you. They know someone has your back."

"You?"

"Me."

Warmth spread through her. "It still feels like hiding. I don't like the idea of being run out of my own home."

"I can understand that, but think of it more as taking precautions. Not running or hiding."

She raised her coffee mug to her lips, thinking. There was some validity to what Travis said. If someone broke into her home again, having Travis there would certainly be better than being alone. And she had to admit, as much as she wanted to go home, she was still a little afraid. A couple more days in Travis's bed wouldn't be a hardship. *In Travis's guest bed*, she mentally amended. Alone. Her cheeks heated again, and she fought the urge to fan herself.

"Okay. Um, I'll stay here."

He smiled. "Great."

"Great." She brought the coffee mug to her lips again.

"I'd like to take you out to dinner tonight."

Chelsea spat coffee onto what was left of her omelet. Travis rounded the table but paused when she held out her hand to stop him. She was embarrassed enough. She didn't need him patting her back like a father trying to burp an infant. She caught her breath enough to sputter, "Dinner?"

"Yes. I would like to take you to dinner." He handed her a napkin.

She wiped at the coffee dripping down her chin. "Why?"

"Because you've made dinner and showed me where I can get the best fish tacos on the West Coast. I'd like to do something nice for you. And you mentioned it had been a while since you went out for a nice meal."

Oh, so that was it. He felt sorry for her. "You don't have to do that."

One of his shoulders rose in a shrug. "I know I don't have to. I want to." He picked up his plate and carried it to the sink before turning back to her. "It's just dinner. We have to eat, and it's not fair for you to do all the heavy lifting. I can't cook dinner, but I'm a champ at paying for it," he joked.

That got a smile from her. Why not? He was right. It was just dinner. Dinner with a colleague, kind of. They were working together, after all. *And living together for the moment*, a little voice chimed in. She ignored it. "Okay. Yes. I'd like to go to dinner with you."

Travis's shoulders relaxed. "Tonight then. Meet you in the living room at 8:00 p.m."

A tingling sensation ignited her body. It had been a long time since she'd been on a date. Even if it was just a friendly dinner date. After she cleared her father and got him out of prison, she would get a life. Aunt Brenda was right about how Chelsea should find someone to settle down with and start a family. Someone better for her than Simon ever was.

Her gaze went to Travis, who was still looking at her in a way that made her pulse pound. Places inside her that had long been dormant awakened.

Whoa, girl. She didn't need to ask to know he wasn't the settling-down type, but her body didn't seem to have gotten that message. Luckily, her brain was still in control. She wanted a real connection with someone, not just a roll in the sack. Not that rolling around with Travis wouldn't be fun. She was pretty sure he would be extraordinary in bed. But the moment would be fleeting. She didn't need the additional emotional drama that playing with a man like him was sure to cause.

No. Friends were all she and Travis could ever be. And she'd keep saying that for as long as it took her to believe it.

Chapter Fifteen

Travis helped her straighten up her house as much as they could while the locksmith fixed her door. Dealing with the paint-splattered walls would take more effort and lots of primer, but she was glad Travis had offered to help. Even though she'd agreed to stay with him for a few days, she felt an urgency to erase the vandal's presence from her home.

The locksmith was not only good at his job, he was also fast. It took him less than an hour to change the locks and add a dead bolt at Travis's request. She had to admit the dead bolt did make her feel safer. She hoped the hesitance she felt being in her own home would pass quickly.

After she paid the locksmith, they headed to Gina's address.

Gina worked the nine-to-nine overnight shift, and when they pulled into her street a little after eleven o'clock, they saw a woman in blue scrubs matching her general description just getting out of a car parked in the driveway.

Chelsea and Travis headed up the concrete walkway to the front porch.

Gina turned toward them, a mask of distrust on her face.

"Gina McGrath," Chelsea said when they reached her, giving her a smile.

Gina's gaze cut to Travis, then back to Chelsea. "Who's asking?"

"My name is Chelsea Harper. This is Travis Collins. We are investigators."

"Investigators? What do you want with me?" Gina was dressed in scrubs, but even with their loose fit, Chelsea could see the woman was painfully thin. Gina's eyes were sunken, and her muddy brown hair was short and straight. Her lips were covered in bright red lipstick. She looked older than her forty-something years.

"We're looking into Lily Wong's murder. We understand you used to be her neighbor."

The frown on Gina's face hardened. "That was a long time ago. I told the police everything I know. I don't have anything more to say."

"We aren't with the police," Travis said. "We're conducting a separate investigation."

"Evidence has come to light suggesting Franklin Brooks may not have committed the murder," Chelsea added.

The comment clearly surprised Gina. She let the bag of groceries slide through her hands. Two apples rolled in opposite directions across the porch floor.

Travis went after them and handed the apples back to Gina.

"Thank you," she said, placing them in the bag again.

"If we can just speak to you for a moment," Travis said, trying again. "Please, it could help free an innocent man."

Gina hesitated for a long moment. "Come on in." She stepped back, allowing Chelsea and Travis to walk into the house, then closed the door and headed to the kitchen. She set the groceries on the counter and took a carton of milk from the bag. She put it in the fridge, then turned to face them, wariness in her eyes. "What kind of questions do you want to ask me?"

"We want to know about the night Lily died."

She reached into the grocery bag and pulled out a loaf of bread, not looking at either Travis or Chelsea. "Like I said, I already told the police everything I knew."

"We understand that, but sometimes things come back to us later. Details that we don't remember right away," Travis said.

Gina sighed. "I don't think I'll ever forget anything about that night. You don't forget the details of the day your neighbor was murdered."

"Can you tell us about it?" Travis asked.

Gina sighed a second time. "I got home from work late. Peter was there. I'd stupidly given him a key, which he took as an invitation to essentially move in. The house was a mess. I remember garbage day was the next day, and Peter hadn't taken the trash out. We argued about it, and I eventually ended up taking it out. That's when I saw Lily and Frank. They were on her front stoop talking."

"On the front stoop. Not in the house?" Chelsea said.

"On the stoop. They weren't arguing or anything, at least not that I could hear, but it kind of looked like Lily didn't want to let him in the house." She shrugged. "That's the vibe I got anyway."

"Why did you get this vibe?" Travis asked.

"I don't know. It was the way she was standing. Like right in front of it like she was blocking it so he couldn't come inside. Like with her arms crossed."

Gina looked at Chelsea for understanding. She got it. Arms crossed, defenses up, the universal signal among women that they weren't interested in whatever the man in front of them was saying at the moment.

"Like I said, it was just a feeling I got."

"So, you definitely didn't see Frank go into the house," Chelsea pressed.

Gina shook her head. "I can't say for sure they didn't go inside, but I didn't see them go inside."

"And Peter didn't go outside with you? You're sure about that."

"I'm sure."

Chelsea cut a glance at Travis. That confirmed the contradiction of Peter's statement at trial and at least suggested that the writer of the note was telling the truth. "In his testimony at trial, Peter said he took out the trash that night. That's when he supposedly saw Frank and Lily arguing and Frank follow Lily into the house," Travis said.

Gina reached into the grocery bag, avoiding their gazes again. She turned her back on them, putting canned peaches into an overhead cabinet.

"Gina, was Peter in the house or not?" Travis asked softly.

"He never left the sofa that night. I'm not a liar." Her back stayed to them.

"But Peter is?"

Gina turned and looked at them. "Peter had problems back then."

"He was arrested for possession about a week after Lily's murder. Carrying enough drugs to have been charged with a felony," Travis said. "It would have been his third strike, which meant he was in danger of serving serious time behind bars."

Gina didn't respond.

"So maybe Peter saw an opportunity," Chelsea picked up the narrative. "Tell the cops what they want to hear about Frank and Lily, and they'd look the other way regarding his charges."

"I don't know anything about that," Gina said, still avoiding looking directly at them.

"But you suspect," Travis pressed her.

Gina flattened her lips into a thin line but stayed quiet.

Chelsea moved across the kitchen and stood directly in front of the woman. "Gina, I'm not just doing this to right a wrong. Franklin Brooks is my father. He has spent the last seven years of his life in jail separated from his family who loves him because of a lie."

Gina sighed and finally looked Chelsea in the eye. "I don't know anything for a fact, but I told the cops the truth. I didn't know about what Peter told them until later. They believed him over me, and the cop seemed pretty sure that Franklin killed Lily so—"

"So, you just left it," Chelsea said, unable to curtail the hint of anger in her tone.

"What was I supposed to do?" Gina challenged. "The cops had their killer."

"Let's stay focused on the night Lily died, okay?" Travis interjected. "Did you see Franklin leave Lily's house that night?" he asked Gina.

"No," she responded.

"Did you notice anything or hear anything at all unusual after you saw Lily and Franklin?"

Gina scrunched her face as if she was thinking. After a beat, she responded, "Unusual, no. I put the trash out by the curb, waved at Lily and she waved back."

"Wait a minute." Travis said. "Did you see Jace Orson? He said he was out with friends the night Lily was killed."

Gina laughed. "Jace? Out? With friends? No way. If

he wasn't at work, he was at home, and I'm pretty sure he didn't have any friends."

"That's what he told us," Travis said.

"Well, then he lied. He was definitely home and I saw him."

There was no mention of Gina having seen Jace in her statement.

"Did you tell the cops about seeing Jace that night?" Travis asked.

"I don't know. I don't think so. They were mostly focused on the argument I had seen between Lily and Franklin."

"Do you have any idea where we can find Peter now?" Chelsea asked.

"Last I heard he'd moved to Monterey, but that was eons ago. I haven't seen or heard from him in years. And good riddance."

They thanked Gina and headed back to the car.

"We need to find Peter and talk to Jace Orson again," Chelsea said as they fastened their seat belts.

Travis flashed her a grim smile. "You read my mind."

Chapter Sixteen

Chelsea Harper just would not back down. He'd watched her house. Seen the locksmith come to fix the door. Watched through the windows as she and the private investigator cleaned up inside. He had a clear view into the house now since he'd slashed the curtains and pulled them from the wall.

It looked like they were pretty cozy with each other. Downright domestic. Maybe the obvious attraction between the two would distract Chelsea from her investigation.

He didn't hold out much hope for that, but women were fickle. Lily had proven that, hadn't she? She'd left Franklin, and then—just when he'd been about to make his move, to show her the right man for her was right in front of her—she took up with that other guy. The memory of seeing her with the new guy sat like a stone in his gut. It still made him want to scream at times.

The memories of Lily both comforted and tormented him. He hadn't meant to kill her. He'd wanted her. He'd loved her. He still did. His stomach churned. Things had just gotten out of control. *He'd* gotten out of control. He had only been trying to make her understand. Understand that they were meant to be together. But it had all gone so wrong.

He'd hoped that Chelsea could be easily scared off her investigation. But when he'd seen her dining room, her research, everything she'd collected on her father's case, he'd known that would never happen. And then they'd gone and tracked down Gina.

This had the potential to be bad. Really bad. Chelsea would keep digging until she found the truth. Until she found him.

He knew what it would take to get her to stop now. But it was dangerous, too dangerous. He shouldn't even be thinking about it, but he was. He had always hoped it wouldn't come to this, but he'd also known that if it did, he'd do what needed to be done.

It seemed like the time had come.

His rage boiled, stoked by once again being forced to do something he didn't want to do. Forced to lose control.

He needed to get out of here before he did something stupid. He'd do what he had to do, but he needed to think. To plan. Whatever he did, it couldn't come back on him. He didn't want the authorities to even think of his name in relation to Chelsea Harper's.

He started the engine and pressed the accelerator. He needed to think. He had to figure out how to stop Chelsea and the private investigator before they ruined everything.

Chapter Seventeen

Jace Orson didn't answer the door at his house when Chelsea and Travis dropped by. Travis had used West's resources to dig up a phone number for him, but Jace hadn't answered his call, either. That, and Gina's surety that Jace had been home the night of Lily's murder, was enough to make Chelsea want to track him down and force the truth out of him immediately.

But Travis pointed out that they had no power to force anything out of anyone. They weren't the police. And Jace not being at home didn't really mean anything anyway. Travis had confronted this kind of thing many times when he'd been on the police force: a witness or neighbor just hadn't wanted to get involved with a police investigation, so they claimed not to have been home or seen anything. It wasn't uncommon, unfortunately.

Travis left a message for Jace, asking him to call, and then suggested to Chelsea that their best course of action would be to give Jace a little time to get back to them. Keeping things cordial went a long way toward getting people to help when you were a private investigator, he explained.

He could tell Chelsea didn't like it, but there was nothing more they could do about Jace right then.

Hoping to get some good news, he suggested they stop by the police station and see if Owens had made any progress finding out who had vandalized Chelsea's house. Travis didn't relish walking into the station, so he called Owens on his cell and arranged to meet the detective in a small park near the station's parking lot.

When they arrived, Travis parked in one of the visitor spaces. It had been almost four years since he'd left the force; been forced to leave, really, since he could no longer trust that his colleagues would have his back when bad stuff happened. Still, he felt a little tug in his chest looking up at the building that had been his professional home at one point.

They got out and made their way to the lone picnic table on the small patch of land next to the parking lot.

"Where is he? I don't see him," Chelsea said, shading her eyes from the glaring sun and scanning the short expanse between the station and where they stood.

Travis checked his phone to make sure he hadn't missed a message from Owens. He hadn't. "He probably just got caught up in something. He'll be here."

"Well, well. I thought I smelled something foul."

Travis stiffened, instantly on alert. He turned and found Detective Robert Ward. Ward had a wrapped sandwich in one hand and a to-go cup in the other. They were from the deli two blocks over that was a frequent cop stop for lunch. Travis missed their pastrami on rye, but he hadn't dared patronize the place since he had resigned from the force.

Ward swaggered toward them, a glower on his face. He cut a glance at Chelsea, dismissing her quickly, for which Travis gave small thanks. Ward hadn't worked on Franklin Brooks's case, so he likely didn't recognize Chelsea.

Ward could have been out of Central Casting playing

the stereotypical not-so-bright middle-aged cop. His shirt strained against his belly, and his sport coat was several years out of fashion.

Travis folded his arms over his chest and angled himself so he was slightly in front of Chelsea. "Ward," he greeted the man without a hint of warmth in his tone.

"What are you doing here, Collins? I hope not looking to get your job back," Ward sneered.

"I've got a job."

Ward snapped his fingers theatrically, as though he'd forgotten. The sound was like the crack of a whip in the otherwise quiet park. "That's right. You're a PI now," he said. "That's a club that doesn't mind a Judas is in their midst."

"Who is this jerk?" Chelsea said from behind Travis. Her voice was low enough that he didn't think Ward heard. Or maybe Ward was just so focused on his hatred for him that he couldn't be bothered to respond to Chelsea's slight.

Either way, Travis gave his head a slight shake and nudged Chelsea a little farther behind him. He didn't think Ward would lash out physically, but the man's disdain for Travis was clear. Who knew how worked up he would get himself?

"Every one of the cops I turned into internal affairs was either fired or forced to resign from the force," Travis responded.

"Internal affairs pigs covering their behinds," Ward spat. "That doesn't mean anything. I knew those men. They were good cops."

"They were supposed to uphold the law, not break it." Travis knew he was talking to a brick wall. Ward was not the kind of cop who would ever see it his way.

"Don't give me that crap. We do what we have to do to get the bad guys off the street."

"Not when it means becoming the bad guy."

"Who decides who's a good guy and who's a bad guy? You?" Ward scoffed.

"Well, it sure as hell shouldn't be you," Travis shot back.

Ward's face reddened. But before he could mount a comeback, Owens jogged over.

"Ward, the lieutenant is looking for you."

Ward cut a glance at Owens, but Owens kept his expression impassive. Ward shot one last venomous look at Travis before stomping away.

"I'm sorry if you're going to catch flak for meeting with me," Travis said to Owens when Ward was out of earshot.

Owens waived his apology away. "Don't worry about it. The vandalism at Chelsea's house is my case. Officially, I'm meeting with her. If she wants to bring you along..." He shrugged. "Who am I to argue?"

Owens was a good man and a good cop.

"So do you have anything for us?" Chelsea asked, getting the meeting on track.

"I wish I had better news," Owens answered. "Your ex-husband has an alibi for the vandalism. He was in surgery all day. Confirmed by multiple people. The fingerprints turned up nothing. They were all yours, Travis's or too smudged to be of any value. Whoever broke in probably wore gloves. I've turned up no witnesses. Not surprising since most of your neighbors were at work. I'm sorry, Ms. Harper."

"Please, call me Chelsea."

Nothing but dead ends, Travis thought, frustrated.

"I have to get back inside, but listen..." Owens stole a glance over his shoulder at the station before turning back to Travis and Chelsea. "I have a bad feeling about whatever you two have gotten yourself into."

"Are we still talking about the vandalism or Chelsea investigating her father's case?" Travis asked.

"Both. As you well know, they are probably one and the same. That's part of why I have a bad feeling. All I'm trying to say is be careful."

All three of them looked at the police station now. Ward had disappeared inside, and Travis had no doubt several of his former colleagues were at that very moment discovering he was currently nearby.

"There are a lot of people who would like to see you go down," Owens said in all seriousness. "By any means necessary."

Chapter Eighteen

Chelsea and Travis stopped by the hardware store and picked up cleaning supplies and paint and primer to cover the mess the vandal had left on her living room walls. When they got back to her house, Chelsea started cleaning and getting the house back in order while Travis broke out the primer and got to work on the walls.

It was slow going, both painting and cleaning. Chelsea made note of items that weren't salvageable and would have to be replaced. Included in that list was pretty much every piece of paper she hadn't had in her binder. Thankfully, the most important stuff she'd scanned and saved to her computer. But printing everything out again would be another big job she'd need to tackle at some point.

She worked on her bedroom first, cleaning until she felt like she'd rubbed out the destructive presence of the stranger who had invaded her private space. She saved the clothing she could; the vandal had cut up several shirts and skirts and several of her bras and panties. The thought of a stranger handling her things made her stomach turn. She gathered the rest of her clothing into her laundry basket to be washed. Then she turned her attention to the other rooms in the house.

The carpet in the living room had been splattered with paint along with the walls and would need to be taken up and replaced, but the kitchen and dining room floors got a thorough mopping. She cleaned until her hip protested, then headed into the living room to see how Travis was faring.

Red paint wasn't easy to cover, and the vandal had splattered all four of her living room walls. Travis had finally gotten enough primer on the walls to cover them, but there was no time to move on to painting.

Chelsea packed a few more clothes, including her favorite little black dress and the strappy heels she'd bought months earlier even though she'd had nowhere to wear them then. She had somewhere to wear them now. Contrary to her frequent reminders that this wasn't a date. They were working together to clear her father, and that was what she had to keep her focus on. But it definitely felt like a date when Travis picked her up in his living room at 8:00 p.m. sharp as they'd agreed. Wearing black dress pants and a button-down blue shirt that hugged his chest under a dark sport coat, he looked…delicious.

She was glad she'd opted for her little black dress when they stepped into the Fireside Grill, one of Los Angeles' nicest steak houses.

"This is a nice place," Chelsea said.

Travis's brow quirked up. "You didn't think I was going to take you to a nice place?"

"I…I didn't mean to imply—"

"I was joking. You made me a gourmet meal. I'm returning the favor." He turned to the hostess and gave his name for the reservation.

Chelsea wasn't sure if her ragù would qualify as gourmet, but she wasn't going to turn down dinner at the Fireside Grill, either.

The hostess led them to a table in an intimate corner

of the restaurant. She handed them each a menu and left them with a promise that their server would be with them soon. Chelsea's stomach flip-flopped. *Not a date*, she reminded herself.

The restaurant was fairly busy. This was probably just one of the only tables available. Still, she couldn't help but feel a little nervous energy. She could tell herself it wasn't a date all she wanted, but she hadn't been out with a man in longer than she was willing to admit, and her body seemed anxious to make up for lost time.

The flickering candle at the center of the table cast a shadow on Travis's face that made him appear even more ruggedly handsome than he already was. Leagues sexier actually. For a brief moment, she wondered what he would do if she rounded the table, sat on his lap and kissed him silly.

"Chelsea?" His voice pulled her from her fantasy.

She shook herself out of her racing thoughts and focused on the present. "Sorry, yes?"

A small, knowing smile crossed Travis's face. "Where did you go?"

"I was just thinking about the menu," she said, heat crawling up her neck. There was no doubt he knew she was lying. The menu was still closed in her hand. She opened it and hid behind it. She spent the next several minutes choosing her appetizer and entrée and reining in her libido.

The waitress stopped by their table and they put in their drink order. They continued to make small talk until the drinks arrived and then ordered their appetizers and entrées.

"So, um, do you have any siblings?" Chelsea asked, taking a swig from her glass of wine.

Travis's lips quirked up. "Do I have any siblings?"

"Give me a break," Chelsea laughed. "This is awkward. I'm trying to make conversation."

Travis chuckled, the low rumble sending a tingle down her back. "Okay. I'll lay off." His smile dimmed. "I had an older brother. He died when I was ten. He was thirteen." Travis lifted his wineglass to his lips.

"Oh, I'm sorry," she said, kicking herself. "I didn't know."

"Of course you didn't. It's fine." He laid his index finger over the rim of his glass. "I don't mind talking about him. Charles, his name was Charles. He was a cool kid. At least I thought so. As far as I was concerned, he hung the moon." He smiled again.

Chelsea laid her hand over his on the table. "How did he die, if you don't mind my asking?"

"It was a car accident. He, my parents and I were in the car when we were hit by a drunk driver. Charles and my mom and dad didn't make it."

Her heart broke for him. "God, Travis. I'm so sorry."

He pressed his lips tightly together. "Thanks. I spent the next eight years in foster care. Twelve homes in eight years to be exact. I think it's why I went into the marines. I craved structure after such an unstable childhood."

"And how long did you serve?"

He turned her hand over and traced the lines on her palm, sending a charge up and down her spine. "Eight years," he said with another chuckle. "A psychologist would probably have a field day with that coincidence."

"Was it just a coincidence?"

"Yes. Maybe. I don't know. After a while, I just felt like my time in the corps was up."

"And that's why you joined the LAPD?"

"Yeah." Now his laugh turned mirthless. "Not my best decision."

"I think it was a great decision." She took another sip of wine. She needed to be careful. She wasn't a big drinker. Not much of one at all really. She didn't want to make a fool of herself tonight. "You brought corruption to light."

"Yeah, well, my former colleagues aren't as appreciative as you are."

"They should be. Dirty cops make the good ones look bad. They should want to out the bad ones, and if they don't, they should get into a different line of work. Preferably one that keeps them away from the public," she added passionately.

He grinned. "You sound like a real-life avenger. Or a member of the Justice League or something. A real-life superhero."

She dipped her head. "I'm no superhero. I just hate seeing injustice go uncorrected."

"I bet you're a superhero to your dad."

Before she could think of what to say to that, their food arrived. She had opted for the lamb while Travis had more traditional fare for a steak house and ordered steak. They both had veggies on the side, and the waitress refilled their wineglasses before leaving again.

Chelsea took a bite of her food and moaned slightly as the spicy flavors mingled with the lamb hit her tongue. "This is amazing," she said around the food.

"I'm glad you like it," Travis said, his eyes sparkling. He cut into his steak. "A buddy of mine is the executive chef here. That's how I was able to get a reservation at the last moment. I was hoping to introduce you, but he's out of town."

"Well, your buddy sure knows what he's doing. You should get him to teach you."

"I think I'll stick to omelets and pancakes." Travis popped a piece of steak into his mouth, and they spent the next few minutes eating in companionable silence.

"I told you something about me," he said at last. "It's your turn to tell me something about you."

Chelsea leaned back a bit, surprised by his question. He hadn't shown much interest at all in her life outside of looking into her father's case. But she had asked him questions about his personal life. It was only fair that she answered his questions about hers. "You already know more about me than most people."

"I know about your father's case," he said pointedly. "I want to know about you, Chelsea."

She took another sip of wine, shifting in her seat. "What do you want to know?"

"Anything. Did you always want to be a teacher?"

She put her glass down and picked up her fork again but didn't bring it to her mouth. "No. I wanted to be an attorney, if you can believe it."

Travis pointed at her. "Now that I can believe. Why didn't you go to law school?"

She shrugged. "Money. After my dad was convicted, I needed to get a job quickly if I wanted to help pay for the appeals. I found a position with a small private school in San Francisco and got my master's degree at night. Then I switched to the public school system and moved back here to be closer to Aunt Brenda and Victor. And my dad. Don't get me wrong, I love my kids—"

"But you still think about law?"

"Sometimes. I mean, it's hard not to consider it. I almost feel like I don't need law school now. I have practically lived the law for the past several years."

"It couldn't have been easy."

"It wasn't. When I got word that Dad lost his last appeal..." She let the thought hang, mostly because she couldn't adequately put into words the desolation she had felt. She guessed this was how he felt talking about his family. Time to get this dinner conversation back on track. "What do you like to do for fun?" she asked, spearing another piece of lamb.

"Fun?"

"Yes," she said with a laugh. "You know, enjoyment. To bring pleasure to your life."

He leaned forward, the candlelight sparkling in his eyes along with a hint of something sensual. "Believe me, I enjoy pleasure, and I know many ways to have fun." His gaze raked over her face.

A part of her wanted to look away, but a bigger part wanted to lean into the suggestion he was making. She felt ready to burst into flames under his gaze.

"How are you two doing over here? Can I get you anything else?" the waitress singsonged, oblivious to the moment she had interrupted.

"We're great, thanks." Travis leaned back in his chair, but his gaze didn't move from Chelsea's face. "We'd like to see the dessert menu, please."

"Certainly," the waitress said, sailing off to get the menus.

"I probably shouldn't."

"Come on now, weren't you the one who just mentioned fun? Where's the fun in skipping dessert?"

Were her eyes deceiving her or had he licked his lips

after the word *dessert*? She was really on the edge of bursting into flames. Any minute now.

The waitress brought over dessert menus, and Chelsea scanned hers, thinking about the unexpected turn the night had taken. When Travis suggested dinner, she figured it was a pity thing. *Poor Chelsea who hasn't been out on a date in forever.* But she was not only enjoying spending time with him and getting to know him a little better, she enjoyed his flirting. *Wait.* Was that a pity thing, too? Was he throwing her a bone?

She glanced at him over the top of the menu. Even if he was, so what? This non-date couldn't mean anything anyway. It was nice getting to know him, and the flirting was a much-needed ego boost. She felt that she understood him a little better and trusted him a little more, but that was all this could lead to.

When the waitress returned, Chelsea ordered the chocolate mousse and he got the seven-layer cake. They both ordered coffee. They chatted more about their lives until the dessert arrived.

This time it was Travis who moaned when he tasted the cake. She was glad she was sitting when he did. Her knees wouldn't have held her up.

Travis placed a bite of cake onto his fork and leaned across the table with it outstretched toward her. "Try it."

Hunger for a very different kind of dessert seared through her.

"You like it?" he asked.

Her first attempt at answering failed. She leaned back in her seat and cleared her throat before trying again. "It's good," she said. "Great, really."

They finished their desserts quickly, and Travis paid

the check. They picked up their coats from the coat check and stepped out into the night.

"Thank you for a wonderful evening," Chelsea said.

"You're welcome." Travis shot her a heated gaze.

The valet rushed toward them, and Travis handed over his ticket.

The brisk wind sent a shiver through Chelsea. Travis put his arm around her, pulling her into his side. "Is this all right? Better?"

The spicy scent of his cologne snaked under her nose. "It's fine. Thanks." She looked up at him and found his face only centimeters away from hers.

Travis sucked in a breath and leaned closer. His lips slowly lowered until they were covering hers. She sighed, opening farther and letting him pull her in closer. The kiss was gentle but hot in a way she'd never experienced before. His hips pressed against her, and she felt the length of him. How much he wanted her. As much as she wanted him.

The kiss went on and on but not long enough. A boisterous group turned the corner, laughing loudly and heading to the restaurant.

Chelsea pulled away, her entire body still ignited from Travis's kiss. A kiss that had been everything she'd imagined and more, but the doubts and second thoughts were already creeping in. She needed him to get her father out of prison. That was the most important thing to her. Even if being in his arms made her forget about all the obstacles she was facing. But she could not mess that up. No matter how strong her feelings for Travis were growing.

She took one step back and then another, putting distance between them. She watched disappointment flit across Travis's face. Disappointment she knew was mirrored in her own expression. But this was for the best.

The valet pulled Travis's car to a stop at the curb in front of them and got out.

Travis turned to the young man.

A loud bang split the air, and Chelsea dropped to the pavement.

Chapter Nineteen

Chelsea jerked to one side, then fell to the sidewalk. In two steps, Travis was by her side, shielding her with his body. Tires squealed, and people were yelling around him, but all he could see was Chelsea's teary eyes staring up at him, her face contorted with pain. Blood poured from her arm, her sleeveless dress giving him a good view of the wound.

"I've got you. I've got you, Chelsea." He stripped off his jacket and button-down shirt and used the latter to press on the wound. She moaned.

"It's okay," he said. "You are going to be okay."

"Oh, man. Oh, my God. He shot her," the valet said in a high-pitched voice filled with panic.

"Call 911. Tell them we need an ambulance and that we have a gunshot wound. And tell the dispatcher that the victim is Chelsea Harper. Ask them to notify Owens," Travis barked out orders.

"Yes, sir. Got it." The valet dashed away.

"It hurts," Chelsea moaned.

"I know, baby. Hang in there. Help is on the way."

How had things gone bad so fast? He'd let down his guard. Been distracted. He'd let his attraction to Chelsea cloud his judgment, and she'd paid the price. If she died… He shook the thought away. She wasn't going to die. He pressed harder on the wound in an attempt to slow the bleeding.

The sound of sirens cut through the air, letting him know that the EMTs were close. Moments later they arrived, a man and a woman in blue. They pushed him to the side so they could kneel next to Chelsea. He stayed close, though, not wanting to let her out of his sight.

She must have felt the same way. Her eyes didn't leave his face even as the EMTs worked on her.

"Sir?"

Travis snapped his head to the right. A uniformed police officer stood next to him.

"Could you step over here and give me your statement of what happened?" the officer said.

"I'm not leaving her," Travis snarled.

The officer frowned. "Sir, I need to get your statement."

Travis gave the officer a succinct version of the moments leading up to Chelsea getting shot without moving away from her side.

"Let's get loaded up," the male EMT said. He and his partner lifted Chelsea onto a gurney and began pushing her toward the ambulance. Travis moved to follow.

"Hey!" The officer he'd been talking to put a hand on his forearm to stop him. "You need to stay here and finish giving me your statement."

Travis shook off the officer's hand. "I am not leaving her," he repeated.

"It's okay, Officer."

Travis and the officer turned as Owens stopped next to them. "I can get his formal statement at the hospital."

The officer scowled at Owen's badge but stepped back.

Travis jogged to catch up with the gurney, and Owens hustled to keep up.

"What happened?" Owens asked.

"Drive-by. I didn't see the driver. Black sedan. I can't tell you anything about the plates. They were covered. Just like with the hit-and-run video, although this was a different car." Travis pulled himself into the back of the ambulance.

"I'll meet you at the hospital," Owens said.

Travis turned and shot Owens a look that had made lesser men tremble with fear. "Owens, when we find this guy, I want to be the one to take him down. Understand?"

TRAVIS WATCHED THE doctor examine Chelsea from the corner of the room where he'd been since the EMTs had rolled her into the hospital on a gurney. Watching over her like he should have been doing before she was shot. He was still kicking himself for letting his growing feelings for her sway his professionalism. Chelsea's injury might not be lethal, but it was painful. He could see that from the semi-glazed look in her eyes.

"Travis? Are you still there?" Kevin's voice cut through Travis's thoughts.

"Yeah, I'm still here," he said into the phone.

"Are you sure you're okay? I can come down to the hospital."

"No, I'm fine. Chelsea's going to be okay, too." The bullet had only grazed her arm, thankfully.

"Good. Then you should know that I was able to get an address for Peter Schmeichel. He does still live in Monterey. I found his name and a photograph in a church bulletin. Looks like he volunteers a lot of his time."

"Send me everything you got." Travis glanced at Chelsea again. "I'm not sure when I'll be able to make a trip to Monterey." The picturesque town was nearly a six-hour drive away. "But I have a buddy who owns a condo there. I'll give him a call. See if I can crash there for a night or two in the coming days."

"If you need me or Tess to head up there for you…"

Travis looked at Chelsea again. He didn't want to leave her side, but he knew this investigation better than Tess or Kevin, and he wanted to see how Peter would respond to his questions. "No. I'll go." He ended the call with Kevin.

Seconds later, his phone pinged with a text containing Peter's address and the church bulletin Kevin mentioned. Travis shot off a quick text to his friend asking if his Monterey condo was available for the next several days and whether he could crash there, then walked over to the bed where Chelsea lay.

"You are very lucky," the doctor said as she finished the last of Chelsea's stitches. Dr. Lacey's curly brown hair was bound on top of her head with a hair tie, and wrinkles creased her forehead. Intelligent eyes indicated that she knew what she was doing. She pulled off her gloves and tossed them onto a metal table next to Chelsea. "I'll prescribe a painkiller, but you'll be able to sleep in your own bed tonight."

Chelsea cut a look at Travis. "Not exactly, but thanks, Doctor."

Dr. Lacey made notes on a tablet. "It may take me a little while to get your discharge papers together. Just hang tight. We're a bit understaffed tonight."

"As long as I don't have to stay overnight, I'll be fine," Chelsea responded.

"You shouldn't be so eager to leave," Travis said after

the doctor left the room. "At least we know you're safe in the hospital."

Chelsea tilted her head and looked at him. "I'm safe at your place, too."

"I'm not so sure about that anymore," he muttered, running a hand over his head.

Chelsea studied him. "What does that mean?"

"It means I'm the reason you got shot."

Chelsea frowned. "Did you hit your head?"

"Chels, I'm serious."

"So am I. Did you hit your head when you threw your body over me? Because admittedly things happened fast, but I don't recall you shooting at me."

"I was distracted. I should have been paying attention. I should have seen the sedan and the gun before the shooter got off a shot. If I had been doing my job—"

"Wait a minute." She held up a hand. "I hired you to help me prove my father's innocence, not throw yourself in front of bullets for me."

"I know, but of the two of us, I'm the professional."

Chelsea pushed herself up straighter in the hospital bed. "Oh, get over yourself. You are no more responsible for me getting shot then I am. You're not a superhero. If you had seen the guy and thrown yourself in front of me, you would have been shot. Would you be saying the same things to me right now if our roles were reversed?"

"I'd tell you that you weren't to blame," he reluctantly admitted.

"Okay, then, I don't want to hear any more of this macho 'I should have protected you' baloney."

Despite everything, he smiled.

A moment later, that smile fell as Chelsea's aunt Brenda barreled through the door.

"There you are. Oh, my God, Chelsea." Her aunt threw herself on top of Chelsea, her sobs filling the room.

Chelsea flinched with pain from her aunt's jostling.

Travis took a step toward them, intending to prod the older woman away before she inadvertently hurt her niece any further. But the man from the photo on Chelsea's dresser, her cousin Victor, strode in after Brenda.

Victor sized Travis up quickly. "You must be the private investigator my mom told me was helping Chels."

Travis nodded, bracing himself for the same anger Chelsea's aunt had thrown his way at her house.

Victor thrust his hand out. "Victor Harper, Chelsea's cousin. More like a brother. Thanks for looking out for my cuz."

Travis shook Victor's hand, surprised by the friendly greeting.

"Chelsea told us how you used your own body to shield her and that you tried to stop the bleeding," Victor explained.

Chelsea had called her family herself after the doctor determined her wound wouldn't require surgery and they'd been waiting for her to get stitched up. She'd wanted privacy for the call, so Travis had stepped into the hall while she was on the phone. Apparently, she had embellished his role.

"I really didn't do that much," he countered to Victor.

"Yes, he did," Chelsea called from the bed.

Chelsea's aunt lifted herself from Chelsea's body and made a half turn. "You," she said, stalking across the room to Travis.

Victor moved quickly, getting out of the path of his mother.

Before Travis knew what she was about to do, Aunt

Brenda had her arms wrapped around him. She buried her face in his chest, still crying.

"Thank you," she said, her voice thick with emotion. "You saved my Chelsea."

Travis rubbed her shoulder awkwardly. "You're welcome, but really I—"

Aunt Brenda reared back, fire mingling with the tears in her eyes. "Don't say it was nothing. It was everything to me. To Victor. Chelsea is family. She told me you ruined a beautiful shirt, and you stayed with her when she was scared. That's not nothing."

"She would have done the same for me," he said, still unsure what to do with the older woman's praise.

"That is true," Aunt Brenda said. "My Chelsea has a big heart." She patted one of Travis's cheeks. "So do you. I can tell."

"Thank you," Travis said, touched by her words.

"I was rude to you the other day when you came to my house. Let me make it up to you? You have to come to dinner. Do you like mashed potatoes and gravy? I make them with real potatoes. None of that powdered junk. Milk and real butter, that's the secret to getting them nice and fluffy." She patted his cheek again.

Victor edged up to his mother. "Okay, Ma. I think now is not a good time to try to feed the man." He wrapped an arm around his mother, but she shrugged him off.

"It's always a good time to feed a man." Brenda turned back to look at her niece. "You hear that, Chelsea?" She winked at her.

"Aunt Brenda," Chelsea groaned.

"Ma," Victor lamented.

Travis held back a chuckle, but he was struck by a sense of longing. He never let himself think about what might have been if his family had lived, but occasionally a memory would creep up on him. They had been a happy family. Content to be in each other's company. His brother had teased him sometimes, and it had annoyed him then, but Travis would give anything to have his brother tease him again. Or fight with him. Having people in his life who cared enough to fight with him and for him... It had been a long time since he had that. Maybe too long.

He told himself he didn't need it, but watching Chelsea with her aunt and her cousin, who had raced to the hospital the minute they learned she was hurt, made him realize he'd been lying to himself. He wanted people in his life, that sense of belonging to a family. Maybe even this family.

He watched Chelsea's aunt and cousin fuss over her while foggy images of what his future could look like played through his head. What if he let Chelsea in?

The door to the room swung open, and Dr. Lacey strode back in. "Well, it looks like the gang's all here. I'm going to have to ask you to step into the hall while I talk to Miss Harper about caring for her wound. When we're done, she will be all set to go home."

Victor ushered his mother out into the hall.

Travis started to follow but stopped at the sound of Chelsea's voice.

"Hey, are you okay?" she asked him.

Was he? He wasn't sure. He felt like a raw nerve at the moment. But he wasn't going to trouble Chelsea with his kaleidoscope of emotions. Especially not when he wasn't sure what to make of them himself.

Instead, he smiled. "I'm fine. Great, now that we know you're going to be okay."

"Okay," she said, a note of skepticism in her voice.

"I'll be waiting for you when you're ready to go home."

Chapter Twenty

Travis helped Chelsea into his guest room, then left her to change into her pajamas. It had been a long and arduous night, and she was exhausted. And despite knowing she was safe now, a thread of fear still lingered. She could hear Travis walking around the house, checking all the locks on the doors and windows, she suspected.

She'd changed and was crossing from the attached bathroom to the bed when he appeared at the bedroom door again.

"Here. Let me help you." He put an arm around her shoulders, walked her to the head of the bed and turned down the bedspread with one hand.

"You know, I'm not an invalid. I can walk."

He eased her down onto the bed. "I know you aren't, but you should take it easy for a while. And speaking of taking it easy, Kevin found an address for Peter Schmeichel. It's in Monterey, so I was thinking I could have Kevin or Tess stay with you while I go speak to him."

Chelsea swung her legs up onto the bed and under the bedspread. "Without me? No way." She shook her head. "I'm going with you."

He sighed. "I had a feeling you'd say that. We'll go in a few days then. Once you've had some time to rest."

"I don't need rest, and I don't want to put off talking to Peter. We can go tomorrow."

Travis pulled the covers up to her waist. "You were just shot."

She tamped down the fear that threatened to rise. "It was a graze."

He rolled his eyes. "Semantics."

Chelsea grabbed his hand. "Travis, please. We're close. I can feel it. I don't want to wait. I need to do this."

He sighed again. "Okay. As long as you're feeling up for it tomorrow, we can go. But if you don't feel like it when you wake up tomorrow, you have to promise you'll tell me." He looked into her eyes, and she saw how serious he was. "I won't compromise your health."

Warmth spread through her chest. She squeezed his hand. "I appreciate you looking out for me." She threw good sense to the wind and leaned forward and kissed his mouth quickly, softly.

He stroked her cheek with the pad of his thumb. "Get some sleep." He stood and headed for the door.

"Travis?" Her heart pounded in her chest. She felt a little foolish, but fear pushed her forward.

Travis turned.

"Would you mind staying with me tonight? Just sleeping. I'm embarrassed to admit it, but I'm still a little shaky after, well, everything."

"You have nothing to be embarrassed about," he said, heading back to the bed.

She scooted over to make room for him. He toed off his shoes and slid in beside her still in his clothes. She relaxed against him. He wrapped an arm around her waist and gathered her close. The faint smell of his cologne still lingered even after the night they'd had.

"I feel safe when I'm with you."

"I'm glad I make you feel safe."

His breath tickled the skin on her neck, causing her pulse to pick up. She'd meant it when she asked him to only sleep next to her, but her body didn't seem to want to cooperate. Lying next to him was sweet torture but still torture. "You do," she said.

"You know, when I woke up in the hospital and the doctor told me that my parents and brother had been killed, that was the most scared I thought I could ever be. Until today. I've never been more scared than I was when I saw you lying on the pavement with a gunshot wound."

"I'm sorry I scared you like that."

He shifted so he could look at her. "You don't have anything to be sorry about. I'm just so glad you're safe." He held her more tightly against his side.

She snaked a hand up around the back of his neck and leaned forward. As soon as their lips met, his control seemed to snap. He ravished her mouth, sending a groan through them both. Blood pounded in her ears. She deepened the kiss, letting her hand move down from his neck to his chest before venturing farther south. He stopped her before she reached below his waist.

"Wait. Chelsea. I…" He panted. "I think we should slow down. This… We… I'm not a relationship guy," he blurted.

She stiffened.

"I mean… I didn't mean. I just wanted to be upfront about—"

"I get it." She slid away from him.

"I'm not trying to hurt you. Obviously, I'm attracted to you, but you deserve a man who is going to be all in, and I'm not that guy."

"I said I get it, Travis," she said, her tone more caustic than she'd intended. She couldn't be mad with him for saying out loud exactly what she'd been telling herself for days now. She let out a breath. "You're right." She laid her head on his shoulder. "You'll stay until I fall asleep?"

"Of course. Whatever you want."

When she woke the next morning, the side of the bed where he'd been was cold.

TRAVIS WAS UP at six the next morning. He normally went to the gym, but he wasn't about to leave Chelsea's side, so he settled for a pared-down workout in his bedroom. The drive to Monterey took about five hours, and he wanted to arrive by early afternoon, but he was loath to wake Chelsea. She needed rest to heal. Part of him hoped she would sleep late so he'd have a reason to put off the trip for another day and give her more time to rest, but he should have known it wouldn't be that easy. He heard her moving around the guest room shortly after 7:30.

He still had a knot in his throat thinking about their conversation the night before.

You did the right thing.

He knew he had. Chelsea deserved the truth from him. He wasn't the type of man who did relationships, no matter how brilliant, sexy and fearless the woman. And Chelsea was all of those things. She deserved someone who could commit to her. That wasn't him.

He'd just finished cooking the first batch of waffles when Chelsea entered the kitchen. She looked much better than she had the night before. The color was back in her cheeks, and she appeared rested. But her body language was closed off. She gave him a weak, polite smile as she headed for the coffee maker. "Good morning."

"Good morning. I hope you like waffles," he said.

"I do."

"How many?"

"Two, please."

He handed her a plate with a couple waffles he'd just taken off the iron.

She took it without meeting his gaze. "Thanks."

He had never done the awkward morning-after dance before. He rarely stayed the night. He blew out a silent breath and put two more waffles on the griddle for himself. When they were ready, he sat across from Chelsea. They ate in uncomfortable silence for several minutes.

"Are you still up for the trip to Monterey?"

"Absolutely." Chelsea dabbed her mouth with a napkin and rose. "I just need to pack a few more things. When do you want to leave?"

The clock on the stove read 8:15 a.m. "Does nine o'clock work for you? We should get there around three if we don't make a lot of stops and don't hit traffic. Peter works the three-to-eleven shift at a plumbing supply distributor, so that will give us a little time to settle in at the condo before going to see him."

"That's fine. I'll go get ready." She all but ran from the kitchen.

He sighed. There wasn't anything he could do about the awkwardness except hope it passed. He cleaned up the kitchen before gathering his own overnight bag. Chelsea met him at the car at nine o'clock sharp, and they headed out.

He headed north on US 101 toward Santa Barbara. It would be marginally faster to take the I-5 north, but the 101 ran along the coast and provided a much better view. They kept the conversation light and mostly talked about the case. As he hoped, some of the awkwardness from the night before ebbed the farther they got from his house.

Chelsea fell asleep somewhere around Pismo Beach. He shut off the radio to let her sleep, content to make the drive in silence. He couldn't help but note how he seemed to be content to do just about anything when he was with her.

She woke as he exited the freeway and drove into what was known as Old Monterey just before 3:00 p.m. They drove past a gallery, specialty markets, several restaurants, pubs and coffee shops. Everything about the area screamed small-town America.

"Do you like seafood?" he asked her, turning the car away from the downtown area.

"Yeah. I love it," she said, stretching.

"Great. I need to make a stop before we get to the condo."

Travis drove a few miles before he pulled into a parking lot twenty-five yards from the wharf.

"Where are we?"

"This is my favorite place to buy seafood." He opened his door.

Chelsea pushed open her door and followed Travis into what looked like an aluminum shack. Inside there were several rows of tables with seafood displayed on ice. Running along the far wall was a counter with more fish behind glass.

The muscular young man behind the counter greeted them. "What can I get you folks?"

"Two lobsters, a pound of shrimp and a half pound of crab."

While the clerk pulled his order together, Travis walked around the shop collecting the other items he'd need to prepare lunch, as well as a six pack of beer.

"This seems like a lot," Chelsea said, following him.

"Trust me," he said.

They went back to the counter and gathered their order. "Anything else I can get you?" the man asked.

"That should do it," Travis said.

The clerk put everything into bags and rang them up. Travis paid, and they got back into the car and headed a little farther up the coast until they reached a strip of beachfront condos. He pulled the car into a short, shared driveway. The ocean was visible just beyond the side of the house, the water a brilliant calm blue past a smooth expanse of sand.

Travis had spent many weekends decompressing here. His friend actually owned a couple condos as investment properties, but it looked like the left side of the house was empty at the moment. Inside, the condo was renovated and well maintained. Two good-size bedrooms opened up off the large living/dining/kitchen area. A wide balcony jutted off the back of the condo, looking out into the ocean.

"Take whichever room you'd like," Travis said, placing the grocery bag on the counter. He grabbed the lobsters and put them in the fridge.

Chelsea carried her bag into the room on the left. It was slightly bigger and had a better view in his opinion. It was the room he usually slept in, but he was happy to give it up to her.

He opened one of the beers and put the others in the fridge. Then he grabbed a large pot from a lower cabinet and filled it with water, setting it on a burner to boil. Next, he got started preparing the easy crab dip recipe he always used, then arranged some crackers on a plate and scooped cocktail sauce into a small bowl. When the water came to a boil, he pulled the lobsters from the fridge. The cool air had done its job putting the crustaceans to sleep. Cooking them this way seemed less cruel than throwing them into boiling water while they were still active.

He was spreading the shrimp out on a platter next to the cocktail sauce when Chelsea stepped out of her bedroom.

"This is a gorgeous place. And these photos," she said, stopping next to a nighttime photo of the ocean just beyond her bedroom door.

Travis poured her a glass of wine. "My buddy who owns the condo is a photographer."

"He's really good." Chelsea crossed to the kitchen and took the glass of wine from him.

He smiled. "He's Myles Messina."

Chelsea's hand froze with her glass halfway to her lips. "Myles Messina, the famous photographer?"

Travis nodded.

"Wow. How do you two know each other?"

"Myles was in foster care with me for a year. We managed to keep in touch after we aged out of the system."

"I didn't know he was in foster care." Chelsea sat on one of the kitchen counter stools.

"Yeah, he's a real success story."

"Both of you are." Chelsea brought the wineglass to her lips.

Heat traveled through him at the compliment. He lifted the plates with the shrimp and crab dip and carried them to the balcony door. "Can you open this for me?"

Chelsea grabbed the door handle and turned it. They stepped out onto the deck. A glass-top table with four wrought iron chairs stood center stage.

"Don't sit yet." Travis set the food on the table, then went back into the house. He returned moments later with two towels and his beer.

They both sat. Travis took a deep breath of ocean air, feeling it calm him. There was something special about the beach air here. Cleaner. He took another sip of beer and watched Chelsea reach for a shrimp and dip it into the sauce.

"Oh," she moaned, sending a spirit of need to his lower region. "This is amazing."

"Yeah, the crab house makes the best cocktail sauce. Homemade by the owner," he said, trying not to think about how his body had reacted to her moan.

Her brows rose. "I thought you said you couldn't cook."

"You'll notice there's nothing that had to be seasoned or braised or anything much more difficult than dropping things into a pot of boiling water or mixing crab dip."

Chelsea laughed. "How often do you come here?"

"Recently, not as much as I'd like to. Work has been busy."

"Well, I can see why you like it." She leaned her head back against the chair and closed her eyes.

God, she was gorgeous.

They said in silence for a while until Chelsea said, "The lobster should be ready by now, shouldn't it?"

Travis got up. "You're right." Chelsea started to follow. "No. You stay. Enjoy the view. I've got this."

He transferred the lobsters from the water onto a large platter and carried it outside with a dish of clarified garlic butter. He went back inside for the wine bottle and dinner plates.

"You know, I can get used to being served like this," Chelsea teased, grabbing a lobster and putting it on the plate he slid in front of her.

And I could get used to serving you. The thought popped into his head unbidden.

No. This was nice, but that's all it was. A nice moment. That's all it could be.

But even as he thought, he couldn't quite convince himself that was all this was.

"Do YOU NEED anything else?" Travis asked her, still standing next to the table.

"I don't think so. Sit. Relax," Chelsea said.

He sat down next to her. They ate in companionable silence until her phone rang. She pulled it from her pocket. Simon. She made a face and declined the call. The phone rang again a moment later.

"If you need to take that, you can," Travis said.

"No, it's just Simon." She declined the call again.

Travis's mouth twisted into a frown.

For some reason she felt she had to explain. "He's been calling me since I, we, threw him out of my house."

"Why?" Travis groaned.

"I don't know. I haven't taken his call."

Travis seemed relieved to hear her say that. She got the feeling he didn't want her taking Simon's call any more than she wanted to talk to her ex-husband.

Chelsea dipped a piece of lobster in butter. "This is the best butter I've ever tasted." She popped the lobster in her mouth. A little bit of butter dripped down her chin.

Travis reached out and swiped it away with his thumb.

The waves crashed against the sand, and electricity crackled between them.

Travis ran the pad of his thumb over her lips.

She knew she would probably kick herself later. He'd made it quite clear he was not available for anything serious, and she didn't do casual hookups. But she didn't care about any of that at the moment. She had to kiss him, the desire more than she had the will to fight off.

She leaned forward, closing the distance between them. Kissing him felt like a strong wave had crashed into her, dragging her underwater. His hands roamed over her shoulders, then down her back. He seemed to feel just as much urgency as she did.

Travis pulled back first. "We shouldn't do this." He slid his chair away from her.

"You're right," she said, turning away from him, her pride smarting. She was a glutton for punishment.

Travis rose. "I'm going to get us a couple of bottles of water." He went inside.

Water. He probably thought she'd had too much to drink. Maybe she had. He was right, she shouldn't have kissed him. No matter how good it felt. It was stupid.

Travis returned with the bottled waters, and she took the one he offered.

"How about a walk on the beach?" she suggested, mostly to get away from the scene of the kissing crime, as it were.

He agreed, and they set off along the beach, keeping a respectable distance between them. Travis told her a little bit more about his older brother, recounting several childhood stories. She reciprocated, telling him about growing up with Victor.

They'd made it about a mile down the beach when her phone began ringing again.

"Are you sure you don't want to take that?" Travis asked.

She silenced the ringer this time. "Absolutely sure."

"You know, I can't see the two of you together. How did you two meet?"

"Aunt Brenda took a fall four years ago. Simon was her orthopedist. I should have known better, but Dad's first appeal had just been denied, and I was in a tough place. We got married too quickly. Only five months after we met."

"That is fast."

"Too fast. We didn't really know each other at all. I think we were both infatuated with how different we were. Or maybe that was just me. I've learned that Simon always has ulterior motives."

"And what was his ulterior motive for marrying you?"

"I think he thought it would upset his father. Bringing a poor, Black girlfriend home. And to be truthful, I think his father was concerned at first."

"At first?"

"Funny enough, my former father-in-law and I had more in common than Simon and I did. Gerald passed away about six months ago."

"I'm sorry for your loss."

"Thanks. Gerald was a doctor like Simon, but he came from nothing. A poor boy from southern Texas. Worked his way through college and med school. He was brilliant and came up with a revolutionary procedure for conducting intestinal surgery. That made him a legend in the medical field and a millionaire many, many times over. I think Simon's issues stem from feeling like he can't live up to his father. I think Gerald thought that I might be good for Simon."

"But you weren't?"

Chelsea laughed. "Our marriage was a disaster. Before the first year was out, I realized I'd made a mistake. Simon was already stepping out with one of his coworkers. Our marriage didn't last much longer. I kept in touch with Gerald, though. He was a good man."

"He didn't have a problem with who your father was?"

She pushed a lock of hair from her face. Gerald had never bought up her father, at least not with her, but she was sure he'd cautioned Simon. "I'm sure he didn't love that his daughter-in-law had a convict for a father, but he was never anything but supportive."

"That's cool. He sounds like a good guy."

"He was. Can I ask you something?"

"Sure."

"You told me you don't do relationships." Her heart thudded uncontrollably. "Have you ever considered it? You know, doing a relationship."

Travis stopped walking and turned to look out at the ocean. He didn't answer her.

"I'm sorry. I shouldn't have asked." Chelsea said as her phone vibrated, indicating another incoming call.

"You should take that," Travis said, turning back to the condo. "I'm going to clean up. Peter should be getting a break soon."

She ignored her phone and watched him walk away.

Chapter Twenty-One

His nerves were on edge. Shooting at Chelsea had been a rash decision. Stupid. Especially since he hadn't killed her. The cops would have no choice but to investigate a shooting. They weren't the brightest bulbs in the pack, but even a dim bulb gave off some light. What if some upstart detective believed Chelsea's rants about her father's innocence?

He'd done it again. Let his emotions, his anger, take over. It was Chelsea's fault, just like it had been Lily's. They confused him. Forced him to take action when he just wanted to be left in peace. Lily had paid the price for angering him.

Blood roared in his ears. He could feel his life veering out of control again. Like it had when Lily was alive. He wasn't sure how to regain control, but he knew he had to. Chelsea Harper had to be dealt with. Once and for all.

Chapter Twenty-Two

Salinger's Wholesale Plumbing and Fixtures was located in an industrial park in Salinas about twenty miles from Monterey. Travis had called ahead and, using the bogus excuse of having talked to Peter earlier about some plumbing part, found out that Peter was scheduled to work that day from three to eleven that evening and that he usually took his dinner break around 7:00 p.m.

The manager of the warehouse pointed Peter out to Chelsea and Travis. Peter was pulling several large boxes on a dolly cart from one end of the warehouse to the other where the truck bays were. He wore a blue-gray jumpsuit unzipped enough for Travis to see the white T-shirt underneath. His name was stenciled on the jumpsuit's left side, and worn work boots covered his feet. He slowed and stopped as Travis and Chelsea approached.

"Peter," Travis said with a polite smile that he hoped would put the man at ease. "My name is Travis Collins. This is my associate Chelsea Harper. Can we speak with you for a moment?"

"About what?"

"Lily Wong," Chelsea answered.

Peter's body stiffened, going on full alert. "I don't have anything to say about that."

"I think you do, Peter," Travis said firmly. "Chelsea's aunt received an anonymous note saying you'd lied at trial. I think you sent it."

It was a shot in the dark, but from the way Peter paled, Travis knew he'd hit his mark. If Peter had sent the note, it meant he felt remorse for what he'd done. That was good for them.

"We have spoken to Gina." Travis paused for several beats, letting that statement percolate in Peter's head, leaving him wondering just what his ex-girlfriend had said about the night Lily was murdered. "We'll buy you dinner. Your manager said your break starts soon. Anywhere you want to go. Just give us ten minutes." Travis could see the man's resolve cracking. "Ten minutes, and you get a free dinner. How about it?"

"Ten minutes," Peter agreed. "There's a Thai place two blocks down. I'll meet you there in fifteen minutes."

"Thank you," Chelsea said before she and Travis turned and left the warehouse.

"You think he'll show?" she asked as they got into Travis's car and headed for the restaurant.

"I think so. If he doesn't, we'll track him down again and ask a lot less nicely."

Thankfully, they didn't have to. Peter arrived at the restaurant fifteen minutes later as promised. Their waiter had already left three waters and three menus on the table. Travis wasn't hungry, and apparently neither was Chelsea. They both had coffee. Peter went all in, getting stir-fry with soft-shell crab, the most expensive item on the menu. Travis only hoped the coming conversation would be worth what this dinner would cost.

When the waiter left to put their order in with the kitchen, Peter asked, "What do you want from me?"

"I don't know if you know, but Franklin Brooks is my father," Chelsea said.

Peter squinted at her from across the table. "I didn't recognize you. Yeah, yeah, I remember you now from the trial."

"My father has exhausted all his appeals. Barring the truth coming out, he's going to spend the rest of his life in jail."

Peter's gaze slid from Chelsea's. "I'm sorry to hear that."

"Are you?" Chelsea leaned forward. "Because I think you know my dad is innocent."

Peter wouldn't look at either of them. "I don't know anything."

"Mr. Schmeichel." Travis jumped back into the conversation. "We are trying to get an innocent man free from prison. We need your help."

Peter remained silent.

"My father's life is at stake. If you don't tell the truth now, he'll die in prison," Chelsea added.

Peter reached for his glass of water and took a long pull on the straw.

Chelsea and Travis waited.

Finally, Peter spoke. "The court said he's guilty."

"In part based on your testimony. But we all know that what you said on the witness stand wasn't true," Chelsea countered.

"Are you calling me a liar?"

"I think you may have seen a way out of a jam, and you took it," Travis said, avoiding the question.

"Oh, yeah? And you got all this figured out based on what?"

"Based on the fact that Franklin was somewhere else at the time you say he was at Lily's house. On the fact that Franklin has always professed his innocence. And on the fact that your recollection of seeing Franklin at Lily's house at the time of her murder is undermined by Gina's statement."

"Gina," Peter scoffed. "The cops didn't believe her."

"No, they didn't," Travis agreed. "But then they had an incentive not to believe her. A woman killed in her own home. The community was scared and demanding someone be arrested. The recent ex-boyfriend is an easy answer. They just needed enough evidence to slap the cuffs on him. But they had enough evidence to slap the cuffs on you."

Peter's angry gaze slipped away but not before Travis got a hint of the guilt there, too. He kept going. "You were arrested about a week after Lily's murder. Your third strike." Travis softened his tone. "No one could blame you for wanting to avoid prison. Did one of the detectives hint that they would be willing to make a deal if you had seen something helpful regarding Lily's murder?"

Travis half expected Peter to erupt with anger and denials, but neither came. Peter looked down at the table and sighed.

"You know how we found you?" Chelsea asked.

Peter looked up and shook his head.

"The church bulletin. Your name popped up as a parishioner of the month. You do a lot of good work at your church."

"I do," Peter confirmed.

The waiter returned with their food then. It took several moments to get settled, but when the waiter left again, Travis decided to push Peter a little harder. "You know, Chelsea and I don't think you were involved with Lily's murder. But I work with a team, and we bounce things off each other. It's been pointed out to me that you could have made up the story regarding Franklin not to get out of the drug charge, or at least not just to get out of the drug charge. That maybe you had another reason for wanting to throw suspicion on Franklin." Travis let the implication hang over the table.

"What are you suggesting?" Peter glared, ignoring his lunch.

"Well, and I'm just spitballing, but Lily was an attractive, professional, intelligent woman. A catch. And she was back on the market. We know she was dating again. And Gina mentioned you two were having trouble. Arguing a lot. Maybe you made a play for Lily. She said no, things got out of hand."

"No," Peter spat.

"Then what really happened?" Chelsea asked. "I know it wasn't what you testified to at my father's trial."

"You don't know anything."

"Oh, but we do." Travis said. "We know you lied. The cops may have dismissed Gina seven years ago, but we wouldn't let them get away with that now. And someone has been targeting Chelsea. Attempting to run her down, vandalizing her home, even shooting at her. That makes me very angry, Peter. It makes me think someone has something to hide. Maybe someone who has already lied under oath. Where were you yesterday between 8:00 and 11:00 p.m.?" Travis asked, giving the time period when Chelsea had been shot.

Peter pushed his chair back and started to stand. "I don't have to listen to this."

"Sit. Down."

Peter hesitated, half standing, half sitting for a fraction of a second before reclaiming his seat.

"Peter, my father has been in prison for seven years," Chelsea said in a soft voice. "You seem to have changed your life, turned over a new leaf. You're helping people now. Help my father. Right this wrong."

There was a long silence where no one at the table so much as moved beyond breathing.

Peter spoke first. "I have to admit I lied."

"You have to tell the truth," Chelsea responded.

"You sign an affidavit under oath saying that your testimony at Franklin Brooks's trial was inaccurate."

Peter laughed bitterly. "Inaccurate is just fancy talk for lied."

It was, so Travis stayed quiet.

"Everyone will know I'm a liar and I could get in real trouble."

"Everyone will know you're correcting a wrong," Chelsea countered. "Making amends for a mistake that you made. There's nothing shameful about that."

Peter's chin dropped to his chest. "I lied." His voice was so soft Travis wasn't sure he heard it. "I lied," Peter said, louder this time, and Travis nearly cheered.

Peter looked at Chelsea. "You said I've turned over a new leaf. Well, I've tried. I kicked the drugs. I started going to church. I got a decent job, but I've always felt guilty about what I did to your father. I don't know if he's innocent or not. The cop said he did it, and I didn't see any reason for both of us to go to jail back then, so I lied. But it was eating me alive that an innocent man might be sitting in prison in part because of me, so I sent the note to your aunt. I...I was too scared to go to the prosecutor myself, but I hoped that someone would look into it. Make sure a mistake hadn't been made."

Chelsea let out an audible breath.

Even Peter looked lighter. Like a weight had been lifted from his shoulders. He looked Chelsea in the eyes. "I'll sign your affidavit. I don't know how much it will help your father, but it's time I told the truth."

Chapter Twenty-Three

"I can't believe he admitted he lied," Chelsea said not for the first time since she and Travis had left Peter. They'd just walked into the condo, and she was euphoric. "I'm going to get my dad out of jail, Travis." She'd always believed that she'd do it someday, but someday finally felt like it was coming soon.

"Slow down," Travis said, probably attempting to temper her enthusiasm. But even he was grinning. "We still have a lot of work to do before we can go to the prosecutor."

But they were closer, and she had him to thank. Without thinking, she threw herself into his arms. "Thank you," she said, wrapping her arms around him and hugging him tightly. "You don't know what this means to me. What it means to me that you've helped."

His muscles flexed under her hands. "I will always be there for you, Chelsea. Whenever you need me."

The air between them was charged. She knew if she looked into his eyes now she'd see in them exactly what she was feeling. Want. Desire. Need. She leaned back, and there it was. She knew that there were a lot of good reasons they shouldn't do this, but she didn't care about any of them. She wanted Travis Collins, and from the look and feel of him, he wanted her, too.

She feathered a light kiss over his lips.

He sucked in a ragged breath. "What are you doing?"

She didn't answer right away. Instead, she kissed each corner of his mouth before dotting light kisses along his jawline. "What do you think I'm doing?"

"Chelsea—"

"Travis, I don't want to hear about all the reasons we shouldn't do this. I already know the reasons not to. I'm telling you that I want you. Do you want me?"

"You know I do, but—"

She pressed a finger to his lips. "No buts. No doubts. Just us, right now."

He growled, placing his palms on either side of her face and pulling her to him. His lips met hers in a kiss that was ruthlessly efficient. He lifted her. She wrapped her legs around his waist and let him carry her into his bedroom.

His chest rose and fell. She felt the beat of his heart and gazed up into his face. A heady desire coursed between them. Then his mouth met hers, kissing, nibbling, suckling. Somewhere in the heat of passion they both shed their clothes. Her lips were swollen with his skill. They were both breathless by the time he slid down her body, kissing her neck and shoulders before lavishing her breasts with attention.

He grabbed her wrists, pulling them both over her head, and rolled her flat onto her back. Then he came down over her, straddling her. He worked his way down her body, leaving a trail of kisses across her belly before making his way lower. She responded by opening herself to him, body and heart. His fingers explored her, and she sighed, giving in to the intimate caress and riding the wave of release when it came. The aftermath of her orgasm was still rippling through her when he came up over her again, having sheathed himself with a condom. Gently he coaxed her thighs open, his large hands clamping around her hips as he eased himself into her, filling her body, heart and soul.

The realization that she had never wanted a man the way she wanted Travis tore through her, frightening and exhilarating at the same time. Then he took up a rhythm, and all she could feel was him. Her release this time was an explosion that sent shock waves through her body, made all the more potent by the fact that Travis found his release right along with her. Within minutes, they fell asleep, wrapped around each other.

They awoke sometime before dawn and made love a second time. She fell back into a satiated slumber, pressed into Travis's side, knowing that her life would never be the same again.

THE EVENTS OF the night came rushing back as Chelsea awoke still in Travis's bed. Her gaze shot to the space where he'd slept, but the other side of the bed was empty. No sound came from anywhere else in the condo, either.

They had driven to Monterey together, and she knew Travis wouldn't abandon her. It wasn't a surprise to find a note from him next to a fresh pot of coffee saying he'd gone for a run on the beach. He was giving her time to wake up and go back to her own room, she knew.

She would never forget the night of passion they'd shared. He had driven her to heights she hadn't known existed. She didn't, couldn't, regret making love with him, but it didn't change anything. A part of her, a big part of her, was disappointed about that, but Travis had been honest with her from the beginning. This thing between them could go no further than the physical.

She poured her coffee and took it with her back into her bedroom.

Travis returned to the condo while she was in the shower. She heard him in his bedroom while she was getting dressed and packing to head home. She took her time getting ready, brushing her hair and applying her makeup and trying to tamp down her nervousness about seeing Travis after their night together.

When she walked into the living room, he was perched at the kitchen counter with his phone to his ear. His expression was serious, and when he waved her over and put the phone on speaker, she forgot all about her nerves. "Kevin, Chelsea is with me now."

"Good morning, Chelsea," Kevin's voice called through the phone.

"Morning." Chelsea shot Travis a questioning look.

"I was just telling Kevin about Peter admitting that he lied on the stand and agreeing to sign a statement saying so."

"It will take some work to iron out the logistics, but we'll get a lawyer started on it today," Kevin said.

"That's great. Thank you," Chelsea responded.

Travis cleared his throat. "Kevin and I were also discussing something else."

Chelsea had a feeling that *something else* was something she wasn't going to like.

"Even with Peter's statement, it's going to be an uphill climb getting the prosecutor to reopen the investigation," Kevin said gingerly.

She knew what Kevin said was true, but it didn't make it any less frustrating. "I sense you have an idea that may help."

"We have been talking," Travis jumped in, "and we

both think it will go a long way if we can get Lily's sister, Claire, to support reopening the case."

"I agree, but she has refused to speak to me."

"I know," Travis said, "but maybe with Peter retracting his statement, and knowing now there was another man in Lily's life, she will reconsider."

"Hey, I'm all for trying," Chelsea agreed.

"Good. Lily's sister lives in Santa Clarita. It would just be a little detour on the drive back to Los Angeles to stop in and see if she'll talk to us."

"I'm up for it," Chelsea said.

She was still high on having gotten Peter to admit to his falsehoods and relaxed from a night of incredible lovemaking. It felt like the tide might finally be turning in her and her dad's favor.

Chapter Twenty-Four

"This is it," Chelsea said, pointing to a mailbox with the address that they had for Claire Wong, Lily's half sister on their father's side. Claire had been twenty-two years old at the time of Lily's murder. She'd been in court every day of Chelsea's father's trial. Chelsea was sure the woman wouldn't be happy to see her, but she hoped Claire would be willing to listen. After all, if she was right, the wrong man was in jail for her sister's death. Claire had just as much incentive to get to the truth as Chelsea did.

Travis brought the car to a stop in front of a slightly rundown home surrounded by a good-size yard with mature trees and bushes. He and Chelsea sat in the car for a moment after he shut off the engine.

"Claire lived in LA at the time of Lily's death," Chelsea said. "She moved out here sometime after she inherited this place from her grandparents."

"It looks like it could use some TLC," Travis said.

"Claire was a community college student seven years ago. I don't know what she does now. Maybe she can't afford it."

"The background check I pulled on her had her employed at a small boutique in town." They sat in silence for another several seconds before Travis said, "Shall we?"

As they got out of the car, Chelsea noticed the curtains in the front window flutter. "Someone is inside, and they know we're here."

They walked up the front steps carefully since they appeared ready to crumble at any moment. The door opened before they had a chance to knock.

"What do you want?"

Claire Wong looked like a much older version of the young woman Chelsea had seen each day at her father's trial. The Claire standing in front of Chelsea now had aged two decades in the past seven years. Her pallor seemed to have a grayish tinge as if she didn't get enough sun. Her brown eyes and hair were dull and lackluster. She wore a sweater that was several sizes too big and jeans that did nothing to flatter.

Travis smiled at her. "Hi, we're sorry to bother you. We're looking for Claire Wong."

The woman's eyes flicked to Travis, then back to Chelsea. "Why? Who are you?"

"My name is Travis Collins."

"And my name is Chelsea Harper, although it used to be Chelsea Brooks."

Claire looked as if she had been slapped. "You're Franklin Brooks's daughter. I remember you now." She started to shut the door.

Chelsea slipped her hand around the door, stopping it from closing in their faces. "Please, we just want to talk," she said quickly.

"I don't care. I want you both to leave now."

"New information has come to light that exonerates my father. Don't you want to know the truth? Who really killed Lily?"

"Your father was convicted," Claire spat.

"What if the police, the prosecutor, everyone got it wrong? What if they just took the easy way out, and Lily's real killer has been walking free all this time? Since I started looking into my father's case, I've almost been run down, had my home broken into, and I've been shot."

Claire jolted, her eyes widening. "Oh, my God."

At least now she was listening. "That tells me someone doesn't want me looking into Lily's murder too hard, and I have to ask myself why that is."

Claire eyed Chelsea for a long moment. She prayed Claire was really thinking about what she had said.

Finally, Claire jerked her head at Travis. "Is he a cop?"

"I'm not a cop," he answered. "I'm a private investigator helping Chelsea get to the truth. We need your help in order to do that. Please."

After a moment, Claire opened the door and let them in. She led them to a kitchen table but didn't offer them anything to eat or drink. They sat.

"What do you want to know?" Claire asked hotly.

"Tell us about Lily," Travis said soothingly, taking the lead.

Claire visibly relaxed, a smile turning her mouth up and bringing some light into her eyes. "She was a great big sister. We had the same father, but he was never around for either of us. My mother died when I was nineteen, and Lily, she just jumped right in as a surrogate mother. Well, she'd always been somewhat of a surrogate mother. She was fifteen years older than me. I looked up to her like she was some sort of goddess." Claire laughed shortly. Then her smile fell, and her eyes hardened. "She was all I had, and your father took her from me."

"No," Chelsea said firmly. "I never believed that, and now I'm this close to proving it."

"How?" Claire crossed her arms over her chest, but a flicker of doubt flashed in her eyes. "What is this information you claim to have?"

Chelsea looked at Travis who nodded.

"We've learned that the eyewitness who said he saw my father leave Lily's house around the time of her murder lied."

Claire blinked, surprise widening her eyes. "Really."

"Yes," Chelsea answered. "He's agreed to sign a statement to that effect, too. He feels guilty for his part in putting my father in jail."

"That…that doesn't mean anything. It doesn't mean your father didn't kill Lily."

Travis interjected quickly, "We've also discovered that Lily likely had a new boyfriend whom no one ever questioned."

Claire's gaze moved away from Chelsea's face. Something about it struck Chelsea. "But you knew that already, right?" she asked.

Tears spilled down Claire's cheeks. "It doesn't matter. Your father killed Lily."

Chelsea fought the urge to reach across the table and slap the woman. She fisted her hands under the table.

Travis must have picked up on her anger. "Claire, do you know who Lily's new boyfriend was?" he asked softly.

Claire was quiet for so long Chelsea began to think she wouldn't answer. "No," she finally responded in a small voice. "She didn't tell me his name, and I never met him. Lily only said she had to be careful."

"Careful?" Travis pressed gently. "Why did Lily have to be careful?"

Claire shrugged. "I don't know. I didn't ask her."

"Did you tell the police this after Lily was killed?"

Chelsea asked, the anger in her voice too potent to conceal completely.

Claire noticed. "No," she said bitterly. "The cops said Franklin did it. I know he drank a lot, and he wanted to get back together with my sister, and she didn't want to. I didn't think it would help to throw some innocent guy to the cops."

"An innocent guy who didn't step forward after Lily, the woman he'd been dating, was murdered," Chelsea shot back. "Doesn't sound all that innocent to me."

"Telling the cops would have just muddied the waters," Claire said angrily. "They would have written Lily off as some promiscuous woman who got what she deserved. They had her killer, and I wasn't going to let him get away with it."

"The killer has gotten away with it," Chelsea said, acid in her voice. "For seven years while my dad sat in a jail cell because you didn't tell the truth."

Claire's eyes hardened. "How dare you? I loved my sister."

"Okay," Travis said. "Let's just everyone take a step back here. Breathe. We all want the same thing. To see Lily's killer pay for his crime."

Charged silence crackled between Chelsea and Claire. Lily's sister was just as bad as the cops and the prosecutor in her father's case. They'd all jumped to conclusions, and her father had paid the price.

"Lily may not have told you the name of the man she was seeing before she was killed, but is there anyone else she would have told?" Travis asked.

Claire pulled her gaze from Chelsea, but her scowl remained. "Maybe her best friend, Gina. But like I said,

Lily said she had to be careful, so I'm not sure if she told her, either."

"Do you still have any of Lily's belongings?" Travis asked. "Any old diaries or address books or anything where she might have mentioned this man?"

Claire hesitated. "I found an old diary of Lily's and some other things out at our father's place after he died."

"At your father's place? Why would she keep them there?" Travis asked.

Claire shrugged. "She lived with him for a while before she moved into her own place. Maybe she just forgot them."

"Would you mind if I took a look?"

Claire hesitated again. "I don't see how it could help." But she rose and disappeared into another part of the house.

"Are you okay?" Travis asked softly.

Chelsea shook her head but didn't give him any other response. She definitely wasn't okay. She didn't know what she was exactly. Livid at the authorities. Appalled at Claire's callousness with her father's life. She couldn't put her current state of mind into words. She wasn't sure there were any words to explain it.

Claire reappeared with a small box in her hands. "You can take it with you."

It was an obvious dismissal, but Chelsea didn't much care. She wanted to get out of this house and as far away from Claire as she could as soon as she could.

"But I'd like to have it back," Claire amended.

"I'll make sure you get it back as soon as possible," Travis assured her.

"I can't believe her." Chelsea said when Travis had driven away from Claire's house.

"I know that was hard to hear, but at least Claire confirmed for us that Lily did have a new man in her life. That was good. Hopefully something in this box will point to who he was."

"I can't wait until we get back to LA to look."

"Okay, how about I find us somewhere to eat, and we can see what's inside?"

They stopped at a diner about a mile from Claire's house. They ordered food, then Travis leaned over to look as Chelsea opened the box.

"A high school yearbook." Chelsea pulled it out. A bear was on the cover with his arms spread wide. A school year was embossed in gold between them. She flipped a few pages. She found Lily's graduation photo and stared for several long seconds before passing the yearbook to Travis.

"We should look at this more carefully later." He set the yearbook aside.

Chelsea reached back into the box and pulled out a small book. This one said *Diary* across the front. Chelsea opened the cover. The first entry was from January of the same year. She sighed dejectedly. "It's probably just her high school diary. It's not going to help us."

Travis took the diary from Chelsea's hands. "I don't know," he said, carefully flipping through pages. "I can understand why Lily may have left her high school yearbook at her father's place, but her diary? It seems like she would have taken it with her to make sure that her innermost thoughts stayed private."

Chelsea shrugged. "She was eighteen when she wrote it. Maybe she just forgot about it."

Travis turned another page. "She didn't forget." He slid the book over so Chelsea could see the date on the page he had open two thirds of the way into the diary. It was dated two months before Lily was killed.

The handwriting was more refined than in the earlier entries, but it was still clearly Lily's.

"It looks like she started writing in her diary again before she died. Maybe she left it at her father's because she was being careful, as her sister mentioned." Travis said.

Chelsea grabbed the book. She flipped through several pages. All of the ones toward the end were dated from that fall. She looked up at him, confused. "Why would Lily have felt she needed to be so careful?"

"My guess is if we read these entries, we'll find out."

She flipped to the end of the diary. "Usually I avoid spoilers, but I'll make an exception in this case. If Lily was having trouble with the new man in her life, and he killed her, her last entries will probably be the most telling."

Travis couldn't argue with her logic although he wanted to read the old diary carefully as soon as possible.

Chelsea scanned over the pages, reading quickly. "She was dating someone, but she didn't say his name. She only gives his initials. WR. She sounds worried." Travis watched as she swallowed hard. "She's worried about telling my dad about the new guy. How he will react," she said, her eyes not leaving the page.

"Does she say why?" Travis asked softly. If Lily was afraid of telling Franklin she was moving on, that gave support to the people who believed Franklin had killed her out of jealousy and possessiveness.

Chelsea didn't answer right away, but the book slid from her hands and onto the table. She turned to look at him, her eyes glazed over as if she'd been stunned.

"Chelsea, what is it?" He reached for the diary, which had fallen closed when she dropped it.

"Lily. She wrote that she was worried about how my

father would take it when he found out she was seeing his best friend. Bill Rowland," Chelsea murmured. "Travis, Lily's new boyfriend was my uncle Bill."

Chapter Twenty-Five

Uncle Bill opened the door and smiled when his gaze landed on Chelsea. It was a smile she couldn't return. She still couldn't bring herself to believe that her father's best friend had been sneaking around with Lily behind his back. There had to be another explanation. Something that didn't involve Uncle Bill betraying her father.

"Well, hello there. Isn't this a pleasant surprise?" Uncle Bill said.

"Uncle Bill, this is Travis Collins, the private investigator I hired to look into Dad's case."

"Nice to meet you, sir." Travis extended his hand.

Uncle Bill started for a moment, possibly surprised by Travis's formality. "Well, it's nice to meet you, too."

"I'm sorry for dropping by without calling first," Chelsea said, both anxious to get answers and terrified of them at the same time. "Do you have a minute to speak with us?"

"I always have time for you, sweetie. Come on in." Uncle Bill led them into the sunroom. "I'm taking advantage of every nice sunny day we have left."

His battered old recliner faced the glass wall of windows. Across from it was a matching love seat, slightly less worn. To his left was an end table with a pitcher of water and a coffee mug on top. The day's paper lay open on the seat of the recliner, clearly having been discarded there when he rose to answer the doorbell. Uncle Bill folded the paper along its creases and tossed it onto the floor before sitting.

She and Travis claimed the love seat.

"Sorry, I don't have any refreshments prepared right now. The market is on my list of things to do today. I can get you water if you'd like?" Uncle Bill made to get up, but Chelsea lifted a hand to stop him.

"That's okay. We're good."

"Okay," he said, sitting back into his recliner. "What can I do for you then?"

"You know I've been looking into Lily's murder," Chelsea said.

Uncle Bill nodded slowly. She could tell this was a subject he didn't want to talk about.

"Lily's sister finally agreed to talk to us. Lily wanted to keep it a secret because her new boyfriend was a friend of Dad's. She found Lily's diary after Dad's trial, and in it Lily mentions seeing a man whose initials were WR."

Uncle Bill's leg jiggled, and he wouldn't look at Chelsea. "I don't know what you're talking about."

"Sir, we could go back through your phone and computer records, if necessary, but it would be better for everyone, for Chelsea, if you told us the truth now," Travis said.

Chelsea suspected he was exaggerating. They didn't have any authority to obtain, much less search, Uncle Bill's computer, and nothing they'd uncovered to date was enough to compel the police to reopen her father's case.

But Uncle Bill didn't know that, and even if he did, tapping into his feelings for her seemed to do the trick.

He looked at her with eyes shining with tears. "Does your father know?"

Chelsea felt tears well in her own eyes. "No, and I'm not sure I'm going to tell him. It depends on what you tell me now."

"Nothing I can say will change anything."

"It will bring us one step closer to finding the truth, sir," Travis said.

Uncle Bill stared out the window for a long moment before answering. "Okay. What do you want to know?"

"How did your relationship with Lily begin?" Travis asked.

Chelsea was happy to let him take the lead questioning her uncle. She had too many emotions swirling through her to focus on asking the questions they needed answers to at the moment.

"We met when she and Franklin started dating. She was an amazing woman. Too good for Franklin. Too good for me as well."

"And when did the two of you begin your separate relationship?"

"Nothing happened until after Frank and Lily ended things."

"Did Lily end things with my dad because of you?" Chelsea chimed in, bitterness lacing each syllable.

"No. Lily wasn't that kind of woman. She was fai~~ to your dad even when he wasn't faithful to her," Bill spat. His gaze flashed with anger that Chel~~ with anger of her own.

"Okay," Travis said in a quelling tone. "Ho~~ it after Lily and Franklin broke up that y~~ gether?"

"I don't know," Uncle Bill said,

Travis. "You have to understand Franklin was very volatile during those days. He was drinking and stepping out on Lily a lot. We were both concerned about him. He'd always been a heavy drinker, but it had gotten so much worse, and neither of us knew what to do about it. We tried talking to him, but he would just get angry. We spent a lot of time commiserating, and one thing led to another." Uncle Bill's eyes shifted back to Chelsea. "But like I said, nothing happened until it was over between Lily and Franklin."

He seemed sincere, but Chelsea wasn't sure she could believe him. After all, he'd been lying to her for the past seven years.

"You visited Lily at her home, correct?" Travis said, pulling Uncle Bill's attention back to him.

"Sometimes, yes."

"What about the night she was killed? Were you two still together then?" Chelsea asked. All the fire seemed to have gone out of Uncle Bill. He stared down at the tiled sunroom floor. "We were."

"Did you tell the police about your relationship after Lily was killed?" Chelsea asked.

Uncle Bill looked up. "No," he answered, his voice small.

"So, you just let Dad take the fall?" Disgust at the man ⸺tting in front of her swept through her body. She hadn't ⸺wn him at all.

⸺ncle Bill looked at her, his eyes imploring. "I didn't ⸺ily. I may be a coward for not telling the cops about ⸺ationship with her, but I did not kill her."

⸺ere were you the night Lily was murdered?" Tra-

⸺ver forget it. I was out with my employees. Celebrating the opening of my second shop. I would have loved to have Lily there with me, but we were still taking things slow. Keeping our relationship to ourselves so we didn't hurt Franklin." Uncle Bill stared out of the windows again, but this time it was clear he was looking into the past. "He was supposed to be there, too, but he never showed up."

Probably because he was meeting with Lily. It was the perfect time, since Lily would have known that Bill wouldn't show up to interrupt them.

"So, you think Franklin might have killed Lily?" Travis returned to his questioning.

Uncle Bill shrugged. "I don't know. He was a mean drunk, but I had never seen him be violent toward anyone. But who else could it have been?"

"Maybe Lily had a third boyfriend?" Chelsea said bitterly.

Uncle Bill's expression turned to surprise as if he'd never even considered the possibility. But if Lily had been playing around with her father and Uncle Bill, it was more than possible she had other companions. It seemed she wasn't as nice as she led everyone to believe she was.

"Did you know if Lily was having difficulties with anyone specific?" Travis asked.

Uncle Bill's forehead crinkled. "What do you mean?"

"We were told she had a vandalism incident and a possible break-in at her place."

"Oh, yeah. I think she mentioned something like that. But nothing came of it. Probably just kids messing around."

"Did she ever find out who did it?"

"If she did, I don't remember. You might try askin' neighbor. Kind of a busybody." Uncle Bill rolled h'

"Knew everything that happened in the neighb'

"Gina McGrath?" Travis asked.

"Gina? No." Uncle Bill shook his head. "I was talking about the guy. John. Justin. Something starting with a *J*. He was always in Lily's business."

"Jace," Chelsea supplied the name.

"Maybe," Uncle Bill said, sounding unsure. "It's been too long for me to be certain."

Chelsea shot a glance at Travis, but his gaze was locked on Bill's face.

"Lily thought he was a nice, if somewhat lonely, guy," Uncle Bill continued, "but he gave me the creeps."

"He did? Why?" Travis pressed.

"Well, he was always finding reasons to come over to Lily's place. And more than once, I caught him looking at her from the windows of his house."

A spidery feeling crawled down Chelsea's back.

Uncle Bill snapped his fingers. "If you ask me the cops should have taken a much harder look at that guy."

Chapter Twenty-Six

Travis spoke to Kevin on speaker as he drove away from Bill Rowland's house.

"So, Franklin's best friend was seeing Lily at the time of her death. Man, that is some friend," Kevin summarized the information Travis had just conveyed.

Travis cut a look at Chelsea who still seemed to be in a state of shock. "Chelsea's in the car with me."

"Oh, sorry, Chelsea," Kevin apologized.

"No, you're right. I'm struggling to wrap my mind around how Uncle Bill could have done this to my dad."

"We will need to check on Bill's alibi for the night of the murder," Travis said.

Kevin groaned. "Confirming a seven-year-old alibi. Give me something hard, why don't you?"

"Sorry." Travis stopped at a corner to let a jogger cross the street before making a right-hand turn. "Bill Rowland swears he had nothing to do with Lily's death but—"

"But he's been lying for nearly a decade, so we can't trust anything he has said," Chelsea interrupted.

Travis stole a glance at her. She was focused on the scenery outside the passenger window, avoiding his gaze.

"Bill gave us the names of the employees he remembers being at the party the night of the murder. So them no longer work for him, so they don't have a strong incentive to lie for him if they were ever inclined to do so." Travis ordered the virtual assistant on his phone to send the list of names to Kevin. Seconds later, he heard a faint ping come from the other side of the line.

"Got it," Kevin said. "I'll get started on running down this alibi. What are you going to do?"

"I think the most important thing right now is to focus on the information Bill gave us," Travis said, slowing to a stop at a red light. "If Jace Orson was at home the night Lily died, and he lied about it, we need to know why."

"Agreed," Kevin said.

"I'm going to drop Chelsea off at her house, and then I'll come into the office," Travis replied.

"Wait, what?" Chelsea finally tore her attention away from the window to look at him. "Drop me off? No way."

"Guys, I'm going to hang up," Kevin said before quickly ending the call.

"Chelsea, Jace Orson might not be involved at all." But Travis's gut was telling him that wasn't the case. "But if he is, he's probably the person who tried to run you down and vandalized your home and shot at you. He's dangerous."

"He's dangerous to you, too, then."

"But I'm trained to deal with dangerous people, and you aren't. You hired me for a reason. Let me do my job."

She looked like she wanted to argue with him. Instead, she pressed her lips together tightly.

"Listen." He tried a different approach. "I'll reach out to Jace again. When we spoke to him, we weren't thinking about him as a suspect in Lily's murder. I'll see how he responds to the suggestion that he lied about where he was the night of the murder. Maybe there is some innocent explanation."

"You don't believe that, or you would take me with you to talk to him." She was too astute for her own good.

"There is a lot West can do, but ultimately we have to turn this case over to the cops and the prosecutor if you want to get your dad out of prison. Let me do my job. I'll let you know what's happening as soon as I can."

Chelsea stayed silent, the tension building in the car to the point he couldn't stand it anymore.

"I can't take the chance that you'll get hurt again if something goes wrong," he said softly. "You've already been shot. I can't—I don't think I could survive it."

Chelsea hesitated for a beat longer. "Okay. I'll sit home twiddling my thumbs."

He let out a sigh of relief and a bark of laughter at the same time. "I doubt that. Actually, I was thinking you could call your cousin, Victor, and have him stay with you."

"Stay with me?"

"I don't want you to be alone. Maybe Victor could help you finish painting."

Now Chelsea laughed. "You don't know Victor. Painting would be the last thing he'd want to do, but I will call him."

She made the call while he drove. Victor was waiting for them in front of Chelsea's house when they pulled up a little while later.

Travis put the car in Park but didn't shut off the engine.

Instead of getting out of the car, Chelsea grabbed his forearm. "This feels like one of those moments in the movies when the hero goes off to face the bad guy and doesn't come back."

He lifted a hand and caressed her cheek. "This is a movie, and I'm no hero."

"I beg to differ with that last part." She leaned forward and placed a fast, hard kiss on his lips. "Promise me you'll be careful and come back to me safe."

He knew it was a fool's promise. Nothing was ever certain in life. But if it alleviated even a moment of her worry, he also knew he'd make that promise a million times over. "I promise."

It was a promise he had every intention of keeping.

Chapter Twenty-Seven

Damn. Damn. Damn. He had been reduced to sneaking into his own house through the back door. It had been all he could do to control his temper and not slam the door as he went in. The last thing he needed was to draw more attention to himself. His neighbors kept to themselves for the most part, but he had no idea who else Chelsea and her private investigator had spoken to. Whether they'd spread their suspicions about him to his neighbors. But he knew they were looking for him. He knew that they knew, or at least suspected, he killed Lily.

He shuddered. Thinking about how it would feel to have everyone know that he killed Lily. They'd look at him the way they looked at Franklin Brooks. Worse than the way they looked at him. The rage was threatening to take over again, but this time he didn't try to stop it. He didn't want to control it anymore.

He headed into his bedroom and went straight for the closet. Pushing aside the clothes folded neatly on the overhead shelf, he exposed two boxes. One held his mementos. The other his gun. Chelsea had left him no choice. His life as he knew it was over. But that didn't mean he couldn't exact some revenge before it all exploded for good.

He took the gun from its case, holding it for a moment,

feeling the steel in his hand, its weight and balance. Then he slid in a loaded magazine.

He'd given Chelsea Harper the chance to walk away before.

He wouldn't give her that chance this time.

Chapter Twenty-Eight

Chelsea took a step back and eyed the newly painted living room walls. It had taken her and Victor the better part of the evening to paint over the walls with the light blue shade that she'd selected, but she liked the results.

Chelsea set her roller down on a piece of newspaper. "Ready to start doing the trim?"

Victor groaned. "We don't have to do it all in one day."

"I want to get my house back together. And I don't want to have to prep the room a second time just to do the trim."

Victor groaned again, shooting a glance at the sand and eggshell paint cans. "Well, can we at least take a break? The pizza will be here soon, and I'm starving."

"Okay, but after we eat, we knock this trim out. I want to get my home back."

The sound of gunfire burst from the television speakers, drawing their attention. Their pending project would have taken considerably less time if Victor hadn't brought along the *Dark Knight* trilogy on DVD. She and her cousin shared a love of action and superhero films, and even though they'd seen the Christian Bale movies nearly half a dozen times each, Chelsea loved watching them again with her cousin.

Victor's attention was glued to the television, but Chelsea's eye landed on a white envelope she hadn't noticed on the television stand earlier.

"Hey, what is this?" she asked, crossing the room and picking up the envelope.

Victor glanced over at her, then back to the television. "Oh, it was wedged between your screen door and your front door when I got here. It must have been delivered while you were staying with Travis."

"Yeah, I guess." She turned the envelope over. The return address was for a law firm in San Diego.

Victor cleared his throat.

Chelsea pulled her gaze from the envelope to look at her cousin. "What?"

"About Travis."

"What about Travis?"

"I know you're a grown woman, but I worry about you. You're my cousin, and you're like a sister to me. I don't want to see you hurt again."

"Travis is nothing like Simon."

Victor held his hands out. "I'm not saying he is. Just that it seems like the two of you have grown close. This investigation is a lot. You're close to maybe finally proving your father's innocence, and that could leave you emotionally vulnerable."

"Emotionally vulnerable?" Chelsea teased.

"Ugh, I mean the last thing I want to do is talk to you about your romantic life. Just know that if that man hurts you, he will have to answer to me."

Chelsea smiled and threw her arms around her cousin. "You know how much I love you, don't you?"

Victor squeezed her in a tight bear hug. "I do. And I love you, too."

The doorbell rang, signaling the arrival of their pizza. "I'll get it." Victor stepped out of the embrace.

"I'll grab some paper plates for us," Chelsea said, heading for the kitchen while opening the envelope she still held in her hand. She stopped just inside the kitchen, shocked at the information in the letter.

Her father-in-law had made her a beneficiary in his will. The letter was brief and didn't get into details about exactly what she'd inherited, but it invited her to reach out to the lawyers to discuss the issue more fully as soon as possible.

So, this was why Simon had been so desperate to talk to her. She wondered if he knew what she had inherited. She was debating whether to call the lawyers right then when Victor screamed, "Chelsea! Run!"

There was a loud crack, a groan and then a thump.

Someone was in her house.

Despite Victor's order to run, her feet felt as if they were glued to the ground. Her brain finally sent the message to move, but she knew she couldn't just leave Victor. "Victor?" She started for the front door.

He was lying face down on the floor in front of the door. The man standing over him looked up.

Jace Orson.

Jace smiled at her, and her stomach twisted into knots. "Chelsea. Good to see you again."

She turned and ran back into the kitchen. Jace's footsteps pounded on the hardwood floors behind her. She grabbed at a counter drawer, reached inside and pulled out a knife.

"Ah, ah, ah. I wouldn't do that if I were you."

She turned to find Jace pointing a gun at her.

"Put down the knife, Chelsea."

She didn't have any choice. A knife couldn't beat a bullet. Her shoulder throbbed at the memory of having been shot. Jace was even closer now. If he pulled the trigger, he wouldn't just graze her this time. It would be a direct hit.

The knife clattered as she let it drop to the countertop.

"Good girl. Now come here."

She didn't move.

Jace crossed the kitchen in three long strides. "I said come here!" He grabbed her arm, wrenching it behind her back in a painful twist, and pulled her tightly against his chest. "From here on out, you do exactly what I tell you. Do you understand?"

Her eyes filled with tears of terror. She nodded.

"Say it!" Jace yelled.

"Ye-yes," she stammered.

"Good. Now move."

"My cousin... He needs help."

"The guy at the door? He'll be fine. At least he will be as long as you do what you're told."

"You didn't... Is he?" A different kind of fear flooded through her.

"He's not dead. I told you he's fine for now. I just needed him out of the way to get to you." Jace pulled on her injured arm drawing a wince forcing her forward. "We need to go."

"I'm not going anywhere with you." She struggled against him.

"No?" Jace yanked her into the hallway where Victor still lay on the floor not moving. "Maybe I'll have to show you how serious I am." He pointed the gun at Victor's head.

"No! No, I'll go with you." If going with Jace kept Victor safe, kept him alive, she'd go. She would trade Victor's life for hers.

She let Jace push her forward, stepping over Victor's prone form and out the front door. Travis would come for her. She just had to do everything she could to stay alive until he did.

THE WEST SECURITY AND INVESTIGATIONS offices were busy with activity when Travis arrived. He'd gone to Jace's house before heading to the office, but no one answered. It looked like he hadn't been there for a couple of days, which didn't necessarily mean anything, but Travis's instincts were buzzing. They were onto something.

The first thing he did when he got back to the office was request a rush background check on Jace Orson. The company they worked with was good and promised to have something to him within two hours. He also tried calling Jace at his accounting firm, but his boss said he hadn't heard from Jace in days.

Travis spent the next couple hours calling Bill Rowland's alibi witnesses for the night of Lily's murder. He'd just gotten off the phone with one of them when his computer dinged with an incoming email. Jace Orson's background report. He read it quickly, then printed out a copy before hurrying into Kevin's office.

"I think I got something." Travis handed the report to him.

"What is it?" Kevin flipped through the pages, scanning.

"Jace Orson has a red Mazda registered in his name." He reached across the desk and helped Kevin flip to the relevant page. "Chelsea and I saw him get out of that vehicle the day we met him. But he also has a black Oldsmobile in his name."

Kevin made the connection instantly. He looked up

from the pages in his hand with a sparkle in his eye that said they'd just hit on something significant. "Just like the car that tried to run down Chelsea."

"Exactly," Travis responded excitedly.

"Okay, it adds to the questions we want to ask Mr. Orson, but it doesn't exactly help us find him."

That, unfortunately, was true.

"Did you find a second residence? Maybe a family member's place where he might be staying?" Kevin handed the papers back to Travis.

"No," Travis said, his frustration doubling. "Both of Orson's parents are deceased. He's an only child. The Oldsmobile was his mother's. It looks like he inherited it when she died three years ago, but the registration is still active, so it's likely he has it stored somewhere."

"Could be in a paid parking spot or in a self-storage unit. If he used it in a hit-and-run, he wouldn't want to park it in his driveway where everyone could see it. That could also be where he's hiding out. Assuming he is hiding out," Kevin added pointedly. "He could just as easily be at a conference or on vacation."

Travis shook his head. "I checked with the IT firm where he works on my way back to the office from his house. He hasn't been in for the last three days. He didn't call in sick or arrange for time off. He probably won't have a job when, if, he shows up."

"So, he's nuking his life." Kevin frowned. The concern in his tone was unmistakable, and Travis shared it.

"Yes." If Jace was at the point where he no longer cared about showing up for work or at his house, he might feel like he had nothing left to lose. That could mean he was desperate, and desperate people were very dangerous. "But it gets worse. The IT firm is a state contractor. I recognized the company's name from my time with the LAPD. They provide the IT guys for the police department's help desk. Orson's boss told me that Orson was assigned to the Hollywood police station until early this year."

"So, Orson had access to all the LAPD's police files."

Travis nodded. "It's possible. I'd even go so far as to say, given what we now know, that he knew Chelsea was looking into her father's case."

Kevin stroked his chin. "It wouldn't be hard for a computer technician to tag a file, so he's notified when it was accessed."

"No, it wouldn't be hard at all," Travis agreed.

"Okay, well, all we can do is keep searching for him," Kevin said, turning back to his computer. "In the meantime, we've got an attorney working on the affidavit for Peter Schmeichel. He's hopeful that it will be done by the end of the week or early next at the latest."

Travis frowned. That gave Peter plenty of time to change his mind. He hoped that didn't happen. Peter seemed remorseful about his lies.

"I reached out to three of the nearly dozen names Rowling gave me," Kevin said. "They all remembered the party and confirmed that, to the best of their recollection, Bill was at the party the whole night. One person was even able to send me photos of Bill with a dozen other people. The metadata from those photos confirms the dates and times Bill gave us."

"That's a pretty airtight alibi."

"Yeah, I'm not feeling Rowland for a murderer," Travis responded.

"But you are feeling Jace Orson?"

The knot in Travis's chest twisted tighter. "I am. Now we just have to prove it."

His phone rang, and he plucked it out of his pocket. "Hello?" The voice on the other end spoke so fast that it took him a moment to realize it was Victor, Chelsea's cousin. "Victor, slow down. I can't understand what you're saying."

"It's Chelsea. She's been... I think she's been kidnapped."

JACE PUSHED CHELSEA toward his car, the barrel of the gun pressed into her back. He opened the passenger door and shoved her over the middle console and into the driver's seat before climbing into the passenger seat himself. He handed her the keys and ordered, "Drive."

She started the engine without protest and pulled from the driveway, praying some nosy neighbor was watching her be kidnapped and was on the phone at that very moment calling out the cavalry. She gripped the steering wheel with white knuckles, her entire body on alert as she assessed her situation.

It was dire. Jace held the gun below the view of the window but pointed it at her with his finger on the trigger. His eyes were on the road.

"Where are we going?"

"Just drive," he responded.

So, she did. When they neared the interchange for an older, underused stretch of road, he directed her to it. "Make this right."

She did as she was told, still trying to formulate a plan. It was late, and the old highway had seen a drop in traffic since the nearby freeway had been built. She hoped someone had seen her kidnapping and called the cops, but she couldn't count on it. If she wanted to get out of this situation alive, she'd have to do it on her own.

She took a deep breath, trying to remain calm and focus on finding a solution. Her first order of business was making sure Jace didn't just decide to kill her and be done with her. He had, she was sure now, killed Lily, but she still had no real idea why. Maybe if she could get him talking, she could get an answer and distract him enough so that she could get away.

She swallowed the ball of terror in her throat and spoke. "You killed Lily."

Jace's body stiffened, but he didn't respond.

Chelsea continued, "You killed her, and you let my father take the blame for her murder. Why?"

"He deserved it. He never treated my Lily like she should have been treated. Like the treasure she was. I tried to tell her she deserved better."

"You tried to tell her?" She remembered he'd said something similar the day she and Travis met him.

"I thought she understood. She broke up with him, but then she started dating that other guy."

Uncle Bill. "Is that why you killed her? Because she wouldn't date you?"

"She was mine."

"She was her own person. She belonged to herself, and she didn't deserve what you did to her," Chelsea growled, forgetting her fear for a moment. She glanced away from the road to take a look at Jace.

He showed no remorse at all. His eyes were cold and emotionless. Empty. "She was mine, and now she is mine forever." He stared out the front windshield, his voice eerily calm.

That was probably as close to a confession as she was

likely to get from him. His calmness was the most ter-rifying part of her current ordeal. Jace didn't seem to be bothered in the least at having killed Lily. Just like he wouldn't be bothered at all by killing Chelsea.

Her pulse raced as an almost uncontrollable urge to get out of the car and as far away from the monster beside her racked her body with tremors. But she needed to keep calm and clearheaded if she had any hope of surviving this. Jace had eluded justice for seven years. He might be a sick monster, but he wasn't stupid. She had to keep him talking until she had a plan.

"So, what now? You can't hope to get away. The private investigator I've been working with knows you killed Lily. The cops probably know I'm missing by now and are looking for me." She hoped that part was true. "They'll realize that you kidnapped me sooner rather than later."

Jace finally showed some sign of emotion, his face twisting into a mask of rage. "Just keep driving and shut up!" His fury blew through the car.

Chelsea stopped talking. She'd blown it, and now he was going to have to drive to some remote area and kill her. Well, she wouldn't go down without a fight.

Several minutes passed in silence. They crested a hill, and Chelsea saw headlights shining a dozen yards in front of them. A hasty, dangerous plan formed in her head. There was no time to think it through.

As the truck passed by them, she slammed on the brakes, her seat belt yanking her back sharply. Jace jerked forward, too, the gun flying from his hands and landing on the floor well in front of him. His head banged against the dashboard.

She wasted no time throwing the car door open and

running toward the truck. It had already passed by them, but their sudden stop had the truck slowing. She ran.

She heard the passenger door to the car open behind her and a gunshot ring out.

Chapter Twenty-Nine

Travis's heart raced. He was more afraid than he had ever been in his life. Victor had calmed down enough on the phone to explain that he'd opened Chelsea's door to a man pointing a gun toward him. After he'd yelled out a warning to Chelsea, he'd been knocked out. When he'd come to, Chelsea and the man were gone. Victor had gotten a quick look at the car the man drove, and although he didn't get the license plate, the description matched Jace's red Mazda.

A patrol car was already at Chelsea's house, but Kevin drove Travis to the police station. Travis burst into the police conference room and barked, "What do you know?"

Detective Owens rose from his seat as did the other man at the conference table.

"You can't just come bursting in here, Collins!" Lieutenant Zach Grady blustered. Grady had been in charge of the precinct while Travis was a cop. They hadn't gotten along even before Travis went to Internal Affairs about his dirty colleagues.

"Slow down, Travis," Owens said, stepping between him and Grady. "We are already doing everything that can be done. The BOLO is out. Squad cars all over the city are on alert. I notified the state police myself, and they're combing the interstate. They're also standing by to offer any other support we might need." He put a hand on either of Travis's shoulders. "We'll find her."

That was all fine and good, but Owens hadn't answered Travis's question. How had Jace gotten to Chelsea in the first place?

"How did this happen?" Travis bit out again.

Owens looked at the lieutenant and got a nod from his boss before answering. "It looks like Jace got the jump on Chelsea's cousin."

Travis vibrated with anger.

"When Victor Harper came to, he called it in. We got there quickly and set up a perimeter, but we think Jace had a ten- to fifteen-minute head start on us."

Ten to fifteen minutes. It didn't sound like much, but a car could turn that into significant distance. Especially since they didn't have a clue where Jace was heading.

"Mr. Harper is in the hospital. He probably has a concussion, but he'll be okay." Owens darted a look at the lieutenant.

"What?" Kevin asked, looking between the two police officers.

"Mr. Harper was pistol-whipped," Owens answered.

Pistol-whipped. Jace had a gun. So, Chelsea might already be—

Travis wouldn't let himself think about it. Except he couldn't stop. Chelsea had been kidnapped by an obsessed killer. A man who had already killed once and who probably knew the authorities knew it. He had nothing to lose by exacting revenge and killing Chelsea.

Don't hurt her. Please don't hurt her.

But Jace would. That was his plan. To kill Chelsea.

Travis had to find them first.

"Like Owens said, we're doing everything humanly possible to find Ms. Harper," Grady chimed in.

"You have someone at Jace's house?" Travis asked.

Grady nodded. "We're executing a search warrant now."

Travis turned for the door, stopping only when Owens grabbed his arm. "Where do you think you're going?"

"To Orson's house to help with the search."

Owens shook his head. "You know you can't be there."

"Chelsea and I have been looking into Lily Wong's case. I have more insight into this guy now than either of you do. I may see something that clues us in to where he's taking her that your guys won't."

Owens looked at Grady again, an entire conversation taking place between the longtime colleagues without a word spoken.

Finally, Grady nodded again. "You can't touch anything," he said to Travis before turning to Owens. "Go with him."

Orson's house was swarming with officers when Travis and Owens arrived. Travis was out of the car before Owens shut off the engine. They stepped inside the house together.

Travis forced himself to take several deep breaths and think. People were creatures of habit. There had to be something in the house that hinted at Jace's plan. He had to find it. He walked through the house with Owens, touching nothing just as Grady had directed. He didn't need to touch anything. Not yet anyway. He needed to get a feel for how Jace lived first. How he used the space. That was likely to tell him where Jace would hide anything of value.

As he did, he thought about Chelsea. She was a fighter.

She had proven that by fighting for her dad when everyone, including him, thought it was a lost cause.

Owens spoke quietly to one of the officers in the hall. When he returned, Travis knew the news wasn't good. "So far they haven't found anything, but we aren't done looking."

Ignoring Lieutenant Grady's admonishment to look and not touch, Travis went to Orson's bedroom.

The officer searching the room spun around as he entered. "Hey, you can't be here!"

Owens stepped into the room behind Travis with his badge out. "It's okay, Officer Johnson," Owens read the name on the officer's chest. "He's with me. Why don't you go help in the basement?"

Officer Johnson trotted out of the bedroom.

Travis marched to the nightstand and yanked the door open.

Owens didn't say a word about Travis ignoring the lieutenant's instructions. Instead, he went to the closet and picked up searching where Officer Johnson had left off. After a few minutes, he called, "Hey, I think I've got something."

Owens pulled a metal box from the closet and set it on the bed as Travis walked over to join him. The box had a flimsy lock. Owens borrowed a flashlight from one of the officers in another room, and with two solid hits, the lock gave way.

Inside were photographs. Hundreds of them of Lily from years ago and dozens that had been taken more recently. Of Chelsea. There were even a few photographs of Travis. Orson had clearly been watching them. Of course he had.

"This is creepy," Owens said. "Jace was stalking Lily Wong."

"And Chelsea," Travis added.

The detective's cell phone rang. "Owens." He was silent for a moment, then said, "Lieutenant, I'm going to put you on speaker so Travis can hear." Owens hit a button on the screen. "Okay, Lieutenant. Go ahead."

"We just got a call from a driver out on Old Route 1. They said they passed a red Mazda, and a woman jumped out. Followed by a man with a gun. The passerby reported shots fired."

Travis went numb. "Chelsea. Is she—"

"The driver who called it in said a man shot at his truck. The bullet didn't hit him or his vehicle, but it scared him. He drove off but called it in as soon as he was sure the shooter wasn't following him."

"So, we don't know if Chelsea—" Travis started.

Lieutenant Grady cut him off. "I've got units rolling in the direction that the man said the car was headed. And the state police are putting a chopper in the air."

Travis looked at Owens.

Owens pulled his keys from his coat pocket. "I'll drive."

CHELSEA THREW HERSELF onto the paved highway. Tires screeched, and she lifted her head in time to see the truck tear off down the highway. Tears rolled down her cheeks as she watched the brakes fade into darkness.

Then Jace was there beside her.

"Get up," he ordered.

She looked up into the barrel of the gun. She stood.

He grabbed her arm and turned her around roughly, so her back was to him. The cold metal of the gun pressed against her temple. His breath touched her cheek, his voice pure rage. "I should shoot you right now but I'm not going to make the same mistake I made with Lily. When I'm finished with you nobody will ever find your body."

She didn't want to die. Not when she was so close to freeing her dad. Not at the hands of the man who had destroyed both of their lives. And not when she had finally found someone, she could see having a future with.

"Pl-please, no," she stammered.

"Don't worry. I have plans to make you pay for ruining my life. You don't deserve a quick death. Now, get back in the car. Move!"

Shaking uncontrollably, she walked with him to the car. Again, he directed her to the passenger side and pushed her over behind the wheel.

"Drive!" he yelled, pressing the gun into her side hard enough to make her yelp.

She got the car moving again.

"Faster! You just made a huge mistake. And I'm going to make sure you pay for it."

"You don't have to do this."

"I'm not going to jail."

"You didn't have any problem letting my father go to jail," Chelsea said, fury rising in her.

"Just shut up and drive!" Jace screamed.

The hysteria in his tone was enough to temper her fury and ignite another wave of fear. She knew she shouldn't antagonize him any further. Her attempt to escape hadn't gone the way she hoped, but the driver of the truck had gotten away. Surely, he had called the police. She just had to hang in there for a little longer.

They'd driven another several miles when she noticed the flashing lights in her rearview mirror. Jace noticed them at the same time.

"Faster." He slammed his hand down on her right thigh in an attempt to push the accelerator to the floor. The car sped up, but the next time she checked the rearview mirror, the flashing blue lights were closer and had doubled.

A voice came over the police cruiser's speaker. "Pull over."

"Don't," Jace said through gritted teeth.

She didn't stop the car, but she slowed. She wasn't sure what the cops knew. Did they know Jace was holding her against her will? Or had they only been told about a man who had shot at another driver? Would they open fire at the car with her in it?

She eased up on the accelerator even more.

"Don't stop." Jace reached across the car again, this time grabbing the wheel. The car veered across the center line in the road.

Chelsea yanked the wheel in the other direction, but she overcompensated. They went off the road completely this time, hitting the ditch beyond the shoulder.

Jace screamed next to her.

All four wheels left the ground for a brief moment, and then they were rolling. Once. Twice. The windshield cracked, and the driver window shattered into hundreds of pieces, scattering glass over the front seats.

Chelsea was completely disoriented, unsure which way was up as the car finally came to a stop.

Jace moaned.

She turned her head slowly, but pain still exploded in her skull. The car was upside down, balanced on its top, but their seat belts held both of them strapped to their seats. Yet somehow Jace had managed to hold on to the gun.

Chelsea's eyes widened, her pain forgotten as he raised the gun and pointed it in her direction.

OWENS AND TRAVIS rounded a curve in the highway, and Travis quickly took in the scene. The Mazda was fishtailing, swerving from one side of the road to the other before it dropped into the ditch at the side of the road. The sickening crash of metal nearly stopped his heart.

Travis watched in terror as the car rolled several times before coming to a stop. "Chelsea!" he screamed, opening his car door before Owens came to a complete stop, and raced toward the accident. The police cruiser that had been following along with them pulled over on the opposite shoulder of the road. Travis drew his gun as he raced past it, pushing aside the nearly paralyzing thought that Chelsea might be dead.

She wasn't dead. She couldn't be dead.

But she could be badly injured. The crash was bad. The Mazda was upside down.

He got to the driver's side of the car and knelt. Chelsea was in there, but the passenger seat was empty. "Chelsea? Baby, answer me, please?"

Chelsea turned her head slowly toward him. "Jace. He got out. Ran away."

"Don't worry about him. We'll get him."

A shot rang out, shattering the back window that had somehow remained intact after the crash.

Chelsea screamed.

Travis ducked down behind the rear of the car. "Jace! Give it up! You're surrounded."

But Orson clearly had no intention of giving up. Travis could hear him moving through the trees and shrubbery on the other side of the ditch. If he got enough distance between himself and the road, he stood a good chance of getting away.

Travis went back to the driver's-side window. "Chelsea, I'll be back. Hang in there for me, baby," he said, and then he took off after Orson.

Orson was fast, but Travis was motivated. He wasn't going to let him get away.

Orson pushed through the branches with Travis right behind, closing the distance. Travis put on a burst of speed and threw himself at Jace's back, slamming the man onto the pine-needle-covered ground. Jace's gun flew out to the side.

Anger flooded through Travis's body. He flipped Orson onto his stomach and drove his fist into the killer's face. He had never been so enraged or scared. This man was a killer. He had kidnapped Chelsea, and he probably planned to kill her.

Orson struggled, but Travis used his weight to hold him down while he pounded his fist into the monster's face. He wasn't sure how many times he hit him before he felt someone pulling him away.

"Travis, stop. Enough."

Owens dragged him off Orson. A second officer grabbed Jace's arms and slapped cuffs on his wrists.

"Go back to Chelsea," Owens ordered. "The EMTs got her out of the car, and they're about to transfer her to the ER."

Travis didn't have to be told twice. He backtracked through the woods at a run. "Chelsea!" he called as he cleared the trees. He spotted the gurney being lifted into the ambulance and raced forward. "Chelsea!" He ignored the EMT's protest as he hauled himself into the back of the ambulance.

"Sir, you can't be in here," the EMT said with a glower.

"It's okay. I want him here," Chelsea said.

The EMT shrugged and closed the back door and called to the driver to get them moving.

Travis sat on the bench across from the gurney and stroked Chelsea's cheek while the paramedic started an intravenous line in her arm.

"Hey, you're going to be okay, Chels." Travis leaned down and kissed her on the lips. "I have never been more afraid in my life. When I saw your car flipped over—"

She took his hand and squeezed. "I'm okay. Did you get him?"

Travis squeezed back. "We got him. He won't hurt anyone else ever again."

She sighed. "Then it's over. My father—"

"It will take a little more time, but your father is coming home." Travis stroked her cheek. "You did it, Chels. You got the truth and freed your father."

THE LAST SIX hours had taken Travis on a roller coaster of emotion, but the doctors had checked out both Victor and Chelsea and declared no permanent damage had been done to either. The cousins would be spending the night in the hospital, though. It had taken Victor, Chelsea and a doctor to get Brenda Harper to go home and get some rest, but she'd finally relented. Now it was time for Travis to do what he knew had to be done and say goodbye to Chelsea.

"They aren't going to let me out until tomorrow," Chelsea said, sounding displeased when he entered her hospital room.

"Well, I'm sure the doctors know what's best."

Chelsea pushed herself up straighter in the bed. "I was thinking that I could make dinner for us tomorrow when I get home. It would be nice to get back in my own kitchen."

She reached a hand out to him, but he didn't move closer to the bed to take it.

"You should probably rest when you get home," he said in a flat voice that sounded nothing like his own.

Chelsea let her hand fall to the mattress. "What's wrong?"

"Listen, Chelsea. We got the evidence you need to prove your father's innocence. Orson is in jail. West Investigations will work with you to get whatever evidence you need to the prosecutor."

"Oh." The hurt look that crossed her face nearly crushed him.

Silence fell.

"I told you I don't do the relationship thing," he said quietly.

"Yes, you did. If that's what you want, I guess that's it."

His heart felt like it was being squeezed in a vise. He wished he could be different, but it wouldn't be fair to either one of them.

"Thank you for everything," she said quietly.

"If you ever need anything, just call, okay? Anytime, day or night. I'll be there."

"Goodbye, Travis."

"Goodbye, Chelsea." He forced himself to turn away from the bed before she could see the tears welling in his eyes and walked out of the room.

You did the right thing, he repeated as he walked to his car and drove home.

Then why did it hurt so much?

Chapter Thirty

A week had passed since Chelsea had been released from the hospital. There was still a lot to do before her father was released from prison, but the prosecutor's office had filed the necessary paperwork with the court. There was little reason to wait once Jace Orson confessed, which he'd done once the police presented all the evidence they had on him. He was behind the call to her aunt, the hit-and-run and the shooting in front of the restaurant. Most important, he'd admitted to killing Lily.

Chelsea couldn't help wondering how different her life and her father's life would have been if the cops hadn't had tunnel vision seven years earlier. Or if they hadn't accepted Peter's lies. When she thought about it, the anger threatened to consume her, so she tried not to. It worked most of the time.

She tried to stay busy and keep her mind off Travis, too, but that didn't really work, either. She felt as if a part of her was missing. She hadn't realized how deeply she'd fallen for him until he walked away. She wanted to be angry at him, but he'd been honest with her. He told her from the start that he didn't want anything permanent. She was the one who had hoped for more.

But it wasn't to be. She needed to get herself together

and get over him. She repeated that mantra a hundred times a day, but it didn't seem to be working. She still ended every day crying herself to sleep.

Aunt Brenda had demanded that she and Victor appear for family dinner at her house that evening. Her aunt had struggled with the news that she'd been wrong about her brother for so many years. It had taken a few days, but she had finally got up the nerve to call Franklin two days earlier. Chelsea had only been able to hear her aunt's end of the call, and there had been a lot of crying, but it seemed like the siblings wanted to work on building a new relationship.

Aunt Brenda set a big bowl of mashed potatoes on the table and took her seat. She had also cooked a ham, cabbage, homemade biscuits and apple pie for dessert.

"You made a feast, Mom." Victor leaned over and planted a kiss on his mother's cheek.

"Yes, well, we are celebrating." Aunt Brenda beamed. "Franklin is coming home to his family, and it's all Chelsea's doing." Her aunt reached for her hand. "You have grown into an amazing woman, and I could not be prouder of you, sweetie."

"Thank you, Aunt Brenda. And I have an announcement to make, too. We have something else to celebrate. I've decided to go to law school."

Working on her dad's case had shown her just how much she loved helping people and the law. There were too many innocent people in jail. One was too many. And she could do something about it. She'd done her research, and there was still time for her to apply for a spring semester at several area law schools. She could even take a course or two at night as a nonmatriculated student during the fall term and have them count toward her degree when she enrolled as a student.

"Wow, Chels. Congrats," Victor said.

"There are so many people out there who need someone who knows the law to fight for them. I think I can do that for others."

"I know you can," Aunt Brenda said.

"I also spoke to Gerald's estate lawyer," Chelsea went on.

Victor scoffed. "Yeah? I bet Simon was none too pleased to hear they'd reached out to you."

"He was not. It was his job to inform me of the bequest as his father's executor." Chelsea piled mashed potatoes on her plate. "He wanted to get on my good side first."

"Ho ho! That means Gerald must have left you something good."

"Half the estate," Chelsea said.

Her aunt's fork dropped onto her plate with a clang.

Victor's mouth hung open. "Half his estate?"

"Apparently, Gerald wrote the will when Simon and I were married, specifically noting that Simon would take half and I would inherit the other half. He never changed his will. It was why Simon suddenly showed up again and has been calling me."

Victor whooped and raised his water glass with a grin. "Here's to Chelsea becoming an heiress."

"No. I spoke to Simon. I told him that I'd sign over my bequest to him as long as I could keep enough to pay for law school. He was more than happy to accept my proposal."

"Chelsea," Victor groaned.

"It's the right thing to do, Victor. I don't know if Gerald just never got around to changing his will or what, but he meant more to me than money. And I think he'd be happy that I'm going to graduate from law school debt-free. I know I am."

Victor groaned again. "You are too good, cuz."

Aunt Brenda tapped Victor's hand. "There is no such thing as 'too good,' Chelsea has made her decision, and that's that. Now let's eat."

They ate dinner and dessert, and when they were finished, Aunt Brenda insisted on cleaning up everything herself. Victor and Chelsea retired to the living room where Victor pulled up *Iron Man*, her all-time favorite Marvel movie, on Aunt Brenda's television.

"So have you heard from Travis?" Victor asked while the opening credits played.

"No," Chelsea said without looking away from the television. "And I don't expect to." She could feel Victor staring. "I don't. I hired him to do a job, he did it adequately, and now it's over."

"He did it adequately?" Victor's tone was incredulous. He reached for the remote and paused the movie. "It was clear that there was something going on between you two. Now it's just over?" He shook his head. "I don't believe that. You don't do casual relationships."

Chelsea tried forcing back the tears that threatened, but one got away from her.

Victor looked mortified. "Oh, I'm sorry. Don't cry. I shouldn't have brought it up." He wrapped her in a hug.

But it was too late. The floodgates had opened. Chelsea leaned into her cousin's arms. "He didn't want me, Victor. He didn't want me."

TRAVIS SAT AT his desk at the West Security and Investigations office. Phones rang. A meeting was being held in a conference room. Kevin had been holed up in his office all day. It seemed like everyone was busy except Travis.

He hadn't been able to get motivated since he walked out of Chelsea's hospital room and out of her life a week earlier. He needed to shake off his malaise, but all he'd thought about in the last week was Chelsea.

This had never happened to him before. Usually when he ended a relationship, he was able to move on quickly. *Because you never really cared about those women. You never loved them.*

It felt like with each day that passed without Chelsea he hurt even more. Missed her more. He needed to get his head on straight, like Kevin had said.

He glanced over the top of his cubicle wall and saw that his boss's office door was finally open. Thirty seconds later, he knocked on Kevin's door.

Kevin looked away from whatever he'd been reading on his computer monitor.

"Got a minute?" Travis asked.

"Absolutely. What's up?"

Travis crossed to one of the chairs in front of the desk and sat. "I wanted to know if you had anything for me. I'm a little light right now, and you know I like to keep busy."

Kevin's head tilted to the side. "To be honest, I'm surprised you aren't with Chelsea. We can manage around here without you for a few days. You should take some vacation time, you have certainly earned it."

"I don't think that would be a great idea. Chelsea has a lot on her plate right now. Recovering and getting her father out of prison." His gaze slid away from Kevin's face. "Her job is over, so I think it's best we both get on with our lives."

Kevin leaned back in his chair and frowned. "That's what you think is best?"

The pain that had been lingering in Travis's chest for days now became more acute, but he continued to ignore it.

Kevin shook his head, a pitying look on his face. "I thought you were smarter than this."

"Smarter than what?" Travis snapped. "You told me to get my head on straight. It's on straight now."

Kevin looked at him directly. "You think this is what I meant when I told you to get your head on straight? Because right now it looks like you have your head up your—"

Travis growled, cutting him off. "What did you mean then?"

"Man, I can't answer that question for you. Only you can. If you really think letting Chelsea go is the answer, then maybe it is." Kevin shrugged. "Maybe you don't deserve her." he turned back to his monitor. A dismissal.

Travis rose. He made it to the office door. "You really think I could make it work with Chelsea?" he asked, his hand on the doorknob but his back still to Kevin.

"I think when two people want a relationship to work, they make it work. The question is do you want to make it work?"

That was the question.

Chapter Thirty-One

It had been two days since his talk with Kevin, and Travis was no closer to figuring out how to live without Chelsea. He had made a little progress on the professional front, though. Kevin had assigned him to a case that was little more than busywork, collecting files from the Parks and Rec Department. He was heading up the steps of the municipal building when he caught sight of Chelsea's cousin, Victor. He considered turning away to avoid having to make small talk with the man, but Victor's gaze fell on him before he could make his getaway.

The anger marring Victor's face had Travis reconsidering turning and walking away.

Victor increased his pace, coming to a stop in front of Travis. "What the hell did you do to my cousin?"

Travis's heart rate increased. "What are you talking about? Did something happen to Chelsea?" She hadn't called. He'd told her to call if she ever needed anything.

"Yes, something happened to her. You. You happened to her."

Travis's chest tightened even more, but this time from confusion. "I don't understand. Is Chelsea okay?"

"No. She's not okay. She's heartbroken."

He felt himself relax a little, but his chest still felt as if an anvil sat on it. Heartbroken?

"She cried," Victor said, a note of mortification mingling with the anger in his voice. "She cried and said you told her you didn't want her."

"I never said that!"

Victor crossed his arms over his chest. "What did you say then?"

"I—" He hadn't said he didn't want her. He couldn't say that because it wasn't true. But he hadn't told her how much he wanted her, either. He hadn't told her that he loved her. And he did.

He groaned. Kevin was right. His head was up his—

"I told my cousin that if you ever hurt her, you'd be answering to me, and I meant it," Victor said, pulling Travis's attention back to him.

"You're right," Travis responded quickly.

Victor looked at him, confused. "I am? About what?"

"Everything. I'm an idiot. I love your cousin, and I stupidly pushed her away because—"

"Because you're an idiot." Victor grinned.

Travis smiled back. "Yes."

"Good. At least we agree on one thing."

"Look, I need your help."

"Is it helping you make a grand romantic gesture for Chelsea?"

"Let's not get carried away."

Victor tsked. "You are an idiot. If you want to make up with my cousin, you very much need to get carried away. It sounds like you definitely need my help."

CHELSEA PARKED HER car in front of Aunt Brenda's house and got out. The interior of the house was dark, but Victor had called her an hour ago and insisted she meet him there. Since she hadn't been doing much, just rewatching the *Black Panther* movies for the umpteenth time, she'd agreed to. Three more weeks of summer, and then she'd be back at work. The new school year, new students and law classes had to take her mind off Travis, right? She sure hoped so.

She turned her key in the lock on her aunt's door, walked inside and gasped.

A carpet of red rose petals lined the hallway leading to the kitchen.

Was her aunt seeing someone? She would be mortified if Victor called her here to break up his mother's date night.

"Aunt Brenda? It's me, Chelsea."

The voice that called back wasn't her aunt's.

"Chelsea." Travis stepped out of the kitchen, and everything inside her melted. He wore a dark suit and held a dozen red roses in his hand.

"Travis. What are you doing here?"

"I needed to talk to you."

Her heart ached, but she wasn't ready to open it up again and possibly have it shattered further. "About what?"

"About us."

She looked away from him. "There is no us. You made that clear. You don't want me. You have your own life, and I'm not a part of it."

His lips flattened. "You think I don't want you? That's the furthest thing from the truth."

Her eyes met his. "Of course I think that. You left. You walked out on me."

"I was wrong," he said. "I swore to myself I wouldn't let myself love anyone so that I never had to hurt the way

I hurt when I lost my parents and brother. But I hurt her anyway. When I lost you. Worse even because I lost you because I was an idiot."

Chelsea couldn't help it. Hope swelled in her chest. "And you're not an idiot anymore?"

"No. I'm not afraid of being hurt. I'm afraid of living another second without you in my life. I want you, Chelsea. I've never wanted anything more than I have wanted you. And I hope you still want me, too."

Something released inside of her, letting her heartbeat again. She ran into Travis's arms. He held her tightly. Tight enough that she could feel the beating of his heart.

"I love you. Don't you ever leave me again."

"Never again. That's a promise."

Epilogue

Chelsea waited in a private room in the prison family area with her aunt Brenda, Victor and Travis at her side. She'd waited years for this moment, when her father would walk out of prison a free man, but the last two weeks waiting for his release had been some of the longest of her life.

Travis took her shaking hands in his and brought them to his lips.

"I've dreamed about this day for years, and now that it's here I'm so nervous," she said, giving him a small smile.

"That's understandable." He pulled her close and wrapped his arms around her. "You're an amazing woman. I don't know anyone else who would have fought so hard for someone they loved. Your father is lucky to have you." He leaned in close and said in a voice that sent a shiver through her, "I'm lucky to have you." He pressed a kiss to her lips.

They broke apart just as the doors opened.

A pair of guards led her father into the room. He'd changed out of his prison uniform and into the new slacks and cotton pullover that Brenda had bought for her brother.

Chelsea couldn't help the cry that tore from her throat when she saw her father for the first time as a free man. "Dad." She crossed the small room quickly and threw herself into her father's arms.

She felt his tears falling on her shoulder as he squeezed

her tightly. It had been so long since they'd had more than a brief touch. She didn't know if she could bring herself to ever let him go.

But after several minutes, her father stepped back and opened his arms to his sister. Aunt Brenda stepped into her older brother's arms, fat tears sliding down her cheeks.

When she turned, Chelsea noted that Victor was also crying. Even Travis's eyes were red. She stepped back to his side, and his arm slid around her waist.

"Okay, enough with the tears," her father said with the widest smile Chelsea had ever seen on his face. "I've been waiting years to say this. I'm going home!" He kept one arm around his sister and threw the other one around his nephew before heading for the door, laughing.

Chelsea watched her family step out of the room, then looked up into Travis's eyes. "I'm so glad you were here to share this moment with me."

He gazed at her with so much love in his eyes, her breath caught. "I'll always be by your side. There's nowhere else I'd rather be."

* * * * *

INTRIGUE

Seek thrills. Solve crimes. Justice served.

Available Next Month

Tracking Down The Lawman's Son Delores Fossen
Twin Jeopardy Cindi Myers

....

Cold Case Protection Nicole Helm
Wyoming Christmas Conspiracy Juno Rushdan

....

Danger In Dade Caridad Piñeiro
Holiday Under Wraps Katie Mettner

Larger Print

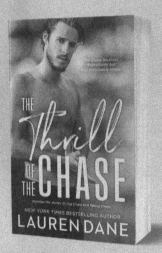
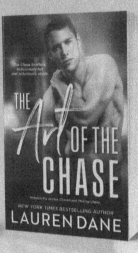

ıbscribe and
ll in love with
Mills & Boon
eries today!

u'll be among the first
read stories delivered
your door monthly
d enjoy great savings.

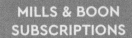

WE
SIMPLY
LOVE
ROMANCE